# An Italian Holiday

Maeve Haran is an Oxford law graduate, former television producer and mother of three grown-up children. Her first novel, *Having It All*, which explored the dilemmas of balancing career and motherhood, caused a sensation and took her all around the world. Maeve has written ten further contemporary novels and two historical novels, plus a work of non-fiction celebrating life's small pleasures.

Her books have been translated into twenty-six languages, and two have been shortlisted for the Romantic Novel of the Year award. She lives in North London with her husband (a very tall Scotsman) and a scruffy Tibetan terrier. They also spend time at their much-loved cottage in Sussex.

# Maeve Haran

# *An Italian Holiday*

PAN BOOKS

First published 2017 by Pan Books
an imprint of Pan Macmillan
20 New Wharf Road, London N1 9RR
Associated companies throughout the world
www.panmacmillan.com

ISBN 978-1-4472-9195-4

1 3 5 7 9 8 6 4 2

A CIP catalogue record for this book is available from the British Library.

Typeset by Ellipsis, Glasgow
Printed and bound by CPI Group (UK) Ltd, Croydon, CR0 4YY

*To Vicki Barrass, for thirty years of fun and friendship —*
*not to mention advice on Italian customs, language*
*and the art of flirtation*

# One

'For Christ's sake, Claire!'

Martin hopped around on one foot, reminding Claire of a balding heron. 'Do you have to leave boxes lying about where people can trip over them? I nearly broke my bloody leg!'

'I'm leaving in five minutes to drive to Mayfair for the lunch I'm catering.' Claire tried to restrain herself from braining him with the box containing the tuna ceviche which was destined to be her starter. She'd already had to deal with one outraged male ego this morning when she'd asked Harry, the fishmonger, if the tuna was fresh and he'd gone ballistic. As Harry was extremely useful to her professionally, she had stroked his ruffled feathers and apologized. Her husband, she decided, was a different story. She had been the breadwinner for years now, but did he lend a hand? Offer to carry her catering boxes to the car? No, he did not. Claire decided that she was becoming a misanthropist or maybe just a good old-fashioned feminist. Taken aback, she stopped shoving plastic boxes of food into the boot of her ancient Panda. She'd never seen herself as a women's libber. In fact, if you'd asked her thirty years ago, she'd have said she was the domestic type; forget bra-burning, she preferred hearth and home. Maybe it was life that made you a feminist. Or marriage.

However you sliced it, and as a caterer there was nothing Claire didn't know about slicing things, there were times when she felt men were an optional extra. She thought of one of her favourite cartoons when the wife said to the husband: 'When one of us dies, I'm going to live in the South of France.' Too right.

'Don't be ridiculous, Claire,' her friend Jan replied whenever she voiced these subversive sentiments. 'You'd never survive without a bloke!'

She suspected Martin thought the same.

Anyway, for now she was going to forget about Martin – and also about their son Evan and daughter-in-law Belinda, both of whom had been 'temporarily' living with them for the past six months since their flat had fallen through; they had been making Claire's life doubly difficult since she now had to prepare all her catering commissions with two more people around – not to mention a fridge overflowing with unfamiliar vegetables and revolting kale shakes. Evan and Belinda only believed in Eating Fresh. Added to which, her precious liquidizer was forever left with bits of green stuff sticking to it.

*Claire,* she reminded herself, *you are beginning to sound like your mother.* This was such a terrifying prospect that, immediately, she switched her mind to the morning ahead. She'd never cooked for this company before, but a caterer she knew had found she was double-booked and she'd asked if Claire could take on the job. The clients were venture capitalists, obviously successful ones, based in a large house in Brook Street, Mayfair. Claire didn't really understand what venture capitalists did and wondered if they were any different to the City types she'd done directors' lunches for in the old days.

They had mostly been harmless if pompous old farts, apart from the occasional really dangerous one with wandering hands who thought the cook was on the menu along with the crème brûlée. Amazing how enduring this breed of man was. Her mother's generation had dubbed them NSIT – Not Safe in Taxis.

Claire typed the company's address into her ancient clipped-to-the-windscreen TomTom and waved goodbye to her domestic irritations. This was her favourite moment. She always left early so that she had plenty of time for breakdowns, traffic queues, parking problems or any other foreseeable disaster. One disaster she hadn't foreseen was a driver going straight into the back of the ancient transit van she borrowed for big occasions and knocking the four carefully stashed whole salmons she was taking to a wedding onto the floor. She had managed to rescue two of them by judiciously placing cucumber slices so that they reminded her of nudists with beach balls disguising their modesty. The other two she had had to make into salmon mousse with the help of a handy freezer – she always carried her salmon-shaped mould – and, thank God, the guests had thought she was being deliberately retro and loved it. Fortunately, by the time she served the mousse, the bride and groom had drunk too much champagne to notice the change in menu.

An hour and a half later, when she arrived at the grand Georgian house in Brook Street, there was a parking space right outside. Remembering Woody Allen in the film *Sleeper*, when he knew something bad was going to happen when he got a parking space outside the hospital, Claire was grateful but suspicious.

She paid the parking charge with her phone and carried

her boxes carefully inside. Margie, the previous cook, had tipped her the wink that the clients were bored with the usual conservative fare and fancied something a bit spicier, hence the tuna ceviche, followed by chicken piri-piri and the ever-popular bread-and-butter pudding, made with Italian panettone instead of Mother's Pride – a touch of Nigella *ooh la la*.

She was busily plating up the ceviche in the tiny galley kitchen, Radio Four on her headphones, when the office manager put her head round the door. 'Glad to see you're so ahead of yourself,' the woman congratulated. 'The last cook was so slovenly we had to fire her.'

'Right.' Claire squeezed out the last of the limes thoughtfully. Margie hadn't mentioned anything about being fired. How very weird. Maybe she was embarrassed. Word spread fast in the catering world, often about appalling clients – bad payers, or customers who treated you as if they were Henry the Eighth and you some menial serf.

Claire went back to *You and Yours* and the topic of whether or not you had invested your pension wisely – or, in her case, not at all, since she'd never had a job that paid enough. She wasn't going to think about that. She'd just have to go on working till she was a hundred.

She could hear the sounds of people beginning to arrive and had a final check: fizzy and still water on ice; white wine, though they wouldn't drink much of that. She finished plating up the tuna ceviche, sticking her finger naughtily in the pungent dressing – just the right mix of chilli and lime – then popped the chicken piri-piri into the warmer and assembled the mini bread-and-butter puddings ready to finish off until they were fluffy and irresistible.

Her final touch was to write out the menus by hand. Her fourteen years in private schools might not have left her with

4

much in the way of educational attainment, but at least she'd been taught her perfect italic writing.

Claire got out her trusty fountain pen and began to write.

Angela looked around the shop with satisfaction. The atmosphere was just as she'd hoped when she'd first had the idea to start a clothes shop.

The whole look was inviting, almost like slipping into someone's sitting room – Persian rugs dotted around, bookcases with ornaments, tables with pots of her favourite bright red moth orchids, and, most vital of all, smiling assistants who actually seemed pleased to see you.

If there was one thing Angela loathed it was shops with forbidding white spaces and daunting salespeople who looked down their noses as if they were assessing whether or not you were worthy to cross their sacred threshold. The location was great too. St Christopher's Place was near enough to the crowds of Oxford Street, but funky and inviting, full of happy office workers overflowing into the pavement cafes, glad to be away from their desks. In fact, it was almost like Paris.

Angela smiled. She could still vividly remember the moment in Hong Kong when she'd tried on a dress in a little back-street shop and couldn't stop stroking it – rather embarrassingly, since the owner was watching.

'Nice fabric,' the little man had insisted, stroking it too. 'Come from bamboo. Very soft. Softer than silk even.'

The dress was like a very long sweater with a scooped neck and long, tight sleeves and Angela knew she didn't want to take it off. Ever.

It was ridiculous but she felt somehow enveloped in softness, almost like a caress. The mad, silly words *a hug in a dress* came into her head, though Angela had absolutely no inkling that she'd just come up with the slogan that would make her famous.

She'd been working for a bank at the time and had worn nothing but tailored suits, certainly nothing with even the hint of a caress. After her dramatic conversion in Hong Kong, she'd researched the clothes market thoroughly and decided that there was enough interest in relaxed and wearable fashion to take a punt, so she'd handed in her notice and started Fabric. Her colleagues all thought she was mad.

Of course the hug dress was only the core of the collection. Long, flattering tops that covered your bum followed, fine-knit cardigans, capsule wardrobes based on luxurious comfort as well as style and all of them flattering to the over-forty woman. By a stroke of luck she hit the gym explosion and her clothes fitted well with women's more casual lifestyles. Her ninety-year-old mother would never have worn anything like this, but then that was the point. Women's lives had changed. Angela added a line of wrap dresses which the fashionistas might declare to be as dead as a dodo but which sold like Harry Potter in paperback. As did the many-coloured pashminas – another item despised by the fashion gurus but beloved by the customers – and lovely exotic silk scarves – which gave her an excuse to keep travelling to India and Morocco.

Angela caught sight of herself in one of the long mirrors she insisted they had everywhere – she hated shops where you had to wander round for hours before you found one.

The face that looked back shocked her. Despite her carefully tended blonde bob, the clever clothes and the bronze beaded necklace judiciously chosen to disguise the crêpey neck, she looked old. Worse than that, she looked hard. Unwillingly she remembered the line in Nora Ephron's wonderful essay on ageing – that it took longer and longer every day just to look like you.

Well, maybe it was a good thing she was hard. She was going to need to be. Three years ago she'd sold a large stake in Fabric to a venture capitalist in order to give her the money to open more shops and expand her business online. The expansion had been a great success with six more shops in prestigious locations and booming Internet sales. Fabric had been so successful, in fact, with her name constantly in the press, that she'd been approached by the popular TV show, *Done Deal*, to be one of its business moguls.

Angela glanced at the expensive watch her success had enabled her to buy. It was half past twelve. At one o'clock she and her deputy, Drew, were due at a lunch at Woodley Investment's smart offices in Brook Street.

Mayfair was where the venture capitalists liked to be, marking the difference between themselves and the old-fashioned City boys.

'Are you ready?' Drew asked, emerging from their upstairs offices.

'What do you think they want?' Angela asked him. She and Drew had been summoned to this lunch by their investors without any advance warning.

'Come on, Angie,' Drew replied with a grimace, 'you must have some idea. I don't suppose it's good. When you get into bed with the devil you expect to get scratched.'

'Scratched is OK. I just don't want to get swallowed whole.'

Angela said goodbye to the smiling sales assistants and they went outside to look for a taxi. There were always loads waiting round the corner near Selfridges. In fact, there were loads of taxis everywhere since the invasion of cheap Uber minicabs. She glanced back at the shop. 'Filling up nicely with lunch-break shoppers,' she commented happily.

'Do you ever stop, Angie?' Drew's voice held the merest tinge of criticism.

'No. Never. It's my business.' She looked back at him, weighing up whether or not to take offence and decided against it. She might need his support. 'I've given Fabric my all. It's been everything to me. And it hasn't let me down so far.'

On the spur of the moment, Angela ignored the line of hopeful black cabs and waved down a bicycle rickshaw from the row of tatty machines with their gaudy fake-velvet seating and ramshackle plastic roofing.

'What on earth . . . ?' Drew demanded. 'They're a rip-off for tourists. Shouldn't you be playing the business tycoon? Famous star of *Done Deal*?'

'To hell with that.' Sometimes she wished she hadn't signed up for the show at all. Especially as she'd been cast as the blonde ball-breaker.

Grinning at the madness of her choice of vehicle, she climbed into the back.

'Aren't you that lady on the telly?' The rickshaw driver studied her. 'The scary one who's nasty to everyone and never lends anything?'

'That's me.' Angela laughed. 'Why? You don't want to expand your business, do you?'

'Not me. I'm a student.'

'What of?'

'Business management.'

Angela laughed. 'Good luck with that. I'm not *always* scary. As a matter of fact, I just do things by instinct.'

'Your instincts must be pretty hard line, then.' The young

man delivered this with such a big grin that it was hard to be offended.

'Even the rickshaw drivers are scared of you,' whispered Drew. 'So you follow your instincts, do you?' They were bowling down Oxford Street at an alarming rate for a bike-powered vehicle. Bravely, Drew tried to take her hand. 'Like getting involved with your second in command?' He and Angela had, very ill-advisedly in Angela's view, been to bed together a couple of times. To be frank, she'd been surprised that at her age anyone still wanted to go to bed with her.

'Come on, Drew, we've been through this. They were moments of madness. Not a good idea to mix business and emotion. Besides, you're too young for me. Remember Rider Haggard's *She*?'

'Before my time.'

'Mine too. He was Victorian, actually,' she pointed out wryly. 'He invented the original She-who-must-be-obeyed. Played by Ursula Andress in the Hammer film. She was really called Ayesha and she was immortal. A nice young man falls in love with her and she tries to make him immortal too. Only it all goes wrong and she becomes two thousand years old – before the poor lad's very eyes.'

'I'm not a lad. I'm forty-five.'

'When you're my age that's a lad.'

'So it's all been worth it, then?' She could hear the hurt in his voice as they turned left into Bond Street.

'What has?'

'You, Angela. No husband. No children. Not even a dog.'

Angela had to fight against slapping him. How *dare* he?

She was so angry that she didn't notice passing her favourite Jo Malone store or the blue plaques for both Jimi Hendrix and Handel.

'You may need my comfort after today,' Drew announced ominously. They were arriving outside a perfect Georgian gem of a building a few doors down from Claridge's. As usual the paparazzi were gathered outside the Queen's favourite hotel, as they often were, to photograph not Her Majesty but Alexa Chung, or Daisy Lowe or Karlie Kloss coming out of yet another celebrity lunch.

Drew helped Angela out of the rickshaw and glanced up at the perfect proportions of the exterior. 'The venture capital boys love this old-school stuff to disguise the fact that they're a bunch of spivs,' he announced.

'A bit harsh, since they paid me a very nice sum for their shares then left me alone.'

'Till now,' was his portentous reply. 'They're not called Vulture Capitalists for nothing, you know. They're not interested in what they invest in, only their returns. Look at that lot who lent to the shoe diva. She said they didn't know a stiletto from a Cornetto. Come on. They can only tear us limb from limb.'

The inside of Woodley Investment's HQ was, if anything, grander than the exterior. A flunkey took Angela's coat and ushered her through a large hall with daunting black and white tiles which led to an even bigger staircase, just like the one Scarlett O'Hara came down, carpeted in deepest red with an ornate black iron banister. A flower arrangement stood on the hall table – so vast that it must have taken two men to carry it in. The whole was lit by crystal chandeliers.

'The Sun King would have been at home borrowing from this lot,' whispered Drew.

A willowy young woman dressed in edgy black, with sleek dark hair, appeared almost out of the panelled woodwork. 'Good Morning, Ms Williams. Mr Northcott and Mr Fisher will join you in one moment. If you'd follow me.'

Angela was suddenly conscious of her rickshaw-blown hair. 'Do you have a Ladies' room first?'

'The nearest is in the basement.'

Angela skipped gratefully down the luxuriously carpeted stairs. It was very much the kind of Ladies you found in a gentleman's club, huge and unmodernized, speaking of old-fashioned class that didn't need stupid Italian taps or silly-shaped basins to proclaim its status.

Angela adjusted her lipstick and brushed her hair. Ten minutes in the open air had brought a tinge of colour to her cheeks. She leaned in towards her image and informed it, in the familiar words from the TV show: 'Come on, Angela. It's a done deal.'

From the far side of the room the diminutive Filipina attendant, who must have been hiding in the loos, jumped out. 'I know it is you when you leave your coat!' she exclaimed excitedly. 'You amazing! You don't take no nonsense from nobody!' The attendant glanced around as if she knew she was behaving out of line. 'Could you give me autograph?' She pulled a sheet of paper towel out of the machine and handed it to Angela.

'What's your name?'

'Nina.' The tiny lady grinned ecstatically.

'To Nina, who is also amazing. Best, Angela.'

Nina held the paper towel against her bony chest.

Angela washed her hands. 'OK, Angela,' she told herself, 'you don't take no nonsense from nobody!'

Angela pulled herself up to her full five feet eight inches and walked into the dining room. What took her aback wasn't the extraordinarily grand décor with a huge boardroom table, elaborately swagged windows and yet more flowers. It was the fact that there were five people seated around the table. Not just the two young men – over-entitled public school boys – whose names she'd already forgotten – Eddie? No, Jamie. And possibly Adam? – but three other people – two men and a woman – who had the instantly recognizable air of lawyers.

Drew caught her eye. He obviously thought so too.

'Ms Williams, hello.' Jamie was holding out a hand. 'So good to meet you in the flesh, so to speak. I'm a great admirer of *Done Deal.*' He smiled ingratiatingly. 'I'm just grateful Woodley doesn't have to lend to any of your contestants.'

'They're not contestants,' Angela replied disdainfully. 'They're genuine business people who want an investment.' She looked round at the gathering. 'Just like I did from you.'

'Fabric had rather more substance than onesies for dogs.' Jamie smiled in a superior way at his colleagues.

'Actually, I made a very wise investment in Poochy Protectors. They've done extremely well.'

'Right,' Jamie continued quickly. 'You've already met Adam Northcott. Mary, Tim and Seb are all from our legal department.'

'How thoughtful of you to forewarn me that lawyers would be present.' The hint of steel in her voice had them all suddenly shaking out their napkins.

'Please, take a seat.'

Angela noticed the caterer hovering in the doorway, eager to serve their starter. She placed a dish in front of each of them, handed out bread, which Angela noted looked delicious, and began to fill their glasses. 'Still or sparkling?'

'Fizzy for me.' Angela held out her glass.

'Excuse me,' Jamie's voice interrupted, waving Claire's

carefully handwritten menu, 'but what is this?' He pointed petulantly at the starter.

'Tuna ceviche,' Claire replied, trying to be polite. 'It's from Peru. Tuna marinated in chilli and lime.'

'If I want chilli I'll go to a Mexican restaurant. What happened to the tomato and basil soup we ordered?'

Claire felt a wave of panic, thinking of the piri-piri salsa she was serving with the next course. He didn't seem to have noticed that yet. What had Margie been up to, giving her a deliberately bum steer? If it was revenge for being fired, then she'd kill her when she next saw her. It was bad enough being humiliated like this, but it would be in front of that steely-looking woman from the telly. And having to put up with being patronized by this overpaid kid . . .

'Well, I think tuna ceviche is delicious,' Drew interrupted. 'Fresh and sophisticated and fabulously trendy.'

Jamie looked at him as if he'd crawled out from under a stone.

Shortly afterwards, Claire collected the plates – the others had eaten theirs but Jamie's remained untouched – and disappeared as fast as she could into the kitchen where she scraped the piri-piri off the chicken breasts. Madly, she chopped some mushrooms she had been going to use as a garnish and sautéed them on the hob. She would just have to use the cream that was destined for the pudding.

As soon as the mushrooms began to cook and release their dark liquid, Claire added the cream, reserving a little which she could dilute with some milk later for the pudding course.

To her relief, the dish didn't look too bad when she plated it up with the rice she had been going to serve with the piri, plus a green salad.

Her eye caught Angela's as she placed the de-chilli'ed

chicken down in front of her. Angela smiled almost impercept-ibly, still managing to convey some of the disdain she was feeling for this public-school idiot.

Angela knew from previous encounters that they wouldn't discuss the real business of the day till the coffee arrived, so she did her best to survive the inane chit-chat about their chil-dren, the state of the stock market, and who was going to win some test match or other.

The pudding, when it arrived, smelled delicious. 'Whose recipe is it?' she asked the caterer before Jamie or Adam had a chance to put the boot in.

'Nigella's.' The woman smiled. She had a very pleasant smile which lit up her rather plump features. *God*, Angela couldn't help casting a professional eye over her, *look at those awful clothes.*

'She can lick my spoon any day,' announced the sleaze-bag Angela identified as Adam.

The female lawyer raised her eyes to heaven.

The caterer cleared the dishes, obviously deciding this wasn't worthy of a reply.

Once the plates were in the kitchen, she returned with a cafetière and placed it on the table with some mints.

'At least the mints are OK,' commented Jamie wittily. He leaned towards Angela and added in a low voice, 'I bet you wouldn't lend to her on *Done Deal*. No Deal for Ms Sour-Faced Caterer.'

'I thought she was extremely pleasant, actually,' Angela replied. 'And unlike venture capitalists, caterers operate on such low margins that I doubt she would have applied to *Done Deal* anyway.'

In the kitchen, Claire smiled. Angela knew how to keep those jumped-up prep-school boys in line.

She was surprised to look round and find that Angela had brought her own dirty plate back to the kitchenette.

'You didn't have to do that,' Claire thanked her.

'Pleased to. Sorry about all that. The food was great – especially the pudding. I adore that Italian panettone.'

'I love all Italian cooking.' Claire found herself responding to this gesture of friendliness. 'My dream would be to move there and run a restaurant with rooms.' She smiled at Angela. 'Fat chance of that. Heigh-ho. I'm Claire, by the way.'

'Excuse me, ladies,' one of the loathsome idiots called out to them. 'This isn't a mothers' meeting. Time for business.'

Angela turned, her eyes sparkling dangerously. She had always loathed patronizing expressions. And, besides, she wasn't even a mother.

'Right.' The one called Adam decided it was time to assert his authority. 'To business.' He leaned forward on the table and steepled his fingers as if he were Henry Kissinger about to announce world peace. 'We have received a very interesting offer for Fabric from a most desirable party, from which both you and ourselves would benefit greatly. In fact, the approach is so advantageous that we would like to proceed immediately and close the deal in two weeks.'

Angela almost choked on her mint. 'But Fabric's not for sale!'

She knew that venture capital investments were more about making a fast profit then selling and that they had invested in Fabric three years ago, but surely they couldn't force her? Besides, you didn't reach this point in a major transaction in this manner. They must have been working on the deal behind the scene for weeks, months even. And all without consulting her! She was being squeezed out! They were trying to sell her own company from under her!

'And who is this desirable party?'

'The Tuan Corporation of Singapore. They have already made several acquisitions of clothing chains and they think Fabric would sit perfectly in their portfolio.'

'Aren't they the people who bought Material Girl?'

'Yes, I believe they are.'

'Then they took a perfectly good clothes range and ruined it! They stuck jewels and sequins on simple, stylish clothing and destroyed it!'

'I understand that since the sale it has been flourishing in Asia.'

'If they want bling in Beijing, then they can get it with their own companies. Not mine!'

'Ms Williams, you would stand to make a considerable amount of money.'

'As would you!'

'That is the purpose of our investment.'

'And to watch my brand destroyed! The brand I developed from my kitchen table, and put all my unpaid time into until it could stand on its own feet. I refuse.'

'Ms Williams,' the female lawyer spoke up for the first time, 'may I remind you of the Drag and Tag rights in the shareholders' agreement?'

Angela realized she had never fully understood this stuff, partly because she had never dreamed it could come to this. 'How long have you been working on this deal without telling me?'

'We have been exploring the option for a little while, certainly, but that is normal business practice.'

'And what would be my role in my own company?'

'Mr Tuan might wish to keep you on as Fabric's figurehead

16

with some kind of continued shareholding, though from what I've heard he does tend to run things himself.'

'Fabric's figurehead ...' she repeated bitterly. 'I'm not agreeing to anything until I talk to my lawyer. And if I can't get her, I'm not agreeing to anything, no matter how desirable the other party is.'

She got to her feet and strode out of the room, Drew at her heels.

'I just can't believe they're trying this on!' she hissed when they were out of earshot.

'You would make quite a killing,' Drew pointed out.

She dragged Drew all the way downstairs and into the Ladies with her, despite the cheeps of protest from the startled guardian at an invasion by someone of the male gender, determined that they wouldn't be overheard. After several fumbled attempts she located her legal adviser and repeated the situation to her.

'So, let me get this straight,' the lawyer spelled out. 'They're saying that if they decide to sell, you aren't in a position to refuse the offer?'

'Exactly. That can't be right, can it?'

There was an ominous pause from the other end of the line.

'I'm afraid it is. That's what you agreed in exchange for a very generous cash offer when you crystallized a large part of Fabric's value.'

Angela knew she had a good head for business but this lawyerese drove her insane. She was sure the woman hadn't made this clear at the time. Maybe she'd been badly advised? If so, she'd sue – but that might not stop her losing her business.

'That was three years ago,' she insisted furiously. 'My hard work and creativity has added huge value to the business since then! The business Mr Tuan of Singapore wants to take from me and ruin.'

'You could always start another. You'll have more than enough cash, Angela.'

'Oh fuck off, will you!'

The diminutive cloakroom attendant smiled encouragingly under the mistaken impression that Angela wasn't taking anything from anybody.

When they got back into the dining room, there was much conferring in hushed voices which stopped when Angela entered.

'Right, ladies and gentlemen,' Angela announced in steely tones. 'It seems you are right.'

Listening from the galley kitchen, Claire was appalled that someone as smart as Angela could be treated so shabbily. All she could think of was to offer more coffee and some of her home-made brownies.

'Whatever happens,' Angela tossed her hair in a gesture Drew recognized as a sign of stress, 'nothing is going to be settled today.'

'Of course.' Jamie nodded sympathetically. He could sense that they were going to get what they wanted. 'But you do understand there is no other option in the end?'

Angela got up and walked towards the huge swagged windows. Claire could sense her anguish, even though no one else in the room seemed aware of it. Under the desk she saw Jamie make a crude gesture of victory and it was too much for her. What with her husband Martin, Harry the fishmonger and now this untalented little shit . . .

As she refilled Jamie's cup, Claire's arm jolted suddenly and the boiling liquid landed in his crotch with all the deadly accuracy of an unmanned drone. Jamie jumped up, yelping.

'Stupid bloody woman!' he accused. 'You can't even get the menu right; now you've injured me for life. You won't be working here again.' He turned to the row of lawyers. 'Can't you sue her or something?'

The meeting descended into chaos.

Drew had been about to offer Angela some discreet support when his phone began to vibrate in his pocket.

It was his old friend and mentor, Stephen Charlesworth, whose business acumen was so legendary that he was sometimes nicknamed the Seer of Southwark. Stephen was not only famously successful but equally reclusive, so Drew knew a call from him was not to be ignored, no matter how unfortunate the circumstances. He withdrew into the galley kitchen, so close to Claire that she could hear his conversation as she tidied up.

'Stephen,' he replied in a low voice. 'Can't talk. In a rather bloody meeting.'

'I know,' was the astonishing reply.

'How come?' Surely even Stephen wasn't *that* all-seeing.

'Someone has been tweeting, "It's a done deal for ball-breaker Angela",' he quoted. '"Telly tycoon's company to be bought from under her." Drew, you'd better warn her. The press will be onto her like maggots on carrion.'

'What a delightful image.'

'Is she OK? Look, Drew, if she needs somewhere to get away, I've got this villa in Italy. If she has to have a reason, you can tell her the owner has had an offer to sell it and turn it into a hotel and would welcome her advice.'

'Right. Of course, you knew her once.'

'A long time ago. And for Christ's sake, don't mention that or she'll never go.'

'Stephen, what are you up to?'

'Kindness of my heart, mate.'

'I didn't know you had a heart.'

'Tut tut, Drew. Just because I'm successful it doesn't make me heartless.'

'They often go together in my experience.'

Claire, hiding in the galley kitchen till they'd all gone and she could pack the dishwasher, let her thoughts dwell on what she'd heard. Would Angela really feel the need to run away? To Claire, she seemed pretty resilient, but she could see what a field-day they might have in the papers about the tough tycoon from the telly losing her business in real life.

She put the plates in neat rows, filled the cutlery basket, and added the glasses on the top layer before stowing away her own stuff in a large orange Sainsbury's bag with an elephant on it.

She wiped the boardroom table and put the sponge cloth back in the sink. There was someone waiting by the door. Claire recognized the woman in charge of hiring who had told her about having to sack Margie.

With a sigh Claire waited for the blade to fall.

'I've just been talking to Mr Fisher. He seems to think you deliberately injured him.'

'Nonsense,' Claire rallied. 'It was a simple accident.'

'And what about the menu changes?'

Claire decided she'd sound mad if she launched into Margie's sabotage. 'I'm very sorry. I had no idea a menu had already been selected.'

'I see,' replied the woman severely. 'Well, I think that possibly your skills aren't quite what we're looking for here. Send your account for today to me and I'll get it settled.'

*

20

Claire shouldered her heavy bag and headed down the thickly carpeted stairs.

'Claire!' a voice suddenly hissed at her.

It was Angela, with a nervous-looking Drew in tow.

'Can you see if there are still two reporters standing outside the front door? The bastards seem to be onto me already.'

Claire peeked out. A small posse of journalist-looking types did indeed seem to be standing on the other side of the street, waiting to pounce.

'Yes,' she told Angela. 'Are you sure they aren't waiting for someone lunching at Claridge's?'

'I don't want to risk it. I wonder if this building has a back entrance.'

'My car's right out front. It's a blue Panda. Here are the keys. Go and get in and I'll distract the enemy with the leftover panettone. Better that than giving it to my husband.'

Before they could object, Claire threw her the keys and strode out across the road towards the huddle of reporters. 'Hello, guys, you look starving. Why not share out this delicious bread-and-butter pudding which would otherwise go to waste?' She handed over the pudding.

The three reporters fell on it like lions on a wildebeest. Claire turned on her heel and smartly crossed Brook Street, halting the traffic with a firm hand. She jumped into the driver's seat of the Panda, relieved to see Angela in the back and Drew in the passenger seat, and tore off before the hacks worked out what she was up to.

'My God,' Angela glanced out of the back window, 'that was brilliant! Thank you so much.'

'Don't worry.' Claire grinned. 'I enjoyed it. Where to?'

'I live in Marylebone but any tube station will be fine.'

'Nonsense. I can drop you home and go back over the fly-over to the A40. Hardly a detour at all.'

'If you're sure.'

'You seem to have had a hell of a morning.'

'Yes. But not as bad as it might have been, thanks to your decoying of the press.'

'Makes a change, I must say. To be honest, my working life is usually a bit dull.'

'Hence the restaurant with rooms idea.'

'Italy's my passion. Maybe my great-great-grandmother dallied with a Neapolitan sailor.' She smiled at Angela in the driving mirror. 'Or looking at her picture, ice-cream maker would have been more likely. Anyway, I've always loved the place.'

'Maybe if your mysterious friend is serious,' Angela said to Drew, 'Claire here ought to come too.' She then turned to Angela. 'I've just had this generous offer from Drew's friend to disappear to Italy for a bit.'

'I'd come like a shot,' Claire announced, 'whether my husband likes it or not.' She suddenly realized this might sound a bit pushy and concentrated on her driving.

They were at Marble Arch already.

'If you could, go left after Selfridges,' Angela said to Claire, pointing to the turning into Duke Street. Half a mile later they passed The Wallace Collection in its beautiful eighteenth-century home, and just as they were approaching St James's Spanish Place, Angela pointed out a small mews entrance. 'That's me here. I really can't thank you enough. You saved my bacon. Or should I say pancetta?' She and Drew climbed out of the car and waved Claire goodbye.

She watched them negotiating the busy road. How weird it must be to be famous. Angela seemed to have so much going for her and yet here she was being hounded and in danger of losing her business.

It was at that moment she noticed the parking ticket tucked under her windscreen wipers. She'd been so busy chatting to Angela that it had escaped her notice till now. Great.

All told, she'd made a loss of about £40. Fighting back the temptation to dissolve into tears she thought about the mysterious man on the phone's offer to Angela and whether Angela could possibly be serious about suggesting that she could go too.

# *Two*

---

Sylvie Sutton edged into her chaotically crowded office in a converted pub on the less fashionable end of the King's Road and attempted to sit down behind her desk.

It always amused her that the road had once been a private one belonging to King Charles II, since he was a king she particularly admired. She adored the transition from puritanism to the louche lust his reign achieved – not to mention those gorgeous off-the-shoulder dresses. In fact, if she had to live in any era but her own, it was the one she would have chosen.

Funnily enough, the pub she had converted had once been the King's Arms, but that was the only thing the derelict, beer-smelling, damp premises had in common with Britain's lustiest royal.

The King's Road had also certainly changed since the hippie days when it had been the epicentre of Swinging London, from the Chelsea Drugstore, immortalized by the Rolling Stones in 'You Can't Always Get What You Want' to The Pheasantry nightclub with its twenty-foot-high Greek caryatids and its wildly exotic clientele. Sylvie repressed a shudder that it was now, of all things, a Pizza Express.

Sylvie herself preferred the chummy Bohemianism of the Chelsea Arts Club down the road with its glorious hidden garden. She'd also loved the now-defunct Queen's Elm pub nearby, home to literary types such as Laurie Lee of *Cider with Rosie* fame, who, once, would regularly prop up the bar and give free seminars on modern literature.

Sylvie breathed in so that she could manoeuvre herself more effectively. The room, and indeed the whole building, was part office, part antiques shop, part storage space for her interior design business and also housed the many exotic fabrics that characterized her decorating style. Sylvie liked to think of her trademark style as exotic and extravagant. Partly, this was due to her childhood following her diplomat father to the far-flung reaches of Syria, Egypt and Iran. But it was also good for business. The 'English country-house look' was too crowded a market, and though some people – usually foreigners – were still mad for it, Sylvie's dramatic, opulent, over-the-top look appealed to people who liked a sense of theatre, as if their homes were stages where some exciting event might at any moment be about to unfold. Sylvie abhorred the thousand and one shades of off-white which tyrannized London's walls nearly as much as she loathed the vogue for shabby chic, which seemed to Sylvie's eyes to consist of a lot of chipped furniture and ludicrous lace with silly pink tutus draped all over the place as though the occupant were about to dance *Swan Lake*.

The walls of her own office were in Sylvie's signature colour – bright cobalt blue – but it was hard to determine this as they were almost entirely covered with photographs Sylvie had taken on her beloved smartphone of anything and everything that had caught her eye. They ranged from silver Moroccan teapots, bits of coloured rope on beaches, goldfinches in the pub garden, orange Penguin paperbacks from the charity shop next door, a dazzling crimson Chinese screen, to the perfect blue of a duck egg.

Her eyes dwelled sadly for a moment on the photograph of her daughter Salome – now determinedly Sal – with the two grandchildren Sylvie rarely saw. Her daughter couldn't cope with a mother as flamboyant as Sylvie and much preferred her safe and conventional mother-in-law.

And yet, Sylvie knew, her flamboyant manner was her trademark, and helped her in business. It was also a good cover for when she was actually really worried, as she was now.

Sylvie had also found that a dramatic manner was a good cover for when she was actually really worried, as she was now. She could toss her long and curly red hair and clap her hands like the stern mistress of a ballet school and people wouldn't notice the panic veiled behind her green eyelids. Her current two-million-pound project was a five-bedroom apartment in Belgravia. The owners were from Moscow and were due to return in three days, when they expected everything to be beyond perfect.

Her Russian clients, Sylvie had discovered, preferred every last detail to be completed, right down to the beds being made as if it were an actual hotel rather than their own home. She often wondered, in fact, why they didn't just move into the Savoy or the Ritz. They liked the feel of a hotel or show home, with every vase filled, every object chosen and every mantelpiece adorned with silver picture frames. In fact, once she had visited a client six months after he'd moved in and admired the photographs of his lovely family only to realize they were actually the models who'd come with the frame. She'd been more careful not to ask questions ever since.

'Amelia!' she called to her assistant, who, like their three designers and Frank, their wonderful furniture mover, was sited on the ground floor. 'Where the hell is Tony?' Tony was Sylvie's husband and, when he could be bothered, business partner.

'I think he went to Belgravia with Kimberley to take some final measurements,' Amelia shouted up the stairs. 'Would you like a cup of mint tea?'

Fresh mint tea was one of Sylvie's minor addictions, though on a very small scale compared to champagne. Most days she had a glass on the stroke of midday, announcing that there was nothing like Laurent Perrier to get your creative juices flowing.

'What on earth is he measuring for at this late stage?' Sylvie demanded crossly, picking up her bag and easing her way down the spiral staircase to the ground floor.

'Kimberley said something about needing a bath mat in the master bathroom.'

'Oh my God, she'll probably pick it up in Primark!' Sylvie ran an irritated hand through her curly hair. 'And Tony would be far more useful making sure those red velvet curtains are up in the dining room. Frank, can you come with me in a minute? I'll do it myself.'

Sylvie didn't like Kimberley, the spoiled daughter of one of their suppliers from Basildon, who would be more at home on *The Only Way is Essex* than in sophisticated Chelsea. God knows why Tony had agreed to give her an internship. The girl seemed to think interior design was all about sparkly cushion covers and putting frilly cloths on every table she could lay her hands on. Sylvie could almost bet her bedspread at home would be decorated with a pile of stuffed animals. She probably even had 'Kimberley' on her bedroom door.

She saw Frank exchange a quick look with Amelia. 'You

don't need to come, Sylvie. I could do it under water. Didn't you say something about picking up that red velvet chaise longue from the upholsterer?'

'Yes,' Sylvie replied, looking at him curiously, 'but it isn't ready till tomorrow morning. Besides, they said they could deliver. They bloody well ought to for that price.' The chaise longue, an Empire find from the Decorative Antiques Fair in Battersea Park, had cost as much as a whole room set from Ikea, even with her decorator's reduction, but it would lend the rather oddly shaped dressing room the hint of drama the owners wanted. She suddenly recalled the famous quote from the Edwardian actress Mrs Patrick Campbell about craving the deep peace of the marriage bed after the hurly-burly of the chaise longue. Did Edwardians really get up to hanky-panky on chaises longues? They looked far too uncomfortable.

And as for the peace of the marriage bed, she obviously hadn't encountered a husband like Tony who considered the duvet his sole property.

Frank brought round their pickup truck, parked opposite the World's End pub, now a concept eatery, and proceeded to load up his curtain-hanging gear. 'You look all-in,' he suddenly said as Sylvie opened the passenger door. 'Do you more good to hop in there and have a glass of fizz.' He pointed to the pub over the road.

Sylvie stared at him. If she wanted a glass of fizz, she'd open a bottle herself. Besides, she was too strung out to relax yet. Perhaps Frank sensed this and that explained his rather strange behaviour. 'Maybe when I get back. Perfection isn't good enough for these clients. If there's a smear on the window, they'll walk straight out and ask for their money back.'

Frank shrugged. 'Okey dokey. Belgravia it is.'

It didn't take them long to get there. It was that dead time of the afternoon after the lunchtime drinkers had headed back to work and before the yummy mummies had got out the Range Rovers and top-of-the-range Lexuses to do the school run. Or got the nanny to do it while they worked out at the Harbour Club.

The Riskovs' apartment was on the first floor, in what used to be called the piano nobile, with a row of magnificent floor-to-ceiling windows that let the afternoon light flood in.

Frank unpacked his stuff while Sylvie searched for her key. On the ground floor the uniformed concierge nodded to them and went back to his copy of the *Racing Post*.

The lift came at once. The door of the apartment had one of those fancy Banham keys which were supposed to be un-copiable, with a fob that turned off the burglar alarm when you held it up to the mechanism. Police round here insisted on fobs as too many rich people couldn't remember their 6-digit PIN numbers and made their alarms go off by accident. Strange, the alarm didn't seem to be on. She would have to tell her staff off for that.

To her great relief the flat looked amazing. All it needed was the red velvet curtains, the chaise longue for the dressing room and fresh flowers from the shop at Bluebird. She might even do them herself if there was time. She had just got out her phone to snap the locations where vases of flowers were needed and to remind herself of the exact colours in each background – this was how Sylvie operated, everything was a snapshot in her mind – when she heard a strange noise emanating from the master bedroom.

Frank was in the huge drawing room, already up a ladder. She padded across the carpet with pile so deep you almost sank to your ankles in it and opened the bedroom door.

She would remember the image that met her for the rest of her life.

Underneath the vast gilded bed canopy, Kimberley, still wearing her jailbait Boohoo dress, lay spread-eagled beneath Sylvie's husband.

Kimberley stared at her like a rabbit caught in headlights.

Suddenly Sylvie realized why Amelia and Frank had been behaving so oddly. They already knew what was going on and were trying to protect her.

The emotion and fury would come later. For now it was her decorator's eye that took in the angles, the light and the dramatic effect of the scene in front of her.

Kimberley suddenly screeched and Tony turned, a look of horror on his face, while Sylvie snapped away on her phone.

'You know, Tony,' she fought to hang on to her dignity, 'apart from me, you always did have terrible taste in women.'

Gwen Charlesworth sat down with her usual plate of bacon, eggs and heavily buttered toast and switched on her beloved iPad. She might be well over eighty but she had never believed in all this muesli nonsense. Her husband Neville had eaten it for years, and look at him: always moaning about some ache or pain while she could keep gardening all day. And as for this nonsense about the old not being tech-savvy, she couldn't imagine the world without Mr Google.

She scrolled through the dull invitations designed for the elderly to invest in annuities, to buy hideous shoes promising comfort for the older foot and her confirmations of orders from Amazon. Amazon was her secret passion. Every day the postman or delivery van brought her a new item – her favourite pens, new gardening gauntlets and unsuitable novels from Black Lace – she viewed each and every one as a present.

'What is it today, Mrs Charlesworth?' the postman would joke. *'Fifty Shades of Grey?'*

To which Gwen would enjoy shocking him by quipping back, 'No chance. I'm too old for all that hanging about. I'd probably die before Christian wotsit got round to seeing to me.'

She was actually hoping for a communication from her son Stephen. He dutifully rang her once a week but sometimes he'd scan a funny cartoon or a piece from the paper he thought would make her laugh.

She thought about Stephen for a moment. He, too, was a successful businessman like that Christian Grey chap, but she hoped he didn't get up to those sorts of weird goings on. Certainly he'd been a happy child. And now here he was, apart from one brief marriage in his twenties, still single. She didn't really get it. He was charming and funny and successful. What was the matter with all the women out there?

'Could you top up my coffee, Gwen dear?' Neville requested.

Gwen ignored him since being called 'dear' particularly irritated her. It made her think of the phrase 'old dears', a group in which she definitely did not include herself. Neville repeated his request, wisely losing the affectionate addition, and she refilled his cup.

Ah, there was a message from Sylvie Sutton. She had liked Sylvie ever since, aged twelve onwards, she'd come to stay with her aunt and uncle every school holiday about half a mile from the Charlesworth home. Now there was a girl who'd had a peculiar upbringing, dragged round the Middle East with two selfish parents who clearly saw having a child as a momentary lapse of concentration. Neither of them ever seemed to think that Sylvie's constant running away from boarding school, or her dressing up in outrageous outfits –

31

clearly to catch their attention – was anything to bother about.

Not long ago, Gwen had called Sylvie in to help her redecorate their drawing room and it had become Gwen's favourite room in the house, all dramatic velvet and lush sofas – a bit like a Beirut bordello, according to her son – and it had horrified all Gwen's conventional friends whose taste ran to flowery loose covers.

'Don't ever mention the C word to me!' Sylvie had pleaded when they'd looked at fabric swatches together. When Gwen looked puzzled, Sylvie had dropped her voice and whispered 'Chintz!'

She wondered what dear Sylvie wanted. Maybe she was going to come and stay and Gwen could get her advice on the front border. Sylvie was so good at colour. Gwen had been contemplating the ruby of Rococo Red tulips and the exotic purple of Arabian Mystery amongst the sea of forget-me-nots which suddenly appeared like wafts of blue clouds in her garden each year. Sex might have disappeared from Gwen's life a long time ago but at least she still had gardening, and, given the state of Neville's knees, that was probably a good thing.

The email seemed to be addressed to everyone on Sylvie's database and simply said: 'Dear All, thought this would make you smile.'

Gwen was already smiling in anticipation when she clicked on the attachment. Unshockable as Gwen thought herself to be, her mouth dropped open in astonishment at what appeared to be Sylvie's husband in a compromising position with a young woman.

Moments later, her phone rang. Instantly she recognized her son Stephen's number. He appeared via Skype, another of Gwen's addictions.

'Have you opened the attachment yet?' he asked with no further explanation.

'I'm looking at it right now . . . My goodness,' Gwen demanded at last, 'what do you think it's all about?' Gwen had always liked Tony Sutton, Sylvie's husband. There was something reassuringly masculine about him. She always pictured him with a moustache, though he had never had one. Besides, he was kind to animals and children. A man who was kind to animals and children was rarely vain enough to be a bounder in Gwen's experience.

And yet here, right in front of her, was evidence to the contrary.

'I suspect that Sylvie has captured her husband in flagrante,' Stephen suggested.

'Good heavens!' Gwen studied it again. 'It looks like one of those awful divorce set-ups from Brighton in the 1950s. But why would Sylvie be sending this round to everyone?'

'I imagine she must be trying to get her own back. She always was a bit impulsive. I just hope it doesn't rebound on her. I'm not sure her Russian and Middle Eastern clients are going to think this is funny.'

'Oh poor little Sylvie!' The image of a lonely little girl parading before her aunt and uncle's astonished dinner guests came vividly back to Gwen.

Poor little Sylvie wasn't exactly the image that Stephen had of Sylvie Sutton, all five foot eight of her. She had always considered him a spineless playmate due to his unwillingness to don tights and a tutu. And, as an adult, Sylvie had seemed well able to take care of herself.

Until now.

'Stephen, you must call her. She's obviously in trouble and, as you say, this could be disastrous for her business. Couldn't she say she was – what's the word, hacked or something?'

'Possibly. Except a lot of people might guess that this is exactly Sylvie's style, if she wanted to get revenge on Tony.'

Gwen paused to think what should be done. She wasn't the type to sit back and let the people she loved suffer. 'What about the gorgeous Villa Le Sirenuse? What better place to tempt her away than a holiday on the Med? She can tell all her clients she's on a little break till all this blows over. I mean, it's not as if you've got a family you need to take yourself.'

She swept on before Stephen could protest at this jibe on his single state. 'It's off-season anyway. The Italians don't even go outside till the beginning of May. They think we're mad to start taking our clothes off before then and saying it's spring. I remember when we used to stay in Capri . . .'

Stephen knew that once they got to Capri it would lead to reminiscences of E. F. Benson and Somerset Maugham and his mother would bring up the latter's bon mot about the Riviera being a sunny place for shady people, which she had decided applied equally well to Capri.

'As a matter of fact, Ma, I have just offered it to a woman called Angela Williams. I'm not sure you remember her, but I knew her years ago when we were at Oxford.'

'Not that frightful woman on *Done Deal*? Your father loves it. Why on earth did you do that?'

'She doesn't know the villa's anything to do with me.'

'Why would that matter?'

'It's a long story. She's just lost her business. You probably saw it in the paper.'

'Good God, you're not opening a retirement home for indigent females?'

'Actually, I hope she's going to give me some good business advice. I've had a very tempting offer on the place.'

'Stephen, not Le Sirenuse!' demanded his mother, scandalized. 'You can't sell that wonderful house as if it were an off-plan studio in Shoreditch! It's unique! What would they do with it? Fill it with oligarchs and Qatari sheikhs?'

Stephen had heard the shady people weren't going to stay in the shade much longer. 'As a matter of fact, they want to open a luxury hotel.'

'In Lanzarella! Surely there are enough luxury hotels there already? When your father and I first visited from Capri it was just a little village that grew lemons, saved from all that horrible tourism by not being on the sea. Stephen, you can't!'

Stephen was beginning to wish that Sylvie's husband had kept his trousers on. It would have saved them all a lot of grief.

'I'll think about it, Ma.'

'Besides, Carla loved that place.' Gwen knew it was a low blow to bring Stephen's long-dead wife into the argument, but did it anyway. Stephen turned his face away from the camera. He knew his relationship with the villa made no sense. But somehow, remembering Carla and how happy they'd been there, he could never sell it. Maybe this time it would be different. 'Sylvie could do the place up for you. She'd make it so beautiful you'd never want to get rid of it.'

Stephen shuddered, thinking of his mother's Beirut bordello. 'Sylvie and I don't exactly share the same taste in decorating.'

'You've spent far too long in the beige world of property development,' insisted his mother. 'In fact, you should go to Italy more yourself. Stop you wrecking London's skyline. I read a whole article about what people like you are up to!

Apparently you can't see St Paul's properly from Hampstead Heath because of all those horrible new skyscrapers.'

Stephen smiled to himself. The fact that he'd made a considerable amount of money from the beige world of property development had never impressed his mother. Maybe it was a good thing.

'Right. I'm going to weed my herbaceous border while you call little Sylvie.'

'Now don't overdo it, Ma.' Stephen swiftly changed the subject. 'You *are* using that kneeler I bought you?'

'Anyone would think I was an old woman,' protested Gwen acidly.

'You'll never be an old woman, Ma. Even when you're a hundred. It's not your style.'

Gwen repressed a wide smile. 'Off with you now. And no handcuffing nude women and leaving them hanging about.'

Stephen stared at the phone. Since he had not read *Fifty Shades* he was utterly mystified. In anyone less obviously on the ball he would have been worried but no doubt his mother would explain the reference to him when she felt like it. For now he was thinking about the Sylvie proposition. As usual there was some solid sense in what his mother had suggested.

And what if Angela accepted? There would be even more reason to take the offer he'd received seriously.

He thought for a moment of the Angela who starred in *Done Deal*. Although he would never admit it to his mother, secretly he watched every episode. The tough blonde who terrified the participants and fought ruthlessly with the other judges seemed a different person entirely from the pretty, shy young woman from the underprivileged background he'd known all those years ago. In those days Angela had been unsure of herself, conscious of her difference, perhaps just beginning to develop the angry spikiness that now seemed to characterize her.

Maybe it was this that had drawn him to her. He'd always liked strong women. Would things have been different between them if her father hadn't died and Angela hadn't been forced to leave university suddenly and look after her mother?

The day they took their first lot of exams came back to him; how they'd had to wear the traditional Oxford uniform of sub fusc – black and white – and how annoyed it made Angela. So annoyed, in fact, that she tore up the white carnation he had in his buttonhole and threw the petals over him.

Stephen found himself smiling. He'd often read about her in the papers, how well she'd done; he'd even spotted her across a crowded room at one or two events and almost gone over to introduce himself.

Yet something had stopped him. Guilt, he supposed. They had all been young and silly, yet he felt he hadn't behaved well towards Angela. Which was why he'd told Drew not to admit that the villa was his.

He stared out of the window, wondering if she would accept.

He just wasn't sure he was up to inviting the whirlwind that was Sylvie into his life again.

'Are you OK, Mum? Why don't you sit down and I'll bring you a cup of tea?'

Claire smiled at her son Evan. His expression was one of kindness and there was a look of genuine concern in his grey eyes. Funny how much he looked like his father; the same build and mop of dark hair, though Martin's was greying now, and, Claire remembered, there had been a time when Martin

37

would have offered her that cup of tea and told her not to overdo things.

'I'd love the tea but I have to keep chopping for this funeral I'm catering tomorrow. Why are you laughing?'

Evan squeezed past her in the small kitchen. 'I didn't know people had their funerals catered, that's all.'

'You'd be surprised. This lady left a complete list of readings, music and poetry plus a detailed menu. Smoked salmon blinis followed by coronation chicken and green salad with no peppers or tomatoes because she thought that ruined the look. Cheese and biscuits. Coffee.'

'I don't suppose she'll be noticing from where she is now.'

'I wouldn't count on it. She was one of those clients.'

Evan handed her a mug of tea. 'Do they vary a lot?'

'God, yes, some of them just delegate to you and forget all about it and the others drive you mad with fussing. She was one of those.' Claire sipped her tea. Sometimes she'd really like to give up the catering and take it easy but they couldn't afford it. Besides, just at the moment, she liked getting out of the house. She found Belinda a difficult daughter-in-law. She seemed almost to expect room service and never offered to cook or even shop. Then there was the state she left Claire's liquidizer in. This reminded her that she'd been meaning to have a word.

'Evan, darling, do you think you could remind Belinda to wash up after her kale shakes? Only I depend on the liquidizer for my work.'

'Maybe it'd be better if you did,' Evan suggested nervously.

Claire sighed. How come nice men like Evan ended up with bossy partners like Belinda? And she, whom she also considered a nice woman, had let Martin get away with letting her do all the earning while he rarely did a thing.

As if to illustrate her point Martin came into the kitchen. 'What are we having for supper tomorrow? Leftovers from the funeral? Or will the grieving mourners have recovered enough to stuff themselves with all the coronation chicken?'

'Why don't you cook something for a change? Or would that be asking too much?'

Martin pretended he hadn't heard.

Claire went back to chopping her onions. She had learned how to do this professionally on her catering course – first cutting the onion in half then turning it on its side and slicing with consummate skill so that every bit was a similar size and it didn't even have time to make her cry. Today, for some reason though, she did feel like crying. It wasn't at all like her.

Evan noticed the tear slide down her cheek and looked concerned.

'Just the onions,' she lied. 'Any news about the flat?'

'Not so far. Trying to get rid of me?' he asked.

'Of course not.' Just Belinda. And maybe Martin.


'What the fuck did you think you were doing, sending that out to all our clients, not to mention my ninety-year-old mother in her care home?' Tony Sutton's face was the kind of tomato colour that suggested an imminent heart attack. If so, she'd wear a red dress at his funeral.

'I hope she's proud of her stupid son.' Sylvie was slightly regretting her rash behaviour but she wasn't telling *him* that. 'And what the hell were you *doing* anyway?' she demanded. 'Forget the betrayal, the indignity of seeing my husband pumping away at that brainless little bitch, the total lack of originality in screwing the intern – haven't you even heard of Monica Lewinsky? What about the Riskovs' five-hundred-thread-count sheets? What if they had arrived early and got a preview of your arse? Have you *no* business sense?'

'Who are you to talk about business sense? You've probably killed ours stone dead. This thing's bound to have gone viral by now. We'll be the laughing stock of London.'

'It'll blow over soon enough.' Sylvie shrugged. She knew she was on shaky ground. She even had a sneaky suspicion it might be illegal. All this stuff about revenge porn. Would Tony minus his boxers qualify?

The sudden look exchanged between her assistant and Frank the curtain hanger came back to her. They had both known about Tony and Kimberley and had wanted to protect her, so this thing had to have been going on for some time.

'May I remind you this is *my* business?' Sylvie insisted. 'You are my occasionally useful husband.'

'Thanks very much,' Tony replied huffily. 'Didn't you even consider what our daughter would think?'

Sylvie tossed her mane of red hair. She had indeed been assuaged by a tsunami of guilt on this front, but so far there had been total silence from Salome. The truth was, she hadn't thought of her daughter at all at the time. She'd been too angry. But of course she should have.

Rather to her surprise, most of the response she had had so far from their clients had been amusement and even a little admiration – especially from the women. She had instantly told everyone that the whole thing was the work of some malicious hacker. The Russians and her grand Middle Eastern clients had chosen to accept this rather than disrupt their decorating plans and, fortunately, Kimberley's father was no longer on their emailing list or he would certainly have been in for a surprise over his cornflakes.

'Anyway,' Sylvie put on her grandest dame manner, 'you'd better bugger right off now and move in with Kimberley.'

'Don't be ridiculous. She lives at home.'

'Do the words "You should have thought of that before" register in that sex-obsessed brain of yours?'

Tony slammed out of her office, tripping on the rolls of fabric as he left. That would have been entertaining, if he'd broken his leg. She had a feeling Miss Kimberley of Basildon might enjoy dressing up in an Ann Summers nurse's uniform but not tending to a temporarily disabled Tony.

She had tried to dismiss Kimberley as the bitch of Basildon, but the memory of the girl's glossy hair, long legs and youthful, dewy skin crept unwanted into Sylvie's thoughts. She glanced down at her own arm, which had once been as smooth and appealing as silk, now dry despite oceans of moisturizer, and at the way it crinkled into a hundred tiny folds when she moved it, just as her mother's had.

And tough, extrovert Sylvie suddenly wanted to cry.

She wondered for a moment what Kimberley *had* been doing sleeping with Tony. A father complex? The hope of a job? Then she remembered with irritation that her husband could actually be very charming and attractive when he put himself out. It was just that it had been a very long time since he'd put himself out for her.

Angela sat staring at her laptop, not even noticing the surroundings that usually meant so much to her. She'd searched for five years to find the perfect mews house in Marylebone, one of the few parts of Central London she felt still had real character. She'd decorated the house entirely selfishly – the privilege that came from living alone when you had no one to please but yourself. Angela hated compromising on taste, or, in fact, compromising at all. Perhaps that was why she had never got married, or even lived with anyone, and now found herself, as Drew had put it so brutally, without a husband, family or even a dog. As a matter of fact, she had thought about getting a dog, but had decided it would be too unfair, given the hours she worked and the amount of time she spent away on buying trips and visiting foreign factories to make sure the suppliers were keeping to her rigorous standards.

Drew had also pointed out the fact that Angela didn't seem to have many women friends.

'Women friends are a waste of time!' Angela had snapped. 'They say they are offering sisterly solidarity but actually they just dump their problems on each other. That makes them feel so much better that they go straight back to the same bad situation they were moaning about. I'd rather not moan to other people but do something about my problems.'

Unfortunately, today her problems seemed insuperable. She'd just been reading how incredibly common it was for founders to get fired from their own companies if they'd opted for outside investment. Outside investors, it seemed, rarely believed that the founder – no matter how successful – was the right person to really make the most money out of expanding the business. Yet according to all the lawyers, she had no option but to take the money and leave.

Angela slammed her laptop shut and strode over to the fridge. Breaking all her usual rules she opened a bottle of Pouilly-Fumé and poured herself a large glass to take to the bath. Even more out of character for one who valued her figure, she decanted a large handful of cashew nuts into a bowl and took them too.

The en suite bathroom was her favourite place in the

whole house. It had a large freestanding bath, thick luxurious carpets you could almost drown in and a lovely antique basin. The crowning luxury was surround-sound music she could operate remotely.

She took off her clothes and left them on the large bed, catching sight of her naked body in the dressing-room mirror. Even at sixty she was tall and elegant, with small high breasts and hardly any puckering of the skin above the cleavage – not that she had much of that. For a fleeting moment it all seemed a waste – her still-attractive figure, the stylish home, the money – what was it all for?

Angela turned angrily away from the mirror. Bloody hell, she was becoming morose!

She quickly filled the bath, adding her favourite wildly expensive bath foam, another of the fruits of her success, and turned the music up loud. Tamla Motown soon filled the steamy room, banishing the blues – at least for the moment.

She lay back, letting the scented water envelop her, and thought about this curious offer from Drew's mysterious friend.

Finding those reporters lying in wait for her had thrown her more than she wanted to admit. Fame was a double-edged sword, which was why she was surprised so many people seemed to court it for its own sake. Well, she wasn't one of them. It also made people somehow want to see you fall, as though you had set yourself up above the average mortal and deserved anything you got.

Of course, in her position, she could go anywhere – a yoga retreat in the Maldives, a spa holiday in Crete. But Angela wasn't good at holidays. This was partly due to her relentless energy but there was something else she didn't like admitting: she feared being pitied. You could stay in the best hotels, eat in the most expensive restaurants, but waiters still came up and loudly enquired if you were dining alone.

A few weeks of Southern Italy, in a private villa, away from the glare of the press and the humiliation of reading about herself, was undeniably seductive. She could even speak a little Italian since she'd been to a summer school in Rome when she was a teenager. It might be fun to brush it up. But the biggest attraction was certainly the business proposition of whether the villa should become a hotel. That was something she would relish. She wouldn't be a lonely holidaymaker but a woman with a purpose.

When she got out of the bath she decided she'd google Lanzarella. Besides, it didn't have to be for long. The press had a short memory. They'd soon be distracted by a politician's affair or a corruption scandal in football. On the whole she thought she'd say yes.

Sylvie had a last check of the Belgravia apartment to make sure everything was in place. The main reception room looked suitably magnificent – Moscow Opera House with just a dash of modern sophistication. The flowers were perfect. She hadn't had time to do them herself, but the florist had managed to get the dark red peonies from New Covent Garden market that Sylvie had requested even though they weren't really in season yet. She had toyed briefly with silk ones, which could look sensational, but her instinct told her the Riskovs would see that as somehow cheapskate, especially if their friends surreptitiously started to feel them and smirk, which was all too possible. The peonies had been arranged in huge Chinese vases.

Sylvie bent down and breathed in the subtle aroma. Perfect. The red curtains looked brilliant. Frank had been putting them up when she had discovered Tony, but she wasn't going to think about that.

She got Amelia to do the bedroom checking, just in case she broke down. She had suggested the Riskovs arrive at midday because the light from the enormous windows looked at its best then, but today the weather was dismal – any sign of spring was shrouded in sheets of sleety rain. She'd just have to hope that, coming from Moscow, they would at least consider it better than home.

The doorbell rang and she stood like a hostess in a reception line, holding a bouquet of glorious white roses, the kind that had their petals fully open but hadn't started to droop yet. Until now it had only been Mr Riskov she had dealt with. The roses for his wife had been Amelia's idea and the look on Mrs Riskov's face when Sylvie presented them told her it had been an inspiration.

'Welcome to your new home. We hope you'll be very happy.' Amelia, standing behind her, almost curtseyed.

Mrs Riskov took the bouquet and smiled. She was stunningly blonde and beautiful. Tall and willowy as Maria Sharapova, she was dressed from head to foot in softest black leather, the shoulders alarmingly studded, but clearly the creation of some shockingly expensive designer, a tiny Chanel bag swinging from her shoulder. Although she must have been five foot ten she towered even higher in Louboutin stilettos. She was also startlingly young.

Sylvie wondered how many previous wives Mr Riskov had discarded on the way up. Probably an unsophisticated local one from whichever region he originally hailed from, then possibly an air stewardess or PR girl. That seemed to be the pattern with oligarchs.

Despite her dazzling appearance, Mrs Riskov had a

beguilingly sweet smile as she looked around her new home like a child at Christmas.

'Your wife is lovely,' Sylvie whispered to Mr Riskov as Amelia held the door open to the enormous bedroom and en suite bathroom.

'Is true,' confirmed Mr Riskov fondly. 'Name Natalya. Was friend of daughter's.'

Sylvie found herself feeling slightly sick and had to hold back from snapping 'And what did daughter think of it?'

They toured the five bedrooms with Natalya appearing to be delighted and Mr Riskov appearing equally delighted at her delight.

Sylvie glanced out of one of the bedroom windows. A fleet of black Range Rovers, all with darkened windows, was lined up outside the entrance. She wondered what exactly it was that Mr Riskov did.

'Does everything meet with your satisfaction?' she asked when they reached the fifth bedroom.

'Yes. Is good. Mrs Sutton, can I have word?'

She had to admit Mr Riskov had a certain thuggish charm. Some instinct told her to leave Natalya with Amelia and lead him into the gentlemen's club of a study.

'Mrs Sutton. Your husband.'

This was the last thing Sylvie was expecting, but she quickly recovered herself. 'I'm sorry, Mr Riskov, that you should have been exposed to such a distressing image thanks to our system being hacked. I can assure you we are trying very hard to get to the, er—' Sylvie stopped herself on the brink of disaster before using the word 'bottom', but floundered, unable to think of an alternative.

'Was very funny. Appeal to Russian sense of humour. But this is not point. You are nice lady. You have made beautiful home for us. Do not deserve such treatment from husband. I have suggestion.'

Sylvie stood frozen to the spot. What on earth was he going to suggest?

'English authorities do not like simplest solution so I have alternative. Would you like husband to visit former Soviet Union? Is very big place. Husband easily get lost.' She could just imagine it, with all those Range Rovers to do his bidding. She wondered for the briefest of moments if they'd take Kimberley too.

'No, no, Mr Riskov,' Sylvie answered breathlessly. 'It's very kind of you. But I can deal with my husband here.'

He bowed. 'Let me know if you change mind. Is easily arranged.'

'Thank you.' She called to Amelia. 'Time we left Mr and Mrs Riskov to enjoy their new home.'

'That seemed to go well,' Amelia offered as they drove back to the office.

She knew Amelia was being thoughtful and she smiled back. Better not to share Mr Riskov's offer of losing Tony in the Siberian wastes.

'Wow,' Amelia added, 'Mrs Riskov was quite something. Though they struck me as an odd couple.' What she really meant was that the beautiful blonde wasn't much older than she was.

Sylvie couldn't help thinking that it must be a strange life for a lovely girl that age to be a trophy wife. This unfortunately led her down the road to Kimberley and Tony. As if Amelia guessed her thoughts, she leaned forward impulsively. 'I just want to say, Kimberley really threw herself at Tony.

I don't think he'd even noticed her till she went for him full-on. We all thought it was disgusting.'

Sylvie didn't know whether to be touched or offended that they were all gossiping about her.

When they arrived back at the office, instead of going to her desk, Sylvie excused herself, pleading a headache, and slipped up to the flat at the top of the building. They had moved to this engaging part of the King's Road – not as posh as Sloane Square or as Sloaney as Fulham – when the children had left home. 'No sense in rattling around in a big house when we have plenty of room over the office,' Tony had suggested. 'Especially with the price we'd get for a family home.'

Sylvie's first gesture now was to turn on all the lights. Mad, and bad for the planet, but somehow it lifted her spirits. Sylvie was addicted to light. She made herself a cup of mint tea and sat down in the kitchen. The place seemed depressingly quiet. Tony, she realized, had always seemed to fill the flat with noise. Jazz on the radio, whistling to himself, banging about in the kitchen, singing snatches of Frank Sinatra off-key.

*Oh for God's sake,* she told herself, *don't start missing the bastard! Remember what he did to you!*

She noticed that there were messages flashing on the answerphone and despite all her advice to herself, her heart leapt. Only Tony left messages there because he distrusted mobiles and thought the landline more reliable.

She was conscious of disappointment when it was another male voice.

'Sylvie,' the unfamiliar tone greeted her, 'this is Stephen Charlesworth, Gwen's son.'

Funny, she hadn't heard from her old playmate for years. She supposed Gwen had made him ring and hoped to God it wasn't out of sympathy. She could imagine Gwen strong-arming him into asking her to do up one of his many apartments just to be kind and she couldn't bear it.

'The thing is,' Stephen's voice continued, 'I have this great place in Italy, above Lerini, and I could do with some design advice. I don't go there much and I was wondering if it would make a boutique hotel.' And then the truth. 'Ma and I wondered if you might feel like going out there for a while and enjoying the Italian spring.'

She'd been right. She smiled at the thought of the irresistible force that was Gwen Charlesworth coming up with the suggestion and Stephen, despite his reputation as a tough businessman, not being able to say no.

'It's very beautiful out there, sunshine and lemon groves. You might like to think about it.' And then he left his number.

Sylvie put down the phone. It was dismal in the flat despite all the lights and exotic décor.

Sunshine and lemon groves.

She thought of all those springs she'd spent abroad as a child, from Beirut to the Bosphorus, the nature of the light, quite different from anything gentle and British, and her heart lifted.

Now that the Riskovs were off her hands, Amelia and the designers could hold the fort for a while. It was a tempting offer, very tempting indeed.

Sylvie never reconsidered for a moment once she'd made up her mind, a quality some of her friends loved in her and others deplored.

She half hoped Stephen wouldn't answer the phone himself and she could just leave a message. His voice would betray his true feelings and Sylvie wasn't sure she could bear it.

Her hope was justified. There was simply a message saying

that if the caller left their number he would return the call as soon as possible.

'Hello, Stephen, long time no see. Thanks for your' – she almost said 'kind' and mentally changed tack – 'terrific offer. Sunshine and lemons sound irresistible. Just email me all the details and any thoughts you have for your design scheme. Love Sylvie.'

She put down her mint tea, feeling better already.

She'd go back down to the office and start planning her escape.

# Three

'How are we getting on with our Italian caper?'

Stephen recognized the mischievous glint in his mother's eye, and wondered quite how it had become *their* caper, or indeed a caper at all.

He was in Great Missenden for his weekly duty visit, though he had to admit time spent with his mother was often fun rather than duty. The duty part applied to his father.

Although she would never have admitted it, Gwen also greatly enjoyed being seen by her friends with her tall, attractive son and batted off all their attempts to diminish his unmarried state by telling her about their hordes of grandchildren.

Gwen had opted for lunch at the golf club, golf being her other passion, and it was early enough for her to bag her favourite table in a commanding position where she was able to monitor who came into the bar as well as what was happening on the green.

She had only just settled herself when her arch-rival Mariella Mathieson appeared, in top-to-toe new tweed.

'Do you know,' announced Gwen in a low voice, 'I saw her

at the Kimblewick point-to-point last week. She's not a day under ninety and she and the two bloody boxers were kitted out in brand-new tweed! At a point-to-point! Talk about nouveau riche. Who does she think she is? The queen of the county?'

As this was a role Gwen had indisputably bagged for herself, Stephen held his peace.

'Oh God, she's got that dreary daughter of hers, what's her name, Maureen? Margaret?'

'I seem to remember it's Monica,' Stephen supplied.

'That's right, Monica. Dull as ditch water. Maybe she does it to spite her mother. You may be a wicked developer but at least you're entertaining.'

'Thank you, Ma,' Stephen conceded.

'Oh my God, she's coming over.'

They watched Mariella's dowager-like procession, graciously talking to everyone as she passed. 'Gwen!' she greeted her rival effusively. 'Not out on the green? I suppose at your age you don't want to overdo things.'

'As a matter of fact, Mariella,' Gwen replied frostily, 'I am having a quiet lunch with my son. I see your daughter's back at home.'

Mariella breathed a gusty sigh. 'Yes. She is. I know I'm too big-hearted in letting her stay. But you know me, generous to a fault. She ought to be finding her own accommodation, but we do have a rather large house.'

She glanced across at Monica. 'You know her husband died? Typical Monica to choose a man with a heart defect.'

'Perhaps he didn't know he had a heart defect,' offered Stephen, straight-faced. 'I expect it came as rather a shock.'

'Anyway, dropped down dead at fifty-nine. Rodney's eighty-four and still plays tennis every day. Left her poor as a church mouse. They were both librarians, you know. Librarians! God help us. Monica always used to say it was different because it was a university library. Can't see it myself. Still stamping books all day. Rodney says she's never been the same since the Internet. Before that the students used to ask her for help all the time. Now they ask Google. Once the university clocked that, they made her redundant.'

They all glanced round at the unfortunate Monica who sat, round-shouldered and oblivious, nursing an orange juice by the bar.

'I mean, look at her. Just like that rugby song. No bloody use to anyone. If I wasn't so kind-hearted I'd chuck her out but she has her uses. She's looking after the dogs when we go on safari.'

Gwen thought about Mariella's revolting boxers, all three of them, who had never been trained and jumped up continually, stealing food from your plate while Mariella and Rodney just laughed and said 'Aren't they a hoot?' Suddenly it was too much.

'Stephen has the perfect solution,' she announced, avoiding his glance. 'She can go to his house in Italy to recover from her loss. Just the place.'

'Oh, she'll never want to do that, not Monica. She's a real homebody.'

'Why don't we ask her? Monica!' Gwen called across to the bar, causing the poor woman to choke on her orange juice. 'Come and join us for a moment.'

Monica reluctantly crossed the room clutching her drink as if it were a talisman.

'Which would you rather do?' Gwen asked gaily, ignoring Mariella's quelling expression. 'Look after your mother's dogs or spend three weeks in an Italian villa?'

Monica glanced nervously at her mother, who was regarding Gwen with obvious dislike.

'The house belongs to me,' Stephen added gently, seeing her distress. 'I have a wonderful library. There are some early religious manuscripts I'd really welcome your view on.'

Monica visibly straightened her slouchy shoulders and looked her mother in the eye.

'I'd rather go to Italy,' she announced with a firmness that took them all by surprise.


Claire parked her Panda and began to empty the boot, feeling unusually exhausted. The lunch she'd just catered had gone on far longer than the invitation had stated so she and her Portuguese servers had been left standing around unable to finish clearing while the guests drank their way through all the alcohol they could find, including a disgusting chocolate liqueur the hosts had bought on holiday five years earlier. She hoped they were all suffering for it. She carried the first box of dirty plates into her kitchen to find a scene of such devastation that she could hardly believe it. Not only were half the glass bowls she used for baking covered in rapidly hardening dough, but her precious liquidizer was sticky and the tool she had hidden away because it was, of all her utensils, the most difficult to clean – her potato ricer – was white with some substance – rice?

Normally, being the peacemaker that she was, Claire would have steeped the lot in the utility room sink or at least stacked them so that they looked less daunting. Today she simply piled them up on the centre of the kitchen table and wrote a large sign in black Pentel with the words WASH ME on it and placed it on the table.

She then calmly stacked her catering plates and poured

herself a large gin and tonic, which she took over to the TV. She switched it on and put up her feet in front of the *Antiques Roadshow*. That's what she needed – a bit of that iron fist in the velvet glove that Fiona Bruce possessed.

Half an hour later, Martin returned. He took one look at the kitchen table and demanded what the hell she thought she was doing.

'It's called washing-up, Martin. You may not recognize it.'

He put on his superior look. 'I'm going to answer my emails. What time's supper?'

Claire took a large sip of her G&T and channelled her inner Fiona Bruce. 'Whenever you feel like cooking it. I've had enough for today. The lamb chops are in the fridge.'

Martin considered her warily as if she might have a case of early dementia.

Once he'd gone, she wondered how she could get in touch with Angela Williams. She decided Angela might well be the type who'd have an account on Twitter. Claire's son Evan had set one up for her and thought it hilarious that she'd only used it twice. Well, now was the time. She signed up to follow Angela and then sent a tweet asking her to get in touch. Most likely, knowing Claire and technology, Angela wouldn't even get it.

She was absolutely stunned when Angela tweeted back almost immediately, including her email and phone number. And, staggeringly, five minutes later they were talking.

'Hello, I'm Claire, the caterer from the other day. I know this will seem unbelievably cheeky, but I wondered if you were going to accept that offer to go to Italy?'

'Do you know,' Angela laughed, 'I think I am.'

'I just wondered' – Claire's nerve almost failed her – 'if there might be a use for a caterer. I could do the cooking and maybe assess the place and get a handle on the facilities it would need if it was going to be a hotel.' She hesitated. 'I mean, you did say maybe I should go too . . .' she faltered.

'Do you know, Claire,' Angela replied, 'I have no idea if that would be useful.' Claire's spirits plummeted. 'But in my view, there'd always be a place for someone who dumped coffee in that little prick's crotch. I'm sure you'd be more than welcome.'

If the mystery owner objected, Angela thought, she could always put Claire up in a hotel nearby. And with Claire there she wouldn't be eating alone.

'Terrific.'

'I'll let you know as soon as I get the details.'

Martin put his head round the door. He was actually wearing a pinny. She was about to say it suited him but didn't want to push things *too* far.

'Why are you looking so happy all of a sudden?' he asked suspiciously.

'Because I may be going to Italy for three weeks, maybe a month.'

'But you don't even know anyone in Italy,' he protested.

'Oh yes I do. I'm going with my friend Angela Williams from *Done Deal*.'

'You don't know Angela Williams!' accused Martin, clearly wondering if she really had lost her marbles.

'Yes I do. I met her through work.'

'But what about us?' he asked incredulously.

'I'm sure Belinda can rustle you up some kale shakes, and maybe even an egg-white omelette.'

Then she poured herself another G&T and waited for the lamb chops to appear. It might be a long wait.

\*

'So you're going to go, then?' Drew enquired, his voice studiedly neutral. Angela had come into Fabric's head office to make the arrangements for the departure.

'Yes, why not? Those bastards can get hold of me if they need to. And Fabric will be fine in your entirely capable hands.'

'They'll be furious you flew the coop.'

'Too bad. As if I should care, the way they've screwed me over.'

'So, sunshine, Prosecco, swimming. There's a pool there, I understand.'

'Good, and for the record, I hate Prosecco.'

'It's a very famous house. Once home to all kinds of stars and celebrities trying to escape.'

'How appropriate. And who is this mysterious owner?'

'Ah.' Drew smiled intriguingly. 'He wants to remain mysterious.'

'Very Howard Hughes. It would be easy enough to find out.'

'Well, don't. Just take it from me he's a good guy.' Knowing Stephen, the villa was bound to be held by one of his companies rather than himself.

'I bow to your judgement. Besides, it'll be fun not to know. As long as he isn't some Middle Eastern arms dealer.'

'He isn't. By the way, you know what Le Sirenuse are?' Drew grinned.

'Surprise me.'

'The Sirens. Those mythical women who lured men to their deaths.'

Angela's laugh – happy and spontaneous – transformed her usually tough exterior and if they hadn't been in the office, Drew would have risked her rebuff and reached for her.

He had to content himself with saying, 'I wish I was coming too.'

'Drew . . .'

'I know, I know.'

A timely interruption meant they had to think about deliveries of a new tunic dress which had proved so popular that it had sold out instantly. It was funny, Angela mused, that the tunic – an object of derision to women when they were young, sexy and eager to display their wares – became instantly desirable when they got older and wanted to disguise the same curves which were no longer quite so shapely!

As soon as Drew left, she walked round her spare and elegant office looking at the few objects she had collected, all of which had some special meaning to her. There were the three pebbles, which had so much stark and understated beauty that a designer might have placed them there – in fact, they came from the beach where she had spent so many childhood holidays; the slender vase she had found in a Copenhagen design shop; and lastly, and perhaps most meaningful of all, a swatch of fabric, framed in wood. That had been that 'softer even than silk' material that the back-street shop owner had introduced her to in Hong Kong and on which she'd founded her business.

It suddenly struck Angela, as she surveyed her sanctuary, that it was entirely free of photographs and that her home was the same. What did that say about her?

The phone rang and Angela answered it, neatly avoiding answering her own uncomfortable question.

Sylvie always found packing a challenge. It wasn't that she was Joan Collins, needing ten suitcases plus one for her wigs, but clothes had always been an important part of who she was.

She hated 'fashion', the ridiculous dictates of a few posy men (and now, thank God, more women) who designed outrageous clothes for fifteen-year-old stick insects. What Sylvie believed in was *style*. The ageless elegance of Audrey Hepburn, the lush seductiveness of Elizabeth Taylor, the aristocratic untouchability of Grace Kelly. But it was colour that she loved best of all and that inspired both the way she dressed and her style of decorating.

Sylvie reached for her biggest suitcase, the metal one that had belonged to her father. It was ridiculous, really, it weighed a ton even empty, but it was incredibly precious to Sylvie. It was covered in labels – Istanbul, Cairo, Beirut, Tehran and her parents' favourite, Damascus – it was so tragic what had happened to that amazing city, where the famous damask rose was always in bloom, according to her mother. When, finally, they came back to England, her mother would only grow her beloved Damascus roses. In their freezing manor house near Beaconsfield, her mother would put a damask rose by the bed of those she loved. Sylvie, at eleven, had once wept because there was no rose in her room.

And it was those first eleven years that had left their indelible mark on Sylvie. Sylvie even *looked* more at home in the Middle East. She knew there was something unusual about her colouring, as well as her strong nose, dark brown eyes and the almost-black hair she now dyed red with her beloved henna. There had been uncomfortable silences between her parents that seemed to concern her, low-voiced conversations that stopped abruptly when she entered a room. Once she had even heard her English nanny rudely whisper 'a touch of the tar brush' to her friend who had come for a cup of English tea. Fortunately, Sylvie had been too young to understand the implications.

England had seemed cold and dull by comparison. If she closed her eyes, Sylvie could still see the souks, the carpet sellers and the snake-charmer with his tame cobra. But, more than anything, it was the scents that were different in the Middle East, the pungent bite of the spice sellers with their piles of dried turmeric (that yellow was still one of her favourite colours for decorating); fresh ginger and the bright red of fresh-picked strawberries; the sweet, cloying aroma of the hubble-bubble pipes in the cafes, and, above all, the irresistible invitation of roasting meat on huge charcoal braziers.

And everywhere – the colour! When she got to England, Sylvie sometimes felt she was the only champion of colour in vast empires of beige, as if Kubla Khan had been handed the colour chart from Farrow & Ball.

She had been lonelier then than she could ever have imagined. If it hadn't been for the kindness of their neighbours, the Charlesworths, and especially the lively mother Gwen, she could have turned into a very sad person.

Sylvie folded her favourite silk kaftan top, in orange with swirls of aubergine and cobalt, embellished with silken rope along the sleeves, which she wore with her jeans and matching nail varnish on her toenails – Sylvie loved to go barefoot whenever she could. Her ankle-length black-and-white zebra dress in softest silk followed, then her midnight-blue velvet number, her sequinned cocktail dress covered in tropical birds, and a variety of sandals and shawls. Sylvie eschewed the cardigan – declaring it an item for visits to Blackpool – despite Michelle Obama's spirited effort to bring it into fashion.

She thought for a moment about Tony.

In the days when he was as excited as she was about the business, they had shared some wonderful trips to the exotic places of the world. And he'd been such fun to be with. But she wasn't going to think about that.

She packed her carry-on with a mini capsule wardrobe, a skill she had learned since the time her case had gone to the Caymans while Sylvie herself was disembarking in Cape Town. She added her laptop and her precious zip-up bag of every known adaptor on the planet, useful for the equally vital tasks of plugging in her electronic devices and using her hairdryer.

Passport, check.

Ticket, check.

Euros, check.

Make-up bag, check.

She cheerfully zipped everything up. Sylvie and her carry-on bag were ready to go.

Monica Mathieson lay on her single bed, the bed of her childhood, and asked herself how she could have ended up back at home. Her mother could make her feel such a failure. One crushing remark could undo years of trying to build her own identity. Her mother would reel off the successes of her friends' children, their grandchildren even, and end with the remark, 'of course, with all your education you chose to become a librarian'.

And it was true she had excelled academically. For a brief moment her mother had been able to boast about Monica's exam results.

But then Monica had turned down the dazzling offers and chosen a provincial university because she had wanted to be ordinary.

It wasn't something she could ever explain to her mother, who would have liked nothing more than to show off about 'my daughter at Cambridge'.

She'd even been offered quite a good job during her gap year but had preferred to go and be an au pair instead. 'Why would you want to go and waste your education looking after someone else's children?' Mariella had demanded. But it had been Monica's first taste of freedom. Maybe that was why she'd jumped at the chance of this villa.

She got up and opened her window. A tiny mouse had managed to nest outside in the dead ivy, cleverly camouflaging itself against the golden bronze of the leaves.

It made Monica think of herself. Mousy Monica.

Why do I never like to be noticed?

But at least, to her mother's intense disapproval, she was going to Italy.

Feeling suddenly panicky about what she would wear there, she emptied her entire wardrobe onto the bed and surveyed it.

She and her husband Brian had led a quiet life. It had been a small life but a happy one, though her mother would never understand that.

The students were colourful. Monica had taken much pleasure in watching them from her desk in the corner of the university library – punks, new romantics, goths, rappers – Monica had enjoyed them all. But she had felt no temptation to emulate them. Which was just as well since she was small, pale and what her mother Mariella often called 'plain'.

She knew she gave the impression of being dumpy but her figure was actually quite shapely – when finally she took her clothes off and she and Brian had enjoyed a surprisingly adventurous sex life, which, since his sudden death, she had sorely missed. Another thing on the long list that Mariella wouldn't understand about her own daughter.

Indeed, one of the attractions of going to Italy was to get

away from her mother for longer than the two weeks she was supposed to be dog sitting. She had only come home because her parents' house was enormous and her financial situation dire. Brian had been a lovely man but naive about money. When he'd met an old friend who advocated the greater rewards they would get if they moved their pensions from the university scheme to a private one, Brian had believed him and had persuaded Monica to do the same.

Unfortunately, the friend had turned out to be on commission from the private scheme which had subsequently gone bust, leaving both of them broke. Monica was sure it was guilt about this that had given Brian his heart attack. She wasn't young enough to get another job (despite the Government's exhortations that they should all work into their late sixties) and the landlord of the flat they'd rented was selling the house to a developer. So Monica had come home. Her father had been delighted but Mariella had seen her as an unpaid skivvy.

Anyway, there was no point in feeling sorry for herself. She loathed self-pity.

Actually, Monica decided, she might as well just take her entire wardrobe, since it would fit into one suitcase. The only item of clothing she possessed which could be called remotely fashionable was the swimsuit she had bought in the sale at Toast. One of the perks of working at the university was free entry to the university pool. With her short easy-care hair, the swimsuit gave her a kind of boyish chic that had once or twice surprised her when she'd caught sight of herself in the dressing-room mirrors.

What would weigh far more was the selection of books she insisted on taking with her when she travelled. Friends had tried to persuade Monica of the far greater sense in possessing a Kindle, but Monica loved physical books too much, especially old books, the smooth feel of their spines, the aroma of decades of use, the amazing thrill to find that some of their pages were still uncut.

And then there were Brian's ashes. She had never yet found the right place to scatter them. Brian had been drawn to the sun, maybe surprisingly for someone born in Lancashire. Perhaps she would find his natural resting place in the sunshine of Lanzarella.

Claire scanned the EasyJet flights to Naples, not quite convinced she was actually doing this.

Martin had been grumping around ever since she'd told him, while Evan gave her little grins of encouragement and Belinda darted her glances of betrayal, as if she had denounced her to the secret police, rather than leaving her to help with a bit of cooking and washing-up.

Claire wondered when Angela was planning to go. She supposed she might be flying British Airways, possibly even Business Class, but that was a whole other world from her own. Still, it might be nice to coordinate their arrival and perhaps even travel from the airport together. Since Angela had given her a mobile number, she decided to call it while she was sitting with all the flights in front of her.

Angela answered with remarkable speed.

'Hello. Angela Williams.'

She sounded wildly impressive to Claire, who always thought she herself came over on the phone as halfway between a charity chugger and her own mother.

'Angela. Claire Lambert here. The caterer,' she added into the tiny silence that followed. 'I wondered when you're flying to Italy? I'm just looking at flights now. Getting from the airport to Lanzarella seems a bit complicated. Two buses.'

This time the silence grew into frank amazement that anyone could contemplate any journey that involved two buses.

'I'm flying in on Tuesday afternoon,' was Angela's instant reply. 'I've booked a car to meet me.'

She didn't suggest, Claire noted, that Claire might like to join her.

'Look, I'll email you all the details and we'll meet there. Apparently, there's a housekeeper in permanent residence so any time you want to turn up would be fine. Sorry, I have to rush now.'

Angela grimaced as she switched off her phone. She hadn't anticipated this woman Claire and she becoming best friends, just that Claire could look into the catering. She hoped agreeing that she could come wasn't going to be a mistake.

Claire looked at the phone. Uppity bitch. She'd seemed so nice the other day compared to those idiotic venture capitalists. But maybe they were all part of the same world. And it definitely wasn't Claire's.

Still, she was definitely not backing down. It would give Martin too much pleasure to patronize her.

She looked at the flights again. The cheapest one meant flying out at 6.30 a.m. She wondered if the trains started that early. Maybe she'd have to spend the night in the airport. She wouldn't check a bag so as to save costs. At least the buses the other end seemed reasonable.

In spite of everything Claire felt a little flare of excitement.

She was going to Italy.

'Our PR people say there's going to be a profile of you in tomorrow's *Times*.' Drew knew how Angela would react, but he had to warn her anyway.

'Do we know what it says?'

Drew had actually managed to see a proof via a mate of his on the paper but he wasn't going to tell Angela that. 'Usual stuff. Charts your rise. Switch from banker to entrepreneur. Success of Fabric. Rumours of imminent sale, what you're like on TV.'

Angela looked at him searchingly. She'd known Drew long enough to tell that he was hiding something. 'And . . . ?'

'It says you're a workaholic with no personal life.'

'A sad woman who takes refuge in her work,' Angela stated bitterly. 'I think I'd better change my flight to today.' Angela stared out of the window at the happy crowds in St Christopher's Place. They had ordinary lives, ordinary homes, ordinary wives and husbands. Why had she not been able to settle for the ordinary?

'You can handle this,' Drew interrupted, taking a step towards her. 'It's only copy, some journalist trying to get an angle.'

Angela put out a hand to stop him. 'I know, tomorrow it'll be covering fish and chips. *I don't believe a word of it*, that's what my dad said about the *News of the World* with all its stories about vicars and choirboys and disgraceful duchesses. But he always bought it just the same.'

'You've never talked about your dad,' Drew said gently.

'No? He was lovely, my dad.' Suddenly Angela's voice became full-blown Yorkshire. 'Told terrible jokes and always backed the wrong horses, fortunately only for a shilling, but he couldn't have been more loving. Then he went and died. Forty-nine. Silly bugger.'

Drew thought for a moment she was going to cry. 'And my mother went into a total collapse. Nervous breakdown, the whole shebang. So I had to leave Oxford and look after her.'

'Bloody hell, I mean – Oxford!'

Angela managed a faint smile. 'Yes, it was tough, especially as I thought I was in love. In some ways it was good for me. Made me practical. No more philosophy for me. I got a job in a bank. It was the dullest job you can conceive. When the Sixties were exploding, I was reconciling figures in the NatWest Bank in Filey!'

Drew laughed. 'I know. I can hear the Northern Lass whenever you get angry.'

'I bloody well hope you can't! I had elocution lessons to lose it. Another thing my dad was good at was sweeping things under the carpet. He would never have liked all this modern baring-your-soul stuff, and that's what I'm going to do with this profile. I'll get a plane this afternoon, drink a glass of champagne and make sure I don't go near any newsstands.'

'You're amazing, you know, no matter what this stupid cow says.'

'Thank you, Drew, I appreciate that. But on the whole I'd rather be amazing in Italy.'

In the end Martin drove Claire to the airport. It was classic Martin – what should have been a kind gesture miraculously turned into a criticism. Claire said she'd be perfectly happy to go the night before and sit and read a book but Martin had insisted that that was impractical and he couldn't see why Claire couldn't have booked a later flight.

'To save money,' Claire had insisted, her irritation growing.

'The best way to save money would be not to go on this wild goose chase at all,' he'd pointed out acidly when they were all discussing it the day before. 'I can't see how you can possibly be qualified to advise on Italian catering anyway.'

'Mum's a brilliant cook,' Evan had attempted.

'But she's never cooked for a hotel in her life,' Martin grumbled, 'and it'll probably mean we won't be able to afford that trip to Prague we were planning.'

The truth was, it was Martin who wanted to go to Prague, to some international exhibition of movie posters. Collecting movie posters was Martin's hobby.

Since they lived in Twickenham it wasn't actually that far to Gatwick but Martin left, as he always did, about three hours early. So early that Claire could have checked in on the flight before, except that it was full.

Equally irritatingly he announced he would stay and see her off. It might have been grudging of her, Claire knew, when he had got up so early, but she actually wished he'd go and give her a little freedom. She might buy herself some nice perfume, which Martin would see as another extravagance. She decided she would suggest she go through security now so there was no point in him staying and delved in her large handbag for her passport. Her hand alighted on a packet of jelly babies (good for your ears on the flight); wet wipes (you didn't get offered a hot towel in Economy); a dictionary; a map of Naples to find the bus station (not being sufficiently technologically evolved to do this on her phone); English money; Euros; her most beloved cook book, Elizabeth David's *Italian Food* (only for the seriously initiated since it had no pictures or illustrations); her ticket and her – oh my God, she couldn't find her passport!

She could just imagine the intense satisfaction Martin would feel at a) her stupidity b) the stupidity of women generally and c) the waste of money which would now render the whole venture the folly he had always thought it was.

She rushed into the nearest loo and locked the door.

What on earth could she do?

Tell Martin some tall story, disappear in a cab despite the enormity of the cost and try to get back in time for the flight? But that, of course, was almost certainly doomed to failure. Fess up and take her punishment and see if there were any later flights, then rush home and get it?

All the options seemed equally disastrous. Belinda and Evan would both have left for work, so they couldn't bring it.

Someone was banging on the cubicle door. She would have to come out.

And then it dawned on her. After a number of occasions when their burglar alarm had gone off, vastly irritating the neighbours, they had been forced to leave a key with a professional firm of key holders who would come out and turn it off and check that there wasn't an actual burglar present, which there never was.

This service was staffed by teams of nice young men, mostly students, who didn't mind staying up all night, being used to clubbing. One of these nice young men had told Claire that they also provided another service – picking up things people had forgotten and delivering them. He had added that she'd be amazed how many CEOs and Top People forgot their passports and that the nice young men – being in possession of their door key – had to rush to their homes on motorbikes, find the passports and dash to the airport in time for them to catch their flight.

Claire delved in her bag, looking for her wallet, heart beating. There was the card. She called them up, describing exactly where she could see the passport in her mind's eye but not, unfortunately, in her handbag, and where she would be waiting at the airport, well out of the line of vision of her husband.

'It will be our pleasure,' commented the man at the key-holding firm without a hint of patronage. They would charge her £30.

'You were a long time,' commented Martin suspiciously.

'A slight touch of the runs,' elaborated Claire.

'I thought you got that when you were out there not when you're still at Gatwick.'

'Probably just a little pre-trip excitement.'

'I can't think what's so exciting about staying with someone you don't even really know,' he commented generously. 'I thought you said you wanted to go through security.'

'I thought, since you'd been so chivalrous as to drive me here, I'd stay a moment or two with you.'

He looked at her as if she were someone needing care in the community.

As soon as she could she'd get rid of him, but there was no way the bike could get here yet. Claire sat down and leaned her head on his shoulder, knowing full well he would be able to tolerate this intrusion into his personal space for no more than two minutes.

She was proved to be incorrect.

In about eight seconds he shrugged her off. 'Really, Claire, I'm trying to read the paper.'

Claire went back to her book. She snapped it shut after she thought enough time had elapsed. 'Look, love, you've been really kind. Why don't you head back and get a kip? Just think, you'll have the whole bed to yourself for once.'

This proved an irresistible enticement.

'Perhaps I will.'

She waved him off, sighing with relief. 'Bye, love. Evan and Belinda will look after you.'

'I very much doubt it.'

So did Claire, but she wasn't going to admit that.

He kissed her rather clumsily and ambled off, remembering that he had to prepay before leaving the car park. 'Ten quid! Daylight robbery!'

Just as he was driving past the drop-off point a motorcycle cut him up and he had to brake. The driver, a young man, waved to him gaily as he parked his bike and removed his helmet.

If Martin had been a more hot-headed person, he would have replied with quite a different gesture.

Claire, standing under the Arrivals board, had a very different reaction. She could have kissed him. Since having a woman old enough to be your mother throw herself on you would have caused the nice young man nothing but embarrassment, she confined herself to smiling and waving as he handed over the passport.

'You don't know how grateful I am,' she breathed.

'Happens to the best of us,' replied her knight in leather motorcycle gear. Then he waved and was gone. *And that,* thought Claire, *is the best thirty pounds I've ever spent.*

Monica looked out of her window and couldn't believe her eyes. The entire landscape of rural Buckinghamshire was buried in deep fresh snow. Only a day or two ago the sun had shone with a powerful heat. People had worn sleeveless tops! Throughout the county the charitably minded had turned out their winter wardrobes and taken their surplus woollies to the Oxfam shops. And now look at this! It was true that in this area the valleys were famed for their curious microclimate: hot when it was cold elsewhere, cold when it was hot. But this seemed almost Hardyesque in its deliberate malevolence. Nature conspiring against her need to get to Gatwick Airport. It wasn't exactly Tess of the D'Urbervilles slipping her note

71

under Angel's door and it getting stuck under the mat with desperate consequences, but, in Monica's view, it wasn't far off.

'This could only happen to me,' she'd sometimes wailed to Brian. Brian, always jolly, a bright-side person, would laugh and tease her out of her pessimism.

But Brian wasn't here.

Was it a sign? To someone braver it would simply be an obstacle, but to Monica it was the curtains coming down on her escape. Her mother would be thrilled.

The truth was her mother liked having Monica there to be the butt of her comments, and she, Monica, didn't have the courage to live alone with no income.

Monica looked at her neatly packed suitcase, her folded Pac A Mac, and had to bite back the tears. Another failure.

In the far distance Monica saw a vehicle ploughing its way along their snowbound drive. Could it be the postman? He normally came on foot, but maybe the county had some emergency vehicles.

As it came closer she saw that it wasn't the postman but Gwen Charlesworth in her ancient Land Rover Defender. Gwen, ever resourceful, turned the Defender round in a wide circle before she stopped so that it was facing back down the drive.

Monica ran downstairs.

'Gwen! What are you doing driving in this?'

'It's glorious out.' Gwen grinned. 'It feels like the Garden of Eden before man put down his size-ten feet on it. Now, where's your suitcase? You mentioned your flight was this morning, didn't you?'

Monica, who had forgotten even mentioning it, nodded vigorously.

'I tried to phone but nobody answered. Let's get off before your mother makes a scene,' Gwen added with an impish wink.

Monica was back down with her suitcase in no time. But she wasn't quite fast enough for Mariella, who had appeared on the terrace in her flowery dressing gown and wellingtons looking like Lady Macbeth in Cath Kidston, clutching her head ominously.

'Don't worry about me,' she announced dramatically. 'I just have the worst migraine ever.'

Monica looked from her mother to Gwen, beginning to weaken.

Gwen grabbed her suitcase and threw it into the Defender, then delved in one of her voluminous pockets. Out came a very fluffy chick, cheeping away at the bright light. Gwen stroked it and put it carefully back in. 'Wrong pocket,' she announced with no further explanation. 'I just have to make sure the sick ferret is as far away from it as possible.'

'But don't they bite you really badly?' Monica asked, entranced by all the unexpected wildlife.

'Not when you're wearing these.' Gwen waved her leather gauntlets. 'Found them on Amazon. Terrific, aren't they?' Finally, she produced a bottle of rosé with a lovely label illustrating the Promenade des Anglais in Nice. 'Well-known cure for migraine, Mariella. Nothing better. Put it in the fridge and we'll crack it when I've dropped Monica at the station. Of course we have to hope the trains are running but Mr Google says they are and he's very rarely wrong. Hop in.'

Bowing to a force of nature greater than herself, Monica climbed up.

They drove carefully down the drive. 'Neville drove this across the Sahara so I don't think we need worry about a little snow.'

Monica glanced back. Her mother was still standing on the terrace examining the label on the bottle.

'I don't think we'll tell her I got it in Lidl for three ninety-nine, do you?'

Twenty minutes later Monica was climbing out of the Defender at Great Missenden station. Trains to London for her connection were indeed running.

She smiled gratefully at Gwen.

'I never thought there was such a thing as a fairy god-mother . . .' she began.

'Fairy grandmother, more like,' chortled Gwen. 'Have a good time in Italy. It's a shame Easter was so early this year. It's amazing in Italy. Anyway, it'll give you time to think about what you want to do next. You're too young to retire. Look at me. Wouldn't dream of it. Too much to do.'

Monica's shoulders began to sag. 'I'm afraid I'm not very good at much.'

'You wait. That's what you think. Things happen in Lanzar-ella. It's a very special place, you wait and see.'

Claire took off her shoes and put them in the tray along with her phone and backpack, clutching her passport so hard that the customs officers probably thought she was smuggling something.

She went through the security arch and submitted to being felt up by the female customs officer, then, with a sigh of relief that she didn't have any unauthorized goods in her carry-on, she put her trainers back on and headed for the nearest Costa. For once she'd forget the extortionate price of a cappuccino and just order one. The Retail Price Index might calculate the cost of modern life by a basket of groceries but Claire knew better. She calculated it in cappuccinos from Costa. How many cappuccinos is that? This was how she measured the extravagances or economies of her life. A new blouse might be ten cappuccinos and a coat twenty-two. On the whole it wasn't a bad method.

As she sipped the milky brew, relishing the free chocolate sprinkles on the top, she noticed that the front pouch of her backpack was unusually bulky. Oh my God, had some terrorist slipped a bomb in or a drugs dealer turned her into an unwilling mule?

Gingerly, hoping it wouldn't be her last gesture on God's earth, she opened the zip and removed a thick plastic folder. It was a detailed travel guide including printed timetables of the train and two buses she needed to take to get her from Naples Airport to Lanzarella.

It was so entirely a Martin gesture that she didn't know whether to be grateful or cry. He had hardly even said goodbye and now this. On the one hand, he relished such challenges, and, of course, it would discourage her from the weak-willed temptation to get a taxi. On the other, it might have been done out of genuine consideration and affection. Love might be pushing it too far.

She put the package back into the pouch and zipped it up again.

Her boarding gate was being called and, after all, she had to admit it was only because of Martin's infuriating caution that they had come to the airport early enough for her to retrieve her passport in the first place.

All in all, thank you, Martin.

Once on board, Claire got out her Anne Tyler novel but for some reason didn't feel gripped and looked out of the window instead. There was sleety rain over Gatwick. Martin said they'd even had snow in some parts of the south-east.

Please let there be sunshine in Italy.

Sylvie, in her usual contrary fashion, since her house was far nearer to the motorway to Gatwick, decided to fly from City Airport. She loved City. She always said this was because it was like a toy airport, but the truth was, huge airports made her feel nervous.

Another of her oddities was that when she was flying she always wore black. It was Sylvie's claim that you always looked tidy in black, so even if you'd got no sleep, and your hair was a mess, you could still pull it off. Also you wouldn't be so noticeable to hijackers looking for a hostage.

She always managed to take a very large selection of make-up, which somehow she'd succeed in getting through security, so that no matter how drained and dehydrated she looked, she could still go into the toilet and emerge glamorous and glowing.

Sylvie never thought too much about her fellow customers who might be crossing their knees outside. On the other hand, she was extremely charming to them when she emerged, which somehow seemed to compensate.

Having perfected her appearance, she headed for her favourite seafood and champagne bar, which had a good view of all the airport's comings and goings, and checked her laptop for any imminent problems at the office. She was very good at hiring, actually, so she knew she could trust her team to do exactly what she would do. The only problem was that clients always wanted Sylvie, and felt short-changed if, for all the vast sums they were laying out, they didn't get her personally.

She also secretly hoped, although she wouldn't admit it, that there might be a communication from Tony.

Nothing. Nada. Nix.

She ordered another glass. 'To the single life!' She smiled all round at the other passengers.

Very subtly the women slipped protective arms around their husbands.

Sylvie almost laughed. Not one of them was the tiniest bit attractive. But, let's face it, at least they had husbands.

She heard her flight being called but stayed where she was. She was skilled at being the last passenger to board and had developed a sense of timing that would have impressed Lewis Hamilton.

# *Four*

---

Angela's flight went entirely smoothly, as her flights tended to do. Delays and inconveniences rarely happened to Angela. Staff were unfailingly polite and helpful and if they slipped momentarily from this standard, a brief flash of Angela's grey eyes put them back on course.

Naturally, she turned left as she boarded the plane, placed her bag in the overhead locker and sat down in the seat she always booked, by the window mid-way between galley and cockpit, then accepted the flight attendant's offer of champagne.

She studied it before she sipped to ensure it had plenty of bubbles. Occasionally an ill-advised flight attendant attempted to give her a glass from an old bottle. They didn't repeat the mistake.

She glanced round at the other passengers, hoping she wasn't going to have anyone sitting next to her or, worse, that she would be stuck with someone who knew her face from *Done Deal*.

Neither threat materialized. Naples wasn't on the usual business route and it was too early in the season for tourists.

The few other travellers in Business Class were Italians going home and one spoiled-looking teenager who, Angela's fashion antennae noted, was wearing low-slung tracksuit bottoms and a top with shoestring straps which tended to fall down when any male approached. No luck here, sweetie, was Angela's bitchy thought, all the stewards are gay.

There was one elderly British couple – well, to be honest, not that much older than her – sitting either side of the aisle, doing a crossword together. They hardly spoke, just passed the newspaper over when they couldn't get a clue, then passed it back. There was something about the easy unspoken intimacy of the gesture that upset Angela and she looked away. Her life was far more interesting than theirs, she was sure.

She drank a second glass of champagne and looked out of the window. Goodbye to grey London, to venture capitalists, and to the hungry gentlemen and women of the press. She hoped in the next few weeks to forget them all.

The flight passed quickly and it was mid-afternoon when they touched down at Capodichino Airport. At the back, in Economy, she heard some Italians clapping at the safe landing and it made her smile. But her smile soon dissipated when she saw the rain that was obscuring the entire landscape, veiling it in deep grey mist. This wasn't what she'd signed up for.

Once she'd collected her case, Angela glanced around the baggage hall in case Claire had been on the same flight. The two and a half hours in the air had made her rethink her position about offering Claire a lift. After all, the woman had done her bit against the vulture capitalists. The annoying little shit wouldn't forget that lunch in a hurry. But Claire was nowhere to be seen. Angela had to admit to feeling relief. She was looking forward to the luxury of another hour or two of peace before she got to Villa Le Sirenuse. She used it by watching Michel Thomas, the language supremo, on YouTube to refresh her Italian. It had been a long time since that summer school.

Even for someone as efficient and well-travelled as Angela it was still reassuring to see a uniformed chauffeur waiting behind the barrier with a sign saying – unusually liberated for Italy – Ms Angela Williams.

The driver rushed forward to take her bag and, moments later, she was settled comfortably in the back of a silver Mercedes. The first part of the drive was on a motorway, but rather like the shock of suddenly coming across Stonehenge when driving to the West Country, nothing had prepared her for the sight of Mount Vesuvius. She had imagined a snow-dusted peak glowing luminescent pink as the sun made a rare appearance but it was actually covered in green and the rain was so thick you could hardly see it, anyway.

And then, not long after Vesuvius, there were signs to Pompeii and Herculaneum. Angela felt a flash of guilt that she hadn't even known these were so close. Still, there would be plenty of time to visit them.

'How long till Lanzarella?' she enquired of the driver.

'Forty-five minutes, signora.'

She closed her eyes and when she opened them again they had arrived at Lanzarella and were at the gates to the villa. They turned left and drove up a well-kept gravel drive. Despite the rain, scented shrubs – choisya, lilac, daphne and banksiae roses – welcomed them in a perfumy embrace from either side of the road. The driveway was also much longer than Angela had expected. The villa must be way beyond the village. Damn this wretched rain!

The car drew up and the driver announced: '*Villa Le Sirenuse, signora,*' and ran out with a large umbrella.

Angela looked around, amazed. The house itself was a sturdy square building but there were several more wings plus arches and towers and cloisters and a green copper dome, amongst huge gardens dotted with statuary. This wasn't a villa – it was more like a whole medieval hamlet!

An old lady with the look of a Dolce & Gabbana granny, her white hair piled on her head in a bun, stood on the back steps smiling and waving.

'*Buonasera, Signorina Gwilliams!*' To Angela's amusement she pronounced 'Williams' as if it began with a G. 'My name is Beatrice. I am the housekeeper. You are the first of the ladies to arrive.'

What a strange statement, Angela thought; there was only herself and Claire coming. She put it down to some oddity of language difference.

'Good,' announced Angela. 'Then I would like to look at the rooms, if I may.'

Beatrice led her through the unassuming back door. If this indeed was to be a hotel it would have to have a more imposing entrance than this, she thought. There followed a maze of dark passageways with small rooms off them leading into a large hall.

Angela stopped dead, transfixed by a vast fresco of *The Annunciation*. The quality of the painting was extraordinary. She had never seen a Mary with so much shining humility.

Beatrice followed her eyes. 'Our greatest treasure,' she announced with quiet pride. 'The villa was once a convent, until it was, how do you say, ravished away by the Prince of Lerini.'

Angela hoped the nuns hadn't been ravished too, and told herself not to be irreverent. Mind you, nuns seemed to be up for a bit of ravishing in those days. 'Quite a posh convent,' Angela murmured.

'What is posh?' enquired Beatrice.

'*Sontuoso?*' attempted Angela. 'Sumptuous?'

'*Sì, sì, molto sontuoso!*' Beatrice nodded enthusiastically. 'But the father of the prioress, he was the Prince of Lerini. He liked to come and stay here and do a retreat and pray to God that he could defeat his enemies the Florentines.'

'Very secular,' murmured Angela to herself. 'I wonder if God would help me defeat my enemies the vulture capitalists?'

'God will help any who pray to Him *onestamente*, from the heart,' said Beatrice and she bowed her head.

'That's me out, then,' admitted Angela. 'Let's see the rest please.'

'Of course. Follow me.'

She led Angela into an enormous hall with a peeling frescoed ceiling and marvellous buttressed arches ending in carved angels. Angela, businesswoman that she was, couldn't help imagining a large reception desk in one corner. It would be a perfect use of space.

They climbed a wide stone staircase which, intriguingly, had a different stair carpet on each level. Angela decided she liked it. It undercut the austere grandness of the stone. Beatrice led her into the first bedroom and Angela instantly decided this would be hers. There were more arches, two floor-length windows and a wonderful canopied bed, covered in some outrageously expensive-looking devoré velvet. There was even an enormous carved stone fireplace along one wall.

'Does it work?' she asked Beatrice.

Beatrice nodded.

'Could you ask someone to light it?'

'In *aprile?*' Beatrice demanded, scandalized.

'We British feel the cold.'

'*Va bene.*' She shrugged. 'You are the guest.'

'What a wonderful room!' Angela enthused to soothe her ruffled feathers.

'It was the Prince's room.' Beatrice indicated an ancient prie-dieu in the corner of the room with a carved wooden statue of the Virgin above it.

'He liked to get round women, did he?' Angela teased. 'Very Italian.'

Beatrice's granite face told Angela she'd managed to insult both her religion and her race in one sentence. Very clever. She must remember she wasn't in London any longer.

'I am sorry,' Angela said penitently. 'That was unforgivable.'

'We know what happens in England. No one goes to church. Men marry men.'

'One more question.' Angela steered her away from this dangerous direction. 'I wondered what happens about eating. Should I go out to a local restaurant?'

Beatrice looked as if Angela had now insulted her mother and quite possibly her grandmother into the bargain.

'Dinner will be provided for you here.'

Angela smiled her most dazzling smile.

'I am so grateful to hear that.'

Beatrice bowed very formally.

'Will my suitcase be brought up to the room?'

'Giovanni will bring it. Luigi is too old. Giovanni also works in the garden.'

'And the fire?' she added, realizing that she was treating the place like a hotel. But wasn't that what the owner wanted to make it?

'Giovanni will light it also.'

'Thank you, Beatrice. You have been most helpful and

83

welcoming.' A tip, she imagined, would make Beatrice jump off the bell tower.

Angela sat down in one of the armchairs and looked out of the window. Nothing but a grey blur. Oh well. Maybe tomorrow would be different. She got out her phone to make a few notes about the villa's hotel potential, grateful that she was here with a purpose. It was more relaxing than just holidaying. For her at least.

After ten minutes of waiting, Angela was feeling a little less relaxed. When she travelled, she made a point of always staying in hotels, no matter how generous the invitations were to stay in the houses of her suppliers, colleagues or even friends. Angela liked to be in control and she wasn't in control now. What she really wanted was to call room service for a Bellini or a chilled glass of Soave. But she couldn't. And where was her damn suitcase?

In another ten minutes she was almost climbing the walls when there was a loud rap at the door. '*Entra!*' she called, remembering her summer-school Italian.

She was glad she was already sitting down because had she not been she would have had to. Positively the most beautiful man she had ever seen had come into the room holding her suitcase in one hand and a large bunch of red roses in the other.

He was olive-skinned and muscular, but not too muscular, with an enchanting smile and thick black hair, a lock of which had fallen over one eye from his exertions. Angela longed to carefully tuck it behind his ear.

'*Buonasera, Signorina Gwilliams.* I have your suitcase, and Beatrice, she is so sorry – these should be in your room before.' He indicated the roses. 'The driver, he bring them from the flower market in Napoli. Very fresh. I arrange for you?'

'Thank you,' managed Angela, grateful she could speak at all.

'Tomorrow you must see around the gardens.' That smile again. 'They were planted by nuns, maybe that is why they grow so well. The good Lord blesses them.' He reached into the pocket of his jeans. They were so tight that Angela was amazed he could fit anything in the pockets. She tried not to stare like some sex-starved sixty-year-old, even if that was what she was. '*Fiammiferi!*' he announced. 'How do you say in English?'

'Matches,' Angela replied faintly.

He bent down to light the logs. The waist of his jeans dipped to reveal not some hideous builder's bum but paler olive skin, hidden and delicate. God, she'd better pull herself together or she'd pass out!

'Enjoy!' he offered. For a moment the old Angela reasserted herself and she almost asked him for a Bellini. Instead she smiled back.

'Beatrice, she want to know if you come down soon?'

'Yes, *sì*. I will just unpack and be right down.'

He nodded and took himself and his devastating smile off, thank God.

Angela put her suitcase on the canopied bed. She hated those stupid suitcase stands which were never big enough for her bag, which opened down the middle and split into two sides like a sandwich. Like Mary Poppins's bag with the lamp standard in it, they seemed to fit twice as much in as any other bag she'd owned and yet when zipped shut they looked quite modest. Angela pitied all those people who'd fallen for the Louis Vuittons, when hers was so much better. But then brands had never appealed to her.

She began to unpack, something she always found soothing because she packed so well. To her it was a science, a thing of beauty. All her clothes were wrapped in tissue paper and stowed in immaculate order. Some people recommended rolling your clothes, but Angela laughed and reached for the tissue paper. The delight of having a suitcase with two halves was that you could put all the bulky things – shoes, hairdryers, lotions and potions, in one side, and stack your clothes in the other.

Angela always had to unpack before she started any business meeting. If possible, she would even buy flowers, if they weren't provided. Only then would she feel at home and relaxed.

She wouldn't need to do that here. She dipped her head down to sniff the perfect red roses. No perfume. But they were certainly beautiful. As she shook out her last dress and hung it on one of the padded silk hangers in a wardrobe so large it looked as if Narnia had to be the other side, she visibly relaxed.

In fact, she felt a new and unfamiliar tingle which, she realized with surprise, was anticipation.

Naturally, Claire noted, Martin's suggestions worked like clockwork. 'Shuttle to Naples Centrale Station. Train to Salerno. Bright blue bus in the Via Vinciprova,' whose picture Martin had helpfully downloaded, 'from Salerno to Lerini. (Buy tickets from *tabacchi* shop if booking office closed, they are more helpful anyway.)' Clearly, Martin had been trawling all the travel blogs for this level of detail. 'From the main piazza in Lerini next to the harbour you'll find the final bus to Lanzarella. If you're lucky, there's an open-top one.' Except, of course, that Martin couldn't have known it would be pouring with rain. 'Last leg takes twenty minutes. Arrive in Lanzarella.'

Of course it was amazing, a real labour of – what – love? Or control, even though she was a thousand miles away.

If it was indeed love, why did it make her so bloody angry?

\*

Monica lifted her backpack from the carousel and strapped it on. She had seen hordes of students striding along with these at the university and had admired the freedom it gave them. She and Brian had even nurtured a long-held fantasy that as soon as they retired they would go backpacking in South America. They had even bought the maps before he had the heart attack.

Monica wiped away a tear, consoling herself with the thought that Brian would approve of this venture. She often heard his voice in her head encouraging her to 'get away from bloody Beaconsfield and see the world!'

Customs was easy and Monica was soon on the airport forecourt.

'*Taxi, signorina?*' asked a smiling tout.

Monica almost replied 'Good try!' Especially the signorina bit, but decided to enjoy it instead. She didn't need a taxi. She knew exactly where she was going because she'd already been here once before on a trip with students to Pompeii and Herculaneum.

She jumped on a bus that took her to the Piazza Garibaldi, in central Naples, and looked around. There was the mainline station and now she had to find the Porto Nolano, the one for the Circumvesuviana train. Just the name thrilled her – the train around Mount Vesuvius! It turned out to be in a much scruffier part of the city, but Monica was reassured by all the other tourists looking for it as well. She watched the amazing Naples traffic, everyone hooting, swerving between lanes, and the way the thousands of *motorini*, the low-powered scooters that seemed the most popular form of transport in Italy, weaved in and out without being squashed by the huge trucks that almost looked as if knocking one down would be an enjoyable game for them.

The ticket office to the Circumvesuviana turned out to be an old railway carriage and the train more New York than Mount Vesuvius – bright red but entirely covered in graffiti. Monica scanned the destination board. The 'direct' train stopped at fifteen stops, God alone knew how many the in-direct one stopped at.

She bought a ticket and stepped on board. Inside, it was just like the tube – only with views. After just a few stops they reached Pompeii. Monica's heart swelled. She would be able to come and spend some proper time here another day; it wasn't that far from Lanzarella. And then Herculaneum! But it was Mount Vesuvius that really thrilled her. She stared at the vol-cano, extinct since 1954, with fascination.

And then the rain began. Proper English rain in dismal sheets, obscuring the volcano and everything else.

'Be careful, signora!' a voice hissed in her ear. Monica turned to find one of those Italian widows, shrouded top to toe in black, whispering in her ear. 'This train is worst in Italy for *borseggiatori*.' She acted out an exaggerated vignette of somebody picking a pocket, almost good enough for *Oliver*.

Instinctively, Monica patted the money belt inside her fleece. It was fine.

'*Grazie, signora*,' Monica thanked her, moving off all the same in case this was an elaborate set-up. The only time she'd been robbed in England was by someone purporting to be collecting for charity.

She was quite relieved when they reached Sorrento. It was still pouring with rain, so she tried to encourage herself by remembering the time she'd seen Pavarotti – bizarrely sharing the stage with Meat Loaf – singing the wrenching ballad '*Torna a Sorrento*' on stage together. It had been quite wonderful.

Now she had a dilemma. The sensible course from Sorrento would be the bus to Lerini. She could even see the orange SITA bus waiting in a line of others. Valiantly, she walked past it towards the harbour.

'Hydrofoil for Lerini?' she enquired of a flower seller who pointed down the opposite street.

The hydrofoil stop was about five minutes away. Monica had to hold tight so as not to lose her balance on the gangplank with her heavy backpack. Maybe she shouldn't have brought *quite* so many books. She was almost knocked over when a handsome young man bumped into her and then made a big performance of making sure she was all right.

'*Va bene, va bene,*' she kept telling him.

Although the journey to Lerini only took an hour it was deeply disappointing. She had to stay inside and the windows had fugged up. The rain persisted and had masked the entire coastline, which, she had been told, was so spectacular she would fall in love with it and never be able to leave.

To cap it all, when she got to Lerini, she'd just missed the bus to Lanzarella and the next one was in two hours.

'Is there an alternative?' she asked the ticket seller hopefully.

'*Mi dispiace,*' was his reply with a shake of the head. There obviously wasn't.

'Taxi or foot,' she was informed by one of those know-it-all Americans who seem to be more familiar with a place than the locals. Still, she ought to be grateful. 'How much is a taxi?'

It was a lot but she was tired after her early start. She delved inside her fleece for her money belt and almost fainted. It had gone! Yet she had paid for her ticket on the hydrofoil! The widow had been genuine but the handsome young man must have been a thief.

She almost collapsed where she stood.

She didn't even have the money for the bus fare. 'How the

hell am I going to get to Lanzarella?' she demanded, on the point of dissolving into tears. Monica pulled herself together. She wasn't the weeping type.

'You could take the short cut,' smirked the helpful American. 'It's only a thousand steps.'

Before she could face it she found a quiet spot sheltered by the yellow stucco front of the cathedral. She heard her mother's voice telling her it had been her own stupid choice to arrive by this circuitous route. Any sensible person would have chosen the bus or train. If she'd been at home, that might have depressed her, but here, far away from Mariella's nagging, Monica realized it just made her angry. There was a fountain to the right of the church and Monica took a long drink. She was sure the water here was fine. In another ten minutes she was ready to start the climb of a thousand steps up the mountainside to Lanzarella.

Sylvie retrieved her three bags from the carousel, piled them on the trolley and headed for the exit. She would have been quite happy to fix up private transport to the villa, but her old assistant Alessandro was Neapolitan and it seemed his manly honour was at stake if she didn't let him meet her himself. As Alessandro was about as manly as Julian Clary in stilettos, this had made Sylvie smile.

She looked along the row of excited families and taxi drivers with their cards, wondering if he was here yet. She didn't have long to wait. 'Sylvie! How long since I have seen you, lovely Sylvie!'

The rest of the passengers watched in fascination as a young man in motorcycle leathers shook out his long black curls, ran across the space between them and physically lifted Sylvie from the floor. No mean feat, given Sylvie's weight.

'I wanted to kill Tony when I saw that email. How stupid can straight men be?'

'I expect gay men are stupid too when it comes to love.'

Alessandro put his finger to her lips. 'No, do not make allowances. Do you give me permission to kill him?'

It struck Sylvie that this was the second offer she'd had to bump her husband off.

'Only in opera. Where's the car?'

'Cars are boring. I have brought my motorbike. My assistant will take the bags but we, *mia cara* Sylvie, we are going to arrive in style. He handed her a black leather jumpsuit. 'Go, put it on! I will mind the bags till Fabio collects them.'

Sylvie made herself smile. The truth was, she was terrified of motorbikes and God alone knew what her already unruly hair would be like when they got there. But Alessandro had always been a hard boy to refuse, and at least they would beat the hideous rush-hour snarl-ups between here and Lanzarella. She headed for the Ladies' toilet.

Putting on a leather jumpsuit in a small and none-too-fragrant cubicle was a challenge worthy of the *Krypton Factor*, but after fifteen minutes Sylvie emerged looking like a plus-sized version of Marianne Faithfull in *Girl on a Motorcycle*. She certainly attracted enough male attention on her way back to Alessandro to satisfy the most sensitive ego.

'Sylvie, *cara mia*, whatever stupid Tony thinks, you've still got it!'

Sylvie smiled back. The day was definitely getting better.

The bus deposited Claire in the main square, in front of the duomo in Lanzarella, just as Martin said it would. She glanced up at the intricately patterned facade with its black and white tiled arches giving it a distinctly Moorish air with just a touch of the Byzantine. No time for sightseeing now. She wanted to reach the villa and just flop. She wondered what they would be doing about dinner. Would she be cooking? And, if so, she hoped somebody had shopped. Welcome packs tended to be no more than the bare ingredients for breakfast.

A man who was optimistically selling Panama hats from a stall under the trees despite the rain had a friendly face so she decided to ask him for directions.

The man looked intrigued for a moment and pointed up the hill. Claire started in the direction he indicated, conscious of how noisy her wheely suitcase sounded banging along the cobbles in the peaceful piazza. No wonder the local authority in Venice wanted to ban them. A little audience of small boys tagged along for a bit then gave up when she seemed tame prey.

Beatrice was waiting for Angela in a long narrow room facing what seemed to be the front terrace. The doors, which would all be open if it were a nice day, were firmly closed, but since the top half of each was glazed, some light came through. The electric lights were the usual dim foreign wattage – she'd do something about that if she got the chance; there was nothing she loathed more than half-light when you were trying to work or read. Beatrice had at least lit candles in giant silver candelabras.

'*Brutto tempo!*' Beatrice shook her head as if this was something even the Prince of Lerini's prayers couldn't solve. 'I am sorry, signorina. Maybe tomorrow sunshine.' She held out a glass which she began to fill with fizzy wine.

'Prosecco?' enquired Angela, seating herself in a medieval churchy-shaped chair.

Beatrice shook her head. Another faux pas to add to her growing list. 'No Prosecco. Prosecco too sweet! Is Franciacorta.'

Angela took a glass and sipped. 'It's delicious!' she commented with surprise.

This was definitely the right reaction. 'Is it from round here?'

'No.' Beatrice looked a little sheepish. 'From Lombardy in the North. Near the Lakes. Not from round here.'

'What a great discovery. No more Prosecco. I will only drink Franciacorta from now on!'

She was about to have another sip when a great clanging started up.

'It is doorbell, Signorina Gwilliams. I go and answer.'

Beatrice disappeared into the bowels of the convent, leaving Angela to enjoy her drink alone.

Moments later Beatrice came back with Claire in tow.

'Is Signora Lambert!' she announced with such delighted surprise it was as if Claire were the last person she was expecting.

'Hello, Angela.' Claire held out a hand shyly.

'I think we're beyond shaking hands, don't you, after you anointed that idiot with boiling coffee. Have a drink?' Angela poured Claire a Franciacorta. 'Don't call it Prosecco, by the way. Extraordinary place, isn't it?'

Claire stared around in amazement. 'I don't know what I was expecting, certainly nothing as grand as this.'

'I think it's the word "villa". Have you met Giovanni yet?'

Claire looked puzzled and shook her head. 'I don't think so.'

'You wouldn't forget, believe me. Shall I show you the rooms so you can choose?'

'I really don't mind,' Claire began. 'Whichever is most convenient.'

'Hey, what happened to the Boadicea of Brook Street? Can I tell you something, Claire?' Angela asked in the way that made her very good at business but less so at friendship. 'Saying you don't mind is really irritating. It's actually much less trouble if you just choose.'

'Oh. Right,' Claire replied, taken aback at Angela's directness. A small smile lit up her slightly doughy features. Angela had forgotten how disarming it was. 'If we're being direct, I thought it was rude of you not to offer me a lift from the airport. Then I wouldn't have had to be given this travel pack by my irritating husband.' She produced Martin's itinerary and handed it over.

Angela took a sip and studied it. 'Wow.' Angela smiled, handing it back. 'And I thought I was controlling.'

'Please don't be. Not here. I came here to get away from all that. Sunshine. Freedom. A change of scenery.'

'I'll do my best,' Angela agreed. 'No promises though. Especially about the sunshine.'

'Signora Lambert, shall I show you the rooms?' offered Beatrice.

'Thank you.' Claire stood back to let Beatrice lead. To her surprise Angela followed.

'I'm afraid I bagged the best one,' Angela remarked unapologetically. 'But this one's good too.' She pointed to the next room down the corridor. It was almost as huge as Angela's. This time the bed canopy was purple silk instead of velvet.

'Oh my God,' Claire's hand flew to her mouth, 'look at that!'

'It's not a mouse?' To Claire's amusement, as someone who'd grown up in the country, ball-breaker Angela looked genuinely scared.

'On that wall opposite the bed. The painting.'

Claire pointed to a huge picture of three women stretched naked across what looked like a giant barbecue full of hot coals with a horrible-looking demon fanning the flames, a look of lust mixed with disapproval on its nasty face.

'Oh that.' Angela studied it 'They're called doom paintings. They're supposed to keep the faithful on the straight and narrow. Funny place to hang it though, they're usually in church. No deviant sex for you in that bed.'

They were both giggling like schoolgirls when the door opened and the divine Giovanni emerged with Claire's bag. He glanced uneasily from the two women to the painting and made the sign of the cross.

Claire thanked him and he put her bag on the suitcase stand, backing out of the room as soon as he could.

'That's Giovanni. Amazing, isn't he? He works in the garden, I think. I wouldn't try seducing him in this room. Something tells me it wouldn't come off under that picture. Though I suppose that was the idea. Medieval aversion therapy.'

The rest of the room was simply luxurious: a deep velvet sofa in leafy green with cushions to match the canopy; a writing desk; two more comfortable chairs; decadently generous purple curtains. And this time the flowers hadn't been forgotten. There was a vast arrangement of dark blue anemones, irises and Canterbury bells.

'Beatrice just told me the owner was very particular.' Angela shrugged. 'Flowers in all the rooms.'

'Amazing. Bouquets and naked women tied to giant barbecues? The owner seems to have pretty weird tastes.'

'I don't think that was him. It used to be a convent, so maybe he inherited the art. I know what you mean though. It is a bit unsettling.'

Claire wasn't the type to need to unpack her bag. 'Why

don't we have a look around? Especially the kitchen. Maybe we'll find clues.'

'In the kitchen?'

'No, but I want to see what facilities they've got. Judging by this painting it'll be cooking on an open fire with a spit dog to turn the meat. Do you know they used to put hot oil on the dog's feet to make it run faster, poor little thing?'

Angela shuddered. 'I'm quite glad I live now, actually.'

They both laughed and made their way downstairs. Now that she was sticking up for herself, Angela thought, maybe it wouldn't be too bad to have Claire around.

Beatrice was ready to refill their glasses in the beautiful salon. Outside the rain was as grey and depressing as ever.

'What time would you like dinner, ladies? Immaculata, she asks if half past eight is convenient?'

'Oh gosh, they have a cook!' Claire sounded almost upset. 'I sort of thought I would be doing the cooking.'

'You can relax. Don't worry, I'm sure you can still inspect the facilities and see what would be needed if the owner does decide to open a hotel.'

Behind them Beatrice suddenly missed the glass she was filling and poured the wine onto the ancient carpet.

Angela and Claire glanced at her, taken aback. She seemed so calm and efficient.

'Is a pity the other ladies have not arrived yet,' Beatrice announced, mopping up the floor, 'but perhaps you eat anyway?'

Claire and Angela were suddenly riveted. 'What other ladies?' Angela demanded.

'Two more English ladies,' Beatrice replied. 'Signora Sutton and Signora Mathieson.'

'Good God!' Angela downed her wine in irritation. 'I didn't

sign up for this. It's like a bloody nunnery. I mean, who are these women? And why the hell are they coming? I think I'm going to ring Drew and find out what this friend of his is up to.'

She opened the door to the terrace in the faint hope her phone might work there. No chance. She came back in, looking livid. 'No signal, naturally. And it's still bloody raining.'

'Giovanni,' offered Beatrice, 'he say best place for phone is down by bed of *asparagi*.'

Angela shook her head. 'And I bet asparagus beds aren't the only beds he knows all about,' she said sourly. 'Where is the wretched bed of asparagus anyway?'

Beatrice opened the door and pointed to the lower layer of terracing and handed Angela an umbrella.

Angela made her way down the gravel path so angrily that she hardly even looked around her. She hated being with other women! She was prepared to put up with Claire because Claire had done her a favour, but two more women she didn't even know were going to turn up and intrude on their peace, yattering on about God knew what. And she still couldn't get a signal!

She made her way back to the villa, noting that her favourite orange suede shoes were probably ruined, when the roar of a motorbike deafened her. It was coming up their drive too.

She couldn't resist going back into the house and announcing it to the others.

'There's a motorbike coming up the drive. Is it Giovanni?'

Beatrice shook her head. 'Giovanni has *motorino*. All the people here have *motorini*.'

Angela grabbed a glass and they all trooped out to the back entrance just in time to see a spectacular arrival. A handsome young man, though not as handsome as Giovanni, stopped the motorbike ten yards from the back door and they watched as his black leather-clad passenger climbed off, removed her helmet and shook out a cloud of curly dark red hair. In what seemed to be one fluid gesture she undid her zip and pulled off the leather jumpsuit, revealing a colourful silk top and jeans.

She stepped forward, as if she naturally assumed they were all waiting for her, a hand held out. 'Hello, there,' she explained, 'I'm Sylvie Sutton and this is my friend Alessandro.'

Before Angela could say a word, a small bedraggled figure with an enormous backpack, making Claire think of an ant carrying twice its weight back to the colony, appeared from a path between two rhododendron bushes.

They all turned, amazed.

'Hello, everyone,' announced the latest arrival, and even her voice sounded as if it needed to be wrung out, 'I'm Monica Mathieson. This is Villa Le Sirenuse?' Her pronunciation of the Italian words was perfect. 'Only I've just had my money belt stolen. That's why I had to walk up from Lerini.'

'Signora Mathieson?' Beatrice ran out, her kind heart touched by Monica's wet and exhausted condition. '*Che cosa terribile!* There is no honesty left in this country! You must come in by the fire. Giovanni! Giovanni! Come and help the signora!'

Giovanni also appeared from the bushes and lifted off Monica's backpack.

Claire watched, quietly amused by Alessandro's sudden interest in Giovanni and Sylvie's obvious irritation at having her dramatic arrival upstaged by this small wet person. Claire also knew at once that she would like Monica and that Sylvie and Angela would be rivals, the female equivalent of rutting stags. It was just a question of when.

She didn't have long to wait.

'You must go and change from your wet clothes and then

we will serve dinner,' Beatrice clucked. 'Giovanni, take the signora's suitcase up to the second floor.'

'Go with Giovanni, signora. He will show you.'

'And where will I be staying?' Sylvie asked, droplets of rain glistening in her hair like silver balls on a Christmas tree.

'Signora Sutton, of course.' To Claire's sharp ears there was a hint of irritation in Beatrice's reply. 'I will take you up myself. Will your friend be staying for dinner?'

Now that Giovanni had gone inside, Alessandro seemed to have lost interest. 'No. I return to Napoli. Now before the darkness comes.'

'Can we offer you some wine before you go?'

He shook his handsome head. Giovanni's looks, it seemed to Claire, were those of the sexy pin-up, whereas Alessandro could have posed for one of the classical statues that seemed to dot the gardens.

'By the way, *cara mia*, you have a famous neighbour, though you will never get to meet him.'

'Why not?'

'Constantine O is a world-famous painter but also a recluse.'

At least that was one extra person she wouldn't have to be friendly to, Angela thought with relief.

Alessandro waved them all goodbye and disappeared back down the drive.

'But where are your baggages, Signora Sutton?'

'Alessandro's assistant is bringing his car to drop them off. Let's go and look at those bedrooms.'

Beatrice led the way up the wide stone staircase. Sylvie followed, taking in every detail. The room she had been allocated was so awful she couldn't bring herself to speak. 'How did you select our rooms, Beatrice?'

'It was *chi prima arriva, meglio alloggia*. First come, first served, I think in English.'

'Signorina Williams arrived first?'

'Signorina Gwilliams was first to arrive, *sí*.'

'Very smart of her. Tell me, are there any other bedrooms? We saw several wings when we were round the back.'

'*Sí*, there are rooms but they are not used.'

'Good. I will stay in this room tonight but tomorrow I will look at the rooms in the wings.'

'*Bene, signora*.' Beatrice looked at Sylvie as if she were mad. No one had slept in the wings for years, but then everyone accepted the English were mad. It was a known fact.

Meanwhile, Monica had changed out of her wet clothes and was standing looking lost on the landing. Sylvie tried not to focus on what she was wearing. It was too appalling.

'What's your room like?' Sylvie quizzed her.

'Wonderful,' enthused Monica. 'I've got my own bathroom and little bottles of toiletries just like you get in a hotel!'

'Right.' Sylvie attempted a smile. She couldn't imagine a universe in which you didn't have your own bathroom. 'Well, I think it's outrageous that just because this Angela got here first she grabbed far and away the best room. I mean, anyone halfway decent would have waited so we could draw straws or something.'

'You wouldn't have chosen that room if you'd arrived first, then?' Monica asked innocently.

Sylvie stared at her, searching for signs of irony, but the question seemed perfectly genuine. 'No, of course I wouldn't,' Sylvie lied. 'I would have waited till we were all here.'

'But Claire says they didn't know you and I were coming.'

Sylvie stared at her even harder. 'Yes. Well, so she says.'

'I'm sure Angela wouldn't make it up just to get the best room. I mean, who on earth would do that?'

Sylvie made a business out of fiddling with the tassel on her top. 'Anyway. Whatever. I'm going to explore the wings tomorrow. Come on, we'd better go down to dinner or they'll have eaten that too.'

As she followed Monica down the wide stone staircase Sylvie wondered how soon she could make her escape and fly straight back to London. Staying here was clearly going to be a complete disaster.

Monica, on the other hand, seemed to be getting happier by the moment. 'Well, I'm absolutely thrilled to be here. Hundreds of miles away from my mother.' She glanced at Sylvie. 'Does that sound awful?'

Sylvie thought of her own mother, bitter and complaining in her very expensive care home. 'No, not at all. Very sensible.'

'With Pompeii and Herculaneum on our doorstep.'

'I prefer the sound of Capri.'

'Isn't that all rich people and expensive boutiques?'

'Exactly.' It was the one thought that was stopping Sylvie calling Alessandro and making a bolt for it tonight.

# Five

_____

Stephen Charlesworth sat looking out at the Thames from his house on Bankside, a stone's throw from the Globe Theatre. One of the contradictions of his personality, and he knew there were many, was that his business was mostly developing luxury high-rise housing, yet he lived in a four-hundred-year-old house on the banks of the river. He loved the feel of old London you got from this small row of houses, and especially the fact that three doors down had once been a famous brothel or 'stew-house', as they were then known, called the Cardinal's Cap, frequented by Ben Jonson and other literary luminaries.

He was wondering, as he looked out at the peaceful river, whether he ought to call Beatrice and make sure everything was all right for his new guests, yet he also knew the staff would take wonderful care of them and he wanted to be a host with the lightest of touches, so that they could enjoy themselves without having to feel beholden. The offer he'd been made to buy the villa from a local hotel chain was a generous one and made perfect logical sense, given the amount of time he spent there. And were it not for his complicated feelings about the place he ought to accept it at once. But, as his mother said, it was a unique home. Some sensible independent advice would be genuinely useful. The idea of turning it into a hotel himself was a bit of a fantasy given how busy he was, but again it would be interesting to hear what Sylvie and Angela would propose.

He found that he was smiling. As his mother had pointed out, they'd have to see how Lanzarella affected them all. It was certainly a place you could fall in love with.

An old London barge glided past his window, its dark red sail flapping gently, leaving a small wave spreading across the river in its wake. Watching it, Stephen felt a rare stab of loneliness. Normally, he filled the void with work, sometimes concerts and a busy social life, but the thought of Lanzarella brought back memories of Carla and what they might have had together if she hadn't died so unexpectedly.

Maybe he should sell the place after all.

He decided to go for a walk and watch the theatregoers straggling over the Millennium Bridge, the mudlarks with metal detectors on the riverbanks when the tide went out, and his favourite view of all London, St Paul's Cathedral, which his mother accused people like him of obscuring with their horrible modern buildings. Just the sight of it made him smile.

'You look happy, Steve,' Sam, the *Big Issue* seller outside the Swan pub greeted him. He was the only person who ever called Stephen 'Steve'.

Stephen duly bought his *Big Issue*, even though he'd already bought one from another seller. Ridiculous really, as his mother reminded him; he should just hand over a tower block to the homeless instead of buying surplus *Big Issues*, but the banks who funded him might have a word to say about that. He did his bit to make sure the social housing he provided as part of his schemes wasn't just on noisy major roads, but overlooking some gardens, much to the annoyance of the financiers, but it hardly made him Bill Gates.

'You need to fall in love again,' Gwen was prone to remind him.

Most men who lost their wives seemed to get over it remarkably quickly in Stephen's view, as if a wife was just someone who made the house tidy and welcoming, but he'd really loved Carla.

And Carla had loved the Villa Le Sirenuse. As he walked back along the river, Stephen saw a woman waiting to go into the Globe Theatre. She was leaning against the river wall, reading a copy of *The Times*.

Angela's face stared out at him from under the headline 'Work is the Way I Relax', and he felt glad she was in lovely Lanzarella.

Everyone told him that Lanzarella had a way of changing your perceptions. Everyone's except his, it seemed.

He wished for the briefest moment that he were there with them all.

Maybe it could finally change his as well.

The table in the dining room of the villa could seat forty but to be cosier, Beatrice had laid it just at one end. Unfortunately, she had put one person at the end with the other three organized round them. To maintain some ceremony she had added white linen napkins, flowers and candles.

As if it were the most natural thing in the world Angela sat herself down in the prime position. Monica looked nervously at Sylvie, who flounced her skirts as she placed herself at Angela's right hand. Claire and Monica took the seats on either side, exchanging a look of unspoken solidarity that neither of them cared where they sat.

Beatrice appeared with the wine and compounded the situation by showing Angela the label in unconscious recognition of her status.

'She thinks you're the boss,' Claire joked.

'Or a man,' Sylvie added under her breath.

The first course appeared, a fragrant pumpkin ravioli with fresh tomato sauce.

'Delicious,' savoured Claire, trying to break the ice. 'Immaculata is a terrific cook.'

Angela took a sip of her wine and looked round. 'Maybe I should put my cards on the table,' she announced. 'I don't really do women friends.'

Claire willed her to stop. She'd come to like Angela once she'd got to know her a little, and saw that this was the best way to antagonize everyone.

'More wine, Angela?' she tried to offer as Sylvie muttered, 'I'm not bloody surprised.'

'But as we seem to be here under rather surprising circumstances maybe we should say a bit about ourselves. I'm Angela Williams. I own a chain of dress shops called Fabric.'

'I've got a top from there,' Monica threw in.

Angela raised an eyebrow as if to say, 'I would never have guessed it.'

'And I do the TV series *Done Deal*.'

'As the ball breaker, surprise, surprise,' contributed Sylvie in a low voice.

'Recently the company was taken over against my will.'

'How awful,' Monica sympathized. 'I didn't know they could do that.'

105

'It's commoner than you'd think. I wanted a bit of a break to get away from the publicity.'

'Yes, poor you, it must have been awful,' Sylvie threw in with a sardonic tone. 'All that money they gave you.'

The irony was lost on Angela. 'Yes, vile. Then I got this offer to come here and see if the house had the potential to be a hotel.'

Beatrice, arriving with the main course, stopped a moment in her tracks so suddenly that a plate slid from the tray she was carrying. '*Scusi! Mi scusi, signora!*'

Claire rushed round to help pick up the food from the floor as Beatrice, still flustered, took the dish back to the kitchen to replace it.

'I wonder what's got to her,' Claire mused. 'She poured the wine on the carpet earlier. Something a bit odd going on.'

'So.' Angela sailed on as if nothing had happened. 'Tell us about you, Claire.'

'I'm very ordinary. No hostile takeovers or TV shows. Though sometimes a hostile takeover sounds rather tempting. I run a catering company. Very small scale. Birthdays, anniversaries, funerals. It just about washes its face with a little bit over, but mostly I love it. And it gets me away from my husband.'

Sylvie laughed in mutual understanding.

'I came to see about the catering possibilities if this were to be a hotel.'

'Sylvie?' asked Angela.

Sylvie looked at her coldly; she supposed she had to join in this stupid charade. 'I'm Sylvie Sutton. I run a successful interior design business with my husband.' She hesitated, wondering how much she was prepared to give away. 'I've been working too hard recently and needed a break.'

Angela looked at her, tempted to say something. She had been shown the email of Tony and Kimberley caught in the act by a business associate and thought it was hilarious. But if Sylvie chose not to mention it, that was up to her. It must have been seriously humiliating after all.

With perfect timing Immaculata filled the awkward pause by arriving with veal saltimbocca and crispy potatoes. 'That smells wonderful!' Monica enthused. 'Is Beatrice all right? *Sta bene Beatrice?*' She surprised the entire room with her perfect Italian accent. Pronouncing Beatrice not like the rest of them in the English manner but 'Bay-ah-tree-chay', as it should be said.

'Impressive,' congratulated Sylvie, who had lived in enough countries to recognize a flair for languages.

'Au pair in Florence.' Monica shrugged. 'I don't recommend it. Underpaid slavery. But then I did get to study in Rome for a term when I was at university. That was fun.'

'Monica obviously has hidden depths,' Angela commented.

'Just as well, since there's not much on the surface.' Monica blushed.

'You'll have to learn not to be so self-deprecating, Monica. People accept the image you give them,' Angela corrected.

'Except in your case, Angela,' Sylvie said sweetly. 'I gather they wanted a new image for your company.'

They all waited for Angela's reaction but she simply looked scathingly at Sylvie. 'Anyway, Monica, you haven't told us about you.'

'I'm Monica,' Monica announced, loathing the confrontation and wanting to head it off, but hating drawing the attention to herself. 'This'll probably make you laugh, people always do for some reason, but I used to be a librarian.' No one laughed but they were all watching her. Angela refilled her own glass. Not the others', Sylvie noted. 'I worked for forty years at the University of Buckingham. That confuses people because they don't know Buckingham has a university, but it was wonderful. I was the university librarian. I met my husband Brian there and we were happily married for twenty-five years. Sometimes people are surprised about that.'

'Monica!' This was a step too far for Angela. 'Stop putting yourself down!'

'I wasn't actually.'

'What happened to Brian?' Claire asked, hoping he hadn't run off.

'He had a massive heart attack about a year ago. For some reason my mother likes telling people that.'

'What a mother!' Sylvie shook her head. 'Why would she like telling people that?'

'Because she thinks I'm a failure to have chosen someone with poor health.'

'But mothers are supposed to be supportive!' Claire exclaimed, thinking of how she couldn't stand her daughter-in-law yet she was her son's choice and she ought to be nicer to her.

'That's exactly what Gwen says.' A mischievous smile crept across Monica's face, transforming it from ordinary to engagingly gamine. 'Gwen says my mother's a complete bitch and that's why she made her son invite me here.'

'How funny!' Sylvie's smile was genuine this time. 'After I accepted, Gwen rang me and said my husband was a complete bastard and she'd persuaded her son to invite *me* to his house in Italy to get away for a bit!'

They both laughed at the coincidence and how like Gwen it was, while Claire smiled and Angela looked annoyed.

A delectable dessert of tiramisu arrived, served by Beatrice, who seemed to have recovered her usual calm.

'Would you ladies like coffee in the salon?' she enquired.

'Fresh mint tea for me, if you have it please, Beatrice.' Sylvie wasn't going to attempt the Italian pronunciation.

'So who is this mysterious Gwen you all seem to idolize?' Angela asked.

'Gwen Charlesworth,' Sylvie replied. 'She was our neighbour. And my lifesaver. My parents were always away, and disinterested in having a child when they were at home. Gwen sort of rescued me.'

'Me too,' Monica smiled. 'I haven't known her as long as you have, but she's always been incredibly kind.'

Angela was struck silent for once and sat staring into her empty wine glass.

Suddenly she looked up. 'You're not telling me that Gwen Charlesworth is the mother of Stephen Charlesworth? And that this house belongs to Stephen Charlesworth!'

'I think we are,' Sylvie stated, studying her. What the hell was the matter with her? All at once bossy bloody Angela had lost her confidence and sat there looking like a deflated balloon.

'But I know him! I mean . . . I went out with him for the first year at Oxford and then I had to leave because my mother had a breakdown, a really bad one.'

'You poor thing,' said Monica with genuine sympathy. She'd seen enough students to know how hard that would be just when you'd started enjoying university life.

'So do I!' Claire grinned, equally amazed. 'Well, I mean I know him too. I went to a ball with him. I was in Oxford as well. Not at the university, obviously. The Ox and Cow!'

'Is that a pub?' Sylvie asked, having difficulty keeping up with all these revelations.

'The Oxford and County Secretarial College,' Claire announced with a flourish. 'Everyone called it the Ox and Cow. Aspiring mothers with dim daughters sent them there in the hope that they'd nab a posh student.'

'My God!' This was a closed world to Sylvie, who'd left school at seventeen and got a job straight away. 'It sounds like Jane Austen.'

'Except it was the Sixties. Lizzie takes a trip. Mr Darcy on ganja.' Claire giggled.

'You didn't go out with Stephen too, did you Monica?' Claire asked.

'Thanks for the compliment. No. We played together when we were kids.'

'So did we,' Sylvie remembered. 'He'd never wear a tutu.'

'But this means we all know Stephen Charlesworth!' Angela pointed out, clearly agitated.

'What's so odd about that?' Sylvie shrugged. 'It's his house!'

'Yes, but two of us haven't seen him for years and didn't even know this *was* his house. I think it's seriously weird.'

'Oh, for goodness' sake,' Sylvie shook her head, 'you're making far too much of it. I suggest we skip the salon and all go to bed. Maybe tomorrow the rain will have stopped.'

The revelation had achieved one thing at least, Sylvie noted. Bloody Angela Williams had stopped behaving as if she owned the place and they were just her guests. And as for not *doing* women friends, who had asked her to be their friend anyway?

Claire was the first to wake; she'd always been an early riser and often leapt out of bed leaving Martin to sleep. She padded over to the window and threw open the shutters. The sun hit her eyes with such force that she had to stand back and shade them. But as soon as she was accustomed to the sunlight she leaned out of her window. The vista unfolding in front of her took her breath away with its loveliness.

The terrace beneath her window was decorated with urns overflowing with pale pink geraniums which gave way to trees of bright, new spring green and below that a dazzling cobalt blue sea. A single fishing boat ploughed its way across her vision, heading inland with its overnight catch, leaving a white trail from its motor.

Claire looked at her watch. Only seven. No one else would be up. And she knew she just had to be outside.

She quickly changed into jeans and a T-shirt, scrabbled around for her trainers and sneaked out through the silent house.

In the gardens that tumbled down the hillside it wasn't just the light that amazed her but a heady perfume she didn't recognize. As she rounded the corner at the side of the house she came across a pergola, half hidden by a mass of purple wisteria, with two chairs placed underneath it. She sat down and breathed in the glorious scent, but it was too lovely to sit for long. At the back of the house almond, cherry and apple trees waved their pink and white blossoms in the morning breeze and she could hear the sound of bees buzzing from one flower to the next.

On the next level down, a small fountain trickled beside a half-hidden grotto with a fresh-water pool built into the rock face. Claire almost clapped her hands in delight. On the edge of the pool a life-sized marble nymph kneeled, staring into the water, an expression of longing on her face. The quality of the carving was extraordinary. This was not the work of some local stonemason. It had to have been chiselled by the hand of a master.

An irresistible temptation overcame Claire. She glanced furtively around, then, satisfied that she was alone, stripped off her clothes down to pants and bra. Oh what the hell, she thought, the nymph is naked, why not me too?

The water was icy cold and clear as gin, but country-bred Claire just held her breath until she got used to it.

She found a small ledge where she could support herself and stared again at the statue. 'Is it your lost lover you're searching for?' she enquired of the stone maiden. 'Banished under the water by some jealous goddess?'

The only answer was a laugh.

Claire swung round to find Giovanni pushing a wheelbarrow, his shirt undone even further than Simon Cowell's, though Giovanni's chest could not have been more different.

'*Due ninfe.*' He smiled with that sly sexy smile that seemed so characteristically Italian. Two nymphs. One nymph and a crone might have been more appropriate. Casually Claire slipped an arm across her breasts, conscious that if she let go of the ledge to protect her modesty she would disappear under the water. She must carry this off with confidence as if English ladies took naked dips every morning. The terrible thought struck her that Giovanni was looking straight at her body through the crystal-clear water.

'*Febbre di primavera.* The fever of the spring,' he stated as if this was a perfectly acceptable explanation for finding a nude woman in a fountain. 'Nobody can resist.'

And then he walked onwards, whistling.

Claire waited until he was safely out of sight and then climbed out. She didn't even have a towel. She pulled her T-shirt on over her wet body, realizing it only drew attention

An Italian Holiday

to her freezing nipples, and scrabbled into her jeans, the dampness of her body making her almost fall over as she tried to yank them on.

She glanced back at the pool.

From where he was standing with the sunlight illuminating the water, she would have seemed as naked as Lady Godiva minus her famous hair.

She wondered for a moment how Martin would have reacted if he'd come upon her nude in a pool. Probably wouldn't have noticed. Or maybe he'd have said: 'For God's sake, Claire, what the hell are you doing? You'll catch your death.' Certainly not called her a nymph. To give him his due he was from Cheltenham.

Angela drew back one of her extravagant devoré curtains and stepped out onto her large balcony, so large that it was really a terrace. For a moment she didn't notice the beauty of the day, still preoccupied with the fact that this was Stephen Charlesworth's house.

She remembered when they'd said goodbye as clearly as if she were still in the moment. He had been so kind when the father she loved so much had died and had even driven her home in his ancient black Austin Healey to take care of her mother. They had both been grateful that for once it hadn't broken down. How he'd loved that car.

And then he'd kissed her goodbye and they'd both promised to keep in touch, but she'd known it was a lie. He was twenty-one and had just found his feet at Oxford. He was attractive and, now that he'd lost his initial shyness, charming. He would be devoured alive by some clever, pretty girl who came from a background like his own, not a council house in Nottingham.

113

Angela had tried not to resent her mother, to accept that she had always been fragile, but there had been some small part of her that thought if she had been in her mother's place she would have done anything to avoid ending her daughter's brilliant university career before it had really begun.

Of course she had heard of Stephen's enormous success since that day. His name often came up in the financial pages, which Angela read avidly, or at least had done until now. The ache, just a dull background pain, suddenly roared out at her. She'd lost her business to the Tuan Corporation of Singapore and when she was twenty-one she'd lost Stephen.

At last the beauty of the day struck her and she almost laughed. It was as if some piece of grey rain-soaked scenery had been rolled away and another rolled into its place of bright blue sea that matched the sky, with small puffy clouds and a child's yellow sun.

She turned back to her room wondering what to wear. Seen in daylight the room was truly spectacular, like the bridal suite in some grand hotel. The unfamiliar thought struck Angela that perhaps it had been a little selfish of her to simply co-opt the best room. She was so used to fighting for what she'd achieved that it didn't leave much room for considering others.

She remembered the other rooms that Sylvie and Monica had been left with and shuddered. Sylvie didn't even have her own bathroom! Maybe she'd wait a few days and then offer to swap. There was a good chance that by then they'd be settled, thank her for the kind offer, and stay put.

Sylvie climbed out of bed and stretched. There was hardly room to swing a cat in. What a stupid expression. Had anyone, apart from in *The Beano*, ever tried swinging a cat? Today she'd find another room even if it was the bloody stables.

She did her five minutes of Pilates, boring as hell, but it did seem to help once you'd reached the big Six-Oh. Not that Sylvie ever admitted she had.

She brushed her springy hair and selected one of her silk tops. She had these in countless colours which she matched with jeans and sandals and she was ready to go. If she had to dress up it was ankle-length silk, which she also possessed in endless different shades. This was Sylvie's look, known to everyone in the decorating world, almost as familiar as her colourful interiors.

She opened the shutter and closed it almost at once. Too bright. With her naturally olive skin and Middle-Eastern appearance the sun meant less to her than most people since she never needed to sunbathe. She was glad the rain had stopped for at least one reason. It made her hair go frizzy. In Los Angeles they even had a hair-frizz factor on the TV weather. Sylvie greatly approved.

She checked to see that the purple Chanel nail varnish she always wore on her toes hadn't chipped, remembering all of a sudden that it was called Vendetta – which, for some reason, made her think of Angela.

OK, so Angela Williams was an uppity bitch but if they were both going to stay in the same house, maybe she'd make a slight effort to be friendly. At least give her one chance and take it from there.

There was a small chip on her third toenail and it almost undid her.

Tony used to paint her toes. It was a jokey ritual of theirs. She would be the haughty duchess and he the humble but sexy manservant. It often ended up in bed with her nail varnish all smudged, but she'd never minded.

She wondered what he was doing now. Had Kimberley's family accepted him as the prospective son-in-law even though he was probably older than her father?

She found the thought only made her want to cry more and she told herself sternly to pull herself together and go and have some breakfast.

Monica climbed out of bed and although she could see the sun splintering through the shutter and longed to throw it open, she made herself do her mindfulness exercises first. Unfortunately, her mind kept wandering to what to wear and had to be 'escorted back' in the jargon of the genre. She had considered her Fabric top, but that raised eyebrow of Angela's had not been lost on perceptive Monica. Finally, her five minutes was up (she was far too excited to go for the full half-hour) and she sprang up.

Though her small room only had a Juliet balcony instead of one you could actually step out onto, she still did her best, opening the shutter and leaning out as far as she could to breathe in lungfuls of the clear, dazzling air. The sun was blazing and the air had that freshness and clarity that came only after heavy rain. To Monica it tasted like champagne.

She surveyed her paltry clothes selection and picked out a taupe linen top. Her mother had said it was the kind of garment psychotherapists wore. Partnered with some harmless linen trousers, Monica decided it looked passable. Perhaps she'd be able to pick up some livelier clothes in the local market. The top of her arms looked a bit pudgy but not actually offensive. Then the big decision – trainers or sandals? She looked out once more at the glorious day that beckoned. On the spur of the moment she checked her phone – avoiding any messages from her mother – and had a look at the weather in Beaconsfield, the nearest sizeable town to Great Missenden. Heavy rain!

With a smug smile, Monica slipped on her sandals and, as an afterthought, a mother-of-pearl necklace, and went down to breakfast. The others might have doubts about the strange set-up and the unexpected company. Monica was just thrilled she was here.

Sylvie couldn't believe it. She went into the dining room at the same moment as Claire, to find that Angela had once again taken possession of the commanding end seat.

'Morning, all,' Angela greeted them cheerfully. 'There's coffee or hot chocolate and croissants called cornettos and wonderful fresh fruit salad. Just help yourself.'

Even to Claire this had the unfortunate ring of a host inviting her guests to dig in. If she had said, 'We just help ourselves,' it would somehow have been far more tactful.

'I'm not hungry, thanks.' Sylvie helped herself to a coffee and went straight outside onto the terrace, all her good intentions abandoned. She found a shady seat and sat down where she could still hear the conversation but make her point.

'What's *her* problem?' Angela shrugged.

Claire took a deep breath. 'I like you a lot, Angela, and admire you too.'

Angela stared. What on earth was the woman about to say? 'But?'

'Maybe it's because – as you say – you don't *do* women friends, but you tend to run things like a meeting with you in charge.'

Monica, standing at the door about to come in, held her

breath. It was brave of Claire to confront Angela head on, but it had been her experience at the university that the very people who told you that you could speak to them directly were the worst at taking criticism when you did.

There was no turning back now, Claire realized. 'Perhaps if you didn't always sit at the head of the table it would seem a bit more democratic.' She wasn't even going to touch on how Angela was somehow making the others feel that it was *her* house, just because she'd got here first.

Outside on the terrace Sylvie smiled. So Claire had more nerve than you'd think, just looking at her.

'How absolutely ridiculous!' Angela spotted Monica hovering in the doorway. 'Monica! Don't you agree that what Claire says is crazy? You don't think I'm taking over, do you?'

Monica tried to dismiss the idea that Angela was actually her mother in disguise. 'Well . . .' Claire shot her a meaningful look. 'There are four of us, so nobody actually needs to sit at the end of the table.'

'That's an excellent idea, Monica,' Claire seconded. She might as well go for broke, Angela was going to hate her anyway. 'And perhaps we should draw straws for who has which room, seeing as they're so very different, or agree to swap after a certain number of days.'

Sylvie swept back in. If these two mice could take on Angela, she'd better have a go herself.

'I've got an even better idea,' Sylvie suggested. 'We've been invited here to see if the place should be sold or could be turned into a hotel so, to make sure no one takes over, I think we should turn ourselves into a cooperative.'

'Cooperatives rarely work,' Angela replied sharply.

'They work for the wine growers! Speaking of which, I'll get Beatrice to bring in some of that Franciacorta.'

'For breakfast?' Angela glowered.

'To celebrate the Lanzarella Women's Cooperative!' Sylvie laughed.

'But what are we trying to achieve?'

'That's what we have to find out. Together. What the hell we're all doing here.'

Angela dropped her head into her hands. But finally she was laughing too and when Beatrice arrived with the wine, all smiles at these ladies who suddenly seemed so happy, she raised her glass in the toast with the others.

'Perhaps we should start by—' Angela began.

The other three looked at her. 'Angela, you're doing it again,' pointed out Sylvie.

'But if no one takes the lead, we'll never decide anything.'

'And maybe that's fine,' Sylvie insisted. 'Maybe we just enjoy being here and it'll all become clear. For a start, I'm going into Lerini to look for some stuff to cheer up the room I'm moving into near the Bell Tower.'

'But won't the bell-ringing drive you mad?' Angela asked guiltily. 'It tolls every quarter of an hour.'

'I'm a little bit deaf. Telling you that is a symbol of my trust, like being blood sisters. I don't tell anyone that.' She lifted her glass. 'OK, blood sisters? Anyone want to come?'

They lifted their glasses.

'I will,' offered Monica.

'Me too,' added Claire.

'If we're a cooperative, I suppose I'd better join you,' Angela conceded, shaking her head, 'in this mad venture.'

As they all went to their various bedrooms to get ready, Monica remembered that not only did she not have any money, but her bank cards had been in the money belt too. Why had she not followed her usual practice of keeping one in her sponge bag? She had almost done so but it had made her feel like a mad old woman, always imagining the worst was going to happen. And it had.

The nightmare thing was that there had been three hundred euros in the belt, half the amount she'd put aside for the whole holiday. Of course her mother had told her not to take cash, but Monica had decided to ignore her. She was a grown-up woman and had often travelled with Brian, nearly always carrying cash because they were a trusting pair who liked to think the best of people, and it had always been all right.

The thought of Brian, the one person she'd ever met who saw beyond her unassuming exterior, suddenly overwhelmed her and she had to sit down. Her mother turned his death into a cruel joke, but it had been the worst thing that had happened in her whole life. She hadn't even said goodbye to him. They'd both been in a rush, she because she was on early duty. The library was open all night for the benefit of the nocturnal students and, amazingly, there were quite a number of them. Brian was giving a lecture to other librarians and he was feeling excited. He was quite high-powered in his quiet way. He'd waved her goodbye and asked her what she'd like for supper that night.

'How about sea bass?' she'd replied. Her last bloody words to the man who had been the love of her life.

The next thing she'd known was a call from their head of department. Brian had died. A massive heart attack. There had been nothing anyone could do, if it was any consolation to her. No one could have spotted it was coming.

She knew he was trying to be kind, that it was in no way her fault, not spotting the symptoms, but it made no bloody difference to the fact that Brian was gone.

And then the reaction from everyone at the university, the

way no one knew what to say. Some had even waited till she'd gone by in the corridors. Others brought out stories about friends and relatives who'd died in similar circumstances.

*But they're not Brian!* she'd wanted to shout out loud. Instead, she thanked them and refused the offer of compassionate leave. The last thing she wanted was to be alone. Work was the only thing that could save her.

And in a way it did. The order and silence of the library had an almost religious quality. They had both worshipped learning. And she missed him so much.

Gradually the pain had receded. Instead of thinking of Brian all day, every day, other things started to come into her mind as well. Small things rescued her – folding clothes for the airing cupboard, morning tea in her favourite mug, walking in the university grounds, nature.

Strangely, it was nature's utter indifference to her pain that she found reassuring. Grass grew, blossom appeared, the sun came up and went down no matter what happened to her or Brian. She would almost have been all right if the landlord hadn't accepted the offer from the developer and arrived one morning to tell her she had to move.

A knock on the door interrupted her thoughts. Maybe it was just as well.

'Hello, it's Claire.'

'Come in.'

'I just wondered about your money belt, whether you had your cards in it too. I could lend you some cash till it's sorted. I didn't know if there'd be a cash machine in Lanzarella so I brought more than I need.' She smiled. It was amazing what effect that had on her face, Monica noticed. 'I didn't tell my husband in case I got a lecture on the dangers of pickpockets.'

'We should get your husband and my mother together.

They'd get on like a house on fire,' Monica suggested. 'Actually, borrowing some money would be incredibly useful. My bank has made an arrangement with one in Lerini till my new cards come, but I don't want to have to keep walking up and down those steps!'

'I should bloody well hope not. How many were there, or did you lose count?'

'A thousand, according to a helpful American.'

'He'd have been a lot more helpful if he'd given you the bus fare. It's only a couple of euros.'

'Yes, but he'd have missed the horror on my face. Thirty euros would be great.'

'Are you sure that's enough?'

'To be absolutely frank,' there was something about Claire that made Monica trust her, 'I'm pretty broke. I'm retired from my job and money's tight. While I'm here I need to try and think of ways to make some kind of a living when I get home. We made some rather stupid pension decisions.'

'Me too. Like hardly even having one.' Claire wished she had more money herself and could just give some to Monica but she'd already dipped into her own savings to come here. Martin's trip to the posters in Prague was getting more remote by the minute. 'I suppose we'd better go down and join the cooperative.'

'Yes, let's. I rather like Sylvie, don't you?' Monica replied. 'She must be hard work to live with but she certainly sorted uppity Angela out.'

'I hope we're not going to get any fireworks between those two. I came here for peace and sunshine.'

Monica glanced out of the window. 'Well, it looks like you've got the sunshine anyway.'

\*

When they assembled at the back of the building to depart for Lerini, four miles down the hillside, they were in for a shock. Giovanni was waiting to drive them in a bright red Mini Moke.

'Oh my God,' Sylvie, swathed in another of her wafting silk tops, shrieked. 'I haven't been in one of these since Mykonos in the Sixties! Tony and I used to drive to the beach and go skinny dipping before breakfast!' Sylvie suddenly realized how old this made her sound and added, 'I was still practically a child then, obviously.' She climbed into the front seat.

Angela took the back, at least partly for safety, though this was an optimistic concept in a car with no back or sides, and couldn't help but notice the knowing look that Giovanni was giving Claire.

'And did you also go, how do you say it, skinny dipping, Chiara?' Giovanni asked, while Claire rapidly turned the colour of a ripe tomato.

'It's Chiara now, is it?' Angela enquired. 'When did that happen?'

'I think it really suits you,' Monica supported.

Once Sylvie had happily reeled off all the other islands she'd skinny-dipped at, Claire decided to enlighten them so that they didn't read more into the situation than it actually merited.

'OK, I think what Giovanni is referring to,' Claire explained earnestly, ignoring his satyr's smile, 'is that earlier this morning I found an amazing little pool with a statue of a nymph leaning into it, and I decided to have a quick dip.'

'Not a nude dip?' asked Monica in startled amazement.

'Er, yes,' Claire admitted.

'Goodness.'

'I didn't think anyone was around, obviously.'

'But somebody was.' Angela indicated the still-leering Giovanni.

'*Due ninfe*,' he announced, nodding his head enthusiastically.

'Claire,' Angela counselled sternly. 'I really think you should tell Giovanni your age.'

'What a bloody stupid idea,' corrected Sylvie. 'Of course she shouldn't. At our time of life she should be grateful for any male attention.'

'But she could be his mother,' Angela pointed out.

'We're in Magna Graecia, Angela,' Sylvie surprised them with her erudition. 'They understand that sort of thing. Look at Oedipus actually marrying his.'

'I'm not sure that's a frightfully good example,' corrected Monica. 'After all, he ended up blinding himself when he discovered the truth.'

'I don't think Giovanni's the blinding-himself type,' Sylvie pointed out gaily. 'He values his looks too much.'

'Let's just get to Lerini, shall we?' Angela insisted. 'Giovanni, can we go now?'

If they'd wanted peace and calm, they had forgotten Lanzarella's eagle's-nest position 1,200 feet above the blue of the Mediterranean Sea, with its dizzying hairpin bends and sheer drops down to what looked like bottomless ravines.

Driving terrified women who had discovered too late that Mini Mokes have almost nothing to hold on to seemed to spur on the testosterone in Giovanni. Ignoring their shrieks he sped downwards, occasionally on his mobile phone, simply hooting optimistically on the blind bends, and passing tour buses on the edge of the ravines with only millimetres to spare, the same wolfish smile lighting up his handsome face.

Eventually they arrived, shaken and speechless, in the main piazza of Lerini.

'*Signorine*,' Giovanni announced with a flourish, '*ecco Lerini*.'

'Thank God for that,' announced Sylvie breathlessly. 'I thought we were going to end up in the cemetery, not the piazza. I need a cappuccino to recover. And personally speaking, I'm going to get a cab back.'

'The bus is only two euros,' Claire reminded her, thinking of her own and Monica's budgets.

'Yes, but it's probably driven by Giovanni's cousin.'

'I just wonder why they need a car like this at all,' Angela shrugged, 'since Stephen never seems to come here.'

'No,' contradicted Giovanni, 'Mr Stefano, he comes sometimes in summer. He like the big heat. That is why we have the car. But usually he drive it himself.'

'I hope he's a better driver than you,' muttered Angela following the others.

Lerini turned out to be a pretty little town, embracing tourism but obviously not entirely dependent on it. Its real charm was that it wasn't one of those sad places that closed up shop in October and remained shut till May. Lerini clearly had its vibrant local life with the butcher, the baker and probably the candlestick-maker too.

Sylvie had chosen the most expensive-looking cafe right opposite the duomo.

'It says in Tour Selector that the one over there is better.' Claire pointed to the cafe opposite.

'I can't bear Tour Selector,' Sylvie announced. 'It's only used by overweight Americans with no taste.'

'Not that I'm ever judgemental,' commented Claire under her breath.

'Anyway, the coffees are on me. I'm wondering who might help me find some stuff for my new room afterwards?'

'I will,' Monica volunteered.

Sylvie tried to look pleased.

'And then I'd like to look around the cathedral. There are some famous doom paintings.'

'Just come to my room and I'll show you one,' Claire giggled.

Their coffees arrived. A cappuccino for Claire and Sylvie and espressos for Angela and Monica.

'Most Brits prefer the frothy stuff,' Angela commented to Monica.

'I picked up the habit when I was living here,' Monica replied. 'Italians call this "*caffé*".'

She smiled but for some reason Angela wasn't listening any more.

'Right.' Angela suddenly stood up, all her bossiness back in spades. 'Drink up, everyone. I only want to spend an hour down here anyway. Lots to do back in Lanzarella on the hotel front. That's why we're here after all.'

Sylvie looked mutinous. Bloody Angela was at it again. 'I'll finish my coffee, thank you.'

Then Angela pulled up Monica. Monica looked at her in surprise. Maybe the rutting stags were at it again. Well, let them get on with it. Instead she stared up at the calming yellow facade of the cathedral.

Unexpectedly Angela threaded her arm through Monica's and began to bodily pull Sylvie out of her chair as if all three were in a chorus line and about to dance the cancan.

'Could you pay, Claire?' she asked, a note of insistence in her voice, as she dragged the other two across the square towards the catacombs under the cathedral. 'I glimpsed a really good antiques shop over here and it'll probably shut in a minute.'

'But it's only eleven o'clock!' insisted Sylvie irritably. How was she going to bear much more of Angela bloody Williams? Who did she think she was, just because she was on telly?

'Their hours are very unpredictable. Look, it's just your kind of thing.'

Some of the eccentric objects in the window – a brass eagle lectern, various stuffed birds, an embroidered silk shawl with a fringe, a five-foot Nubian slave light-holder – did indeed look just up Sylvie's street.

As if drawn by a magnet, Sylvie forgot her complaints and disappeared inside.

'What was all that about?' Claire asked huffily when she caught up with them. She'd only just had enough change to cover the coffees now that she'd lent some to Monica.

Angela gestured discreetly to the other side of the square.

'Because sitting right over there in the next cafe is Sylvie's erring husband Tony with the blonde bimbo who was the cause of all the trouble. I recognized him from the infamous photograph she circulated. Someone sent it to me because they thought it was funny.'

'Oh my God, poor Sylvie!'

The surprising thing, it struck Claire, was how determined Angela had been to protect Sylvie from seeing him.

Maybe she was beginning to *do* women friends after all.

# Six

---

'Oh my God, do you think she saw him?'

Claire couldn't keep her eyes from the older man and the young woman who seemed to consist mainly of hair and high heels.

Angela shook her head. 'No, because she would have exploded if she had. But she still might if we're not careful. I wonder if he's staying in Lerini. Why don't you go and keep Sylvie and Monica busy? Make sure they don't go back to the piazza and I'll try and find out what they're doing here. Maybe they're just on a day trip. Explain to Monica if you can do it discreetly. I never thought I'd ever say this but we need Giovanni to drive us all back pretty damn quick.'

'That's good because he's lounging on the car over there watching the schoolgirls coming out for their lunch break.'

'One thing you have to say for Giovanni,' Angela conceded, 'is that he doesn't practise age discrimination.'

Claire couldn't suppress a giggle. 'Too true. When do you think we should try and go?'

'Can you head off Sylvie for fifteen minutes?' Angela asked.

'I hope so.'

'That should give me time to strike up an intimate acquaintance.'

'Right. I'll tell Giovanni now.'

By the time Claire approached Giovanni he had stopped eyeing the junior talent and was in the middle of a heated exchange which, weirdly enough, seemed to be on the subject of zucchini. A man in a chef's uniform was slitting open a zucchini and had cut out a chunk which he then threw on the ground, shouting '*Ecco! È marcio!*'

Giovanni was waving his arms and shouting in return. As soon as he saw Claire approaching his smile appeared as swiftly as a rainbow after a shower.

'*Chiara! Ciao!* Are you ready to go back now?'

'In ten minutes. But can we go from somewhere other than here?'

Giovanni looked as if nothing would delight him more. He gave the chunk of zucchini back to the chef and waved his arms again. 'The street at the end of this one.' He pointed towards the back of the town, repelling all further attempts to have vegetables stuffed into his arms.

Claire headed off towards the antiques shop in search of Sylvie and Monica. The catacombs were amazing. A whole hidden city of white-painted tunnels away from the heat of the day with a hairdresser's and several wine bars with murky interiors, where old men sat reading papers and drinking red wine and young men drank cold beers and argued about football and cars; there were even restaurants hidden away underground.

Claire found Sylvie and Monica smiling delightedly at the old lady who ran the antiques shop.

'Claire,' Sylvie greeted her, 'Monica's been absolutely brilliant. Not only have we haggled for all those goodies there

– she pointed to a pile of their spoils – but this wonderful lady is selling us these.'

She picked up one of several rolls of taffeta and silks, which frankly looked a bit moth-eaten to Claire but which were certainly in the wonderful jewel-like colours she knew Sylvie specialized in. She couldn't help wondering why Sylvie was going to all this trouble for such a short stay. Unless she was trying to persuade Stephen that he really ought to turn the house into a hotel with herself as the designer.

'The signora here was saving them for when they moved to a palazzo in Rome but Monica discovered they'll never be going because her husband has had a stroke. Isn't that lucky?' Claire couldn't help feeling that it was not so lucky for the husband in question. 'So she'll sell them to us instead. They couldn't be more perfect. I can make a silk canopy to go over my bed and there'll be plenty left over for the other rooms. I can't tell you what a fun morning we've been having.'

'You don't think Stephen will mind?' Claire tried to imagine how she'd feel if Belinda decided to completely re-decorate the spare room in magenta and orange while she was in Italy.

'It's all just for show. I could take the lot down in a couple of hours if he objected. Besides, nobody seems to have even been in the wings for years.'

Claire racked her brains, wondering how to get Sylvie away without going to the piazza. 'Fantastic! By the way, I saw a design shop you'd love in that road away from the square. I'm dying to show it to you.'

'What about all this stuff? Would you be able to deliver, signora?'

The old lady nodded her head. 'Yes. Yes, my nephew bring. He has – how do you say? Pickup truck.'

'Perfect vehicle for an Italian,' Monica murmured. 'Seeing as they spend most of their time trying to do just that.'

'Where do you stay?'

'At the Villa Le Sirenuse,' Monica told her. 'Do you know it?'

'Ah yes, the wedding house.' Monica looked at Claire and shrugged. It seemed an odd description but maybe Stephen had lent it to his friends in the past to get married in. That would create lots of work and be very popular. 'Very beautiful. My nephew will bring tonight. Or maybe my second cousin.'

'I love Italy,' Monica whispered. 'They always have a nephew or a second cousin.'

Sylvie, who knew her business, left her credit cards in her wallet and got out a roll of cash, even managing to negotiate her usual designer's discount.

'Right,' she waved to the old lady, who beamed away. In this wonderfully satisfactory transaction both parties seemed to think they had achieved the coup of the century.

In fact, Sylvie was still so delighted with her finds that she didn't notice the absence of the promised design shop until they came upon Giovanni smiling and holding open the door of the Mini Moke.

'Where was this shop you thought I'd like, then?' she asked Claire, eyeing Giovanni warily.

'We must have walked past it. But do you know, I'm not feeling very well. Do you think, just this once, we could hop back into the car with Giovanni? Only it'd be so much quicker than looking for a cab.'

'I'm not sure being driven by Giovanni is the best prescription if you're off colour, but whatever you like.'

*

131

Maeve Haran

Angela, meanwhile, had found a table next to Tony and Kimberley.

Kimberley, an avid reader of style supplements, instantly recognized her from the television.

'Look,' she announced to Tony in a loud voice, 'it's that woman from *Done Deal*. Angela something. The one who's just been sacked.'

Tony had the grace to look embarrassed.

Angela pretended not to hear and smiled. 'Espresso please,' she requested from the waiter, then turned to Tony and Kimberley. 'Lovely town, isn't it?'

Tony looked like someone who had lost a lot of weight, yet somehow it didn't add to his attractiveness. Like Nigel Lawson, he just looked like a thin person in someone else's skin. Poor Tony, she began to feel, I bet she's put him on a diet.

'Are you Angela . . . ?' Kimberley began.

'Williams. Are you staying here in Lerini?'

Kimberley nodded. 'Yes. For a few days.'

'The cathedral's supposed to be wonderful,' Angela insisted. 'There's a world-famous mural of Jonah and the whale.'

Kimberley looked blank. Tony, on the other hand, looked weary.

Too much sex perhaps.

'The shops are crap.' Kimberley pouted. 'I've never heard of any of them.'

So much for independent retailing. Angela thought fast. 'Where are you staying?'

'The Belvedere Grand.' Tony pointed towards the seafront. 'Any good?'

'Dull. Dull. Dull,' Kimberley replied. 'Everyone's over fifty.'

132

'You booked it,' Tony snapped. 'You said it was an amazing deal.'

'We may move on to Positano soon,' Kimberley announced.

'Except that we've already paid for three days,' Tony pointed out gloomily.

'Still,' Angela encouraged, 'more of a waste if you don't like it. I hear Positano's fabulous. Full of the beautiful people.'

It was also at least an hour away along the winding hairpin corniche.

'Come on, darling.' Kimberley snuggled into his shoulder, and looked up at him. 'Let's go tomorrow.'

Angela drank her espresso and, mission accomplished, said goodbye and headed for the meeting point at the back of the town.

'Look, there's Angela,' Sylvie pointed out. 'I hope she hasn't spoiled your morning by going off on her own. Everything seems to be beneath Angela's touch.'

Claire just smiled and held the door open for Angela. This time she climbed into the back.

Any thoughts of errant husbands were forgotten in the journey back up the mountain. If they had hoped it might be less scary going upwards they were wrong. This time Giovanni entertained them by turning round and asking them if they had enjoyed their morning just as a tourist bus appeared round the blind corner with a thousand-foot ravine beneath them to their right. Claire and Angela screamed.

Smiling with pleasure – this was the way ladies should be in Giovanni's view: terrified yet in his more than capable hands – he edged inside the bus with only millimetres to spare, pushing the bus with its forty occupants towards the outside edge, and somehow managing to ease past. 'Foreign driver!' He shrugged dismissively.

Angela glanced at the back of the bus. It was from Salerno, forty miles away. But maybe round here that was foreign.

Sylvie, blissfully unaware of all danger, was mentally decorating her room, while Monica tried to read the guidebook so she didn't have to look. Angela studied the landscape to distract herself and discourage further conversation from Giovanni.

It was truly an amazing place. She had rarely seen such a dramatic outlook except in the Alps. It was as if a mountain range had been sharply concertinaed into high peaks with vertiginous ravines that cut off dramatically when they came to the sea, making Beachy Head look tame by comparison. Small towns like Lerini had squeezed themselves into narrow inlets then expanded up the hillside and down to the beach. The houses that clung perilously to the hillside made Angela think of pink and white limpets clinging to a bare rock.

'*È bella, no?*' Giovanni turned again at the sharp hairpin just beneath Lanzarella. Angela had the feeling he had practised this before to give maximum scare factor.

'*Sí, è bella,*' Angela replied flatly, gazing determinedly at the distant prospect rather than the near one of Giovanni.

'OK,' he turned back sulkily, 'all want to go to the villa?'

'Yes,' insisted Angela assertively. They were going to need a plan if they were going to keep Sylvie from encountering Tony.

When they got to the villa, Beatrice and Immaculata were waiting eagerly on the steps. 'There was phone call for Signora Lambert,' Beatrice explained excitedly. 'Her husband ring. Want her to call soon as possible.'

Claire's heart thudded. Had something happened at home? And why the hell couldn't Martin just call her on her phone? She knew Martin had a thing about mobiles, but really. Had something happened to Evan? Don't be so stupid, Claire told herself. Evan is a grown man, he would call himself. It was probably just that Martin couldn't find the TV remote. She'd call him after lunch.

Meanwhile, Giovanni was jabbering away to the housekeeper and cook in machine-gun Italian, with much waving of arms.

'What are they saying, Monica?' Claire asked, fascinated at this sudden outbreak of emotion.

'It's all in dialect. I can't follow a word except maybe zucchini. Giovanni was having one of those quiet Italian chats with someone when we were in Lerini. That was about zucchini too. Or at least I think it was.'

'Don't talk about food,' Sylvie suddenly burst out. 'I'm starving!'

Lunch was already laid out when they went into the dining room. A salad of tomatoes, fresh basil, and on top of the sliced tomatoes there was a round little parcel of something white tied up at the top, and a bottle of pale white wine.

'It looks like something my granny would have used for her wash,' Claire giggled.

'It's called burrata.' Monica sniffed hers. 'That means buttered. It's mozzarella on the outside and inside it's all oozy and creamy and divine.' They all sat down and studied their plates. 'The version from round here comes wrapped in a lemon leaf and only stays fresh for two or three days. After that it's rubbery and no good.'

'Imagine a cheese you have to eat in two days.' Sylvie cut into hers carefully. 'In my house we have cheese you have to eat in two months. Occasionally two years. I'm not very strong on sell-by dates. Two days! What a country! Hey, this is divine!'

They had hardly finished when Immaculata arrived with a dish of home-made ravioli stuffed with *cinghiale*, Italy's famous wild boar.

'Immaculata, your cooking is wonderful!' The little white-haired cook broke out into a dazzling smile. 'Is nothing. What you give men working outside.'

'Not the men in my life,' Sylvie laughed. 'They're lucky to get a sandwich from Boots.'

'Is all OK at home?' Immaculata asked Claire as she served her pasta.

The others looked at her too.

'I haven't rung yet.'

'Putting it off?' Sylvie winked. 'Not overwhelmed with excitement at the thought of a phone call from your darling hubby?' She suddenly seemed to sag at the thought of husbands and, despite the colourful clothes and wild hair, looked suddenly old and deflated. 'Take my advice and hang on to him.'

Claire and Angela tried not to catch each other's eye.

'Husbands don't grow on trees at our age,' she sighed. She took a sip of wine and brightened up. 'I used to love that song "It's Raining Men". Completely untrue, of course, especially at our age, but cheering somehow.' To the amazement of Immaculata, who had brought the pudding, Sylvie stood up and treated them to the rousing anthem in an impressively loud contralto.

'I've always thought husbands were rather overrated,' Angela announced as she helped herself to some chocolate and mascarpone cheesecake.

'You may be bloody right.' Sylvie took another gulp of wine. 'God, I'm going to be the size of a battleship after staying here.'

'I rather liked mine,' Monica said quietly.

They all looked at her as if she'd sworn in church.

'And then he went and died.' Sylvie shook her head and looked as if she might burst into tears at the unfairness of fate. 'You get one of the only good ones and then that goes and happens.' She stared into space for a moment. 'Tony and I used to have a lot of fun. Before the gym bunny came on the scene.' She shook her head as if to banish the thought from her memory. 'How long *are* we all going to stay here, by the way?'

The question had an odd effect on all of them, as if they didn't really want to think about it.

'Let's see how it goes, shall we?' Angela realized she was taking control again. 'Lanzarella Women's Cooperative. Do we all agree?'

They all raised their hands.

Immaculata appeared with coffee. Sylvie had another drink before the bottle disappeared. 'There's one thing wrong with this place. No minibar.'

'Perhaps you could install one in your new room,' Monica joked.

'Now that, Monica, is a brilliant idea. You know one thing that I've wondered about. What do all the staff *do* when they haven't got people like us staying? I wouldn't have had Stephen down as one of the super-rich who keep their residences fully staffed just in case they're going to grace it with their presence. As far as I can tell, Stephen never comes near the place.'

'Giovanni says he comes in the summer. Maybe they're ancient retainers he can't bear to sack.'

'Giovanni isn't that old,' Claire pointed out with a grin.

'Now now, Claire,' tutted Sylvie, 'sorry, Chiara. Or is it his Nymph today? Just because Giovanni's got the hots for you.'

'If you ask me,' Claire raised her glass, 'the only person Giovanni's got the hots for is Giovanni.'

They turned to discover the object of their humour, for some reason now dressed in skin-tight white jeans and a sweatshirt made of some sporting material that showed every line of his biceps and pecs plus what seemed to be permanently erect nipples. His black hair tumbled down to his shoulders and he completed the look with wrap-around sunglasses which he now removed to give them the full benefit of his wounded expression. 'I come to ask if you ladies need the *auto* this afternoon. Otherwise I have request from Beatrice for some business in Maggiore.' Maggiore was the next town along the coast.

Angela looked round to the others. They all shook their heads. 'No thanks, Giovanni. Feel free to have the car.'

'And we all know what kind of business it really is, dressed like that,' pointed out Sylvie after he left. 'Unless it's a local Lothario beauty contest. He'd certainly win. By the way, underneath all the cute "I no understand" number, I bet Giovanni speaks perfect English. Beware. Right, I'm going up to start on the room transformation. The stuff has arrived, apparently. Anyone fancy giving me a hand?'

'I've got to make that call,' Claire announced.

'I fancied a stroll around the gardens,' said Monica. 'I will later though.'

'Not really my scene.' Angela shrugged. 'I seem to like my surroundings more neutral.' She thought of her house and its curious absence of personality.

'What rubbish! Your shops are lovely,' Sylvie contradicted. 'I mean, I never actually go into them because I go more for the ageing hippie look but they still look really inviting. I'd say you have quite an instinct for it.'

Angela looked at her, genuinely taken aback.

After lunch she wandered up to her room and opened the doors to her terrace. Lanzarella really was an extraordinary place, seeming to hang in the air, leaning out vertiginously above a sparkling blue sea, and the Villa Le Sirenuse, at the top of the village, like a hidden gem. She wasn't one for nature, apart from the walks with her dad in the Yorkshire dales; she preferred cities. She liked the modern lines of city living, and its anonymity. The chat over the garden wall wasn't for her. What seemed like friendliness to some was busybodying to her. She supposed it came from the days of her mother's break-down, before there was all this caring and sharing, shrinks and daytime TV confessions. In those days mental illness was still a disgrace. She and her mother had to cope with it alone. And it had been frightening. The way her mother had regressed and become entirely helpless.

Suddenly, at the age of twenty-one, Angela became the parent to a mother who had never tried to earn her love and affection. Still, she told herself, enough of this whining. Plenty of children gave up their childhoods to look after an ailing parent, children far younger than she had been. Of course they hadn't had to give up a place at Oxford. Once again, she pushed out of her mind the suspicion that her mother had never wanted her to go in the first place. That was too horrible to contemplate. And of course she'd also lost Stephen. But then, she told herself brutally, that would probably have happened anyway.

She looked around at the umbrella pines that were so characteristic of Lanzarella, gazed down at the bright geraniums and petunias planted round the house and breathed in the air full of the scent of apple blossom – and was that narcissus?

She would go downstairs right now and see if there was indeed narcissus growing and pick a big bunch for her room.

Angela headed straight for the garden where she was overwhelmed not with narcissus but with the scent of the wisteria draped over the pergola and the rose arches shaped like ropes. She walked round the side of the house near her terrace, but there was no sign of any narcissi. On the point of giving up she spotted a whole flowerbed of them and, getting out the scissors she'd taken from a drawer, she cut off an armload and carried them inside, together with some red banksiae roses.

On her way to the kitchen to request a vase she was intercepted by a screeching Immaculata. '*No! No! Porta sfortuna to mix the red flowers with the white!*'

Angela smiled to herself. This was just what her mother used to say. Red and white flowers signified blood and bandages and must never be brought inside. Immaculata and her mother would have got on famously.

She found a large milk jug and filled it with the fragrant blossoms.

Immaculata watched her depart, shaking her head in silent disapproval. She would have to visit the church and say some extra prayers or who knew what bad luck would fall upon the house.

The only question was how soon.

Monica loved gardens. She and Brian had visited famous gardens from Boboli to Great Dixter. Once she'd moved back to her parents' house, Monica had put herself on the flower rota for their local church, not out of religious devotion but because she loved to arrange them. She had even earned a bit of a local reputation and to her mother's amazement had been requested to do the odd trendy wedding.

Most of the other arrangers stuck to the well-loved favour-ites like roses and delphiniums but Monica had developed what she liked to think of as the Old Master style of arranging. A lot of people dismissed flower painting as something Victorian ladies used to do to pass their time but Monica had discovered that the old Dutch masters loved to paint flowers and did so with what Monica recognized as sly and subversive wit.

They filled vast canvases with gleaming oils of everything from peonies and blowsy full-blown roses and bearded irises in rainbow colours to striped tulips. But then they added the joke. The growing things that could never be flowering or fruiting at the same time. A branch of blackberries would be merrily sitting next to early tulips or snowdrops, a drooping bluebell side by side with a late-flowering ruby-hued dahlia. And all before air freight from Kenya made any of this remotely feasible.

Sometimes they would add to the joke by inserting a red admiral butterfly, or a bird's nest full of eggs, and once even a small cabbage. In one Monica had spotted a ripe fig, split open, which clearly had some sexual significance she didn't want to think about.

Monica wandered on down the first level of terracing, all visible from the house, and was surprised to find separate areas to the right and left of the wide central paving, separated off by surprisingly thick and impenetrable hedging and to which she could find no obvious entrance. This ran the full length of further terracing, for four or five levels. Strange, because this was the sunniest area – and already as hot as the loveliest English summer. It was the kind of garden anyone at home would die for.

Finally, after several attempts to penetrate at the lowest level, leaving her scratched and irritated, she broke through and stood in amazement looking up at serried ranks of flowers. If her arrangements were old masters, this was an Impressionist's fantasy.

There were rows and rows of petunias, stocks, wallflowers, irises and the lovely pale-hued anemones she had only glimpsed in the hippest of London florists. And at the sun-trap top corner, the roses! Even at this time of year there were highly scented old China roses, banksiae, Bengal and damask among a bed edged with early lavender.

It was amazing. The curious thought struck Monica that though there were flowers inside the house they were completely different – roses with no scent bought especially from the flower market in Naples? How very odd. Why would the gardeners be growing all this stuff if they didn't even use it in the house?

Intrigued, she decided to see what was on the other side, behind the opposite hedge. Again this seemed as strangely impenetrable as a safety deposit box. How did anyone get to pick the flowers? Finally, she found a small space to squeeze through, scratching her arms as she did so.

This time she almost gasped. In a row of small polytunnels, hidden from view by a blossom-covered pergola, lettuces of different colours stretched in long rows to the far end and cucumbers grew on a trellis next to vast beefsteak tomatoes. In the next small tunnel were rows of zucchini, some still attached to their flowers, interspersed with rosemary and basil.

Monica stared at the profusion of vegetables and herbs, even more surprised. How could they possibly need all this for a house that seemed to be very rarely used? And then it hit her. The argument over the zucchini! This had to be some kind of scam. She wondered what on earth to make of it. Surely dear old ladies like Immaculata and Beatrice couldn't be involved?

It was still only mid-afternoon so she decided to go and offer her services to Sylvie.

'You look as if you've been in the wars,' commented Sylvie from up a ladder.

'Yes, I'll tell you all about it later.'

Monica looked around the room. She could see now why people admired Sylvie's style, though it was a million miles from her own. The room was large with windows at the back and front, both of which had shutters. Even so, Sylvie had hung curtains in a yellow-ochre silk with a tie-back in the same fabric at each. A pair of chairs stood each side of the largest window in matching fabric. Sylvie had sawn the wooden chandelier she'd bought that morning in half and had fixed it to the wall as a kind of coronet to hold the swathes of leaf-green silk which formed a glamorous canopy over the bed.

'You don't want it too matchy matchy,' she said grinning down at Monica, who stood almost speechless at how much Sylvie had achieved in a couple of hours.

Sylvie climbed down. 'It's all down to this.' She brandished what looked like a large metal hairdryer at Monica. 'My staple gun. Forget men. This is the best tool of all time. With that and my trusty gaffer tape I can achieve miracles.'

She smiled round at the impact. 'It's all set dressing really. Like those TV makeover shows. It'll fall apart in a month. Obviously, I don't do this on a proper job, but it certainly gives you an idea. I had a look around the wings. There're another fifteen rooms. The place is enormous!'

Monica leaned back to get the best look and knocked a

card off the dressing table. It said: 'Husbands come and go. Friends are for forever'.

'From Gwen. I think she wanted to cheer me up. The thing is, since I've been here with you lot, I can almost believe it.'

Monica looked at her. She wasn't even teasing. Larger-than-life Sylvie Sutton had implied that Monica was a friend!

'Actually,' Sylvie grimaced, 'it's my birthday. Sixty-two. You have to be a friend for me to admit that. That's a state secret and yes, I know I don't look it, but it's still true!' She looked at herself in the tarnished mirror. 'No wonder Tony left me. I'm an old bag. I'm just like this room. Looks good from a distance but tacked together with staples!' And to Monica's horror Sylvie, who seemed as if she couldn't care less what anyone thought, began to cry.

'Oh shit,' she started to rub her heavily mascaraed eyes, 'what's worse than an old bag? An old bag who looks like a fucking panda because her eye make-up's run.'

She looked around her mistily. 'I know,' she brightened, 'let's have a drink. I haven't got the minibar sorted but I've got a bottle of red somewhere.'

Monica was on the point of saying that she didn't usually drink at five in the afternoon but decided it would come out prim and disapproving and not at all what Sylvie's friend would say.

'Where's the corkscrew?' she enquired instead.

They found it under a pile of fuchsia taffeta. 'I'm afraid we don't have glasses. See what you can find.'

Monica unearthed two painted vases that looked as if they'd come from Pompeii and hadn't been used since.

They clinked their earthenware. 'Bottoms up. Except that mine's been going south for some time now. Do you know, I thought you were a bit dull when you arrived. Vicar's daughter type. Straight-laced.'

Monica toyed with telling Sylvie that she and Brian had bought *The Joy of Sex* and tried every position, but decided it might shock her as well as making her start missing Tony again.

'People can have more in them than you see on the surface,' she said bravely. 'Sorry if that sounds like a bumper sticker.'

Sylvie looked out of the window. 'Sometimes I think I've got *less*.'

'Sounds like the beginning of a beautiful friendship.' Monica grinned, surprised at her bravado.

They clinked their vases happily.

Claire went out to the garden, looking for the famous asparagus bed. There seemed to be a lot of hedges you couldn't see over but finally she located it round the corner at the side of the villa. The cook in her noted how it was almost time for it to be picked. Even the earliest British asparagus wouldn't be ready for weeks. What a wonderful climate it was here.

Someone had thoughtfully put a bench next to the bed. Was this the phone-signal bench? She noted a statue of Mercury nearby and wondered if this was someone's little joke, Mercury being the messenger of the Gods and thus the inspiration for the naming of numerous telecom companies. She decided the joke was a bit beyond Luigi or Giovanni. In fact, she had a strong inkling that Giovanni wouldn't get the joke, even if you explained it to him. But what about the mysterious Stephen?

'You're putting this off, Claire,' she chided herself. 'What if it's a genuine emergency?' But she had an instinct born of long experience that it was probably just Martin. She guiltily acknowledged that the reason she'd kept her phone off and he'd had to call her on the landline was to try and discourage him from ringing her every five minutes because he'd lost his socks.

She dialled the home line and waited. Maybe he'd be out.

Naturally he wasn't.

'Claire, hello. How's life in *La Bella Italia*?' He had his jovial voice on, the one he usually used when he wanted something.

'Great. Hard work,' she lied since so far she hadn't had to do a hand's turn.

'How's the weather?'

'So so, pouring with rain when we got here.' That was true as far as it went. Why was she painting such a dour picture? To emphasize that this trip wasn't a scam or holiday in disguise?

His next question answered that for her. 'It's lonely here without you. Evan and Belinda have started going out a lot for some reason.'

Oh dear. She could imagine why.

'The thing is, I've been looking up some flights to Naples and they're incredibly cheap. Everyone seems to be taking their kids skiing or to Tenerife. Naples isn't much of a holiday destination at this time of year. So I was thinking I might pop over and see you.'

Claire could already imagine him looking up bus timetables to Lanzarella and shuddered.

'Actually, love, that wouldn't really work. It's just us four women here working and no one's brought a partner.'

'It'd only be for a couple of days,' he wheedled. 'I'd make myself useful. Not lie around the pool or anything. And I see you're not far from Pompeii. I've got a wonderful book called *Life and Death in Pompeii and Herculaneum* out of the library.'

Oh God, he really was taking this seriously, and when Martin got an idea, he was like a terrier with a tennis ball. 'The pool isn't even filled yet,' she lied. 'And we're really busy.'

'Maybe I could run up some nice meals for you all. Jamie Oliver's got a good book on Italian cooking. Give you a bit of a break.'

'Well, actually, there's a cook here.'

'What are *you* doing there, then?' he asked suspiciously.

'Sussing out what catering facilities would be needed if it became a hotel. I told you,' Claire snapped.

'Well, if you don't *want* to see me . . .'

'Of course I want to see you, but this is business, Martin.'

'If it's business, why aren't you being paid?' The terrier wasn't letting go that easily.

She could hardly admit she just needed to get away or she'd implode.

Some doves started to coo noisily next to her in the tree.

'What's that noise?'

'Oh, just some birds. Probably sheltering in the tree from the rain.' She'd better lay off or, knowing Martin, he'd go and look up the weather forecast. 'Anyway, obviously, I'd love to see you but it just isn't on. Sorry. How are Evan and Belinda?' she said, changing the subject abruptly.

'Going around looking like love's young dream for some reason. Even they say they're out when I offer to cook.'

'Poor Martin. Maybe they've had good news about their flat.'

'I certainly bloody hope so.'

'Look, love, I've got to dash. My battery's low.'

'Can't think why when you never have it on,' he pointed out grouchily.

'Bye, love, bye.' She turned off her phone and gazed out at the glorious vista beneath her. The terraced landscape fell in deep ravines right down to the sea yet every inch seemed to be used for growing something, lemons, figs, olives, grapes. The sun was just beginning to set and it glowed with a soft pink light. In summer it was a busy coastline with traffic jams and crowded bars and restaurants. But not yet. A deep peace unfolded over the sea and the land beneath. The doves cooed as if they had been put there deliberately.

And Claire knew one thing for certain. She didn't want Martin to come.

For some reason Angela felt like changing before they ate tonight. She slipped on a simple shift dress, one of her own, of course, and softened it with a swirly paisley silk scarf in shades of dusty pink and purple. It somehow seemed to go with the darkening landscape.

*Whoa, love,* she told herself, *don't say you're getting all romantic because you're in Italy. Not your style.*

She stood on her terrace. Claire was sitting on a bench at the side of the house looking out to sea. They'd better all get on with what they'd come for. Tomorrow she'd start checking out the other hotels in Lanzarella. Always start with the competition, that had always been her motto in business, and it had worked.

Claire got up and went inside.

Angela breathed in the evening scents. Somehow they were stronger as the sun went down. Stocks, lavender and something else she didn't recognize, as well as the narcissus

An Italian Holiday

she'd picked earlier. She looked round her huge terrace and decided now was the time to offer to change rooms.

She was the first downstairs. The table was laid in the dining room. Beatrice appeared and poured the usual fizzy Franciacorta. 'Maybe sometimes we could eat outside?' Angela asked.

Beatrice looked genuinely scandalized, as if she'd been asked to cater for an orgy. 'But is too cold!'

'For lunch, perhaps. Or breakfast?'

Beatrice simply shrugged.

Angela, glass in hand, wandered into the salon next door. It was an amazing room with its vaulted ceiling and carved angels. She wondered what the nuns had used it for. Or maybe it was just for the Prince of Lerini?

She wandered over to the mantelpiece where Beatrice had put more red roses. In an automatic gesture, Angela dipped her head to sniff them and as she did so she caught sight of a photograph in a plain silver frame which seemed too modern for this medieval setting.

She lifted it up and looked closer. Her heart jolted. It was Stephen, young and handsome, with a beautiful Italian-looking girl on his arm. She was wearing a wedding dress and smiling up at him, standing under an arch she recognized from the garden. Angela studied it for almost a minute, transported back forty years. It couldn't have been that long after she and Stephen had parted. He could only be about twenty-two or -three.

The day he'd dropped her home in that mad open-topped car came vividly into her mind. So Stephen hadn't been so conventional after all. He hadn't married the 'girls with pearls' type she'd assumed he'd fall for. But Italy was still a long way from Nottingham. Maybe his bride had been rich.

149

*Oh stop it, Angela,* she told herself angrily. *It was all over and done with years ago. Why do you keep picking the scab? Stop behaving like some latter-day Miss Havisham.* But if the wedding had been all that time ago, then what had happened to the marriage?

She heard a sound and turned, ridiculously half expecting to see the young couple walk in through the open window from the terrace.

Beatrice was standing behind her with the bottle.

'*E bella, la Signora Carla.*' She shook her head. '*Molto triste.*'

Angela's summer-school Italian ran to understanding that *triste* meant sad. 'Why, what happened?' she asked softly.

'She was a beautiful bride. It was *la Signora Carla* who fell in love with this house. She was Italian,' Beatrice stated proudly. 'But from Sicily.' This was clearly a point against the beautiful Carla. Like the French were to the English, the Sicilians were the traditional enemy here.

'But why here, why not Sicily?'

'Because of her family. She had many uncles, aunts, her parents, grandparents and, if she lived in Sicilia, they would want her to have babies. Many babies. And Carla, she wanted to enjoy life. To be young and happy and live here with Stefano.' Beatrice looked fondly at the photograph and sighed. 'The house here was *abbandonata*, empty, very cheap. That was why they could afford to buy it.'

'So what happened?'

'They were very happy. Immaculata and I would hear them laughing and smile. And then she died. From bleeding in the brain. It happened in her family before. They were there.' She pointed to the terrace. 'Stefano, he would speak to no one. After the funeral he go back to England.'

Angela stared at the photograph again. Poor Stephen. No wonder he came here so rarely. She wondered why he'd held on to it at all. Perhaps it held happy memories. Or perhaps it was one property among many. Now it seemed he'd decided to sell it or convert it into a hotel. She couldn't blame him, no matter how lovely it was.

One of the things about Beatrice's revelations had struck her forcibly. Beatrice and Immaculata had worked here all the time. Perhaps Luigi too. No wonder Beatrice had dropped a plate when she'd mentioned the hotel. It looked very much as though Stephen had forgotten to tell them.

'Hello, Angela, you look nice.'

Monica had just come into the room.

Unfortunately, the same couldn't be said of her. In Angela's view Monica looked like a sack of ferrets tied in the middle. One of these days she was going to have to do something about Monica and her clothes.

'I wanted to show you something interesting in the garden, but you'd probably get that nice frock torn. Maybe tomorrow, then.'

'Some Franciacorta, Signorina Monica?' Beatrice offered.

'Thank you and I think we can forget the signorina.'

'In Italy it is . . . how do you say?'

'*La cortesia,*' supplied Monica, 'good manners. *Capisco perfettamente.*'

Beatrice gave her a long hard look as if she had no idea Monica could speak and understand Italian this well and was wondering what secrets or indiscretions she might have already picked up.

# Seven

When Claire joined Monica and Angela in the salon, she decided not to even mention Martin's call. She knew how they'd react, at least how Angela would. Husbands were not invited.

For no reason she could think of, Claire had dressed up too. Well, she had added a necklace her son Evan had given her for her birthday. The thought made her smile and as she joined them it struck Angela again how pretty she was when she did.

Angela had planned to tell them about Stephen and his marriage as soon as they were all assembled but suddenly she didn't want to. It was ridiculous but she had to have it to herself for a little while, not as some childish secret to give her an advantage, but because she needed to deal with it in her own way. Tomorrow she'd tell them. For tonight it was just hers.

'I just wanted to mention before she comes that it's Sylvie's birthday,' Monica half whispered. 'She only had one card. From Gwen.' She and Angela exchanged a look of mutual understanding.

'Gosh, this Gwen,' Claire commented. 'She sounds like an amazing old lady.'

They both grinned. 'Don't ever say that to Gwen. She doesn't think eighty-five is even middle-aged.'

'We'll have a celebration for Sylvie. I can make my famous lemon tart,' Claire offered.

'Let's hope she doesn't find out about Tony being here with the brainless bimbo,' Angela said in a low voice. 'Thank God they're staying at the Belvedere Grand in Lerini and not here in Lanzarella. I got the impression it's bad luck he's here rather than deliberately malicious. Apparently, Kimberley booked it but doesn't appreciate all the over-fifties!'

'She'd better get used to them from now on,' Claire commented with satisfaction.

'Time I started to do some work tomorrow,' Angela announced decisively. 'I'm going to check out the hotels. You'd better take Sylvie off somewhere just in case.'

'How about Pompeii?' Monica asked hopefully. She'd been longing to get there as soon as she could.

'Have you met Sylvie?' asked Claire. 'I don't think Pompeii's up her street.'

'Capri! She said she wanted to go to Capri!'

'OK, why don't you persuade her to go on a day trip. I gather it's quite easy from Lerini.' With any luck Tony and Kimberley would have moved on to Positano, despite their three-day package.

'By the way,' Angela grinned, 'it didn't strike me that all was entirely well with the lovebirds.'

She didn't have time to elaborate as they saw Sylvie arriving.

'Evening, girls!' Instead of her usual palette of vermilion through to aubergine, Sylvie was wearing jeans and a paint-stained top. 'Sorry, I didn't know we were dressing for dinner, but the good news is, I've finished! Tours will be available from tomorrow morning when the paint's dried.'

'Actually,' Claire grabbed a glass and filled it with fizz, 'Monica and I thought of going to Capri tomorrow and wondered if you'd come?'

Sylvie contemplated them. A few days ago she would have seen it as being picked for the losers' team, but now they were a cooperative. Yet she still couldn't help wondering why Angela wasn't coming. 'What about Angela?'

Angela saw the trap. If she said she was going to look at hotels, Sylvie would insist on joining her. She'd be safer in the care of Claire and Monica on Capri.

'Actually,' lied Angela, 'I thought I'd ask Beatrice to show me how the housekeeping works.'

Sylvie looked at her in astonishment. 'Well, count me out, then. The only thing I want to know about cooking is what time's dinner? I'd better go to Capri, then. As long as it isn't too early.'

Monica kept her mouth shut. She'd been about to suggest eight o'clock so that they could fit in Emperor Tiberius's villa before the crowds.

'How about ten o'clock?' Claire suggested.

Sylvie agreed, looking pained at such an early start.

'We'll check out the ferry times. I suppose a bus down to Lerini's out of the question?'

Sylvie's expressive eyebrows answered that one. 'It'll have to be Giovanni in the Mini Moke, then,' suggested Claire innocently.

'There has to be some form of transport that doesn't threaten life and limb. How about a cab?'

'They're meant to be worse than anything. They all think they're Emerson Fittipaldi.'

'Perhaps Luigi's got a mule.' Monica grinned.

'I do hope you're joking.'

'I am,' conceded Monica.

Beatrice announced dinner. 'Thank God,' insisted Sylvie. 'I could eat a wild boar. Whole.'

Monica was virtually certain Angela had had no intention of asking Beatrice about the housekeeping. Which was just as well, because if Monica's suspicions were right, Beatrice would have some pretty tricky questions to answer.

As usual, Claire was up the next morning long before the others. It was a time she treasured. But she certainly wasn't going to take any more dips in the hidden grotto. All the same, she looked again at the nymph, smiling to herself at Giovanni's outrageous Italian audacity.

In her quiet way she had been observing Italian men since she'd arrived and had come to her own conclusions. They were individualistic, charming, aggressive, warm-hearted, self-important, hedonistic, industrious, impatient, sexist, happy, as well as suicidal drivers and, most importantly, complete football fanatics. And good luck to any woman who fell in love with one. If this was contradictory, so, as far as she could tell, were they.

But they certainly made a change from Twickenham.

She decided to go and see if Immaculata was up and about. She came across Beatrice laying the breakfast table on the terrace with much tutting and looking up at the cloudless blue sky for signs of rain.

Immaculata was making coffee in those ridiculously tiny coffee pots with the comical little man on the side. The idea of making one large one for four people was clearly not something to be contemplated.

'*Buongiorno, Immaculata.*'

'*Buongiorno, Signora Chiara.*' Rather like their nosy neighbour when Claire was growing up who counted the number of sheets on the line whenever her boyfriend had been to stay, Immaculata had immediately sussed the signoras from the signorinas, and stuck stubbornly to it.

'Would you mind if I used your kitchen to make a lemon tart?'

Immaculata studied her with a gimlet eye. 'You do not want my *torta al limone*? I can cook tonight for you, is very good!'

'Immaculata, I am a cook too. I would like to make this as a present to my friend Sylvie.'

'*Sì, la Signora Sutton.*' She nodded her head vigorously. Thank heavens Sylvie was the other signora. 'I see. But if you want lemons, you must go and see Beatrice's nephew Luca. He grows the best lemons in Lerini.'

Claire was hoping just to pinch a few from the garden but could see this was the price Immaculata was going to extract for trespassing on her territory.

'Can I go tomorrow?'

'I will ask my nephew to see. He or my second cousin will go and ask Luca when is free.'

Claire could see that etiquette demanded this procedure rather than the more conventional one of ringing him up, which was odd since every Italian under eighty seemed to have a mobile phone permanently attached to their ear. She supposed at least it ensured full employment for the nephews and second cousins.

'Thank you. We are going to Capri today so perhaps you

could let me know when I get back, and maybe I will visit him tomorrow for the lemons?'

'*Sì, sì. Va bene.*'

She went to sit on the terrace, poured herself coffee from one of the tiny coffee pots, and glanced down at the sapphire sea. It was calm, thank heavens.

Looking around her she felt such a sense of well-being here, almost like being part of a family. But instead of a family that made constant demands, this was one that seemed to want to nurture you. As if to underline this, Immaculata arrived with a tasty-looking pastry filled with ricotta that looked like a shell, informing her that she must try it as it was the local delicacy. The only clouds looming were the thought of calls from Martin and the much worse threat of Sylvie discovering that Tony and Kimberley were on their doorstep.

'Just get straight onto the hydrofoil and steer clear of the hotel on the point, the Belvedere,' Angela whispered to Monica. 'Giovanni's going to drop you right by the waterfront, so it should be quite straightforward.'

'Right, OK.'

'With luck, little Miss Kimberley will have dragged him off to Positano. Much more her style anyway.'

'You don't think she booked round here to rub it in for Sylvie?'

'There're plenty of posh hotels in Lanzarella, if she did. I think it's just bad luck.'

Claire arrived, holding a guidebook to Capri. 'Where's Sylvie?' Monica looked at her watch anxiously. 'I certainly don't want to experience Giovanni hurrying for a hydrofoil.'

They both shuddered as Sylvie appeared in sunglasses and

a straw hat, looking like a celebrity trying to avoid the paparazzi.

'Come on, Sylvie.' Monica looked like a little brown hen next to a showy rooster. 'Giovanni's waiting.'

'Oh goody.' Sylvie clambered into the back, under the mistaken impression that it was safer there. 'Surely,' she announced, 'Stephen must have some vehicle other than this death-trap?'

'I thought it made you think of Mykonos?' Claire suggested naughtily.

'I had a crap time in Mykonos, now that I remember. Nobody told me it was as gay as San Francisco.'

Claire and Monica giggled and tried to concentrate on the spectacular scenery. It was as though nature was trying to make the most of all the heavy rain of the other day and you could almost hear things growing. Claire half expected to see the bright yellow lemons in the groves that surrounded them spring straight out of the blossom as in slow-motion photography. Everything was exaggerated. The sky bluer. The sun more brilliant. The sea even more sparkling than before.

All was going well and they were chatting away about what they might do on Capri until the final stretch of corniche down three hairpin bends into Lerini when they found themselves behind a battered pickup loaded down with vegetables, driven extremely slowly by a tiny old man who could barely see over the steering wheel.

Every time Giovanni attempted to overtake he miraculously moved into the middle of the road.

Monica was impressed at the moderation of Giovanni's responses given the range of Italian insult possible until he said, 'Mi *fa cagare!*'

'What's he saying?'

'That it makes him want to shit.'

'Well, no shitting in the car please!' Sylvie commanded just as the old man braked and two boxes of cucumbers somersaulted onto the road ahead of them.

Rather than stop and help, Giovanni took this opportunity to overtake, adding another stream of tender insults.

Just as they rounded the final bend, Monica watched the old man climb from his pickup, yell, '*Borsanerista!*' and spit on the ground.

Monica watched him thoughtfully. She was pretty sure that a *borsanerista* was a black-market profiteer.

Thanks to this colourful incident they arrived on the quay just in time to see the hydrofoil departing for Capri without them.

'Bugger!' declared Claire, her anxiety making her uncharacteristically vehement.

Giovanni watched her with new admiration.

'Calm down, there'll be a boat soon,' Sylvie reassured.

This proved inaccurate. Spring might be considered well advanced in England but not so in Italy or by the ferry line. To them it was winter and that meant no boat for two hours.

'That hotel over there looks nice.' To their horror Sylvie was pointing at the Belvedere Grand. 'We're supposed to be researching hotels after all.' She began to walk purposefully towards it.

'No!' announced Monica with such forcefulness that they all stared at her, even Giovanni.

'Why not?'

'It's market day.' Monica groped blindly for a reason.

'*Sì, sì,*' endorsed Giovanni. 'Is market day.'

They all listened expectantly.

'Look at me!' Monica indicated her usual ferrets-in-a-sack appearance.

159

'Must I?' Sylvie asked, cutting the insult with a smile.

'Exactly. I must buy new clothes.'

'In Lerini market? You'd do better waiting for Capri.'

'That would be beyond my budget. Besides, we've got two hours to kill. Come on, Sylvie, rise to the challenge! If you can decorate a room, how is decorating me any different?'

Sylvie refrained from arguing, merely giving Monica a pained look.

'I'll help,' offered Claire.

The thought of Claire giving sartorial advice to anyone galvanized Sylvie.

'All right, then, you're on,' she agreed. 'Come on, Giovanni, where's this market?'

For once Giovanni proved surprisingly coy. Clearly, Monica guessed, he didn't want to elicit any more reactions like that of the old man in the pickup truck.

Instead, he indicated the area towards the small beach.

They wandered past rows of stalls, under cheerful green-and-white-striped umbrellas selling everything from shoes and kitchen utensils to fish and fabrics. Sylvie halted at a pair of fluffy mules on the shoe stall. 'Actually, I rather like those. Very Italian housewife entertaining handsome gigolos while hubby's at work.'

'Sylvie,' reminded Claire sternly. 'Back to Monica.'

With a sigh Sylvie progressed through the chattering crowds, past men holding espressos, and women pushing buggies and hoping the tiny occupants would stay asleep while they enjoyed the exuberant atmosphere of the weekly open-air bazaar.

Sylvie led them past the fruit and veg stall, stopping amazed at a stall that sold entire men's suits. And then a shift dress caught her eye, hanging from an awning next to the shoe stall. It was patterned in a bold combination of black, white and tan, with a dash of dusty pink in an attractive art deco-ish design.

'That's possible,' she announced suddenly, pointing to the dress.

'Sì, *signora*.' The stallholder had it down in a flash. 'Try on?' she asked, this time in English. 'Lady try on?'

Sylvie pushed Monica into the tiny cubicle, which was sectioned off by a tablecloth from the leering interest of Lerini's male population.

Monica slipped on the dress and stayed hidden in the cubicle. This was so not her style.

'Come on, Monica, be brave!' instructed Sylvie. 'I'm not wasting my time otherwise. You've got to wear the bloody thing in public anyway so there's no point skulking in there!'

They were all surprised at the sight of Monica in the art deco dress.

'My God, you've got a figure!' announced Sylvie.

'It's probably the dress,' protested Monica.

'Stop it now, it's you, not the dress.' She felt up Monica's arms. 'You haven't even got bingo wings!' she announced enviously.

'I used to swim a lot,' Monica countered, her tone almost apologetic, 'before I lost my job at the university.'

'Well, it certainly worked. I have to keep my arms covered. Now let's have a look and see what else there is.' Starting to enjoy herself, Sylvie hunted through the circular racks and pulled out two more dresses and a pair of tailored cotton trousers. 'We'll take these,' she announced to the delighted stallholder.

'Oughtn't I to try them on?'

'My dear Monica, I am famous for furnishing an entire

room at a single glance. I can tell what will fit you. How much is that, signora?'

When she heard the reply Sylvie almost had to sit down. 'But that's incredible!'

'Is there a problem? Do you want me to put it back?' Monica asked, reaching for the zip.

'I think she's staggered it's so cheap,' whispered Claire and they both began to laugh.

'Sandals, scarves, jewellery,' announced Sylvie decisively.

Claire and Monica followed the phenomenon that was Sylvie through the rest of the market.

They picked up two pairs of sandals – one brown, one gold – both flat and with toe posts. When Monica tried to protest that she didn't like toe posts, Sylvie ignored her.

'You have to suffer to be beautiful, as the French say.'

'I think I'm a bit old for that,' protested Monica mildly.

'Then buy yourself some trainers.' Sylvie swept on. She had spotted some large plastic necklaces which, although they looked cheap on the rack, somehow looked expensive when worn with the dress.

'She really can do it, can't she?' Claire commented admiringly.

'You're not the one with the toe-post sandals,' whispered Monica. 'It's not beauty I'm suffering for, it's Sylvie's marriage.'

But Sylvie had stopped as if turned to marble just a few feet ahead of them.

'It's a miracle!' she announced in a hushed and fervent tone.

Monica and Claire studied her apprehensively. Had she really witnessed some religious manifestation as Bernadette had at Lourdes? Would she become St Sylvie of Lerini?

They tried to follow the path of her gaze but could only see a glamorous middle-aged woman selling shoes from a trestle table.

'How old do you think she is?' Sylvie whispered.

Monica and Claire shook their heads, wondering if they ought to get Sylvie to sit down.

'I don't know.' Claire guessed. 'Fifty? Maybe even sixty?'

'Look again. At the hands. I would say she's seventy.'

'So what's the miracle?'

Sylvie turned to the others in amazement as if water had been turned into wine in front of them and they hadn't even noticed.

'Her hair, of course! It's a complete masterpiece!'

They both studied the stallholder's shoulder-length hair. It was indeed very attractive, but hardly miraculous.

'Look closer. It must be grey and yet it is the most natural brown I have ever seen, and see those strands of gold? No junior with pieces of foil has been near those – they are as realistic as if she were a golden-haired child! It's amazing!'

By this time the owner of the miraculous hair had begun to notice that she was the object of their awed attention.

'Signora!' Sylvie stepped forward. 'May I congratulate you? Your hair is the most beautiful I have ever seen!' The signora bowed, as if used to this kind of compliment to her crowning glory and considered it only her due.

'Where can I find the artist who has created a thing of such consummate beauty?'

The stallholder turned round and pointed to a slightly down-at-heel hairdresser. The kind that offered pensioners perms on a Tuesday for cut prices.

'Monica,' Sylvie announced, still surrounded by the kind of glow that would have made simple peasants believe in

Bernadette's visitation by the Blessed Virgin, 'follow me. You are going to get your hair done.'

'But . . .' Monica protested nervously. 'What about Capri?'

'Capri can wait.'

'Besides, I really can't afford it. I usually cut my own.'

'Exactly,' agreed Sylvie. 'I will pay.'

Monica considered mutiny. Wasn't this another example of her own wishes being overridden, as her mother had done so often? And then it struck her that her mother had never suggested anything that might be remotely to Monica's advantage.

She glanced again at the signora's miraculous hairstyle and followed Sylvie into the humble hairdressing salon.

Despite Monica's fluent Italian it took Sylvie almost fifteen minutes with many gestures, finally fetching the stallholder herself, to demonstrate exactly what she wanted Monica's hair to be like.

'Ladies, please,' the hairdresser announced imperiously. 'Leave now! I cannot create with so many people in my salon!'

Sylvie was greatly miffed when the signora shooed her out along with the rest. 'There is very nice restaurant next door.' The shop owner pointed deep into the catacombs. 'Tell them Rosmarina send you.'

'It's probably where they took the Christians to fatten them up for slaughter in the good old days,' murmured Claire.

'Or it's run by her nephew or second cousin.'

The name of Rosmarina certainly seemed to do the trick. 'How long you have?' asked the smiling cook. 'Wash and blow dry or cut and *colore*?'

'I'm not sure what it's called,' Monica translated. 'Hair like the lady who runs the shoe stall in the market.'

'Ah, Silvia,' she nodded. '*Riflessi dorati*. Golden highlights. This will take *due ore*. Two hours.'

'Well, we've learned the Italian for highlights,' Claire giggled. 'Look, she's brought us a drink.'

'Is my own limoncello, but I make it not so strong and mix with soda. Is very nice.'

They sipped it doubtfully but actually it was refreshing and delicious.

'Here is menu.' A small plate of amuse-bouches, tiny octopus dipped in tempura, had arrived. They were absolutely delectable.

'Wow, this place is quite a find.' Claire hoped it would take the full two hours to keep Sylvie away from any temptations of popping into the Belvedere Grand. At least this was hardly the kind of restaurant Tony and Kimberley would seek out for lunch.

And more fool them, Claire and Sylvie discovered, as course after tempting course was produced from what seemed to be a hole in the wall. More of the burrata they were getting to recognize, followed by a saffron-scented mussel soup and then the best seafood risotto either of them had ever tasted. Claire was about to comment that Italians don't really *do* puddings apart from the universal tiramisu and zabaglione when a plate of passion fruit sorbet arrived, decorated with chocolate strands, like the net that came with chocolate money at Christmas.

They finished with tiny cups of eye-wateringly strong espresso and little almond biscuits.

Sylvie looked at her watch. 'Better go and look at how the miracle's progressing.'

The owner handed them a ridiculously small bill which they loaded with a hefty tip. 'Thank you so much. It was wonderful!'

But not as wonderful as the sight that awaited them at the

hairdresser's. The owner had used the ten minutes or so since she'd finished Monica's hair to add some make-up.

She whipped off the hairdresser's gown to reveal Monica in her new shift dress and necklace, subtly made up complete with amazing hair. Somehow in the space of two hours she had managed to make Monica not only elegant and soignée, but also slightly Italian. The effect was startling.

'My God, you've turned into the other Monica – Monica Bellucci! Any minute, they'll be asking you to be a Bond girl.'

'I do hope not.' Monica grinned. 'I volunteer once a week in the library so I'd have to turn them down.'

'Please don't change from that Monica.' Claire embraced her. 'I would be disappointed in you!'

On the other hand, she couldn't help enjoying the stunned expression with which Giovanni greeted Monica. It bordered on reverence, as if some holy transformation really had taken place in the hairdresser's.

'Watch out, he'll kiss your hem any minute,' whispered Claire.

The ultimate accolade was that he drove them back to the villa at a careful thirty miles an hour, even forgetting to over-take a tourist bus on the inside.

'Wow,' congratulated Sylvie. 'St Monica, patron saint of careful driving.'

'I wouldn't have many followers in this country,' Monica pointed out as a motorbike streaked past them with total dis-regard for the thousand-foot ravine beneath.

An even more glowing reaction awaited them at the villa. Beatrice and Immaculata clutched each other and Angela whistled softly as she got out of her seat on the terrace where she seemed to be entertaining a strange man wearing a Russian fur hat, despite the twenty-five-degree heat.

When he stood up to greet them, they noted that the rest of his outlandish outfit consisted of a rather expensive-looking floor-length trench coat, tied at the waist, with large pockets, from one of which peeped a bright-eyed furry white head.

'Monica, Claire, Sylvie, may I introduce Constantine O'Flaherty?'

Sylvie had known about their celebrated and reclusive next-door-neighbour from her ex-assistant Alessandro, but neither Claire nor Monica knew they were living next door to one of the most celebrated and eccentric living painters.

'And this is . . . ?' Monica asked, indicating the dog as she shook the old man's hand.

'Hetti. It's short for her full name, Spaghetti. She's a Bolognese,' he stated.

Further questions seemed somehow not to be expected.

'The naughty girl ran away and was discovered by your gardener.' He pointed to Luigi, who crossed himself as soon as he found himself being indicated by Constantine. 'Signor Luigi does not approve of those of the homosexual persuasion. I fear he thinks the condition may be contagious.'

'He needn't worry about Giovanni,' Claire giggled.

'Who is Giovanni?' Constantine glanced around hopefully.

'He is the under-gardener. Rampantly heterosexual.'

'If he is under the gardener, perhaps there is hope for him yet, though looking at Luigi, I fear the worst.'

'Do you live here permanently?' Sylvie asked, trying to remember colour supplement articles she must have read about him.

'Yes. Once I found my eagle's nest,' he pointed through the

trees to his extraordinary house which seemed to be built right into the cliff face thousands of feet above the sea, 'near civilization yet far away from it, I immediately purchased it. The outback without the drawbacks, you might say.'

'And do you have a studio there?'

'Indeed. I am very modern, like a robot making Renaults. I have created a production line of my work and now I only have to fill in the outlines to keep me going for the rest of my life.'

When he made a statement like this it was hard to tell whether Constantine was serious or winding his audience up for asking blindingly banal questions.

He smiled at Sylvie with what seemed like genuine humour. 'I have a reputation to live up to for being disconcerting,' he announced.

'Congratulations,' Monica replied, fast as a whip, 'you're doing very well.'

'Hetti got lost in the gardens and Constantine came to look for her,' explained Angela. 'Fortunately, Beatrice had the idea of putting out some chicken livers which did the trick.'

'I'm surprised you don't have people to cook for your dog,' Monica commented.

'Oh, I do. I felt like a stroll. And to see the four English ladies I have heard so much about. You are the talk of Lanzarella, my dears.'

'But we hardly ever go there,' protested Claire.

'Exactly. They wonder what you are all doing up here in your hilltop fastness. And, of course, the mysterious Stephen too.'

'He isn't here.'

Constantine took a sip of his Franciacorta. 'Precisely. He's rarely here, which pricks the curiosity of the locals.'

They all looked at each other. Instinctively, they felt they shouldn't be telling their intriguing neighbour that Stephen was assessing the potential of Le Sirenuse as a hotel.

'Of course everyone in the village knows of the interesting offer he has received.'

'What offer is that?' Angela asked with a sphinx-like smile. Beatrice certainly hadn't known.

'To create yet another luxury hostelry.' He stroked Hetti's head. 'Just what Lanzarella needs.'

'And quite annoying for you,' suggested Monica. 'If it were true, that is.'

'Ah quite, and I hear you are all with us for quite different reasons, to nurse broken hearts and bruised egos. And to soak up our restorative sun.'

'How do you know so much about us?' Claire challenged.

'Calm down, I promise I am really not interested. I find things out because I dislike *not* knowing, not because I wish to know them to gossip or make use of them. Can you appreciate the difference?'

'Knowledge is power?' asked Claire.

'No, not at all.'

'Knowledge is protection?' enquired Monica.

'Smart girl.'

'So could I extend the welcome and visit you in return?' Monica asked, knowing she was pushing her luck. 'I've always thought art was overrated.'

This was such a lie that they stared at her, but Constantine O'Flaherty laughed so loud the dog almost jumped out of his pocket. 'It would be churlish of me to refuse.'

'Has that held you back before?'

'No.' He laughed again. 'I rather think I might enjoy your

company. Monica, isn't it? An invitation will arrive forthwith. Thank you all, and I'm sorry if my dog caused you any inconvenience.'

As he ambled off down the path at the side of the house and disappeared into the scrubby holm oak wood, Claire commented, 'I bet you he let the dog out deliberately.'

'Of course he did.' Monica grinned. 'He's quite outrageously dishonest and deceitful.'

'But you liked him. And he liked you. Whatever's happened to Mousy Monica from Great Missenden?'

Claire got ready to visit Beatrice's nephew's lemon groves and tried not to feel that it was all a bit of a nonsense. She could just pick a lemon or two for her tart and it would be far more straightforward. Monica had been talking about a trip to Pompeii, and she'd much rather do that.

She'd seen little golf buggies in Lerini advertising Luca's Lemon Tours and, frankly, it all felt rather like a tourist trap.

Still, she consulted her bus timetable and tried not to feel she was becoming Martin. You had to depend on bus timetables here if you wanted to avoid death by taxi or being driven by Giovanni. The thought of Martin made her feel guilty. He had been surprisingly quiet recently. Maybe he and Evan and Belinda had come to an accord and life was running smoothly. She certainly hoped so.

The lemon groves were steeply ranged up the next valley, another white-knuckle bus ride on from Lerini. Claire was finding, to her surprise, that she was getting to rather enjoy these rides, hair-raising though they might be. The local bus drivers seemed to know every tight corner and terrifying hairpin bend as if it were tattooed on their memories. She was beginning to know when they would hoot just before every blind corner and didn't even have to cling on the whole way any more.

The bus stopped on the seafront in Maggiore, the next town along the coast, and Claire walked for ten minutes, the whole length of the town, until she arrived at the address Beatrice had given her.

She pushed open a big wooden door and found herself in a shop selling limoncello, the strong lemon liqueur so common around here, in every different kind of bottle you could think of. A young woman stepped forward. 'Are you the friend of Beatrice? From Le Sirenuse?'

Claire nodded and smiled.

'I am Fabiella, a cousin of Luca.'

'Everyone is a cousin of someone, or a nephew.' Claire smiled, hoping that didn't sound rude.

'Family is very important in Italy, and in business also – more, I think, than in England, especially this family. They have grown lemons for five generations. Now they have big problem. Luca will tell you.'

And all I wanted was some lemons to make a tart, Claire thought, but the girl was already leading her into a dark side room full of old photographs and ancient artefacts about the lemon-growing trade.

A faded photograph, probably from the thirties, caught her eye. It was of women carrying enormous baskets full of lemons down to a boat.

'Each basket is fifty-seven kilos,' Fabiella enlightened her, 'they carry on their backs, and are paid by the number of trips they make in a day.'

Claire looked at the huge baskets, clearly the same as the

ones that were in the photo, that were piled up in the room. Her eye was caught by one which had an extra little extension.

'To carry the bambino,' Fabiella explained.

Claire studied it in amazement. And women thought they had it hard now!

'Every morning they had their nails inspected in case they could scratch the lemons – the skin of the lemon is very important. If the boss could smell lemon they were all in big trouble! Now we go and see how they grow.'

She opened a door into bright sunshine and the overpowering aroma of lemon blossom. But what really surprised Claire was that the lemon groves rose almost vertically up the mountain in narrow strips, so steeply that she wondered how they could be reached by anything but a mountain goat.

'Everything is done by hand.' Fabiella pointed and breathed in the powerful scent. '*La zagara*, they say when you smell lemon blossom, it is a sign of summer.'

Claire stood underneath a lemon tree, amazed that the tree was full of lemons but also with blossom, all on the same tree.

'The flowers will become the fruit.' Fabiella leaned forward and breathed in the scent of the tiny white flowers. 'We are only organic here, no pesticides, only natural manure, but it make it hard to compete against the producers who don't care. Big problems for us.'

'*Ciao, Fabiella, la signora* just come for lemons, not to hear such a sad story!'

Claire turned to see two men approaching. One was old, perhaps even eighty, weather-beaten and tanned by a life outside, with a humorous glint in his eye. It was hard to tell the age of the other; despite his labourer's clothes, he had an unexpected charm and polish, yet he must have been near enough to Claire's own age, she decided.

It had been the younger man who spoke. Now he held out his hand. 'I am Luca, the nephew of Beatrice. Welcome to our lemon gardens. They are always called gardens here, not groves, as you English call them.'

'*E anche paradisi*,' added the old man. 'And also paradises.'

'The Arabs who first planted them sometimes called them paradises, because they were away from the noise of the world.'

Claire looked around, still breathing in the sharp scent of the lemons. 'I can see what they meant.'

'We wondered if you would join us for a refreshment?'

'Thank you, that would be lovely.'

She followed Luca down the steep slope, and would have fallen at one point if it had not been for his steadying hand.

'I can't believe how high up you grow your lemons,' she said, to cover her slight embarrassment.

'Every inch is needed,' he replied with a grudging smile, as if he was making light of something he knew to be serious.

She was offered coffee on a fragrant terrace with a small kitchen attached overlooking the groves, or gardens, as she must learn to call them, shaded by wisteria and lemon blossom.

'This is where we offer cooking lessons to the guests on the tours who wish to have them.'

'And how many tours do you do a day?'

She wondered if perhaps such a question was intrusive; she had only come to buy lemons, but oddly, perhaps because of Fabiella's candour and Luca's polish, which she sensed covered up his worry, somehow she felt they wouldn't resent her interest.

'One, perhaps two occasionally.'

Rather than ask him how much people paid she decided she would quietly grab a leaflet as she left.

Fabiella arrived with coffees and the most delicious lemon cake she had ever eaten. The sponge was warm and the lemon melting, like the most intense lemon drizzle cake straight from the oven.

'My aunt Beatrice says you are a cook too.'

Claire smiled modestly. 'I am what we call a caterer, I cook for other people's parties.'

'Do you like doing this?'

'Most of the time. As long as the customer is not difficult.' For the first moment in what seemed like weeks she thought of Brook Street and the horrible young man she'd drenched in coffee.

'And you?' she asked, realizing that perhaps this was a dangerous question. 'Do you enjoy what you do?'

'*È la mia passione!* It is a passion for me. Until last year I was a lawyer, I travelled all round the world, I live in a big house, I go on expensive holidays. And then my father come to me and say, "The family business is going to die unless you come and save it".'

'That must have been a very difficult decision for you.'

Luca shook his head without speaking for a moment. 'For my wife, yes. And for my children. Not for me.'

Claire felt an odd jolt of disappointment at the mention of his wife. How ridiculous.

'How did you resolve it?'

'I was at that moment when you realize you are not young, maybe you are not old, but you wonder what you have achieved, what is life worth, is it the money you make for yourself and for other people, or is it something bigger?' He leaned across the table towards her. 'Have you ever felt that, Chiara?'

She realized he had slipped into the Italian pronunciation of her name and she felt it was because he was taking her into his confidence.

'Not as you have, perhaps because I haven't had a decision to make, like yours. But I have felt a dissatisfaction, wondering if that is all there is, I suppose, to use a cliché.' She thought of Martin and her irritation with Evan and Belinda and looked away, aware of the intensity of his scrutiny, and the blue of his eyes, surely unusual in an Italian. 'I suppose, in a way, that's why I'm here.'

'You are escaping your life?'

She hadn't seen it like that. The thought was disturbing.

'So you chose lemons,' Claire said gently.

'Yes, I chose lemons. And my wife chose another rich businessman. My children went with her. I could not blame them; in my new life I could not pay for expensive schools and the kind of holidays they were used to. But I still see my daughter.'

Claire knew from his clipped and unemotional voice how deep his hurt really was and wished she could do something to help. 'So what are your plans for saving the business? Or is that private? Do just tell me if I am asking too many questions.'

'It is good that you are interested. We have three sources of revenue – the lemons, which are difficult, as we are so organic we cannot compete on price, only on our quality; the lemon tours, and selling our limoncello.'

Claire was no hard-headed businesswoman but it sounded a slender plan to save a business and to provide a living for Luca's father and a future for the whole family.

Fortunately, she wasn't called on to comment because Luca's father arrived with his arm round an extremely pretty young girl.

'*Ecco Bianca!*' He made Claire think of a very jolly garden gnome.

Luca jumped up. '*Bianca! Carissima!* You didn't tell me you were coming.' His whole demeanour changed with the arrival of his daughter. He turned to Claire. 'My daughter, Bianca. This is Chiara, she is staying up at the Villa Le Sirenuse and she is interested in lemons.'

The young girl gave Claire a quick assessing glance. Obviously, she didn't see Claire, with her unstylish appearance and slightly messy hair, as a likely object of interest to her father.

'I must go,' announced Claire and she smiled at Luca. She stopped for a moment to buy some limoncello on the way out and was standing in the street working out the best route to the bus stop when Luca suddenly appeared. He was carrying a brown paper bag.

'I thought Aunt Beatrice said you were coming to get some lemons.'

In her fascination with listening to Luca she had completely forgotten why she had come.

'Yes, of course,' she managed faintly. 'How much do I owe you?'

'For the lemons?' She could tell even without looking at Luca how much he was enjoying the moment. He pointed upwards. They were standing under a large tree bursting with lemons. 'The business may be less than flourishing but I think we can afford to let you have a few free. I will ask one small thing in return. I would like to show you my lemon gardens the other side of the valley. It is very special there and then you will come and have lunch with me.'

Claire headed for the bus stop on the seafront clutching her lemons in a daze. The locals shopped and sat in cafes drinking their espressos, the children ran up and down begging their mothers for ice creams, the old ladies in black gossiped and hung out the washing from their balconies, the young men rolled down their car windows to let their music blast out into the morning sunshine and impress the pretty girls who pretended not to notice. Claire waited for the bus, oblivious to it all.

Luca wanted to show her his special lemon gardens and to have lunch with her. No one had invited her to have lunch alone since she'd been married to Martin, let alone a dazzlingly attractive Italian man.

And he hadn't, she realized, in all their revelations, even asked her if she was married.

The question was, knowing that she was definitely attracted to him, ought she to go?

'Oh, for goodness' sake, Claire!' she told herself sternly. The Italians were famous flirts, everyone knew that. Stop treating a lunch invitation as if it were something serious!

# Eight

Angela armed herself with a notebook and her iPhone for her tour of Lanzarella's hotels. To her surprise there were more than twenty listed on Booking.com, far more than she'd suspected could be dotted around the maze of back streets, but most were small and not grand enough to rival the villa.

She started with a simple but charming ex-convent. It had about ten rooms, some of which faced the bay, all organized round a small fountain. It was the kind of hotel the well-informed budget customer would stay in. She moved down the small cobbled street to the next one on her list. This one boasted a swimming pool, an attraction since Lanzarella was above the coast with spectacular views of the sea but not actually on it. Yet when Angela asked to see the pool she had to hide a laugh. It was hardly long enough to swim five strokes before you had to turn round. The rooms were simple and clean, but again this was budget territory.

The next two hotels had simple entrances that masked hidden grandeur within, but it was a chilly grandeur – vast flower arrangements, universal pale cream marble floors and sometimes walls as well, which might be cooling in high summer, but were discouraging earlier in the season. Also they had that terrible over-staffed feeling. Angela suspected that at these establishments your wine glass would be continually filled in the restaurant, and you would be asked every two minutes if everything was all right. So many hotels, it struck her, were obsessed with the idea of 'service', i.e. staff constantly bothering you, rather than with comfort.

After visiting ten hotels, none of which she had the slightest desire to stay in, Angela made for the final one on her list, the Grand Hotel degli Dei. The Hotel of the Gods. She hoped it lived up to its name.

It was certainly in an amazing position, suspended high above the bay, with large gardens and a glorious pool. Angela made straight for the bar, the initial way she judged any hotel. This at least ought to feel welcoming, even if the reception area was a little over-formal.

As she sat down Angela wanted to scream. It was all white again, white sofas, white curtains, white floors. She longed to drop a glass of red wine on the upholstery or, at the very least, unleash Sylvie on the décor. She had begun to think that though Sylvie's 'opera house meets bordello' style wasn't her own, a hotel that featured it might do very well just by contrast to all these arctic wastes.

'Can I offer you a drink, madame?' asked the waiter in that creepy five-star hotel way. Angela longed to say, 'Why, are you paying?' but made herself behave. 'A glass of champagne, please.'

She noted with interest, when he brought her drink, that he wasn't even Italian. 'Do you mind if I wander around while I drink it? I'm looking for venues for a wedding.'

'By all means, madame. Perhaps you'd like to look at our

179

wedding book?' He fetched an enormous weddings tome from behind the bar.

'Thank you so much. I'll look at it out by the pool.'

She wandered out into the dazzling midday sun, noting that the entire terrace and pool area was empty. She sat down with the book open on a table in front of her, remembering what her taxi driver had told her: anyone sunbathing in Italy before the end of May was bound to be a foreigner. But there weren't even any foreigners. There was one advantage to that. It meant that Angela could happily take lots of photographs of the place and also the contents of the wedding book.

The hotel certainly pulled out all the stops where weddings were concerned. In one photograph the whole garden had been filled with huge urns of white hydrangeas, and dotted with candles and white fairy lights. In another the pool area had been lit like a Disney movie. She had to admit it would be a lot of brides' dreams. She must remember to check out the costs.

Usefully, there was a scale of charges at the end of the book, beginning with the most staggering sum. Given that this would be simply for the wedding itself and you would have to add drinks parties the night before and maybe brunch on the day after, you would need to be Donald Trump to afford it.

It was a ten-minute walk back to the Villa Le Sirenuse. The weather was utterly perfect. The sun was hot without being burning. Below, the sea dazzled with the tiniest hint of mist.

All around her birds sang.

Almost accidentally she noticed two figures leaning against a wall half hidden by a tumble of purple wisteria, locked in a passionate embrace. To her shame, something made her slow her footsteps and watch, mesmerized, as the young man's hand disappeared under her skirt. The girl closed her eyes and leaned against the wall pushing her body against him until her back arched and she cried out. As they pulled apart she saw that the man was Giovanni.

Angela hurried on, feeling ashamed and yet also aroused. It had all been so surprising yet so powerful. She suddenly thought of Stephen and how, both innocent at the start, they had learned to explore sex together. For her especially it had been a revelation that making love could be so glorious and uninhibited. Having to give up Stephen and the lovemaking had been the worst thing that had ever happened to her.

Of course she had had many encounters over the years but sex had become a functional thing for her, as it had been in her brief relationship with Drew, separate from emotion. But somehow, here, she was remembering the connection and it struck her as very sad.

As she reached the gates of the villa, she rather hoped that there was a time when you were too old to feel stirred. Yet clearly she hadn't reached it.

She passed through the kitchen on her way to her room, to find it full of happy clamour. Claire, wearing a navy-blue pinny covered in flour, was showing Immaculata, so tiny that she was standing on a block so that she could see, how to make her famous lemon tart. Immaculata declared herself shocked that no ricotta or mascarpone was involved. And positively scandalized that the pastry was to be baked blind. But the thing that most amazed the old lady was that Claire was accessing the recipe on her iPad.

'Is like watching television!' Immaculata declared, charmed.

Claire measured out the ingredients on the digital scales she carried everywhere with her. Immaculata inspected these with the intense amazement that must have greeted Galileo's first telescope.

# Claire's Lemon Tart

*For the pastry:*

250g plain flour
75g icing sugar
180g butter
3 egg yolks

*Put the flour, icing sugar and butter, cut into small cubes (as cold as possible straight from the fridge), into a bowl and mix until it resembles fine breadcrumbs. (Immaculata protested she didn't believe in food processors so this had to be done by hand!) Add the yolks and stir thoroughly. Bind by hand. Leave it to rest in the fridge wrapped in cling film for 45 minutes.*

*Roll out the pastry and press into a 24cm flan base. You can ease it in with your knuckles so don't worry if it's not perfect. Bake blind with baking beans on greaseproof paper to stop it rising at 150°C for 20 minutes, pricking the pastry first.*

*For the filling:*

300g butter
300g caster sugar
6 eggs
9 egg yolks
130ml lemon juice
Zest of 6 lemons

*Mix lemon zest, juice, sugar and butter on the hob until butter is melted slightly but not so hot that it will curdle the eggs when you put them in. Whisk the eggs and add to the saucepan. Stir over a medium heat until it thickens into a custard, then whisk lightly (NB: Albert Roux, the king of lemon tart, advises not to over-stir the custard) and pour into the pastry shell. Fill halfway then up to the top, as full as possible. Cook the tart for 40–50 minutes at 150°C until set on top. When cooled down dust heavily with icing sugar and finish off with a blow torch. You can put it under the grill but it tends to burn the pastry, so a blow torch is preferable.*

'Right, where are we going to find a blow torch?'

The response was that there might be one in Luigi's shed.

'*Aie!*' cried Immaculata when they managed to light it. '*È pericoloso!* It will be dangerous!'

'It would be if you let Giovanni near it.' But Claire was made of sterner stuff.

'Why have you made two tarts, Signora Chiara?' Immaculata wondered.

Claire smiled and handed her one. 'One is for you and Beatrice and the others.'

Immaculata took the tart with the reverence usually accorded to Holy Communion.

Beatrice had laid out dinner on the terrace. Monica was down first, wearing her new trousers with the best of her old tops. She helped herself to a glass of wine and stared down at the sea. It was one of those amazing pearly evenings when the sun had just gone down and left a soft pink glow over the terraces and the gardens, and a gentle mist had settled over the sea as if the hard lines of daytime had been rubbed gently by an unseen finger.

Claire appeared next, having showered off the flour from

her cooking demo. Monica looked at her closely. She, too, had a glow like the setting sun. How interesting. 'I hear you've been making mayhem in the kitchen.'

Claire laughed. She looked like a different person from the rather careworn woman who had seemed to carry the burden for her entire family. 'Yes, I have shocked Immaculata with my twenty-first-century cooking tools. The results come later.'

'Hello, girls, plotting the downfall of Western civilization?' Sylvie swished past them and breathed in the night air theatrically.

Claire giggled. 'Well, I made a start. Immaculata wants digital scales.'

Sylvie shook her head. 'Where will it all end? How were the lemon groves?'

'We have to call them "gardens". The locals are very particular. Or "paradises".'

'So you've been in paradise all day. How was it?'

'Heavenly,' Claire laughed. 'Actually, it *was* pretty heavenly. The smell of lemons and lemon blossom. Do you know they have the flower and the fruit on the branch at the same time?'

'Oh my God, she's going native. She'll give up catering in East Cheam and move in with the lemon grower.'

'Twickenham, actually. Anyway, don't be so ridiculous, Sylvie,' Claire replied with sudden brusqueness. 'Where on earth's Angela got to? She's much more likely than I am to abandon us for one of these five-star hotels she's been checking out. You know how she's been missing room service.'

'Not tempted to do any such thing.' Angela had just joined them on the terrace. 'I was just having a rather delicious bath. It's such a glorious night I left the window open. Though point taken about room service. It would have been even more perfect if I could have ordered a glass of fizz.'

'You should have shouted your order out of the window,' Monica suggested. 'You might have got Giovanni!'

Angela suddenly walked to the balcony and looked down at the lights below, which were just beginning to come on. 'It's quite a place, isn't it, the Villa Le Sirenuse?'

'So how were all the posh hotels?'

'Surprisingly uninviting. The last one had potential, though. Sylvie, I wondered if you'd come and look at it tomorrow? There are aspects of it we might find useful.'

Beatrice arrived with the first course of squid in tempura and they all sat round the table on the terrace. Angela didn't seem even to think of sitting at the head.

'Let's get it clear what we're doing here.' Sylvie sipped her wine. 'We know Stephen has had an offer to sell the place to a hotel chain. How serious is it, I wonder?'

A sudden silence followed, almost like the announcement of a death as they contemplated the villa being handed over to a soulless hotel chain.

'I don't think I could bear to see this lovely place ruined.' Claire voiced what they were all thinking.

'Surely it would be better if Stephen did it himself?' Sylvie suggested. 'And I'm not just pitching for the work.'

'But would he really?' Monica enquired.

'He'd have to get someone else to run it,' Angela pointed out.

'Yes, I suppose so,' Claire conceded.

'Well, thanks for the enthusiasm,' replied Angela.

'Unless, of course, he's considering a major life change.'

'I can see why the staff would be so worried.' Monica hesitated for a moment, wondering if this was the moment to voice her suspicions about what was happening with the fruit and vegetables.

185

'Well, of course. They've worked here forever. They'd lose their jobs.'

Monica decided to take the plunge. 'And a nice little side-line. I think they've got a scam going on selling flowers and vegetables. I was walking round outside the other day and came across a veritable market garden with polytunnels and everything, all hidden behind high hedges and pergolas of wisteria and clematis. There's far more of everything than we could ever eat. And flowers too, yet they keep buying them in Naples. It's really fishy.'

'Don't be ridiculous, Monica,' Sylvie scoffed. 'Beatrice and Immaculata as black-market profiteers? It's like accusing your granny.'

'Remember Giovanni and the argument with the chef over the zucchini?' Monica reminded them.

'That was nothing. Everyone does that. This is Italy after all.'

'And why do they import roses from Naples when they've got glorious roses growing everywhere here?'

'Maybe they don't like garden flowers? They might believe posh long-stemmed roses are more sophisticated.'

'Oh well,' Monica shrugged, 'I could be wrong.' All the same, she'd have another word with the antiques-shop lady about why it was 'the wedding house'.

As if to demonstrate the madness of Monica's suspicions, Immaculata came out onto the terrace at that moment carrying Claire's lemon tart as if it were more precious than gold, frankincense or myrrh, with Beatrice behind bearing a candle and Luigi and Giovanni in their trail singing the Italian version of 'Happy Birthday to You'.

'It's a bit late, I know,' Monica whispered, 'but best wishes all the same!'

Beatrice held out the candle for Sylvie to blow out.

'We did not want to put the candle in the tart,' Beatrice explained.

Sylvie then had the honour of trying to cut it, which actually proved quite difficult, as the top layer was the hard and shiny crust of sugar, but all was well when she tasted it.

'Claire, this is divine! Absolutely the best lemon tart I have ever tasted. Are you going to try some, Beatrice?'

'Signora Chiara has made a tart just for us. We are going to eat it now in the kitchen. Would you like some coffee to go with your *dolce*?'

'Too late for me,' Claire said, and she and Monica both shook their heads, but Sylvie and Angela, the alpha females, both opted for espresso.

'Let me know what you think,' Claire asked the housekeeper. 'Of course, it isn't better than the Italian version, just different.'

'Oh, Claire,' Sylvie shook her head, 'how can we stop you being so irredeemably *nice*?'

'Isn't nice a good thing?' Claire asked.

'Not always a good thing for *you*,' Angela said, smiling.

'Come on,' Sylvie got up, 'we've got to see what they really think of a British tart.'

The others followed as Sylvie tiptoed down the dark passage towards the kitchen, her finger on her lips.

In the kitchen, the staff were all gathered around the big table. They each had glasses of limoncello, plus a plate of Claire's wonderful creation. They also had an unexpected guest. It was Luca, Beatrice's nephew. They tasted the tart in turn and nodded their heads approvingly. A lemon-flavoured bomb had clearly hit Lanzarella.

Luca was about to propose a toast when he noticed Claire

and the others watching from the passage. He beckoned them into the kitchen and led Claire to the front, taking her hand. 'Thank you for taking my lemons and performing a miracle.'

He raised her hand to his lips and kissed it.

Sylvie, watching the scene with fascination, whispered to Angela. 'I think we may have witnessed a serious threat to Claire remaining nice.'

They were about to leave when Luigi approached Monica. 'There is a message for you, Signorina Monica. The old *ommosessuale* who lives next door would like you to join him at Antonella's Pizzeria *domani* at one o'clock.'

Monica had to hide her face so as not to laugh. She wondered if Constantine had given Luigi a message deliberately to wind him up rather than using more conventional methods of getting in touch.

'Claire gets Luca and his lemons and I get the old *omosessuale*,' Monica whispered. 'Do you think we could persuade Luigi to be a bit more PC?'

Angela nodded vigorously. 'Absolutely. Why don't you give him a brief resumé of why he should describe homosexuals as gay people?'

Claire, up early as usual, stretched in the sunshine and smiled for no reason at all. Maybe it was the place, the jewel-like beauty of it, the flowers everywhere, the overwhelming scent of wisteria. She tried to pin down what was so utterly special about the Villa Le Sirenuse and decided that it was the sense of being almost out of time.

She was tempted to have another dip with her nymph but twice might look deliberate, as though she actually wanted to attract Giovanni's attention. She couldn't help comparing Giovanni and Luca. The one so obvious, his attractiveness that of the bad boy at the fairground, and Luca, subtle, sophisticated, full of passion not for seducing random women, but for continuing a way of life full of beauty and meaning.

Claire had to be honest with herself. It must have been hard for his wife when he changed his lifestyle so dramatically, but wasn't that part of marriage? With a pang of guilt, she thought of Martin but the only thing he was really passionate about was his movie posters. What would she do if he suddenly announced he wanted to move to Eastbourne and open a poster shop? That it was the dream of his whole life? She didn't want to think about that.

She remembered what the others had said. Maybe it was true that she was too bloody nice. So she stopped worrying about the implications and decided to accept Luca's invitation to show her his other lemon gardens the other side of the valley. After all, it couldn't do any real harm, could it?

Angela sat on the terrace looking very smart in a white linen trouser suit with an attractively battered Panama hat.

'You look nice,' Claire commented, pouring herself a coffee.

'Thanks.' Angela smiled back.

Sylvie had clearly decided that visiting a grand hotel needed a more than usually colourful response. The orange of her Matisse-inspired silk outfit could have blinded a receptionist at twenty paces. It also perfectly matched the colour of the toenails peeping from her vertiginously high-heeled sandals.

'Will those be OK on cobbles?' Angela enquired. 'We're not going by taxi.'

Sylvie looked shocked. 'Why ever not?'

'Because it might be a half-hour taxi-ride down to Lerini but Lanzarella's only ten minutes down the drive!'

'I'll be fine. I'm tougher than I look.'

Angela smiled. She suspected there was a resilience in Sylvie, possibly born of a lonely childhood, or maybe as a side effect of her boundless energy, that would see her through most things. Though maybe walking on cobbles in four-inch heels might not be one of them.

The grandly named Hotel degli Dei – the Hotel of the Gods – in Lanzarella was busier today but the staff and other guests could hardly fail to notice the arrival of Angela and Sylvie, since Sylvie's first action was to walk up to the receptionist and ask for a corn plaster.

Unsurprisingly, this was met by a blank stare.

Sylvie pointed to her toe, now looking red and uncomfortably swollen.

'Ah,' the barman today was Italian, given to standing for long periods in too-tight shoes and suffered from corns himself, 'the signora has need of *un callifugo!*'

'*Un callifugo!*' Sylvie repeated authoritatively, as if she'd known the word all along. Unfortunately, the hapless receptionist was not Italian but Romanian. 'A corn plaster!' insisted Sylvie, 'I need a bloody corn plaster! Oh Good Lord, what kind of hotel is this where you can't even supply a corn plaster?'

Angela dismissed all thoughts of trying to have a quiet look around and suggested that Sylvie go out and sit by the swimming pool and she would join her with some kind of first-aid treatment as soon as some could be located.

This arrived sooner than she expected. A suavely handsome man of roughly her own age in beige chinos and a crisp white shirt was approaching, a distinct smile of amusement lighting up his tanned features. He shook her hand. 'Hugo Robertson. Welcome to the Grand Hotel degli Dei. If I'd known how damn hard that is to pronounce, I'd have insisted on something simpler. Unfortunately, I was only twelve at the time. I rather think your friend would like one of these.'

To Angela's utter amazement he held out a corn plaster. 'It was my mother's. She likes to come for the whole of March.'

There was something in his tone that told Angela this was not an unalloyed pleasure. 'Thank you. I'm Angela Williams. That was my friend Sylvie. We're staying up at the Villa Le Sirenuse.'

'I had heard of the interesting English ladies up at the villa. Lanzarella is roughly the equivalent of Little Snoring. And twice as gossipy.'

'I didn't think we'd done anything worthy of gossip.'

'You'd be surprised. We have very little to talk about off-season. Any drama will do, no matter how small.'

As if on cue, a high-pitched woman's scream came from the swimming pool, followed by a loud splash and a man's shout of angry protest.

Angela, deducing correctly that this was something to do with Sylvie, instantly rushed outside.

To her horror she found Sylvie's husband Tony waist-deep in the pool next to a bedraggled Kimberley, whose mascara had run, creating two black tram lines down her furious face. Clearly they had not gone to Positano after all.

'How dare you, you overweight old harridan!' she accused Sylvie.

Tony, meanwhile, was attempting to rescue what looked like an exercise bicycle from a row that had stood at the side of the pool for use by the more energetic guests and was now heading for the deep end.

'Don't mind me, just think about the bike!' Kimberley berated him.

'Oh dear, what a silly accident,' Sylvie tittered. 'I mean, who would be stupid enough to want to ride an exercise bicycle next to the pool in one of the most beautiful places on earth?'

'Just because you've given up on your ballooning body it doesn't mean the rest of us have to!' Kimberley spluttered.

Two waiters appeared from round the corner, looking horrified and debating what should be done.

'Perhaps you could assist my husband in removing that object from the swimming pool,' Sylvie requested and swept grandly into the Ladies' loo, leaving the hapless waiters to deduce which object she was talking about.

Angela followed her. 'Excellent. I think we have more than succeeded in our goal of having a quiet snoop around the hotel without attracting too much attention, don't you?'

Before she could answer, Tony suddenly burst in. 'Sylvie! I just wanted you to know that I had absolutely no idea that you were even in Italy, let alone staying in Lanzarella!'

Sylvie's face softened for a fraction before she recovered herself. 'Oughtn't you to be soothing the ruffled feathers on your gym bunny rather than wasting your time with overweight old harridans?'

Tony looked as if he were going to say something then he shook his head and backed out of the Ladies'.

'*Can* you soothe ruffled feathers on gym bunnies?' Angela asked, trying not to laugh. 'Sorry, Sylvie,' she pulled herself together, 'it must have been awful for you.'

'Actually,' Sylvie brightened, 'I've been itching to do something ever since I caught them together. Where on earth did you get the corn plaster?'

'You can thank the owner, a Mr Hugo Robertson. For the

owner of a grand hotel he seems to have quite a sense of humour.'

As soon as Sylvie had tidied herself up and applied the corn plaster they went back upstairs to the bar. There was no further sign of Tony, Kimberley or indeed Hugo Robertson but the waiter approached them with two glasses of champagne and a distinct twinkle in his eye. 'With the compliments of the management,' he announced. 'We hope we will see you again.'

'Well,' Sylvie sipped happily, 'that's very broadminded. I thought they were going to throw us out.'

Monica arrived at Antonella's Pizzeria, another restaurant that hung dramatically over the clifftop, at ten minutes to one but Constantine was already installed in the only part of the restaurant that didn't share the view. He still wore his Russian hat and trench coat.

'Is Spaghetti in your pocket?'

'Ssh,' Constantine tutted as a furry head peeped out, 'Italians don't approve of dogs in restaurants.'

Constantine poured them each a large glass of wine. 'I hope you don't mind but I have ordered the wine. There is only one that is drinkable and, anyway, you have to have red with pizza.' He gestured to the other tables whose guests were also drinking the red, apart from one table of Americans who had Coke.

'I will never understand Americans. Do you know, I was once in the Colombe d'Or in St Paul de Vence, one of the most famous restaurants in the world, and these Americans ordered Coke. The chef came out and begged them on bended knee not to drink Coke with his food. It was a travesty. Water, maybe, but Coke, no. Do you know that they did? Kept on drinking the Coke.'

'I thought you were meant to be a famous recluse, not eating in La Colombe and Antonella's Pizzeria.'

'St Paul de Vence is full of painters, and at Antonella's Pizzeria no one has an idea who Constantine O is so I can remain a famous recluse and still go out to lunch.'

Monica giggled and looked at the menu, her attention suddenly arrested, not by the margheritas and the capricciosas but by the flower arrangement on their table. This featured scented roses in a very distinctive shade of purple, which she had definitely seen before – in the villa's gardens.

'What is the matter with you, Monica who notices so much?' Constantine was watching her with the bright eye of a small bird.

'It's the flowers.'

'Are they so unusual?'

'Let's order and I'll explain.'

She chose a four seasons and Constantine a calzone. The order placed, he refilled their glasses. 'I always find wine clears the brain.'

Monica giggled. 'In contrast to all medical evidence to the contrary.'

'Doctors! What do they know? I have spent a lifetime avoiding them. Now tell me about the flowers.'

Monica sipped her wine. 'None of the others believes me, but there's something very fishy going on at the villa. The garden is full of flowers yet the ones in our bedrooms were brought all the way from Naples.'

'Maybe they think garden flowers are just weeds. The Italians have some funny ideas about flowers. For instance never, ever give an Italian chrysanthemums.'

'Why ever not?'

'They signify death. Lilies. Gladioli. Big showy blooms.

194

Those are what the Italians call flowers. Perhaps they wanted to impress you.'

'Maybe. But I am pretty damn sure these roses come from the villa gardens. And we saw a chef in Lerini having an argument with Giovanni, the gardener, about the quality of a zucchini. I'm convinced there's some kind of scam going on.'

'And if there is?' Constantine looked stunned at Monica's naivety. 'The owner lives miles away, he doesn't seem to care what happens to the house, so naturally they do what they can. My dear Monica, this isn't Brightling-by-the-Sea. This is Italy.'

'But these are family retainers. Immaculata's been there since before Stephen came.'

'Then they have all the more right. Besides, they will all know by now that their esteemed proprietor has been talking to the silver-tongued Hugo Robertson.'

'I'm not sure they do know. Who is he anyway?'

'The owner of the Hotel Castello and the degli Dei, the two best hotels in Lanzarella.'

That would explain Beatrice's sudden clumsiness, certainly.

'Though perhaps they don't know what he has been offered.'

'But you do?'

He nodded.

'How on earth do you know that?'

'I make it my business to know things that might affect me.'

'All right, so if you know so much, what has Stephen been offered?'

The sum was so enormous that Monica put down her fork and stared.

'Yes, indeed. Mr Robertson, it seems, has his reasons.'

Monica was so shocked that she couldn't think of anything else to say.

Constantine insisted on paying. 'Do you think I should sign the tablecloth and get us both thrown out?'

'But that would blow your cover as a famous recluse.'

'Indeed it would, Monica, indeed it would. By the way, wise not to share that information with your fellow travellers. Not the most discreet of houseguests, from what I've heard. Would you like me to make some discreet enquiries about your zucchini scam?'

Monica hesitated. It seemed so awful. Reluctantly she nodded.

'And perhaps one day soon you might like to visit my studio.' It was a statement rather than a question.

'You'll have to watch it,' Monica quizzed him, 'or your reputation as a recluse will be in serious trouble.'

'Surely even as a recluse I'm allowed to invite people I would like to pose for me.'

Monica stared at him and had to stop herself saying, '*Me?*'

'There is something elusive about you I find interesting.'

She could hear Brian's voice in her ear urging her to 'Go for it!' It drowned out her mother Mariella's saying, 'Are you sure there isn't some mistake?'

'I would be absolutely delighted,' she replied.

Of course, when the time came, she might well have changed her mind.

# *Nine*

---

As the others were busy, Claire found herself a shady spot underneath the wisteria-covered pergola and thought about home. Things must be all right because she hadn't heard from either Martin or her son Evan. Maybe some miracle had happened and they were all living in harmony and sharing the cooking and washing-up. This scenario didn't seem very convincing so she banished it from her mind. She was going to swim in a moment, take advantage of the empty pool.

There seemed to be no one about, so she put on her swimsuit and walked down through the gardens to the lowest level. The pool sparkled in the Mediterranean sun, blue and inviting as a Hockney painting, but without the bums. She sat on the top of the scalloped steps and got used to the tingle of the cold water, then gradually lowered herself in.

She turned over and stared up at the perfect blue sky. How on earth could Stephen own a place as beautiful as this yet hardly ever come here? Was making money from horrible modern developments so much more tempting? She laughed, imagining Satan taking Stephen to the top of a skyscraper in London and saying, 'All this can be yours for the price of your soul.' And now he was thinking of selling it or turning it into a hotel. Claire suddenly felt fiercely protective of it, of its seclusion in the middle of a busy coastline, its dramatic beauty, its strange timelessness, even its motley staff, no matter what Monica was suggesting.

She told herself not to be ridiculous. It was nothing to do with her and she hardly knew Stephen. He probably didn't even remember taking her to a ball at all. It was up to the others who at least had more of a link to Stephen and ought to advise him. She climbed out of the pool and concentrated instead on the message she'd just found which must have been waiting on her signal-less phone. She wondered how he had got her number. From Beatrice, she assumed. They'd all given her their numbers so that she could keep in touch when they were out and about.

Luca wanted her to go and visit his lemon gardens and she felt as excited as a teenage girl on her first date. How ridiculous was that?

When she got back up to the terrace, she found Angela was sitting with a glass of pale wine, her eyes closed, drinking in the sunshine. She wondered if she dare tease Angela and decided she definitely could. 'Glorious here, isn't it? And great to see you finally taking off your suit.'

Angela looked at her, perplexed. 'But I'm wearing a suit.' She gestured to her white linen.

'I meant metaphorically.'

Angela laughed. 'Now there's a word I haven't heard since university days.'

Emboldened, Claire dared to ask another question. 'Did you know Stephen well at Oxford?'

A shutter came down. Angela visibly straightened in her chair. 'Quite well,' was the crisp answer.

At home Claire would have clammed up too, and spent the day feeling guilty for intruding. But things were different here. They were all escaping something in their different ways, Claire was sure of it.

'What happened between you?' she persisted.

Angela was clearly struggling with how to reply. Intimacy was obviously something she avoided, whether she meant to or not. She looked away. 'Actually, we were in love. Or at least I was, then my mother had a breakdown and I had to leave. He was kind and understanding. He drove me home.' She turned and looked Claire steadily in the eye. 'And I never heard from him again.'

'Angela, how awful!'

'Yes. But he was twenty-one. I was a girl from a council estate. Oxford soon swallowed him up. Parties. Balls. Girls with brains and pedigrees to match.'

'I met plenty of the ones with pedigrees at secretarial college. Not much evidence of brains. You must have been in love since?' Claire was quite prepared to have her head bitten off.

'Only with my business,' Angela replied with a wry smile remembering Drew's criticism. 'Of course I had affairs. I'm not a nun. Not even the kind of nun who lived here.'

'But you had independence. That's the one thing I've never had.'

'Funny old thing, life.' Angela got up. 'I might go and take off my metaphorical suit.'

'By the way,' Claire enquired, 'how did it go with Sylvie and the grand hotel? Did she actually get there in those shoes?'

'You missed a rare treat. Tony and Kimberley were staying there. They must have been moved from the Belvedere Grand.'

'Oh my God, no!'

'Kimberley was on an exercise bicycle next to the pool. Well, I mean, who could resist the temptation?'

'She didn't?'

'She did. And the funny thing was Tony seemed more concerned with telling Sylvie he hadn't known she was here than pulling the gym bunny out of the pool.'

'Interesting.'

'I thought so.' They couldn't say any more because Sylvie arrived and joined them. But Sylvie needed no such discretion. 'Gossiping about me, girls?'

'I could hardly leave Claire out of the drama, could I?' Angela admitted. 'The story's too good to miss.'

'Stupid cow. I hope she's still at the bottom of that pretentious hotel's pool.'

'She probably is for all Tony seemed to care.'

Sylvie grinned delightedly. 'Yes, but poor lamb, did you see how thin he's got? I bet she put him on a diet.'

Angela and Claire couldn't resist exchanging looks.

Beatrice arrived to announce that lunch was on the terrace. 'And my nephew Luca say he showing Signora Chiara his other gardens tomorrow.' She beamed fulsomely.

The Villa Le Sirenuse was clearly no place for secrets.

Luca came to collect Claire in a pickup truck, under the proprietorial eye of Giovanni, who stopped weeding and stared rudely until Beatrice asked him if he'd given up working because it was a saint's day.

It was another set of death-defying hairpin bends over thousand-foot ravines, but Claire found she'd begun to find the stomach-clenching journeys rather enjoyable. Now that was a miracle.

They stopped at a little patisserie and had melting lemon

cakes and espressos. 'No one Italian drinks cappuccino,' Luca asserted waving his hand at all the German, British and American tourists eagerly spooning the foam off their coffees. 'You will have to learn to drink coffee black if you want to be an Italian!'

The look that accompanied this harmless statement seemed to be so loaded she had to look away. Was he implying that *he* wanted her to become an Italian?

'And is everything around here connected to lemons?' she asked eventually.

'Everything,' Luca asserted, smiling.

Back in the truck, they climbed up the other side of the mountain to a series of terraces clustered round a bell tower. 'All ours, the campanile also.' He pointed to the crumbling but still beautiful tower.

A lark soared above them and all was silence and peace, yet only ten minutes away from the busy coastline. What a place to live and work.

They watched as Luca's pickers carried enormous plastic packs of lemons on their backs, their heads cushioned by different kinds of pillows, each individually fashioned by its carrier.

Luca shook his head sadly. 'But it is very difficult to make a profit. Sicilian lemons are much cheaper but not organic like ours. To them it is only money; to us it is not just a product, but a way of life. These lemon gardens have been here for a thousand years.'

Claire looked around her in surprise.

'That is why I will find a way of saving the family business.' She could hear the passion and determination in his voice. He hesitated a moment. 'Perhaps you would help me?'

'I have no business experience,' Claire replied, taken aback and wondering why he should ask her such a question.

'Yet I think you are very wise.'

One of the helpers arrived with two cups of espresso. In each saucer was a slice of lemon, freshly picked.

'Come, sit over here.' He led her to a table and chairs in the shade of the campanile. The bell began to ring across the stillness of the valley. In the past it must have summoned people to their noonday sleeps in the shade of the lemon trees. 'The tower is falling down but the bell still rings!' He showed her how to squeeze the lemon into her coffee and it was delicious!

'So tell me how the business works. Where do you make most money?'

'From the lemon production, from the tours and the limoncello. Soon the limoncello will be best.'

Claire realized that she'd seen the pale yellow liqueur on sale everywhere from patisseries to cafes to dedicated shops.

'But surely the trouble with that is that so many other people make limoncello,' she suggested, not wanting to offend him, but trying to be realistic. 'Even the waiter in the restaurant we were in the other day gave us some of the limoncello he made himself! Isn't it just too easy to make?'

Luca looked anxious. 'Only the best is allowed the special marque on the bottle, but you are right and of course the Sicilians, they cheat with their cheap lemons! *Bastardi!*'

Claire tried not to smile. Those thousand years of rivalry were obviously still very much alive.

'Luca, your family history is so amazing! We have a lot of places to visit in England. It is a national pastime. We visit things called stately homes and there is a saying in the stately home business that you need three things to succeed: you must give people something to see, to eat, to buy. That is what you should be doing with your lemon gardens, build up your family history into a museum and add a proper cafe. If they have fun, people will buy the limoncello as a memory of a nice day out.'

Luca reached out and touched her face. Claire tried not to flush the unbecoming tomato red she often did when suddenly moved.

'I knew you were wise. There is only one problem. I have no money since I gave up my job. I am already supporting the business, my father and brother, and also I give to my wife for the children, although now they are grown up. There is no money for investment.'

'Would a bank not lend it to you?'

'To a lemon grower? No.'

'But surely there must be grants?'

'Yes, there are grants. But the grants end up in the swimming pools of the politicians.'

'But you're not bitter?'

'No, I am not bitter. My life is a thousand times better than when I was a lawyer. Lawyers are not happy people. They do not look out at lemon blossom and lovely Englishwomen – well, perhaps they look at lovely Englishwomen but not the kind I am looking at, with a smile that lights up the sky like dawn on a spring morning.'

Claire laughed happily at the extravagant compliment. No one had compared her to a spring dawn in Twickenham. And the amazing thing was, she could tell he meant it. She thought about the fantasy she'd always had of running a restaurant with rooms in Italy and how she'd known it would never happen. But this – Luca's lemon-growing business – this was real and solid. How much more satisfying would she find it to give her energy and commitment to something like this than cooking endless coronation chicken for fussy clients in London?

Slinging her rival in the swimming pool – though eminently satisfying – meant that Sylvie hadn't had the chance to really look around the Grand Hotel degli Dei – the Grand Hotel of the Gods – only slightly pompous, as hotel names went. She would have to either go in disguise or satisfy herself with looking online. Fortunately, the hotel's website was as pretentious as the place itself. It guided the potential guests around the gardens, the pool and the main rooms of the hotel, as well as one or two of the major suites – in 360-degree detail, all to the sound of Vivaldi's *Four Seasons*. Mr Hugo Robertson's taste in hotel décor was about as similar to her own as opera was to easy listening.

But what really took her breath away was the hotel's charges. A thousand euros a night for a beige box with a white orchid thrown in to save on the flower bill. If Sylvie decorated a hotel, she would insist on fresh cut flowers – no matter how small the posy – in every room, along with free mineral water and sheets so comfortable you never wanted to get out of bed. And you could forget chocolates on the pillow for a start.

When she came down to dinner, Angela was slightly embarrassed to find Beatrice thrusting a large bouquet of white roses into her arms with a note from Hugo Robertson inviting her to lunch in Positano and a walk along the famous clifftop path – the Sentieri degli Dei, the Path of the Gods, after which the hotel had been named. 'Sensible footwear advised.'

Piqued at the casual assumption of her acceptance, and unwilling to endure the teasing the invitation would evoke, Angela slipped up the back stairs and put them safely in her bedroom. She thought about whether she wanted to go. She would actually rather like to see the celebrated Positano, the St Tropez of the Italian coastline, and it would be useful to know more about the man's intentions, not towards her, but towards acquiring the villa. There was also something intriguing about Hugo himself, and no one who found you a corn plaster, then sent you a glass of free champagne, could be all bad. Not to mention the roses.

She opened the windows to her terrace and felt the fresh and cooling breezes that seemed so characteristic of the Villa Le Sirenuse. If Stephen was serious about the idea of selling and wanted to know what they thought, why hadn't he told them a few more facts?

Monica opted to make the most of the sudden activity in the house to walk down the hillside path to Lerini and talk to the lady in the antiques shop. It was a glorious morning and she decided to forgo either the bus or the offers from Giovanni, currently being shouted at by Luigi, who obviously considered all this driving of ladies to be a scam to get him out of digging and weeding.

Instead she would walk down the thousand steps. She stood, looking down into the deep valley, its terraces already fragrant with orange, peach and almond blossom – and, of course, the universal lemons. Myrtle, broom and holm oak vied with the bright acid-green of euphorbia. Bees buzzed in the blossom, and birdsong echoed from one side of the valley to the other.

'It is the season of love for the birds,' Giovanni had offered suggestively when she and Angela had sat outside yesterday.

Angela had shaken her head and asked, in a loud voice,

'Where does he get the script? Do you think they're handed it at birth?'

'In a sense he's right,' Monica had replied. 'The birds don't sing for our delectation, after all, but to attract a mate.'

As she stood on a small viewing point, about fifteen minutes into her descent, breathing in the verbena and herbs and trying to resist picking the wild anemones and violets, an amazing thought struck her.

She was not the same Monica who had struggled up the mountain, damp and depressed and convinced that coming to Italy was a stupid mistake. She was someone entirely different. Someone with miraculous hair, who wore shifts and was going to pose for a famous painter.

And most wonderful of all, she had friends to share it with.

An hour later, she emerged by the side of the yellow stucco cathedral, sat in the small piazza, and ordered a coffee. Lerini, she decided, was a lovely town, unpretentious and bustling, touristy in summer but still a real place when the tourists packed their bags and departed for their cold climates and sophisticated lifestyles.

She ordered a '*caffè*' and sat back to watch the babies and the grannies, and the fat pigeons begging between the tables.

One man caught her attention. He was sitting alone facing away from her, and while everyone around him fiddled with their various gadgets, he looked around peacefully and tore off pieces of his croissant for the small bird that bravely darted from under his seat, grabbed a crumb and retreated. As soon as a bully-boy pigeon arrived on the scene, he shooed it away and waited for the little one to work up its courage and make for the croissant. Something about his protectiveness touched Monica and she found herself smiling.

The man turned towards her to look at the clock on the front of the town hall opposite the cathedral. He had a crumpled air – crumpled linen trousers, crumpled shirt, even a slightly crumpled face.

She realized with a shock that it was Sylvie's husband, Tony. And he seemed to be not only alone, but also in no expectation of meeting anyone.

Storing away this interesting information, Monica paid her bill and headed for the antiques shop in the catacombs under the cathedral.

The lady in the hairdresser's came out and greeted her like an old friend, then pulled her into the shop to have a free comb-through so that the masterpiece could be viewed to its fullest advantage. '*Bella, bella!*' she clucked as Monica got up to leave.

How did Italians have this knack of making you feel good about yourself? she wondered. Was it a national characteristic, were there no self-hating depressives who had fallen through the happiness net?

The owner of the antiques shop was equally fulsome, congratulating Monica on her fluency in Italian and asking after each object that Sylvie had purchased, right down to the individual bolts of moth-eaten fabric, as if they were old friends, sorely missed but happy they had found a good home.

This satisfactorily negotiated, Monica was able to bring the conversation round to the Villa Le Sirenuse.

'I wondered, signora, why it was you described it as "the wedding house"?'

The owner looked at her as if the answer were self-evident. 'Because of the wonderful weddings there. My niece, she have her wedding feast at the villa last *primavera*.'

She went into raptures of remembrance. 'She look so beautiful under the *glicine* – how do you say in English?'

'Wisteria.'

'There are candles everywhere and tables to sit at in the gardens.'

'But wasn't it very expensive, *molto caro*?' Monica slipped in slyly.

'No, no, is not expensive. If the owner come home, must be cancelled, so is very cheap.'

So Stephen hadn't given his permission. The weddings were happening behind his back.

Monica had a sudden inspiration. 'Do you have any photographs?'

The old lady rooted about amongst phone books and files of receipts and finally cried 'Here it is!'

It was a photograph of a smiling young couple standing under a flower-covered pergola. And it was definitely the Villa Le Sirenuse. Now, whatever had been going on, Monica had firm evidence for it.

# Ten

-------

Angela dressed carefully for the trip to Positano. It wasn't an easy brief. Combining visiting a chichi resort with a fairly strenuous walk in sensible shoes was at least going to involve some kind of change – if only of footwear. She went out onto the terrace to look at the weather. It was funny how she no longer simply enjoyed the pure luxury of having her own terrace but felt a twinge of guilt. '*Angela,*' she had said to herself when it first happened, '*stop this. What's happening to you?*' She grinned. Maybe it was something to do with taking off the metaphorical suit.

The day was cloudless and blue. Still, they'd be going on the ferry or hydrofoil, so it might be cooler.

Her final solution was a pair of grey Fabric linen shorts teamed with one of their dusty-pink sleeveless tops. She wished her legs were browner or she'd had a spray tan, but the only alternative was trousers and they didn't seem right for walking.

She was taken aback at her reaction to seeing the Fabric label as she pulled the top over her head.

She had pushed the whole business so successfully out of her mind since she'd been here – if the offer had been due to kindness on Stephen's part, it had certainly worked – now she couldn't help wondering how it was all going. She knew Drew would contact her if it was really necessary, and, equally, that he would protect her from intrusion if it wasn't.

The thought occurred to her that two different men were trying to shield Angela the ball breaker, but instead of finding it funny, or being angry about it, she felt oddly touched. Maybe after all this time her feminine side was emerging. How surprising would that be? Would the next stop be a fluffy dog in her handbag?

She stuffed a pair of trainers and socks into the basket she'd picked up in Lerini market and went down to face the others. As far as she knew, they were unaware of today's invitation from Hugo and since it had nothing whatsoever to do with hotel research, she would have to make up some excuse for a day's absence. Not an easy task. The Lanzarella Women's Cooperative always seemed to know what the other parts were doing. Somehow Claire had managed to escape with Luca without too much comment, but possibly his connection with Beatrice gave her some cover.

Angela decided she might as well come clean and say where she was going. After all, she could pick up some useful information about how serious Hugo was about acquiring the villa at the same time.

The other three were all installed on the sun-drenched terrace consuming bowls of tempting fruit salad prepared by Immaculata. 'You have to try this, Angela,' Sylvie insisted. 'It's the food of the gods.'

'That's funny,' Angela replied lightly, 'I'm going for a stroll on the Path of the Gods, maybe I'd better propitiate them with some of the divine fruit salad. A little libation.'

'Libation is drink, isn't it, Monica?' Claire asked.

Monica nodded. 'I don't think there's a word for food offerings.'

Angela sat down, grateful this diversion into mythology might have averted any awkward questions.

She was wrong.

'So what time's old smoothy-chops Hugo coming to pick you up, then?' Sylvie smiled blandly.

Angela decided to ignore this. 'Actually, I'm going down to the ferry in Lerini. By bus,' she added firmly.

'Oh, goody.' Sylvie smiled. 'I'll come with you. I want to have a look round the market. Beatrice says they have a kind of Italian boot fair on Tuesdays. Just up my street. I thought I might crack on with one of the other rooms. Give me something to do.'

'Don't you ever sit still?' Monica asked admiringly. She'd never encountered a force like Sylvie before.

'Not if I can help it. The idea of sunbathing on holiday would be like Guantanamo Bay to me.'

'Sylvie,' Monica looked horrified, 'that's an awful thing to say.'

'Don't come to me for political correctness.' Sylvie shook out her orange and purple dress. 'I came out of the womb tactless. Anyone else fancy the market?'

Angela held her breath. She could just envisage the entire cooperative watching her departure.

'I do,' Monica offered.

'Goody. You can bargain for me in Italian, so they don't think I'm some stupid tourist in a silly frock.'

'Actually,' Monica said firmly, 'I want to see if there are any old books.'

'Have you run out? I can lend you a Jackie Collins. It's quite sexy in parts.'

Monica hid her face under her shiny new hair, thinking of Brian and how they hadn't needed any racy novels to get them going. Brian's ashes! She suddenly remembered how she had brought them. How ridiculous of her. She'd better try and think of a suitable scattering place. That made her wonder exactly how long they would all be staying and she instantly knew she didn't want to raise the question.

It might break the spell, and there was something magical here. She didn't know if it was the sunshine, the beauty of the place, the friendly acceptance of the Italians, or being part of this unlikely little group, but she was happy and she no longer felt like a failure. How had that happened?

'I was thinking of old books.'

'Oh, Monica, you're so wonderful!' Sylvie decreed affectionately. 'Only you would come to a resort in the Med and look for old books! I bet you're still itching to get us all to Pompeii!'

The idea of Sylvie in her four-inch sandals trailing around one of the most famous historical sites in the world was so funny Monica had to laugh.

'She thinks we're lightweights,' Sylvie announced mournfully. 'Come on, less of this weighing up of our intellectual calibre; if we don't get a move on, we'll miss the bus and have to risk Giovanni. And not the usual terrifyingly casual Giovanni either, this is the brooding jealous Giovanni because his nymph's gone off with a lemon grower!'

Claire shook her head in embarrassment.

To their huge amusement it was an open-topped bus that arrived, and they all made for the back as if it was some middle-aged school trip.

'Don't let Sylvie sing,' whispered Angela to Monica. 'I don't think I could bear the mortification.'

But there was greater mortification to come when they arrived in Lerini.

After they had alighted, Sylvie dragged Monica down to the quayside to wave her off, only to find that there was no sign of Hugo in the queue for either the ferry or hydrofoil. 'I expect he's a bit late, why don't you two go off shopping?' Angela encouraged.

'I may be wrong,' Sylvie declared innocently, 'but I think someone's waving to you from that speedboat.'

And indeed, at the bottom of the steps to the waterside, Hugo was standing up in a small powerboat shouting to attract her attention, plus that of the entire quayside, who watched Angela's progress down the slippery steps to the boat with great interest.

'And all because,' Monica commented just loud enough for Angela to hear, 'the lady loves Milk Tray.'

Monica and Sylvie both spent a happy hour at the market, which to Sylvie's delight turned out to be more antiques market than boot fair. She hunted away through the assorted tables, happy as a robin digging for worms, and twice as colourful. Monica watched her negotiating for the gold cherub she had decided was just what was needed in her new room. She certainly didn't need Monica's help; there was clearly a streak of market trader somewhere back in Sylvie's DNA. Monica felt quite sorry for the poor antiques dealer.

At the other end of the row there were several bookstalls, mainly selling dog-eared paperbacks, old maps, and the occasional copy of Elena Ferrante, whose Neapolitan quartet Monica had already read. She moved on to the next stall.

There was a rather funny cartoon about golf, which her mother might quite enjoy. In some ways, she didn't think Mariella really deserved a gift from her but she decided that was small-minded and bought it anyway. Then, to her delight, she suddenly noticed a hardback book with a bright orange cover on which a wonderful stylized beast, just like something from a medieval painting, illustrated one of Italy's most famous novels, *The Leopard* by Giuseppe di Lampedusa. There was something about its bold yet simple lines she knew instinctively that Constantine would enjoy. She would take it with her if she really did go to his studio.

She glanced round and saw Sylvie approaching loaded with moth-eaten velvet cushions, antique fabric and a small statue of a 1920s flapper which, on close inspection, turned out to be a lamp.

'Monica, I'm disappointed,' Sylvie began, taking the book out of Monica's hands. 'It isn't even in Italian.' She stopped as if frozen, a momentary look of pain flashing across her face before the customary sarcasm returned. 'So, the gym bunny can read,' she suddenly lashed out.

Monica looked up and saw that Tony was standing on the other side of the table, an old copy of an Agatha Christie in his hand. Under his suntan he looked rather tired and old.

'Are you sure that isn't too advanced for her?'

Tony stood still, accepting the bitter irony as if it were only his due. 'Kim's gone home. She decided I was a disappointment in every department but one.' He paused then added, 'I give good massages.'

'I'm sure we're delighted to hear that. Maybe you should do it for a living. So what are you doing here, then?'

Tony looked Sylvie in the eye. 'I was rather hoping I might bump into you.'

'Well, now you have, so you can get the next flight out of Naples.'

'Sylvie, please . . . I deserved to be humiliated and you very successfully turned me into a laughing stock. Can you accept that I did something hurtful and I would very much like to make amends?'

Monica found that she was hoping Sylvie would say yes. Maybe it was the little bird he'd been feeding in the piazza but she couldn't help feeling that there was something kind in Tony and kindness was a quality not to be wasted.

'Absolutely not. You made your bed, as my mother would say.'

'As you are the first to admit, your mother is a bitter old woman. You aren't the easiest person to live with, you know.'

Monica couldn't help feeling that this line of defence was a mistake. *Shut up, Tony! Tell her you miss her!* she wanted to shout.

'You have to dominate every room you enter,' he went on. 'You never acknowledge other people's opinions. You are entirely convinced you're right.'

Sylvie stood impassively, stony faced as a sphinx in a kaftan. Monica thought he might turn and go away.

'And I miss you like hell.' He stepped towards her but she held up the flapper girl as if it were some kind of offensive weapon.

He laughed and shook his head. 'Where did you find that thing?'

'Back there in the market.'

'Knowing you, it'll turn out to be a hidden masterpiece. I am just about to buy this paperback.' He waved the Agatha Christie. 'To give me something to do in the evenings. I am not taking the next flight to Naples, despite your kind suggestion.

Should you want to get in touch with me, I'm still staying at the hotel.'

'Ridiculous place.'

'I paid for the room in advance.'

'You always were a mean sod.'

'And you have no idea of the value of money.'

Monica sighed. The small window of reconciliation seemed to be closing.

Tony finally noticed Monica's book. 'I've tried to read that three times. Too deep for me, but the cover's great. Goodbye, Sylvie.' He paid for the book and walked off back towards the piazza.

'I didn't know he'd ever read that book,' Sylvie said.

'Maybe there's lots you don't know about him. Did you know he feeds little birds with croissants and shoos off the big ones?'

Sylvie looked at her as if she was mad, but Monica noticed that her eyes were following her husband's back until he turned down a small alley and disappeared out of sight.

'This is all a bit flash,' Angela commented, arranging herself on the boat's leather seating.

'Actually, the hotel keeps it for visitors who want day trips away from the hoi polloi. And don't correct me that it should be hoi polloi, not "the" hoi polloi. You look like an Oxbridge type to me,' he stated provocatively.

Angela looked him over. Was that just a lucky guess or had Hugo been doing his homework? Everyone googled each other in London, it was true, though she seemed so far away from that world of competition and mutual measuring that it struck her as odd and faintly unpleasant.

'Yes, I did go to Oxford, but only for a year.'

'Why was that?'

She shrugged. 'Let's enjoy the view. I'm told this is one of the most beautiful coastlines on the planet.'

'It is. Sorry, you start to take it for granted.'

They swept round the bay in a giant arc and overtook the hydrofoil. One or two of the passengers waved. Angela waved back, feeling rather stupid, then she willed herself to enjoy it. The noise of the engine and the slap of waves against the hull were so loud that it was difficult to talk unless you shouted, so thankfully she gave up on conversation with Hugo.

And it was true, the scenery was wonderful. The sea was a deep turquoise, shaded at the edges with paler blue like an ombre silk. How silly to see a likeness with fashion; Angela laughed at herself. Behind them, Lerini, with its pale pastel houses and yellow-painted duomo, clung to the shoreline, and above it, Lanzarella, like a jewel, was set into the rock face. She could just make out the statues that lined the lowest terrace of the Villa Le Sirenuse. In front of them, the island of Capri tempted both the history-lover and the serious shopper.

'Good thing it's off-season,' Hugo shouted as he quietened the engine. The sea became flat as they headed in towards their destination. 'We're here before the beautiful people, thank God. I once saw a girl in a leather bikini leading a Borzoi along the seafront in August. That's Positano for you.'

They moored the boat and walked up the steps into the town, passing a string of lively beachside bars and cafes. A stunning young woman in a tiny white minidress with knee-length boots and a straw cowboy hat walked past them.

'I see what you mean.'

'Do you want to look around and shop a little? I'm not sure Positano style is up your street, but it might be fun.'

217

'And what do you mean by that?' Angela enquired, wondering if he was implying it was only for the young.

'You'll see.'

They turned towards a tiny street, lined on both sides with boutiques selling white lawn dresses, like sawn-off Victorian nighties, identical to the one worn by the girl on the quay. 'My gran would say, "She's no better than she should be in that dress",' Angela laughed.

'Mine wouldn't. She was a stripper at the Moulin Rouge.'

Angela looked at him in amazement. 'You have had a colourful life.'

'I'll tell you about it when we're walking. Walking always leads to self-disclosure, I find.'

Angela looked at him curiously. She'd been prepared to distrust and dislike him, but she was finding it harder than she expected.

'How about that?' Hugo suggested, pointing to a shop that seemed entirely full of fake flowers. Fake flowers were loaded onto hats, bags, belts and the hems of dresses. 'That looks just your style.'

'If you want to look like Eliza Doolittle at Glastonbury Festival.'

The next little street was full of sandal shops where Angela spotted an elegant pair of silver sandals. She decided to buy them, despite knowing that she could get them cheaper in London. It was fun to find something in places you visited. You got the wear plus the added pleasure of the memory.

'Very you,' Hugo approved.

'Now what do you mean by that exactly?'

'Simple, sophisticated, elegant. Rather like that.' He pointed to a necklace in the next shop window. It was a pendant made of some kind of ceramic, glazed in a dark green with intriguing splashes of silver and a tiny silver disc at its centre. The annoying thing was, she might well have picked it out herself.

'Do you like it?'

Angela nodded and, before she could stop him, he had disappeared into the shop and emerged with a small package tied up with lavender ribbon.

'For heaven's sake, you didn't need to do that.'

He grinned. 'My grandmother, the celebrated stripper, could have taught you a thing or two about how to accept presents from gentlemen.'

'I'm sure she could. In fact, I can hear her saying, "Take the bloody present and stop making a fuss".'

'Actually, it'd be more like, "What's this stupid bit of pottery? Show me the diamonds". Now we have a major decision. Walk first and lunch after, or the other way round?'

'Oh I think walk first, don't you? As long as we can turn round when we're hungry and head for a restaurant.'

'You're a woman of decision, I can see. Thus it shall be. The easiest way to get to the start of the path is by bus.'

'You disappoint me. After the speedboat, I'd have expected a helicopter, no less.'

'The helicopters are all booked by the shady people who own private islands.'

'There can't be private islands here!'

'Indeed there are. Nureyev owned one.'

To Angela's amusement they had to buy their bus tickets from the tobacconists. It seemed so Italian somehow.

The journey was a ten-minute ride up the mountain. 'You've been very frank about what you think of me,' Angela stated, 'so I'll be the same. I just don't see you on a bus.'

'You mean because of my suave James Bond manner in arriving to collect you in a speedboat?'

She looked at his perfectly ironed chinos and immaculate crisp blue shirt. It hardly seemed the outfit for a strenuous walk. 'More that I can't picture you nipping into Snow & Rock or The North Face to pick walking gear.'

'I should hope not. But then, what I have in mind today is a light stroll. We will let the serious walkers overtake us.'

'Will we now? Maybe you have underestimated my competitive side.'

'I'm sure you've got a very competitive side. You strike me as an eminently competent woman.'

'Don't say that. That's how my father used to describe my mother's best friend. And he loathed her.'

The bus stopped at what was clearly its final destination and it emptied. Everyone else was far better equipped for walking than they were, though Angela at least produced a pair of trainers from her voluminous shoulder bag.

'Are you really going to walk in those?' She indicated his smart brown loafers.

'Absolutely. These are Timberlands. I could walk five hundred miles in these, as the Proclaimers put it.'

'I certainly hope not. I was thinking more of two or three.'

Angela had to admit that the walk was stunning. A narrow path looked straight down a thousand feet to a duck-egg blue sea, the air so clear you could almost taste it, and all around was the scent of thyme and wild freesia.

'You can see why they call it the Path of the Gods,' Hugo pointed out.

'I'd better look out for some, then.' Angela pretended to glance behind her. 'Pan maybe, or one of those unfortunate nymphs who were always being turned into something nasty by Hera for attracting too much attention from Zeus.'

They walked on in peace, overtaken not by a nymph or

goddess, but by people with backpacks and those funny ski-pole things that shout 'I'm a serious walker, get out of my way.'

Some of them looked curiously at Hugo. It wasn't often that people appeared on this path in chinos and loafers, Angela guessed, and especially if they showed not the slightest sign of exertion.

To her surprise, she found that she didn't feel the need to talk all the time and neither did Hugo. They listened instead to the silence and birdsong.

'It really is amazing.' Angela breathed in the air and closed her eyes.

'Hungry yet?'

'I am, as a matter of fact.'

'Good, because I've just spotted an entire walking club approaching from the other direction. Fortunately, I know a little restaurant not far away.'

Angela grinned.

'What's so funny?'

'You strike me as the kind of man who always knows a little restaurant.'

'Is that a bad thing? You should be grateful I'm not abandoning you to the parka hordes. I've heard they give no quarter,' he added with a twinkle. 'Especially to the women.'

'Maybe I'll stay on, then,' Angela replied, then looked quickly away. *Angela Williams,* she told herself, *you're flirting with the enemy!*

It turned out to be a delightfully unpretentious clifftop restaurant half full of tourists, the odd walker and a couple of local families. One table, Angela noted, was made up of six rather sober-looking Americans, who were determinedly drinking water, while next to them a French couple were already into their second bottle of rosé.

221

The owner nodded to Hugo but was oddly unwelcoming as they were shown to a table.

How strange, when he was bringing them business. Maybe they thought he was a city slicker or someone from a yacht who'd be a difficult customer.

Angela wondered what Hugo would opt for. Some grand wine to impress her?

She was quite surprised when it turned out to be half a carafe of the local red.

'They make it themselves. It's excellent. Anything you fancy?'

Angela scanned the menu. It all looked a bit samey. The inevitable caprese salad of tomatoes and mozzarella, various pastas, a fish stew, veal chops.

'I apologize. It's often worth asking about what isn't on the menu.' He called over the waiter.

It turned out to be zucchini in tempura with parmesan, and a black risotto. Angela ordered them both and Hugo did the same.

'So,' Angela couldn't wait to ask, 'tell me the story of your grandmother the stripper.'

'She was a very classy stripper, of course. She had a celebrated aquatic act, swimming with dolphins.'

'Sounds rather charming.'

'Yes. The dolphins removed her bra and knickers.'

Angela was glad she wasn't drinking her wine or she would have choked.

'It made her quite famous.'

'I imagine it would.'

'And then she met my grandfather. He was some minor British aristocrat, very eccentric. An early conservationist.'

'Perhaps that was what drew him to your grandmother.'

'Why on earth?'

'So he could save the dolphins. It must have been quite cruel to them, you know.'

Hugo couldn't stop laughing. 'How very British. I don't think it was the dolphins he was thinking of. And of course they moved to Italy and lived in the Villa Le Sirenuse.'

Angela almost spilt her wine. 'I didn't know they lived in the villa.'

'Oh yes. Until my grandfather gave up conservation and got into gambling.'

'Oh dear. He should have stuck with the dolphins.'

'So they had to sell. The new owner just neglected it; that was why it was such a wreck when your friend Stephen and his wife found it.'

The zucchini arrived. They were the best Angela had ever tasted.

'So how did your family get into hotels?'

'After my grandfather went bankrupt, my father had to start from scratch. No silver spoon for him. He rented a convent in Lanzarella from the nuns and turned it into a small hotel.'

'There seem to be a lot of convents in Lanzarella.'

'In medieval times a lot of ladies became nuns. If they couldn't find a husband, it was far more pleasant than being a poor relation. Especially if their family endowed the place.'

The risotto suddenly appeared and Angela had to admit it was completely wonderful.

'So did you grow up in hotels?' she asked.

He nodded. 'Brazil, Buenos Aires, Fiesole, and then here.'

'How was that?'

'Strange. Your classmates always wanted to come and stay,

especially when I was a teenager, but you never knew if it was for you or the minibar.'

He raised his glass. 'Anyway, welcome to Italy. I hope you're enjoying it.'

'I am indeed. Far more than I expected.' They clinked glasses. 'And now I suppose I'd better ask you the million-euro question. Why did you invite me? To try to get me to talk Stephen into selling?'

'Wouldn't that be a little unsubtle? You're an experienced businesswoman – indeed, the tough blonde on a TV show, or so I'm told – wouldn't I be a little foolish to imagine I could win you over with my rather fading glamour and charming ways?'

She studied him over the rim of her glass.

There was a slight air of the passé playboy about him. Something to do with his hair being a shade too long and the way he habitually tucked it behind his ears, and maybe he was a tad too generous with the cologne. But all in all, the package certainly wasn't unattractive.

Angela shook her head. 'I'm not so sure about the fading, so why did you ask me?'

'As a matter of fact, I asked you because I liked you. Italian women are beautiful but complicated, you seemed straightforward and it was a breath of fresh air.'

Angela studied him sceptically. 'You obviously make up your mind about people quickly.'

His eyes held hers for a second. 'Yes. Yes, I do.'

The waiter arrived with the dessert menu and for once Angela didn't brush him off with her usual 'I don't eat puddings' announcement.

'The cheesecake is very good. It's made of passion fruit.'

They both laughed.

'We'll have one of those. And two spoons. And two espressos, *grazie*.'

'How did you know I like espresso?' she asked him. 'I might have wanted a macchiato or even a cappuccino.'

He shook his head, smiling. 'You would have the taste to know that cappuccino is for breakfast.' He looked at his watch. 'We'd better hurry with the coffee if we want to catch that bus.'

She reached for her wallet. Hugo took her wrist in his strong grip. 'No. You are in Italy. My territory. I pay.'

Angela knew arguing would be undignified and somehow she rather liked it. The old Angela would have been livid, but this Angela, the one who'd taken off her metaphorical suit, was perfectly happy. What was happening to her in this soft Italian spring?

Hugo was speaking again. 'By the way,' he added, a slightly new note in his voice, 'your friend Claire – she's been seen in the company of Luca Mangiani.'

'Luca the lemon producer? She has been looking around his lemon groves certainly,' Angela's tone was wary. 'He is the nephew of lovely Beatrice, our housekeeper.'

'Tell your friend Luca is not the simple lemon grower, full of passion for the land. There are things in his past. Ask her to find out why he gave up being a lawyer so suddenly. Was it really all about his precious lemons?'

'Look, Hugo, I really don't think this is the business of either of us,' Angela cut him off.

'I hope you're right, Angela.' He shrugged.

'Are you really going to Constantine's studio?' Claire asked Monica. 'Giovanni says no one from the town ever goes there.'

'Why, is he like Bluebeard and his many wives?'

'More like Bluebeard and his many boyfriends.'

'I expect I'll be all right, then.'

Monica took the path through the rhododendron bushes which led further round the hillside. A few minutes later she was greeted by furious barking and Spaghetti appeared, looking remarkably fierce for a small furry animal.

Monica emerged from the overgrown path onto a sunny terrace at the back of the house where a smiling young man of indeterminate age stepped forward to welcome her. 'Signorina Monica. *Il Capo* is inside.' He led Monica and the still-yapping dog into a whitewashed building. Constantine, in his increasingly shabby trench coat, rose to his feet. 'Thanks, Guido. Welcome to my eyrie. Would you like to look around?'

With a hint of pride disguised by his constant complaining about this and that, Constantine took her on a tour of his extraordinary home and studio. It was a large modern building which had been literally hewn out of the cliff face, so that it had more in common with a cave or bird's nest than any house she'd ever seen before.

'God knows how they did it,' Constantine agreed. 'Amazing, isn't it? The whole thing was done by men with pickaxes lowered on slings. Just as well they weren't into health and safety.'

Inside it was open-plan and dazzlingly white. A whole wall was devoted to a vast mosaic of Jonah being devoured by a whale who looked more like a demon, complete with wings and clawed feet.

'Copied from Ravello Cathedral. I love the fact that Jonah appears to be waving goodbye.' He indicated the naked and bald Jonah with his hand raised in what did indeed look remarkably like a farewell wave. 'I like to think he's saying, "See you in three days, loveys". Outside is even better.'

He led her proudly past a tiled terrace so hot you could even feel it through your shoes, to secluded shady paths which could almost have been in an English woodland, apart from the occasional carved stone lion or giant urn full of brightly coloured flowers.

'I find I like the shade more than the sun these days. It's about getting old. I am drawn towards the night in life's diurnal run. That and I keep reading Donne. I half suspect he loved death more than life.' They had come out onto a shady platform housing a small swimming pool full of water as green as a newly unfurling fern.

'Do you fancy a dip? I won't look.'

'I'm not sure about the colour,' was Monica's dubious reply.

'Hockney wouldn't like it, but then I think Hockney's overrated. Guido checks it every morning. It's perfectly safe. You've met Guido – he's my eyes and ears in the outside world. A delightful young man but not quite all there, as we used to say. A lot of Italian families have a Guido. He doesn't like his. They're cruel to him and say he's useless, so he works for me. He hears everything because no one bothers to be discreet in front of him. A great mistake, as it happens. Here he is with some refreshment.'

Guido appeared carrying a tray with two glasses of a bright orange drink. 'Aperol. I loathe the stuff but that means I don't drink the whole bottle. Quite a risk when you're a recluse. I wouldn't be surprised if that saint who stood on the pillar for forty years did it to keep off the sauce. Must be quite hard to order a G&T when you're thirty feet up.'

They drank the Aperol, which didn't taste as bad as it looked, and went inside again.

'And now. My studio. Are you ready?'

227

Monica nodded. She was actually feeling quite excited.

The space was extraordinary. How, in this house, Constantine had created a vast studio with the magical artist's north-facing light was amazing. Monica was fascinated to see that the walls were lined with easels on which were ranged a series of huge outlines: faces, figures, landscapes, a large blue Moroccan-style gateway.

'I copied that from Matisse,' Constantine admitted. 'Not a bad painter in his way.'

'But why are they all just outlines? Does it signify the emptiness of the soul?'

Constantine cracked with laughter. 'My sweet Monica! I have done it so I can just fill them in when the market needs another work by Constantine O. Or if I need the money. It's my response to ageing. Once I lose my inspiration or my abilities, I will just take an outline and fill it in with my celebrated electric colours. The critics and collectors will fall over themselves to praise my authenticity of vision and my simplicity of design. Everyone's happy.'

'I'm tempted to call you less a towering genius of the twenty-first century than an old fraud.'

'Dear girl, they're often the same thing. Besides, I'm damned if I'm going to end up like poor Matisse doing cut-outs like some kid in kindergarten! This way I can keep going till I'm gaga.'

'Right,' he clapped his hands, 'time to get your clothes off. And if you've any qualms, remember, you're not in Great Missenden now, and besides, I'm mostly interested in your outline. As it happens, you have a very interesting outline.'

'Do you know, Constantine,' Monica began to undo her shirt buttons, 'that's the nicest thing anyone's said to me in a very long time.'

The curious thing was, Monica, the university librarian, who had always made it her business not to be noticed, found she wasn't embarrassed. Maybe it was her familiarity with *The Joy of Sex*, but she felt surprisingly unashamed of her body. This was art, after all, not some hideous catwalk or indeed any kind of contest. She liked Constantine and, in a funny way, trusted him.

'If you could sit over there,' he pointed to a chair draped in an orange blanket, 'and put this on.'

It was a sort of kimono in grey with bold midnight-blue flowers decorating it. She sat in the chair.

'Now undo the wrap so that your body is revealed.' Without the slightest shame, Monica did as she was bid. 'Now lean back, and put one leg over the arm of the chair.' The pose revealed Monica's fluff of pubic hair. She smiled, thinking how embarrassed she'd been growing up, how she'd never shown her nakedness to anyone but Brian and now she really didn't care.

'That's it,' Constantine shouted, 'keep that smile! Sweet and sardonic, it's perfect for what I want.'

Monica tried to hold the smile, thinking back to how horrible her classmates had been to anyone shy or even slightly different, and bookish clever Monica had been both. Yet her new image, this one created by Sylvie, had released something in her, something she felt comfortable with. With a sudden shock, she realized that, in spite of her age, she really felt rather sexy.

'Monica, Monica,' Constantine shook his head when he stopped three hours later. 'Who would have thought it? You are a natural model! It's not just that you hold the pose; you give something of yourself, something essential and eternal!'

'I'm delighted to hear it,' the brisk librarian Monica was

back, 'because I can't sit here all day with my clothes off. How much longer is this going to take?'

'Come and see.' Constantine smiled.

Monica came round the other side of the easel and gasped. Constantine had produced an almost finished painting. 'How could you have done that?' Monica demanded.

'I told you, Monica darling, I prepare all the backgrounds beforehand so that all I need to do is tweak the outlines and capture your expression. The rest I can finish alone.'

She studied it again. The whiteness of her body had the polished sheen of a pearl next to the dark shadow of her pubic hair. But it was her expression that made the painting so arresting. *I am opening my body to you,* it seemed to say, *but I am not inviting you in. This is my body alone.*

The painting was not yet finished but the essence of it was there.

'What do you think?' he asked.

'It makes me think of Whitman. *I Sing the Body Electric.*'

'You mustn't intellectualize. Art is about feeling.'

She looked at it again. 'I think it's a very good painting.'

'So do I, Monica, so do I.'

Monica stared at it once more. It brought back her husband more powerfully than anything since he'd died. Neither of them had possessed physical beauty, but looking at this, Monica saw the body he had enjoyed and had treated with tenderness and sometimes with startling passion.

'I miss you still,' she murmured to herself.

Constantine seemed to understand.

'Thank you, Monica. This is a body that has loved and is happy to tell the world so.'

'Let's hope the world appreciates it. And now I really must go.'

'By the way,' he added with one of his most impish smiles, 'Guido has had his ear to the ground and found out about your scam. It's really rather endearing and positively un-Italian. The staff insist on returning half the profit to the kitty for the upkeep of the villa! They worry that Stephen might find the place too expensive since he's hardly ever there. Isn't that just too dear? They try and keep it a secret. It would shock the village if it got out. The black economy would grind to a halt, probably the whole country, if everyone behaved so honourably to their absent employers. So you won't have to denounce your white-haired grannies after all.'

Monica thanked him and hugged the information to herself as she headed back. It would be an enormous relief to everyone.

Claire held the yellow plastic basket and helped Luca fill it with the huge fragrant lemons the area was famous for. All around them was the scent of lemon blossom and the only sounds they could hear were the rushing of water down the hillside, the joshing of Luca's labourers and the very occasional hoot from a car. It was hard to believe that this little bit of paradise was only a half-mile from the centre of the town. The baskets were filled into a larger container and then weighed using a curious bronze scale that looked as if it had survived from the medieval era so that each was exactly fifty-seven kilos. They were then carried down the hillside on the labourers' backs.

'Are you volunteering, Chiara?' laughed Luca.

'No thanks. Would you like me to help with the lunch? I am a cook after all.'

'But you're on holiday,' he reasoned.

'I can't just sit here and watch you all working. I'll see what

I can rustle up.' It charmed her that right in the middle of the lemon gardens there was a large terrace with an outdoor kitchen bigger than the one she had at home. She found prosciutto, olives grown here among the groves, burrata, tomatoes, and some hard cheese she didn't recognize but which smelled delicious, plus some old, hard bread. Using the tip she had learned as a student she doused it in water and placed it in the outdoor oven turned up to high. Meanwhile, she mixed tomatoes with garlic for a bruschetta.

By the time the men came down with Luca and his father it was all laid out appetizingly on the big table with water and some of their home-grown wine. They all grinned gratefully and got stuck in to the bruschetta but when she produced the hot bread they looked at her as if it were a transformation akin to the loaves and fishes.

She enjoyed the praise and didn't admit it was the oldest trick in the cook's book.

While Luca organized the washing-up and his dad snoozed under a tree, Claire realized again that she was genuinely worried for Luca and the continuation of this way of life. She didn't see how, without some more genuine miracle, it could ever work. They were making far too little money, and none of the schemes to expand sounded possible without investment. She wondered if Angela would have a look; after all, she was a successful businesswoman who had actually worked at the sharp end of buying and selling.

'What are you thinking about?' asked a soft voice. Luca was standing behind her with a tiny cup of espresso. He put the cup down and suddenly stroked away the line of worry from her forehead. 'You are worrying about me,' he said, and before she could agree or deny, she felt his arms go round her and his lips, soft and dry, on hers. 'Do not worry about me,

*Chiara mia.* We will be all right somehow. I am not going to let all this history just die out.'

She smiled back, and then suddenly, assailed with guilt, was overtaken with the idea that she ought to admit she was married.

As if Luca sensed a protest he put his finger gently on her lips. 'One thing, Chiara.' A line of worry rippled across his forehead. 'Alfredo, who works for me, saw your friend Angela get into a boat with Hugo Robertson.'

Claire nodded.

'He is not a good man. Tell her to find out about the family he cheated who owned his palace of a hotel before he bought it. Many people around here know the story. Tell her it is better not to trust him.'

Claire bit her lip. Angela would not be an easy person to interfere with, she suspected. So much for asking her advice about the lemon groves.

She had a feeling this was not a good omen.


It was so hot that Monica and Sylvie decided the only solution was to lie by the pool. It was, like so much at the villa, a particularly beautiful pool, its water green-tinged and enticing.

'I hope it isn't green for the wrong reasons,' speculated Sylvie, looking into the deep end. 'Algae or something.'

'It's just the tiles,' Monica reassured her. 'It takes the colour from them, like the sea does when the sky's blue. Look how lovely they are. They're painted all around the edge with a wave pattern.'

'So they are.'

Monica looked around at the glorious garden, the roses out in wild profusion, pink against the clouds of morning glory. 'God, this place is beautiful. I just don't get why Stephen doesn't come here more.'

'Too busy, I suppose.'

'And now he wants to sell it or turn it into a hotel.'

'You sound rather sad.'

'I suppose I am a bit. Do you think it could work as a hotel?'

'Definitely.' Sylvie was more enthusiastic. 'If they opened up the wings and turned the hall into a reception. I just hope it would be a lovely boutique one, not some ice palace.'

'By the way, Constantine's come up with the answer to the disappearing zucchini. The staff sell it and put half back towards the running costs. I suppose secretly they've been worried that something like this might happen.'

'Yes, poor things. They've all worked here so long. It would be a real shock for them. Let's hope it never happens.'

Monica began to undress down to her stylish Toast swimsuit. Sylvie watched her, head on one side.

'Monica, you really are full of surprises. I thought it was my magic touch that created the new Monica, but even I couldn't have found a swimsuit like that.'

Monica laughed. 'Thank you.' She wondered what Sylvie would make of the fact that she'd just taken all her clothes off and posed naked. The unshockable Sylvie would probably be quite stunned. But then Monica had no intention of telling her.

'Hello, you two,' Claire's voice called to them. 'I'm in the kitchen experimenting with cocktail recipes. Trying to save Luca's lemon groves with an exciting new cocktail. Do you remember how no one had heard of Aperol, then the whole world seemed to be drinking the stuff? He needs something like that.'

'How are you getting on?'

'Would you like to try my latest?'

They both nodded. Who cared about it only being four o'clock?

Sylvie leaned towards Monica's sunbed. 'She's getting pretty involved with Luca and his lemons, isn't she?'

In a moment Claire was back with two long glasses which she handed to each of them.

They sipped their drinks. 'Nice. What's in it?'

'It's part limoncello, part Prosecco, and a dash of spritz, but it needs a mystery ingredient to make it different from all the other drinks that use limoncello.'

'The reason Aperol is so successful,' Sylvie sipped her drink, 'is because it's very low-alcohol. It's only eleven per cent proof. How much is Luca's limoncello?'

Claire slumped down onto a spare sunbed. 'Thirty-two per cent! Though Crema di Limoncello is lower.'

'You'll have to get him to make some low-proof stuff. Now who do we know who knows about cocktails? I'll have to ask Alessandro. His friends are all party people. And you'll need a name that will catch on with the YouTube generation.'

'Aperol isn't that catchy,' Claire protested.

'The Women's Cooperative will have to brainstorm it,' Sylvie suggested.

'Sylvie, you're brilliant! By the way,' Claire looked embarrassed, 'Luca says we ought not to trust Hugo Robertson.'

'The man who's just whisked Angela off in a speedboat?' They all looked at each other. 'And you're going to be the one to mention it, are you?'

Sylvie's phone beeped, an unfamiliar sound since none of them could get a signal.

Sylvie checked who it was. Her assistant Amelia. She'd told

the office not to contact her unless it was an emergency. Bugger. Might as well get it over with.

'Hi, Amelia, what's up?' Sylvie had to psych herself up. Lanzarella might be on the same continent as London but it felt as if they were on a different planet. 'Has Mr Riskov changed his mind?' Sylvie teased. 'I know, the Queen's invited us to come and remodel Buckingham Palace?'

'Nothing like that. Everything's going pretty smoothly. It's Tony.'

Sylvie almost choked on her drink. 'What about Tony?'

'He says he's coming back to work in a few days. And we all wondered, is that all right with you?'

'No! For God's sake, don't let him in!'

'That's what we thought. Don't worry, Sylvie, it'll be over our dead bodies!'

'You don't have to go that far,' Sylvie smiled, 'maybe just change the locks.'

'We'll get right on to it. Bye, Sylvie, and don't worry, everything's fine here.'

'New developments,' she told the others. 'Tony wants to come back into the business. I've told them to change the locks.'

Monica sipped her drink thoughtfully. How stupid of him. He should have laid low here and kept up his campaign. She liked Tony, and she was usually right about people. Her nimble brain began to turn over ways that might improve the situation.

# *Eleven*

Hugo dropped Angela back at the quay in Lerini and blew her a kiss as he steered the boat to its mooring.

The thought of going back to the villa and being pounced on by the others made her shudder. She'd never been one for sharing personal information and she certainly didn't want to share what she thought of Hugo Robertson.

So she sat in a cafe in the piazza and ordered a coffee and wondered what she *did* think of him.

If she was honest, she'd liked Hugo a lot from the moment he'd sorted out a corn plaster for Sylvie. Hardly a romantic gesture, yet its very practicality had appealed to her. It was true he was the smooth type, but under that there was a certain self-deprecation that had won her over. He could laugh at his own image. And they'd had more fun than she could remember having in a long time.

The trouble with putting the business at the centre of her life was that it hid a void that she'd never before wanted to face in herself. Drew had touched on it, but she'd refused to acknowledge the truth in what he'd said and just felt angry.

Now she'd lost the business what was she going to put in its place?

She tossed back her espresso, dismissing all thought of Hugo from her mind. For God's sake, was she building a schoolgirl fantasy on one day together?

She hailed a taxi from the rank and dozed for the fifteen-minute ride up the hill to Lanzarella. Half expecting a reception committee, she was relieved to find only Sylvie in the salon.

'How was the divine Mr Robertson?' Sylvie enquired.

'Remarkably down to earth.'

Sylvie considered her. In Angela's book that was high praise. Maybe this wasn't the time to mention Luca's accusation that he'd cheated the old owners of the Grand Hotel degli Dei.

'Where are the others?' Angela enquired. 'Claire is presumably off with Luca the lemon grower. She seems to spend every waking minute with him.' Angela paused. 'By the way, Hugo says Claire should be wary. Luca isn't quite the simple saviour of his family business he seems. She should ask him why he gave up being a lawyer so suddenly.'

Sylvie almost wanted to laugh. First Luca had warned Claire about Hugo. Now Hugo had sent a warning about Luca. 'And you're going to tell her?'

'I'm not sure.' Angela hesitated, surprised at herself. She didn't want to hurt Claire. 'I'll just go upstairs and freshen up.'

'Angela . . . maybe let me tell Claire?'

'If you think it would help.'

'I do. The thing is . . .' This time it was Sylvie's turn to hesitate. 'I know this sounds a pretty ironic situation, but Luca told Claire something about Hugo.'

'What?' Angela flushed angrily.

'That he acquired that hotel of his unfairly. Luca said everyone in the village knows it.'

'What complete rubbish!' Angela stormed.

'Quite probably. But that's what he said.'

'Tell the others I won't be coming down to dinner. I'll see them all tomorrow.'

Sylvie sighed. Now she had to tell Claire what Hugo had said about Luca. And to think she'd come here to get away from emotional trauma.

'I just don't believe this stuff about Luca,' Claire protested angrily. She was helping Monica pick a bunch of crimson glory roses from the bed at the side of the house to put on the dinner table.

They were gorgeous roses, bright red and velvety, with a heady scent Monica found irresistible. She had been given a special dispensation by Luigi to pick them.

'Why don't you ask Beatrice? She's his aunt and obviously she's going to protect him, but you might find something out at least.'

Claire nodded thoughtfully, picking a rose and managing to prick herself on a particularly vicious thorn at the same time. Blood poured from her thumb, staining her jeans and top.

'Go and ask her now. All that blood will distract her and you might get more out of her.'

Claire found Beatrice in the kitchen getting plates out of the dresser. 'Signora Chiara!' Beatrice reacted as if Claire had been seriously wounded. 'Your finger! What has happened to it?'

'I pricked it on a rose,' confessed Claire feeling rather silly, given that she'd produced enough blood for three nosebleeds.

'Come with me and we will bandage it up. *Che brutte*, those roses! Why do you English love them so much? They are dangerous!'

'But beautiful.'

This deadly combination seemed to strike Beatrice, who stood nodding her head, ignoring the blood dripping on the floor.

'Do you have a clean cloth?'

Beatrice produced a sparkling square of muslin usually kept for polishing.

Fortunately, after five minutes under the cold tap, Claire's life-or-death injury seemed to clear up.

'I just wanted to ask you, Beatrice,' Claire was careful to use the exact words of Hugo's accusation, 'why did Luca give up being a lawyer so suddenly?'

It was as if a small explosion took place in the kitchen next to her. Beatrice, white-haired and smiling, the epitome of a cartoon granny, became a wildcat of uncontainable fury.

'*Merda!*' she almost spat. It didn't take a UN translator to work that one out. 'Who is it that has been telling you these lies, Signora Chiara? What a world is it, I ask you, when an act of goodness cannot be taken for what it is? Just because Luca give up the rich life, the fast car . . .'

The expensive wife, Claire stopped herself from adding.

'. . . the big house. Everyone, they ask why this is? They cannot believe he do it because his father ask him to. That if he do not help the family business, it is over for them.'

Suddenly she grabbed the crucifix off the wall and dropped down to her knees. 'On the body of our Lord Jesus Christ, I swear this is the truth!'

Claire pulled her hastily to her feet. 'Don't worry, Beatrice. I promise I believe you!'

\*

'Why don't we have our brainstorming session to think up a name for this new drink tonight?' suggested Sylvie. 'It might take our minds off all the emotion swirling about. We could do it over dinner. Make it into a game and see how many drinks we can remember. On second thoughts, maybe I'll bring my iPad. I've got such a crap memory. I expect it's all that champagne.'

The others agreed but by the time they sat down there was still no sign of Angela.

'Sulking upstairs, I expect.' Sylvie flipped open her tablet just as Beatrice arrived with a mouth-watering starter of spaghetti with clams.

'I'll just read some out, shall I?' She began to spool down a list of drink names on her screen. 'Aperol – an aperitif with rhubarb, chinchona, genziana, whatever on earth that is, and a secret ingredient. Campari – a bitter aperitif made from a secret recipe of aromatic herbs and spirit. Cinzano – vermouth made from a secret blend of ingredients. Martini – hey, have you noticed anything they all have in common?'

'They all have secret ingredients,' Claire suggested.

'And they're all Italian!' pointed out Monica.

'Do you remember those funny ads for Cinzano with Leonard Rossiter as the awful fake smoothie who always threw his drink over Joan Collins?' Sylvie giggled.

'I loved those,' agreed Claire. 'You see,' she beamed, 'Italians really love their aperitifs!' She produced a bright orange bottle from her bag. 'OK, who's tried an Aperol?'

'We're too old!' Sylvie lamented. 'It's after our time.'

'I have,' Monica announced, impressing Sylvie and Claire. 'Twice. Once with Constantine and again in the piazza when I was waiting for the bus. I even asked the barman how you make them. Fifty millilitres of Aperol, a hundred millilitres of Prosecco, and top it up with soda water.'

Claire produced the other ingredients and sploshed the liquid into their glasses.

They all sipped the barley-sugar-coloured potion.

'It tastes like Tango,' pronounced Sylvie.

'No, no,' insisted Monica. 'It looks like Tango. It tastes like Tizer! With added alcohol, of course.'

'Monica's right!' insisted Sylvie. 'Come on, Claire, I'm sure Luca's new drink could be just as popular as this!'

'It will.' Claire nodded, with touching certainty. 'But what are we going to call it?'

'How about Lemon Heaven?' suggested Sylvie.

Sylvie shook her head. 'Too like a cocktail.'

'I know,' Monica said excitedly, 'what's most famous round here?'

'Apart from lemons?' supplied Claire. 'Old churches?'

'That's not very useful,' Sylvie replied.

'Hmmm . . . the sea? Blue something?' Claire persisted.

'Makes me think of curaçao . . .' Monica mused.

'Sunshine?' Claire offered.

'Coastline? How about Costara?' threw in Monica.

'Not bad,' Sylvie approved, 'but it doesn't have much of a zing.'

'Cellono!' announced a voice from above them. 'It picks up the "cello" of limoncello without making it too obvious.'

They stared up to find Angela leaning down from her terrace.

'Actually, that's not bad. Cellono,' Sylvie repeated slowly. Then, in a dreadful cod Italian accent, she said, '*Cellono, per favore!* That actually sounds quite convincing. Cellono it is. Thank you, Angela.'

Sylvie squinted upwards so that she could see Angela's face and was relieved that she was smiling.

'It struck me that men come and go but friendship lasts forever,' said upside-down Angela.

Monica and Claire looked at each other. 'Did she just say friendship?' Monica whispered.

Claire nodded.

'Right, Claire,' Sylvie grinned, 'now all you have to do is get Luca to lower the proof in his limoncello and find those mystery ingredients!'

Claire couldn't wait till the next morning to meet Luca and see what he thought of the name they'd thought of for the drink that hadn't even been invented yet.

The good news, Luca told her excitedly, was that they had produced a version of the liqueur with only half the alcohol. And they had collected a range of herbs and spices to try out with the drink to provide the all-important mystery ingredient.

Luca, his niece Fabiella and daughter Bianca were seated round the terrace table with small piles of herbs and spices, while his father rampaged up and down muttering that this would be a travesty of his limoncello and, as if things weren't bad enough, this would make them all into a laughing stock.

Rows of small glasses containing the new liqueur stood ready to be mixed with the various ingredients for tasting, including cardamom, juniper, thyme, coriander and lemongrass and a mystery ingredient whose identity Luca insisted on keeping from them.

Some were too overpowering, others disgusting and some plain weird, but after an hour they were agreed on a couple of flavours that had potential.

'Now we add some Prosecco and a dash of soda – and this!' Luca swirled the tiniest amount of a ground powder into the glass and handed it round.

'God, Luca, that's absolutely delicious!' Claire was genuinely amazed. The others tried and nodded enthusiastically. 'What is that you've added?'

'Our secret ingredient, handed down through my family for generations!' He winked at his father who crossed himself and picked up the glass.

They all waited for him to throw it to the ground in disgust.

He sipped suspiciously, then, to their delight, knocked back the rest in one gulp.

'Cellono,' the old man repeated suspiciously, savouring the word almost as much as he had savoured the spicy yellow drink. 'Cellono. Not for me but maybe some fools would pay good money for it.'

'You wait,' whispered Luca to Claire. 'In a month, he'll be claiming his grandmother put it in his baby bottle to make him sleep!'

'What is it,' she whispered back. 'The mystery ingredient?'

He drew her away from the rest of the group. 'You will love this, *Chiara mia*. But it must be a true secret between you and I. It is called grains of paradise.'

'It's not a drug, is it?' It sounded so like something from Claire's student days.

He shook his head, laughing. 'A species of ginger from Africa. It tastes a little of pepper and you will laugh now, Chiara. It was used in cordials in your country for hundreds of years until it was banned by your King George!'

'Luca, that's wonderful.' Claire found she was glowing with happiness that she had been a part of his adventure. At home, in the day-to-dayness of marriage and work, she rarely felt she was being useful. But here things were somehow different.

He looked serious for a moment, his warm brown eyes

holding hers. 'Thank you, Chiara, for caring about our little lemon gardens, for wanting to help us. For bringing us Cellono!'

She thought for a moment he might kiss her again, but his daughter Bianca, suspecting an imminent display of affection, rushed in. '*Papà, andiamo!* You said you would give me a ride back to school!'

Luca smiled at her. 'Goodbye, Chiara. *Mille grazie*, though a thousand thanks is not enough.'

Claire smiled, fizzing up with joy, without the slightest premonition of the fact that this might be their last carefree meeting.

Monica realized with a little thrill of belonging that she actually knew the bus timetable from Lanzarella to Lerini off by heart. She enjoyed knowing, as all the locals did, that you had to buy your tickets not from the machine that never worked but from the *tabacchi* on the corner of the street.

As usual, the bus was full to bursting with giggly schoolchildren, surly teenagers, disapproving old ladies and the regulation pair of young lovers who looked as if they would devour each other like amorous boa constrictors.

Monica looked out of the window, thinking that Lanzarella was beginning to seem more real to her than Great Missenden. To think, without Gwen she would have been looking after her parents' revolting boxers. She smiled a small smile of satisfaction. But had she really changed in ways that would survive when she had to leave the magic of this place?

They arrived at the bus stop near the quay. It was market day again and Monica spent a happy half-hour looking through the stalls. A black dress with gold buttons and a slightly military air caught her eye. It was sexy and chic, the kind of dress she would never in a million years have considered before. Monica smiled to herself as she bought it.

The bell on the duomo clanged as she left the market and Monica decided to slip inside. Her parents had had a very English attitude to worship, viewing it as a civic duty, but they'd been embarrassed by any real manifestations of belief. When Monica, as a teenager, had gone through a brief period of devotion to God rather than going out with boys, her mother had pronounced it was because she was fat and un-attractive and preferred the safer embraces of the Almighty.

The interior of the church was dark and quiet, the few sounds of people moving around, kneeling at the various small altars, were muffled, with only the faint murmur of the con-fessional in the background.

Monica was moved by the sudden urge to light a candle. She didn't quite know what for, maybe that this lovely un-expected interlude would continue. To her irritation she discovered that the candles in Italy were electric. It might be better for health and safety, but what about the soul?

She paused at the statue of the next saint, a friar in a brown robe with an immensely sad and kind face. Someone had placed a bunch of real forget-me-nots into his hand and it made him seem almost a living man. She realized it was St Anthony, patron saint of lost things.

As she knelt down, not even sure what she would pray for, her eye caught the glint of something shiny a few feet away. Monica leaned over and picked it up. It was a small silver heart. Was it a locket? And yet the metal seemed too light and thin for a necklace.

She glanced to her left. On the wall, masked by a praying figure, was a large black board covered in tiny silver symbols: hands, feet, legs, faces, and several hearts just like the one in her hand. As soon as the old man who was praying moved off, Monica hung the heart onto the board.

It suddenly struck her as significant. She would pray for Sylvie and Tony's reconciliation.

She waited a moment then made her way out of the cathedral and towards the sun-filled piazza. This was where she had seen him before, feeding the birds. It was a remote chance, but still.

She ordered a coffee and cornetto. The local name for a croissant always made her smile.

'Excuse me,' a voice asked her from the next table. It was indeed Tony. 'Monica, isn't it? Aren't you staying up at the villa with my wife Sylvie?'

Monica agreed that she was indeed Monica.

'I'm Tony.' Monica noticed that he was looking even more crumpled, and it was not just his clothes. There was something deflated and sad about him, like a balloon left over from a party. The carefree charm had dissipated into thin air.

'Is Sylvie still furious with me?'

'What do you think?'

'I think she still thinks I'm the biggest shit on earth.'

'Asking her assistant if you could get back to the office didn't help.'

'Sylvie won't speak to me, what am I supposed to do? It's my home too. I'm a partner and half my stuff is there.'

'I thought for what it's worth, that it would have been better not to criticize her the other day, just to tell her you missed her.'

'Why should she believe me?'

'She knows the gym bunny's off the scene.'

Tony smiled and ran his hand through his hair. It was the kind of bouncy, unruly hair she liked in men. The kind of hair that couldn't do what it was told. For a second he looked like the attractive man she'd glimpsed before. 'Is that really what you call Kimberley? It suits her, I suppose. Oh shit, Monica, I've screwed this up. I haven't behaved well to Kim and I've betrayed Sylvie. I don't really know why I did it. I was flattered, I suppose.'

Monica thought for a moment. 'Let's have a drink,' she suggested.

Tony looked at her in surprise.

'And don't say, "What, at this time?" or "I had you down for the librarian type", or I might have to pour the water in that vase over you.'

Tony laughed and called over the waiter.

'*Un bicchiere di Franciacorta, per favore*,' Monica requested.

'No idea what that it is, but make it *due*, please.'

'You'll like it.'

'You speak very good Italian.' The charming smile was beginning to peep over the black horizon again.

'Yes. Anyway, enough about me.'

Their drinks arrived. Monica raised her glass. 'To mending broken hearts!'

'I don't think Sylvie thinks I've even got one.'

'Now, now, cut the self-pity. You'll have to persuade her. Sending flowers is too clichéd. She'd just chuck them in the bin. I want you to really think about your relationship. Something that made you both happy, it doesn't matter if it's small.'

To her surprise, Tony blushed.

'Hang on,' Monica assured him, 'look, if it's kinky, maybe keep it between yourselves.'

'It's not kinky – well, not very.'

The people at the next table, two elderly Germans, were suddenly leaning forward.

Monica turned towards them and raised her glass. 'We charge for the fruity bits,' she informed them.

They quickly buried themselves in their beers.

'She liked me to put nail varnish on her toes. She was the countess and I was the obliging butler.' He smiled nostalgically. 'And afterwards—'

'Yes, fine, I can well imagine afterwards. So that's what you should do.'

'Dress up as a butler?'

'No, send her nail varnish. What colour?'

'Purple, as a matter of fact.'

'Yes, it would be purple.' She knocked back her drink. 'Come on, drink up! 'We've got to find the pharmacy before they close for the afternoon.'

Tony got up obediently.

'Are you feeling ill?'

Monica shook her head at the obtuseness of the male gender. 'No. We need the pharmacy because you're going to find some purple nail varnish.'

The pharmacy was just next to the bus stop and, frankly, was uninspiring; its shelves were rather dusty and the assistant looked almost surly at the sight of two more tourists who were probably going to request ridiculously high-factor sun cream, diarrhoea treatment or hangover cures.

But when Monica explained that they were looking for expensive nail varnish that they wanted gift wrapped, she perked up quite amazingly. She was a dab hand at bows and furbelows, and rarely got a chance to exercise her skills.

Tony chose the nail varnish and the assistant wrapped it with infinite patience, ignoring the growing queue of old ladies who swore under their breath at the extravagance of this foreign invasion.

Monica turned and announced in flawless Italian that it was a gift to the woman he had betrayed by having an affair with someone many years younger and she was sure they could appreciate the care that must be taken in this delicate attempt at an apology.

A black-clothed widow, leaning on her stick, demanded if he was genuinely repentant and when Monica answered in the affirmative, nodded her head and announced that men were all the same and she hoped the woman would forgive him rather than face a lonely old age as she herself had suffered.

This led to a heated discussion as to whether the woman should or shouldn't, with some yeses, a few noes and one suggestion she leave it to the Good Lord.

Tony just smiled uncomprehendingly and handed over his credit card.

'And now,' Monica smiled, 'you need to summon one of those taxis.' She pointed at the rank over the road.

'Couldn't you take it?' Tony asked, mystified.

'Of course not! This is private business between you and Sylvie. She would hate to think that I even knew about it. By your age you really ought to understand women.'

Tony smiled, a glimmer of his old self returning. 'So you know everything about the male sex, I assume, Ms Monica . . . ?'

'Mathieson,' supplied Monica, realizing he'd probably collapse if he knew how little she knew of men, apart from Brian.

'What a lovely name. With a name like that you ought to be famous. What do you do, in fact?'

Fortunately, the taxi arrived with breakneck speed so she didn't have to admit that, as a matter of fact, she was a retired librarian from Great Missenden.

\*

'How about dinner tonight?'

Hugo Robertson, Angela had discovered, was flatteringly persistent. He had left various messages and texts and his male ego seemed not a whit dented by the fact that she hadn't returned any of them.

This might, of course, have been the difference between men and women. Women, when they didn't get an instant reply – especially after they'd double checked their phone that their message had actually been delivered – immediately imagined rejection, that they were ugly, unattractive and might as well 'get them to a nunnery'. Men, on the other hand, simply assumed that the woman hadn't got the message.

'I know a little place . . .' he persisted before she could refuse.

'Hugo, we established that you always know a little place.' Then she thought, why not? None of those accusations levelled by Luca had been proven in any way. They could just be an unsuccessful businessman's jealousy of a successful one. 'All right,' she agreed eventually. 'When and where?'

'I like a woman of decision. The Balcony. Eight p.m.'

Angela couldn't help laughing as she surveyed her wardrobe. It was all so bloody tasteful. For a mad moment she felt envious of Sylvie. Not that Sylvie didn't have a style every bit as rigidly defined as her own; it was just that Sylvie's was joyous and colourful, while her own was neutral and subtle and, dare she say it, a little dull?

What the hell, she'd go and borrow something.

Sylvie was busy with her trusty staple gun, transforming another room from convent to bordello, when Angela knocked on the door. There were bolts of fabric all over the floor, cushion covers in dazzling jewel shades Sylvie had run up on her sewing machine, the very one she had insisted on carting across the desert on a camel. The intrepid Sylvie had ended up redecorating the tent of the headman of some tiny Saharan village in fabric by Designers Guild.

'Sylvie,' Angela laughed, 'I need your help.'

Good God, she was actually a bit shy; Sylvie couldn't believe it.

'I'm going out tonight and I'm fed up with being me. Have you got anything I could borrow?'

Sylvie thought about it. 'Do you want to go the whole hog or just the half-Sylvie?' She led Angela over to her massive wardrobe. Everything was ranged extraordinarily efficiently in colour tones ranging from dark aubergine to orange to nude pink. 'A silk top to wear with your own trousers might be a good compromise, so that you aren't too out of your comfort zone.'

But Angela was already reaching for the black-and-white zebra-pattern silk dress.

'I love that,' Angela announced.

'What size shoes are you?'

'Seven.'

'Here you are, then.' She produced a pair of black patent toe-post sandals. 'They go perfectly. Only the Italians know how to make sandals that are elegant and sexy at the same time. One problem though. Your date may not recognize you. I don't suppose we need ask who it is.'

Angela didn't answer. 'Thanks, Sylvie. I'll try not to spill red wine on it.'

Angela had gone by the time Sylvie appeared on the terrace for a pre-dinner drink.

'Have you seen the sunset?' Claire was sitting on the wall of the terrace in jeans, with her arms clasping her legs, and by a trick of the light she looked amazingly young. Or maybe it was something else that was transforming her. Sylvie felt a sudden moment of fear for Claire. Her situation would not be easy, whether Luca had a murky past or not. At some point Claire was going to have to remember she had a husband. But surely even she could see this thing with Luca was infatuation. Maybe it was because she was in love with Italy rather than him, temporarily enchanted by a way of life so different to her own.

'Glorious, isn't it?' Sylvie smiled. 'If it wasn't for that rain when we arrived, I'd almost believe the weather here was enchanted as well as the house.' They were silent for a moment and Sylvie sensed the subject none of them seemed to want to address hovering between them: how long could this Italian idyll really go on?

Beatrice arrived bearing the usual glasses of fizz and a small package which she handed to Sylvie.

'This arrive for you, Signora Sylvie. By taxi,' she added, clearly impressed with the extravagance of ordering a taxi for so small a package.

'Good heavens.' Sylvie picked it up just as Monica emerged from her room to join them wearing her new black dress.

'Wow, Monica,' Claire commented, impressed. 'Where did that come from?'

'The market in Lerini again; would you believe it, all of fifteen euros.'

Behind them, Sylvie let out a sharp cry. She was staring at the bottle of purple nail varnish which she had just removed from its wrappings.

To Claire's utter amazement, and rather less to Monica's,

she burst into tears and sat down at the table, clutching the nail varnish as if it were a diamond as big as the Ritz.

'Sylvie,' Claire jumped off the wall, 'what on earth's the matter?'

'It's from Tony,' Sylvie sobbed. 'I told you this silly thing we used to do. He'd paint my toenails and I'd pretend to be the countess and he was the manservant.'

Claire tried not to giggle at this vision. It obviously meant a lot to Sylvie.

'He hasn't gone back to London, then?' Monica asked innocently.

'He must still be here,' Sylvie reasoned with unassailable logic.

'He must be very sorry,' Monica suggested.

'For laying out ten euros on nail varnish?' Claire asked, surprised at Monica.

'It isn't the money, though, is it? He was obviously trying to say something significant.'

'That he wants to play the butler and paint her toes?' Claire asked sarcastically.

But this only set Sylvie off again.

Beatrice was back, this time in a flutter. 'There is a gentleman here to see you. Shall I lay another place?'

Sylvie felt her heart beat as if it might explode. Tony had obviously decided to appear in person to press his advantage. OK, he'd been stupid, but the truth was she still loved him. She stood up, ready to fold him to her ample bosom.

'Thank you, Beatrice.' She smoothed her hair down and pulled her tummy in, in the age-old gesture of women who found themselves suddenly needing confidence. 'Ask the gentleman to come in.'

Monica poured herself a glass of wine. She was surprised

that Tony had come to the villa so quickly, but maybe he'd decided to strike while the iron was hot. Good for him.

Beatrice reappeared, carrying a tray of nuts and olives to go with their drinks. 'Your guest, signorine,' she said, beaming. A male caller was definitely an event in this strange all-woman environment.

'Hello, Claire.' A tall, tired-looking man waved a railway timetable. 'Not bad going. I left this morning at eight and I'm here in twelve hours, one plane, a train and two buses.'

Claire went suddenly as white as the snowy tablecloth in front of her.

'Martin!' she blurted. 'What the hell are you doing here?'

'Heavens, Claire,' was his mock-jovial response, 'anyone'd think you weren't pleased to see me.'

Claire turned to the other two. 'This is Martin. My husband.'

Beatrice's tray of nibbles crashed to the ground, scattering olives all over the priceless carpet.

They all bent down to help gather them up. 'That woman is always dropping things,' Sylvie complained in a low voice to Monica.

'Bit of a shock for the old dear,' Monica replied softly as they pursued a rogue olive under the drinks table. 'What with her being auntie to the lovely Luca.'

Claire was still staring at her husband as if he were Marley's ghost.

'Hello, Martin,' Monica shook his hand with a friendly smile, 'welcome to the Villa Le Sirenuse.'

'Yes.' Claire was finally coming to. 'How's everything at home? Not any disasters or anything?'

'We seem to have been rubbing along quite well – after we worked out where the bin liners are kept.'

Monica smiled at this rather feeble attempt at a joke, but Claire was still suffering from acute shock.

'Would you like a drink?' Monica offered. 'The sparkling wine's very good.'

'Can't bear fizzy wine.' Martin screwed up his face in distaste. 'Do you have a beer?'

'I'll go and ask Beatrice,' Claire offered and dashed out towards the kitchen.

Beatrice was quietly weeping, being comforted by Immaculata, with Giovanni hovering in the background, his eyes pools of burning reproach.

'You are a bad woman, Chiara,' he accused in a loud and angry voice.

Claire looked at the door nervously. Fortunately, Martin wouldn't connect Chiara and Claire.

'You encourage the nephew of Beatrice. He is a sad man until he meet you and now he is happy because he thinks he fall in love with you. And never do you tell him you have a husband!'

The fact that he'd never asked didn't seem an adequate response. 'I'm so, so sorry—' Claire began, just as the door opened and Martin appeared.

'Look,' he interrupted, 'it really isn't that important. Claire, you know how I hate making a fuss.'

Beatrice and Giovanni stared at him incredulously. What kind of man was this who could announce that his wife's infidelity was not important? They had heard of the stiff upper lip but this was scandalous.

Fortunately, Monica was right behind him. '*Beatrice, è ora di mangiare,*' she announced firmly in her fluent Italian. 'It's time to eat.'

This had a miraculous effect. Passion, betrayal, jealousy, none of this counted in the face of dinner.

Beatrice began to chivvy Immaculata to prepare the pasta and shooed Giovanni out of the kitchen.

Monica grabbed Claire and Martin and pulled them back to the salon.

'So Martin,' Monica attempted normal conversation, 'what's the weather like in England?'

'Bloody awful. That's why I thought I'd pop over here.'

Through all the drama Sylvie had been sitting apart from them, staring at her purple nail varnish, thinking about Tony, lacerated with disappointment that the unexpected guest had been this insignificant little man whom Claire clearly didn't even want to see anyway instead of her errant husband.

She had already begun rehearsing speeches of magnanimous forgiveness in her head, and maybe even a sexy reconciliation featuring the nail varnish.

For a moment she considered tossing it out onto the terrace and watching it shatter in a pool of purple rejection, but actually she quite liked the shade. While the others were conversing, she dropped it into her handbag and poured herself a large glass of wine.

'What would you like to do while you're here?' Monica asked, desperately trying to keep up the flow of chat.

Martin visibly cheered and got out a Lonely Planet guide to Naples, Pompeii and the Amalfi Coast, thick with Post-it stickers. 'A whole day at Pompeii and Herculaneum, obviously; another for Vesuvius, especially the crater. Have you read Robert Harris's book?' He reached into his backpack, surprisingly small since it seemed to be all he had with him. 'I can lend it to you, if you like.' He pressed the book into Monica's hands. 'Walking the coastal trails, obviously.' He delved into the backpack again and recovered a guide to walking the coastal paths. 'And of course the Greek temples at Paestum; I wouldn't want to miss those.'

'Goodness,' Monica commented, surprised that these were exactly the things she'd wanted to do herself.

'Bloody hell,' Sylvie muttered into her wine. 'How long's the man planning to stay?'

'Depends how long my wife can put up with me,' Martin joked with an attempt at a jaunty smile. There was a forlorn tone to his voice that rather upset Monica, but Claire, pre-occupied with what she would tell Luca, didn't even seem to notice.

They were rescued by the arrival of the first course, a subtle pasta with seafood and saffron.

'Fantastic.' Martin grabbed a piece of bread to accompany it. 'I could murder a spaghetti.'

Almost as soon as they'd finished, Claire announced she was shattered and was going up to bed. She didn't offer an invitation to Martin, Monica noticed. Surely she wasn't going to make him sleep on the sofa or in one of Sylvie's stapled room sets?

Martin, full of red wine and plans for excursions, had got his second wind and hardly seemed to notice.

But Claire hadn't gone to bed. She was just outside the door to the salon frantically signalling to Monica, who got up as subtly as she could.

'Monica, could you do me the most amazing favour?' Claire whispered. 'Take Martin to Pompeii or somewhere tomorrow so I can go and talk to Luca before Beatrice publicly brands me a two-timing tart?'

Monica nodded. 'But what on earth are you going to do about Luca?'

Claire sighed, as if her whole soul were in torment. 'God knows. I think I'm falling in love with him, Monica.'

'Oh, God, Claire.' She looked over at Martin, happily thumbing through his guidebooks, swigging back red wine, and jotting down bus timetables while Sylvie stared moodily into the distance, as if completely unaware of his existence, which she probably was. 'Poor old Martin.'

Angela walked down the cobbled street from the villa towards the main square, enjoying the feeling of the almost-transparent silk fluttering round her in the evening breeze.

The Balcony was right at the bottom of the town, even beyond the bus stop, hanging over the opposite side of the bay from the villa. To her surprise it was French.

Hugo was already sitting at a table looking out over the sea, immaculate as usual.

'A French bistro in the middle of Lanzarella?' Angela smiled at him. 'That's a surprise.'

'Makes a change from all the pasta. Besides, in London you have Chinese, Indian, Italian, every nationality under the sun.'

'True,' she conceded with a smile. She studied the menu and opted for duck paté, followed by monkfish.

Hugo ordered steamed mussels and mixed fish from the Gulf of Salerno.

'Well,' Angela teased, 'you're full of surprises. To think I had you down as a red meat man.'

'Maybe you should challenge your prejudices a bit more,' he replied, raising an eyebrow. He really was a very attractive man.

This was the moment, she decided, to be direct.

'Speaking of prejudices, I heard a rumour that you cheated the previous owners of the degli Dei on the purchase price.' There was no point not being direct in Angela's view.

'What is cheating and what is good business?' Hugo replied levelly. 'Besides, no doubt this rumour is emanating from Luca Mangiani. The man's got a positive obsession with me.'

'He said everyone in Lanzarella knew.'

'People don't like change, Angela. You must have encountered that in business. Especially in small places like this. They want to keep everything little and local, but the world's changed. It's big and global.'

'Funny that,' Angela teased. 'The world being global.'

'The Oxford undergrad will out.' There was an edge of unmistakable sarcasm in his tone.

'You mean I'm trying to be intellectually superior? I gave that up when I started working in a bank in Filey.'

They had both finished their meal. An unfamiliar silence descended.

'Come on, let's have a mocha espresso and share a tarte tatin, then I'll walk you home.'

'Very chivalrous,' Angela replied, surprised, since it was barely ten o'clock. Maybe he really had taken offence.


'So,' Hugo enquired as they walked back through the town, 'any word from your absentee landlord? Will he be putting in an appearance?'

'Stephen? No, I don't think so. Too busy being global in London.'

When they got to the villa gates, at the moment when he might have leaned over and kissed her, he smiled enigmatically.

'A delightful evening. I greatly enjoy your company, Angela.'

Angela couldn't help smiling back. 'Me too.'

She watched him stroll back down the hill towards the hotel.

Was he offended? If so, she was surprised at how much she minded.

# Twelve

Tony Sutton sat gloomily in the bar of the Grand Hotel degli Dei, nursing a margarita and feeling stupid.

Why had he listened to that woman and sent Sylvie some nail varnish which she'd probably already thrown in the rubbish instead of a grand bunch of flowers?

What's more, the hotel seemed to be full of posh hen parties, not to mention prospective brides, their mothers and the odd hangdog bridegroom-to-be who seemed to view the whole process with all the joyousness of someone awaiting the tumbril.

'Can I get you another? On the house?' asked a well-dressed man in an immaculate camel-coloured suit, who had suddenly appeared at Tony's elbow. 'Hugo Robertson, my family own this place.' He held out his hand.

Tony shook it, taken aback that this glamorous-looking man had a surprisingly damp handshake. 'Tony Sutton.'

'Married to Sylvie Sutton?'

Tony nodded, scanning the man's face for any mockery, the usual response from anyone who'd seen that damn phone-shot of him with Kimberley, but he found none.

Behind them the hen parties whooped, drank expensive champagne from the bottle, and frolicked raucously in their tiny tutus, minuscule bra tops, bridal veils with tiaras and insanely high heels.

'It's the fashion,' commented Hugo. 'They all dress like a porno version of the bride. It doesn't seem to matter if they're from Knightsbridge or Basildon, they still behave the same.'

The Basildon reference pained Tony. Kim had been from there after all.

A very pretty and extremely drunk girl flashed past them through the open doors of the bar and jumped into the pool.

'Isn't that a bit dangerous?' Tony asked, suddenly noticing that his margarita had been replenished without him even noticing.

Hugo laughed. 'I ask the waiters to keep an eye on them.' He winked. Like the handshake, Tony was surprised at the faint leer on Hugo's face, which seemed to undercut the sophisticated image. 'There are plenty of volunteers, I can assure you. So what are you doing down here on your own?'

'I'm in the doghouse. I was having an affair with a work colleague and my wife walked in.'

'Bad luck. Still, there's plenty around here to take your mind off it. In fact, there's a rather hot young woman over there waving at you.'

To Tony's amazement, since he was feeling particularly rumpled and unattractive, a girl dressed in what looked like a Cinderella outfit chopped to just below the crotch was beckoning him over.

Tony smiled and shook his head. 'Too young for me, I'm afraid. I've made that mistake once. I'm sticking to women who know who Pink Floyd are,' he grinned disarmingly at Hugo, 'and can name them.'

'You won't get too many takers here, then.'

'Maybe that's the point,' agreed Tony.

Hugo sat on the stool next to him. 'As a matter of fact,' he glanced at two almost identical bottle-blondes except that, at second glance, one was obviously quite a lot older than the other, 'the mothers are often up for it.' He leaned against the bar looking at the blondes speculatively. 'Sometimes with their daughter as well. Now that's an experience to remember.' The barman topped up Tony's margarita yet again. 'I might try those two a little bit later. The bridal suite's empty and a bottle of Bolly usually breaks the ice.'

Tony looked at him in frank amazement. 'But they're completely rat-arsed.'

'All the better. They won't remember anything in the morning.'

'But you're the owner. Don't you have a duty of care or something?'

Hugo shook his head and laughed at him. 'They see it as all part of the fun. I know your problem. You're a romantic.'

'If not screwing two drunk women who're paying my hotel for the pleasure makes me a romantic,' Tony replied, trying to work out how soon he could get away from the man, 'then maybe I am.'

'Your loss.' Hugo shrugged. 'I might have a crack anyway. If they're still conscious.'

'My, you have high principles.'

'Don't be so pompous.' Hugo turned to Tony, transforming back into the cosmopolitan charmer again. 'So what are those four women really doing up at the villa?'

Tony looked at his watch and started to climb off the bar stool. 'I really wouldn't know.' Sylvie hadn't shared much with him but his instincts told him Hugo wasn't to be trusted.

'I made Stephen Charlesworth a ludicrously good offer for the place,' persisted Hugo, 'and he still hasn't accepted it.'

'And what would you do with it? Fill it with more drunk mothers and daughters? Maybe he's just careful who he does business with.'

'And who are you to lecture?' Hugo flashed back nastily. 'Great photograph of you and your intern. I'm told everyone in London had a laugh.'

'Thanks. Maybe I'll drop in at the bridal suite later,' Tony replied with a silky smile, 'capture some of your touching memories for Instagram.'

'Claire seems to have gone to bed,' Martin announced, as if he hadn't noticed before.

'So she does,' yawned Monica, who had stayed up with him through another bottle of red wine, after Sylvie had pointed to her watch and finally took herself upstairs as well. 'Would you like to show me her room?' Monica offered.

Martin got up, a sudden look of doubt on his face which touched kind Monica. Doubt, she suspected, was not one of his usual sentiments. 'Do you think I should sleep somewhere else? Not disturb her if she's tired?'

The trouble was, in this enormous house only the four bedrooms were properly usable. Sylvie's room treatments were amazing, but so far they were just for show to demonstrate their potential.

'Don't worry,' Monica soothed, 'she's got a big bed. I expect you can slip in without waking her. So would you like me to show you up now?'

'Thank you,' Martin said gratefully, stumbling a little as he spoke. Five more minutes and he'd be so asleep he could doss down in Trafalgar Square without waking.

Monica led him, holding his small backpack, up the grand stairs and pointed to Claire's door. Good luck, she almost added.

Five minutes later, before Monica was even undressed, there was a piercing scream, as if someone in the house had seen a ghost. Three women rushed out to the landing, in various stages of waking.

'What the fuck?' asked Sylvie, from beneath a layer of a crusted white substance, rising in peaks across her face. 'Egg white,' she explained, and tried to rub it off. 'Meant to be brilliant for the skin.'

They pushed open Claire's closed door.

A naked Martin was standing in front of the life-size doom painting, lit from below by a nightlight, staring fixedly at the equally naked women stretched across red hot racks, screaming in agony, being prodded by leering demons with animal faces and long monkey tails.

To the embarrassment of Monica and Angela, and the wild amusement of Sylvie, he had an enormous erection.

Meanwhile, Claire slept on unaware.

Becoming suddenly conscious of his priapic state, Martin grabbed a T-shirt which, given his continued tumescence, merely had the effect of looking like a tent at a rock festival.

'What the hell is that?' he demanded, indicating the picture.

'I think,' Angela tried valiantly to keep a straight face while the others collapsed in giggles, 'it's a medieval painting intended to warn fallible mankind against the pleasures of the flesh.' She didn't add that it seemed to be having the opposite effect on Martin.

Finally, Claire sat up and noticed four people in the bedroom, including her naked husband. 'What the hell is going on?' she demanded.

'Martin's discovering the lessons of medieval morality,' Angela explained. 'Perhaps you should have warned him he was sharing a room with four life-size women being sizzled alive to punish them for the error of their ways.' She wondered if Claire might see the message as relevant to her.

'Oh that thing.' Claire shrugged insouciantly, clearly not in the least affected by its warning. 'I never even notice it any more. For God's sake, Martin, put something on and get into bed!'

'Thanks a million, Monica.' Claire grabbed her next morning. 'I'm really sorry about last night. All my fault. I was so angry with Martin for just turning up that I didn't take him upstairs myself.'

'I think we all quite enjoyed it.' Monica grinned.

Claire looked at her, puzzled. 'And you really will take him off somewhere today?'

'He seems to have plenty of places he wants to visit.'

'That's Martin for you.' The tone of bitter resentment in her voice took Monica aback. 'Claire . . .'

'Yes?' Claire was grabbing a quick croissant and slathering it with home-made jam.

'I probably shouldn't say this . . .'

Now she had Claire's attention.

'This thing with Luca. Are you sure you aren't falling for the idea rather than the man? Growing lemons in the lovely sunshine of Lerini? Miles away from Twickenham and all your boring responsibilities?'

'You think it's all a sad mid-life fantasy?'

'Well, you know, staying here, in this amazing house, waited on, fed, the sunshine and the beauty, able to go and do what we want and answer to no one, it is all a bit unreal, isn't it?'

'But that's not what I've fallen for. It's Luca himself.' Her voice softened. 'I feel with him I could be part of something. And I think he actually wants me to be.'

'But you've only met the man a couple of times. I mean, obviously he's very attractive, but aren't you getting a bit carried away? And now that Martin's here, oughtn't you to spend some time with him?'

Claire poured herself another coffee without answering. It was true she hardly knew Luca. Maybe it was right that it was just a powerful attraction. But there was no way she was going to spend the day with Martin instead of him.

'OK, well, good luck. I'll certainly look after Martin today.'

Ten minutes later, Claire sat in the back of the bus down to Lerini hardly even noticing the beauty of her surroundings or the rollercoaster nature of the journey. In spite of what she'd said to Monica, she was feeling sick and guilty. But the awful thing was, it wasn't about Martin. It was about Luca.

She knew that Beatrice would have somehow conveyed the existence of Martin to her nephew and even though no actual words had been spoken between them about her marital state, she could sense that he was starting to have feelings for her.

The bus disgorged its passengers in the small piazza near the quay and Claire followed the happy holidaymakers and giggling schoolchildren, feeling depressed and at a loss.

She walked slowly towards Luca's lemon gardens, passing his niece Fabiella, who had shown her around on her first visit. Was it her imagination, or was Fabiella's greeting less than friendly? She rang the bell and one of the pickers let her in. As she climbed up towards the covered terrace where the family usually gathered, she passed Luca's eighty-year-old father. His smile was as merry as usual, but Claire feared that his grasp of things wasn't what it had been.

Finally, she came across Luca making himself a coffee in the smallest of the funny little Italian coffee pots that always made her smile.

But Luca wasn't smiling.

He turned towards her. He seemed to be waiting for her, to see what excuse or explanation she was going to try and offer.

'Luca . . .' she began. 'I am so sorry.'

'Me also,' he seconded bitterly. 'Very sorry. When were you going to tell me that you had a husband? Next week? Next month? Never?' The coffee pot boiled over like his anger and he picked it up and threw it onto the soft ground, burning himself in the process.

Claire rushed forward and took his injured hand in hers. 'I didn't tell you I had a husband because I thought it might be the end between us, or at least change everything.'

'Of course it would change everything! I saw how you wanted to understand what I was trying to do here, the way you cared about it as much as I. It seemed to me that it was more than the interest of a visitor who would soon be gone.'

'It was. I do care very much about what you are trying to do here and I would very much like to be a part of it.'

Claire wasn't even sure herself what she meant by this, but Luca opened his arms, his anger melting. '*Chiara mia.* Then I do not know what we are going to do.'

Behind them they heard the sound of clapping. It was Luca's father. 'I am so happy, my son, that you have found love with so kind a lady as this.'

'My poor father,' Luca looked careworn for the first time, 'he no longer understands life as he used to.'

Claire allowed herself to be hugged delightedly by Luca's father.

'Maybe he's the lucky one.' Luca sighed and sat down at the shade-covered table and dropped his head into his hands.

Angela dived into the pool and felt its greeny embrace surround her. Under the water was a separate world, the sound muffled, the silence exaggerated, but wasn't it actually a metaphor of the entire time they were staying here?

She surfaced, shook out her hair, and leaned on the edge of the pool looking down towards the coast. The sun sparkled on a sapphire-coloured sea and the heady scent of wisteria was almost overwhelming. But it wasn't just the beauty of the place that affected her. She liked Beatrice and Immaculata. Even the silent Luigi and the smouldering Giovanni had become familiar. And as for Claire, Sylvie and Monica, women she wouldn't even have noticed before – well, maybe Sylvie, no one could miss Sylvie – without her knowing it was happening they had become part of her emotional landscape.

A pang of guilt assailed her. Stephen might have intended this to be a haven for them, but the offer from Hugo was serious. Would the villa make a lovely hotel? There was no doubt it would. The views alone were spectacular, and its hidden, almost secret location made it incredibly desirable. Sylvie had already shown the potential of the wings in a few days with some moth-eaten fabric and her staple gun. The pool would need to be enlarged and the curious high hedges with the mysterious vegetable gardens Monica was so excited about would have to be flattened to make bigger gardens. Angela smiled. Something would certainly have to be done about communication, though oddly, this sense of being cut off had contributed powerfully to how she felt about the place.

And then there was Hugo himself, and how she was beginning to feel about him. Angela leaned over the edge of the pool and hid her face in her cool wet arms, her chest suddenly painful. This was dangerous. How the hell had it happened?

She got out of the pool and dried herself, pushing away this unfamiliar self-doubt. She was always someone who looked on the positive side. She stretched. Physically she'd never felt better.

Passing the bench near the asparagus bed she couldn't resist checking her phone. To her amazement she thought twice about opening a message from Drew, but it was nothing to do with Fabric. He hoped she was enjoying herself. He'd just seen Stephen, who'd asked how it was all going for them.

She sat down under the pergola breathing in the wisteria and thinking of Stephen. What a strange and curious man he was. So generous but she was still not quite convinced of his motives. Could anyone be that altruistic as to lend his gorgeous house to four women, some of whom he didn't really know, simply because he wanted some advice? She was unlikely to find out, so why bother thinking about it?

Instead, she opened another message from Hugo. Did she want to go to Capri for lunch?

Angela found she was smiling. She'd better go in and get changed.

'You're looking happy,' commented Sylvie, sitting on the terrace wearing motorcycle leathers.

'And you look sexy.'

'What a waste,' laughed Sylvie. 'I'm going with Alessandro to an art exhibition.'

'Where are the others?'

'Claire's gone to Lerini to explain to Luca that she finds she has a husband, and Monica's babysitting the husband while she does it. What are your plans?'

Angela found she was blushing faintly. Bloody ridiculous. 'Capri for lunch,' she announced.

'Better get your skates on. I think I can guess who with.'

Tony woke up and ordered breakfast in his room. He didn't fancy any more unpleasant male banter with Hugo Robertson, or to discover whether he had indeed attempted to seduce the mother or daughter, or indeed both. Hugo, he suspected, was the kind who would tell.

The waiter arrived with an enormous tray, complete with a red rose and snowy white tablecloth, and placed it on a stand which he carried out onto the balcony. Tony ate his brioche staring down into the turquoise blue beneath him and pondered what to do. He was half tempted to cut his losses and go back to London, regardless of what Sylvie said. If she hadn't responded to his gift even with a message, then he might as well chuck in the towel.

And yet if his indiscretion had taught him one thing, it was that he loved her. He grinned to himself. After his anger had died down, he'd even admired her tactic of sending out that phone-shot. Of course it was embarrassing but how many women would have thought of it and then dared to do it? And she hadn't followed it up with cutting the arms out of his suits, or putting his wine on the doorsteps of all their neighbours, as various celebrated dumped wives had done. Not that he had any posh wine. Sylvie was the type to blow her top but not hold grudges.

Be original, that woman Monica had insisted, but where had that got him? Maybe it was time for one last attempt – with flowers. Not that flowers would be easy. Sylvie had always made flowers a special feature of the homes she designed, no daffs or carnations for Sylvie. She refused even to order through Interflora because she wanted to be absolutely sure what she was getting. Sylvie's houses were full of forests of foxgloves or dwarf cherry trees.

But he couldn't think what else to get her. Jewellery was too individual, especially in Sylvie's case, and clothes were a minefield because, let's face it, Sylvie was no waif of a model. But if he bought L, it was often too small and if he bought XL, she wouldn't speak to him, so clothes were out. Scarves were a possibility but she had enough to last several lifetimes already.

Flowers it would have to be.

He went down and on the way out asked the hotel's concierge if there was a florist in Lanzarella. The man eagerly got out his weddings book to show him and insisted they could order for him but Tony politely refused. These were his last-chance flowers and he wanted to choose them himself.

The only proper florist in the area, the concierge conceded finally, was in Maggiore, the next town along the coast.

Half an hour later and forty euros poorer for a taxi, Tony found himself in a dingy cul-de-sac in the backstreets of the small town, outside a very unpromising florist full of fluffy toys and hideous chrysanthemum wreaths and crosses.

Tony was on the point of leaving when a young woman with short-cropped red hair and a flower tattoo emerged from the shop carrying a spray of almond blossom.

'That's more like it,' Tony pointed to the branch excitedly, 'do you speak English?' he asked the girl.

'*Sì*, a little, but only from pop records.'

Tony decided to come clean. 'I need a wonderful bunch of flowers to win back my wife.'

'"Love Will Find a Way",' agreed the assistant.

'Yes? I mean Yes, the band.' Tony nodded delightedly.

The girl laughed. '*Sì, sì.* Yes the band. What flowers you like?'

'My wife is very stylish, she only likes dramatic arrangements.' He held out his arms to signify that Sylvie liked things big.

The girl nodded. '"Whole Lotta Love".' She nodded again.

'Led Zeppelin!'

She disappeared into the back while Tony waited. He suspected these flowers would be hideous and cost an arm and a leg plus the forty euros taxi fare there and another forty back but it was certainly a shopping experience with a difference.

In a surprisingly short time she was back, but, curiously, holding a wooden stool for him to sit on and a glass of murky-looking liquid which she handed to him. '*Amaretto di Saronno*,' she announced proudly and patted him on the shoulder. '"Love Hurts",' she sympathized.

'The Everly Brothers,' stated Tony, feeling ludicrously cheered. The girl seemed to take forever but when she finally returned he was shocked into silence. They were the most stunning flowers he'd ever seen. Pale pink peonies, bearded irises in cream, purple striped tulips drooping gracefully, almond pink ranunculi, ivy, ferns and two huge sprays of pale pink roses, whose scent filled the room.

'"Ah sweet darlin'",' she quoted gleefully as she handed them over, '"you get the best of my love!"'

'The Eagles!'

The assistant bowed and charged him far less than he was expecting.

He summoned a cab and had to take the greatest care to fit himself and the flower arrangement in without mishap.

The florist clapped and waved goodbye.

Tony found he was still grinning by the end of the half-hour journey to Lanzarella. If Sylvie didn't like these he might as well give up and go home.

Beatrice answered the door and told Tony that she was very sorry that Signora Sylvie had gone out earlier that morning.

Tony almost handed them over, then some stubborn determination that would have surprised Sylvie overtook him. 'Please put these in water. I will stay till she gets back. What time is she expected?'

'I do not know, signore. Only that she go off with young man on motorbike.'

'Did she?' Tony's features set in a line of grim disapproval. 'Where would you like me to wait?' It was only eleven o'clock so it could be some time.

'On the terrace would be best. Would you like some English tea?' Beatrice offered proudly.

Tony loathed tea but he could see that a refusal would disappoint her. 'That would be absolutely lovely.'

He had only been seated for five minutes when a sultry-looking young man with a spade started to dig gloomily at the bottom of the terrace steps. When Tony greeted him he stuck his spade into the earth and leaned moodily on it. He was, Tony noted, extraordinarily good-looking. 'Tell me, signore, is it the custom in your country for four ladies to live without a man? No wonder there are *omosessuali* and *tradimenti!*'

He only had a smattering of Italian but even he could deduce this had something to do with homosexuals and infidelity. On the other hand, his morning so far had been so wonderfully bizarre that nothing would surprise him. He had always thought life in the King's Road was Bohemian but Italy, from his limited experience, seemed to be a full-scale opera.

His tea arrived and he duly drank it. Apart from the garden the place seemed empty, so he decided to wander around. What an extraordinary house it was! The position was obviously unique on the top of a hillside hanging over cliffs with the sea far below: completely private. And these incredible gardens with roses, tulips, wisteria and God alone knew what. Tony left the flowery aspects of life to Sylvie; anyway, it was all very scented and somehow he realized the word for it was *English*.

He wandered back up the terrace steps and into the house. There was a quiet stillness with only the sound of clocks ticking and muffled voices, perhaps from the kitchen. There was a smell of lavender and beeswax which took him straight back to childhood. A fly buzzed quietly on the window ledge. He rounded a corner and stopped, dodging quietly behind a pillar. Hugo Robertson was standing in front of the fresco of *The Annunciation*, taking photographs on his phone. It might have been just because he was amazed by it. After all, everyone captured things that interested them on their phones, but there was something about the intensity of his attitude and the detail he seemed to want to capture that made Tony suspicious. What the hell was he up to?

'You seem very interested,' Tony challenged him. 'What makes it so special?'

Hugo jumped and turned round. Tony could see his first reaction was one of intense annoyance, quickly covered by the usual charming smile. 'Tony, old man, good to see you!'

Tony could see that it was anything but. He was tempted for a moment to needle him with references to last night but decided against it.

'Are you looking for your wife?' Hugo asked. 'Angela said she was out.'

Angela came skipping down the stairs at that moment. 'Hello, Tony, we're off to Capri. Sylvie's gone off with her friend Alessandro.'

'Ah, I wonder if that would explain your gardener's curious allusion to homosexuals?'

Angela laughed. She was looking ten years younger. He very seriously hoped it wasn't anything to do with the presence of Hugo Robertson. 'That would be a reference to Constantine, our neighbour. He's a world-famous painter but to Giovanni he's just an old homosexual.'

Tony decided he wouldn't pursue the accusations of infidelity in case they had any connection to him.

'Did she say what time she'd be back?'

'I'm afraid not. I'm sure Beatrice would rustle you up some lunch, if you want to wait.'

'No, no.' He could just imagine Sylvie's reaction if she came back and found him being fed.

'Let me at least get you a drink, then. Fizz all right?'

He grinned. 'I haven't been married to Sylvie for thirty years for nothing. Fizz would be fabulous.'

She came back carrying a long-stemmed glass. 'Take it out onto the terrace. By the way,' she added in a low tone so that Hugo couldn't hear, 'the nail varnish was a definite hit. Except that I think she was a bit disappointed you didn't deliver it in person.'

'Do you think she might forgive me, then?' Tony replied in an eager whisper.

'I think she might,' Angela agreed. 'But for God's sake be humble. Tell her she's wonderful. And don't criticize her. You can do that when you both get home,' she added with a wink.

'Thanks, Angela.'

'I must admit, I've got a bit of a soft spot for Tony,' Angela confessed to Hugo as they got into his car, round the back of the house.

'After the way he behaved to your friend? Betraying her so publicly?'

'From what she's told us it was she who made it public,' pointed out Angela.

'He's a bit of a shit, if you ask me. When I got back last night he was chatting up the Essex girls on their hen night at the hotel.' Hugo paused for effect. 'Not to mention their mothers.'

'Oh bloody hell, was he?' Angela looked really upset. 'I thought he'd learned his lesson. I wish I hadn't given him that glass of fizz, then. I hope Sylvie doesn't come back and believe he's sorry.'

'You can always put her right, can't you?' Hugo smiled.

'No, Hugo. I hate sneaks. I have ever since schooldays. I'll watch out for what happens next.'

'Suit yourself.' Hugo shrugged. But Angela got the distinct impression he was annoyed with her. Now why would that be?

Tony sat drinking his fizz on the terrace thinking that though the place was amazing, it was also a bit unreal. Here they were tucked away in luxury, but what for? Stephen had known Sylvie as a child and had probably wanted to give her respite from what he saw as a shitty situation. She was also, or so she said, meant to give some advice about the villa's potential as a hotel. Was that because of Hugo Robertson's offer?

He thought about Hugo's hotel where he'd been staying. It was ludicrously expensive, horribly pretentious and yet, as he'd witnessed last night, rather sleazy. Tony found himself hoping two things: that the villa would stay as it was, and that

Hugo wasn't pursuing Angela for his own purposes. And why was he taking photographs of that fresco?

He could hear the sound of a motorbike roaring up the drive and a wave of protective anger came over him. Had Sylvie been speeding around on the back of one of those things on these crazily dangerous roads? Doctors didn't call owners of motorbikes organ donors for nothing. And yet, it also hit him, he had no right to criticize. He'd sacrificed that back in the stupid flat in Belgravia.

The sounds of Sylvie's usual noisy entrance and then the excited tones of the housekeeper told him that Sylvie had been given his flowers.

A moment later she appeared holding them, her long red hair blown in the wind from the motorbike ride, every inch a diva, and he felt suddenly lost for words.

'Hello, Tony,' she studied the amazing flowers. 'Thank you for these.'

'I chose them myself in the florist. I didn't want anything clichéd.'

'They're fabulous. You remember Alessandro?'

Tony noticed the exotic young man for the first time. Alessandro had worked for him briefly, he recalled, and to his relief, he was clearly gay. Yet when he'd played this scene in his head, there hadn't been anyone else in the room. How stupid. Sylvie was never alone.

'The roses are scented. I know you love scented roses.'

Sylvie breathed in the glorious scent. 'They're wonderful. And so English.' She studied them for a moment. 'What a coincidence. We have these roses in the garden. I remember because I liked them so much I looked them up. They're called Maiden's Blush.' She laughed her fruity unmaidenly laugh.

'And thanks for the nail varnish.' She pointed at her toes and all three of them studied them carefully.

'You should not wear them with that dress,' Alessandro tutted. 'Purple and green together are too strong.'

'What nonsense, remember that room I did in Rome for the Austrian countess? Green and purple!'

Tony's words of apology dissipated into the hot air like millions of motes of dust. He couldn't do it in front of this cool young man. 'I'm glad you like the flowers.'

Sylvie held his gaze for a second. Maybe she should send Alessandro away. But Tony was already on his feet.

'I'll say goodbye, then.'

'Yes. Tony?'

He turned, a look of hopefulness in his eyes.

'I'm sorry about the office, but you can't just walk in like that.'

'It's my home too. And my business.'

'The lawyers will sort all that.'

'Will they, Sylvie?' He was angry now at her inflexibility when here he was, apologizing and trying to mend something broken. 'Will they really?' He made a decision. 'I'm going back to London. I'll let you know where I'm staying.'

He walked out silently, his body stiff with anger and hurt.

Sylvie watched him go. When he had left the room, she began to cry quietly.

Alessandro watched, mystified. 'You know, Sylvie, you are a strange lady. I would have bet a million euro you wanted him back.'

Sylvie collapsed onto the velvet chaise longue in the salon. 'I do,' she wailed, even forgetting her mascara and how old she looked when it ran. 'But he's hurt me so much, he's made me question myself all the time. He must compare me, my body, my face, my tits, with a twenty-year-old's. I can't look in the mirror any more without seeing this old hag. I used to see someone who looked good for her age. Now I see every wrinkle and age spot!'

'Sylvie, Sylvie,' Alessandro kneeled down beside her and stroked her hair, 'men aren't like that. It doesn't make any difference if they're straight or gay. They're opportunists. This girl came along and fancied him, or maybe she had her own reasons, but he *thought* she fancied him. So he couldn't resist. Maybe, same as you, every time he look in the mirror he see someone old.'

'Yes, but what the hell do we do about it?'

'We ask your housekeeper for a glass of that nice Franciacorta.'

Sylvie had to laugh. 'The universal panacea. At home it's a cup of tea.'

Alessandro grimaced. 'You British. No wonder you're all so dull and straight. Now you must think carefully. If you were Italian, you would lose three kilos and buy new clothes. On his credit card.'

'I loathe shopping. Dieting means I have to give up everything I love,' Sylvie sighed.

'Then you have to ask yourself if you can live with this stupid looking in the mirror. Sit up.' Sylvie pulled herself into a sitting position. 'Say after me. I am Sylvie Sutton and I am beautiful in every way!'

Sylvie burst out laughing. 'Alessandro, I love you!'

Alessandro smiled naughtily. 'Now that would add an interesting dimension to your problem.'

Monica and Martin were sitting in the sunny piazza with the guidebook between them. Monica actually found his obsession with guidebooks rather restful because she didn't have to think what to do, but he said it annoyed the hell out of Claire.

First on his list was the famous mosaic of *Jonah and the Whale*. Apart from the argument with the ticket office that he couldn't have a senior ticket because he had no proof of identity, which threatened to turn into an international incident until Monica stepped in and paid herself, their expedition had been restful.

Now they both stood in front of the huge mosaic and studied it carefully. It was exactly the same as Constantine's copy. Jonah was depicted as a very lifelike man in his fifties, anxious and balding, with an almost hipster beard, with his hand stretched out, perhaps hoping someone would catch it and pull him out.

'He looks as if he's saying "Goodbye, cruel world. See you in ten days", or whatever,' said Martin.

They looked at the other end of the mosaic and realized this section was actually Jonah coming out rather than being swallowed.

'I love the whale.' Monica studied it. 'It has wings and feet like a demon.'

Martin laughed suddenly. 'He reminds me of the demon last night.'

Monica grinned and had to look the other way, remembering Martin's reaction.

'Belief was so literal then, wasn't it?' Martin studied Jonah again.

'If you were bad, demons came and barbecued you on red hot coals.'

'Only on the Day of Judgement,' Monica reminded him. 'You could have a bloody good time first.'

For some reason this made them both giggle until an irate

official emerged and berated them. 'This is the house of God, please leave!'

They ambled out, still giggling.

Martin turned to Monica at the top of the flight of steps back down to the piazza. 'I feel like Adam expelled from the Garden of Eden.'

'Well, I don't feel like Eve,' she insisted, still laughing. 'Let's go and have lunch.'

They found a trattoria in the back streets away from the cathedral crowds and ordered burrata grilled between lemon leaves, just as Monica had had at almost their first lunch here. What a long time ago it seemed, yet it wasn't much more than a moment.

'They seem to use lemons with everything around here,' Monica pointed out.

The observation made her think of Claire and what a horrible situation she and Martin were in. She wondered for a moment what she would do if she were Claire, but found it hard to imagine. She'd only had one serious relationship in her life and that had been with Brian and they'd been so content with their small and happy life that neither of them would ever have thought about falling for someone else. And then he'd died.

Martin was still busy looking at the wine list and comparing it with the wines recommended in his guidebook when Monica almost choked on her water.

Down the street, about fifty yards away from their trattoria, Claire and Luca were walking towards them, looking ludicrously happy and holding hands.

# Thirteen

---

'Excuse me a minute, Martin!' Monica jumped up. 'But I think I left something in the cathedral. Won't be a moment. You go ahead and order the wine.'

'All right,' Martin agreed, 'but Monica,' he shouted, making the other customers glance at him in disapproval, 'you're going the wrong way!'

Martin shrugged. The wine arrived and he took an exploratory sip. It was quite good for the price. He got out a small black book from his rucksack and busied himself with writing down the name of the wine, the year, and where he had drunk it.

Five minutes later, Monica reappeared looking flushed from running. She'd just managed to head Claire off, thank God.

'I tried to tell you,' Martin explained, looking concerned. 'The cathedral's the other way.'

'I always did have a lousy sense of direction,' Monica lied. She'd actually been a star at orienteering, much to her mother's disgust. 'Fortunately, I found a short cut.'

'Did you find what you were looking for?'

Monica racked her brains for what it was she'd lost. 'My wallet. And it was in my bag all along!'

'I've got a special section in my rucksack so I can just pat it and know my wallet's there. You should do the same.'

'What happens if someone steals your rucksack?'

'They can't.' He indicated his rucksack under his chair. 'I've got this clever thing that ties it to my chair.'

Monica couldn't help giggling just a little.

'You think I'm ridiculous,' he stated with a rueful grin that made Monica crease up with guilt. 'I suppose Claire does too. Funny old Martin. I was angry with her when she said she was coming here.'

Their burrata arrived and they dipped their wonderfully crunchy bread in the tomato-infused olive oil provided at every table. 'It seemed so selfish, just leaving us. And to be honest, I thought all this assessing it for a hotel was nonsense. Claire's a local caterer, not someone with experience of cooking for a smart hotel, even if she has always had this thing about Italy.' He sipped his wine thoughtfully. 'But then I thought maybe she needed a break from me.'

He looked up and smiled. 'I wasn't always this dull. When she met me I wanted to be the new Bob Dylan. I expect you think that's funny too.'

But Monica, who had heard people laugh when she said she was a librarian, and laugh again when she said she was a librarian at the University of Buckingham, didn't think it was funny at all.

'Good for you, Martin.' She raised her glass and clinked it against his. '"Tangled Up in Blue"!'

Martin raised his glass, looking stunned. 'Do you know, that's my very favourite of all Dylan's songs?'

'Me too,' Monica replied, thinking of Claire and Martin and

Sylvie and Tony, and the mess love got people into. 'You should keep playing,' she said finally.

'I haven't touched a guitar in years.'

They noticed that they were the last in the restaurant.

'So, where do you want to go now?'

'There's a walk I'd love to do. Steps that would take us all the way up the hillside to Lanzarella.'

Monica laughed helplessly as Martin looked on, wondering what on earth he'd said. It was the same walk she'd done in the pouring rain with her backpack when her wallet had been stolen.

Monica stood up and called the waiter over in her perfect Italian to pay the bill.

'Gosh,' Martin said, impressed. 'You are full of surprises.'

As they set off towards the route for Lanzarella, Martin glanced guiltily at Monica's feet. 'Will your shoes be all right?'

'Oh yes, I always wear sensible shoes.'

'You sound rather mournful about that. Do you yearn for high heels?'

'Absolutely not. Actually, I have a pair of black patent sandals which are definitely *not* sensible.'

'I'm glad to hear it. You look as if your feet are the same size as Claire's.'

'Bigger,' Monica admitted. 'Size seven! She tried to borrow the sandals and they were too big.'

'Sounds like you've all been having a lot of fun.'

They had, Monica admitted, had a lot of fun. There was nothing, she'd discovered, like female friendship to make you feel good about life.

They walked along the narrow path, once used by mules, the only means of transport between the port of Lerini and Lanzarella at the top of the mountain. It was a glorious afternoon and everywhere the scent of wild thyme and purple sage filled the air as they trod it underfoot. 'It really is an extraordinary landscape.' Martin stood for a moment, entranced. 'The mountains so high, these amazing, deep ravines, and yet so near the sea.'

Monica nodded, realizing how much she'd come to love it.

'Look,' Martin suddenly ducked behind a rock and pulled Monica with him, 'it's a honey buzzard! They used to massacre them as they migrated. Skylarks, song thrushes, goldfinches too, seventeen million a year. They're trying to stop it now.'

Monica could hardly speak at the terrible thought. To think that perfectly ordinary Italians like Giovanni or Luigi might come out and hunt songbirds was too appalling.

'We hunted poor old Reynard the fox for long enough,' Martin reminded her. 'Man isn't very civilized under the skin.'

The librarian in Monica wasn't having that and for the next hour, sitting in the moss-covered nook so that they could see any more passing honey buzzards, they happily argued about man's inhumanity to man, and to other furrier creatures, and whether or not cruelty was intrinsic to the human character.

They were passed by several labouring Italians who thought they were entirely mad until they caught the strains of their English accents, and then they knew it for certain.

Eventually they started up the path again. When they finally got to the top step and walked along the narrow path to the villa, they found Angela already on the terrace reading a book. 'You've been a long time,' she commented.

'We've walked all the way from Lerini,' Monica pointed out gaily, 'arguing all the way.'

'Sounds glorious.' Angela leaned back on the wicker lounger. 'How was Capri?'

'Crazy and beautiful as ever.'

'You've missed Tony's attempt to win over Sylvie with the biggest bouquet out of captivity.'

'Did it work?' Monica asked hopefully.

'Not really. He seems to have decided to go home.'

Martin started walking towards the house but Angela grabbed Monica to keep her a moment. 'I thought you ought to know. Hugo says Tony was hitting on the hen parties staying in his hotel. And their mothers.'

Monica stared out at the mist settling on the distant blue horizon. 'What crap. I've spent more time with Tony than the rest of you, and I don't believe a word of it. They might have been hitting on *him*, you know what it's like when hen parties get going; they eat men alive just for fun. And I just don't believe Tony would make that mistake again.' She fixed Angela with her best your-book-is-six-weeks-overdue expression. 'And if I were you, I'd wonder why Hugo Robertson wants you to think so.'

She disappeared down into the garden to let Angela think about that one. Monica wasn't sure why he was making this accusation, but she didn't trust Hugo Robertson. He reminded her of those chocolates that were sweet and soft on the outside with a hard centre you could break your teeth on. She just hoped Angela wasn't going to break a tooth.

Angela watched Monica disappearing down the steps into the garden with mounting irritation. What did she care whether the others liked Hugo or not? But, oddly, she found that she did care, that she wanted them to like him.

It struck Angela again what a curious bunch they were: Sylvie with her hippie silks, Claire still mumsy, Monica now oddly smart but still a librarian underneath, and herself. And yet somehow they all got on. The other night Monica had shocked them all by suggesting that maybe Stephen had asked them because he felt sorry for them.

No one needed to feel sorry for Angela Williams. She could take care of herself. Couldn't she?

From the bottom of the garden, Monica could see Claire walking up the drive from the bus stop and ran down to intercept her.

'Bloody hell, Claire. What were you thinking, walking around holding hands like that in broad daylight?'

Claire shrugged as if she'd had no choice. She had an irritating little smile that really annoyed Monica.

'If I hadn't thrown water over myself and rushed over, you'd have walked slap bang into Martin!'

'Maybe that would have been for the best.'

'No, it damn well wouldn't. You might think you've fallen for Luca and his sodding lemons in record bloody time, but you could at least consider the feelings of the man you've been married to for thirty years!'

Claire had never seen Monica so angry. 'OK, OK, maybe you're right, we should tell him in a way that won't be such a shock, but I don't get why you're shouting and swearing about it.'

'Because I've lived with my mother, that's why, the most selfish being on the planet, who never even thinks other people *have* feelings!'

'OK, Monica. Thank you for keeping Martin occupied, and if you could do it for just a few more days, Luca and I will think about what to do next.'

'You're completely sure, then? How do you think your son and his wife will take it?'

'They're grown-ups, they'll deal with it. They might even decide to find their own place.'

'Poor Martin.'

'Yes, well, Martin doesn't tend to notice other people anyway. He'll be fine. Beatrice'll be calling us for dinner soon. I'd better dash up and change. Thanks, Monica, I couldn't do this without you.'

Monica sighed. It suddenly struck her that she was trying to help Tony get back with Sylvie and Claire make up with Martin, she who'd always believed you should never interfere in other people's lives. How had it happened? She looked around at the beauty of the evening garden. This place seemed to have a magic microclimate of its own. The morning glories were closing their heads, while the scented stock and nicotianas were just beginning to release their heady night-time aromas. Banksiae roses tumbled among the pale pink fragrant daphne – Luigi told her they started flowering in February, imagine, and kept on till June – while statues peeped out of the vegetation as if at any moment they might come alive. There was some kind of strange enchantment in this place, even practical Monica couldn't deny it.

But surely they were all too old to be a Rosalind or a Perdita?

The sudden thought of Angela as Titania and Hugo as an upmarket Bottom made her crack up with laughter.

'You sound happy,' said a voice behind her. It was Martin, spruced up for dinner in a striped white shirt, and jeans which he'd probably ironed.

'Yes,' she replied, 'and for God's sake don't ask me why.' She skipped up the steps to the terrace and accepted the glass he was holding out. Monica took it, thinking as she did that Claire was wrong. Martin did notice other people's feelings.

'So what's the plan tomorrow?'

He waved a map at her. 'Are you up for tackling Pompeii?'

Monica nodded. 'Do you think Claire might like to come?' she suggested.

'Oh no.' Martin clearly had no suspicion of what was going on with Luca. 'She wants to go and find out more about lemons. I suppose it's useful, if you're a cook. She's never been the slightest bit interested in history.'

'Pompeii it is, then.'

'Great. I'll work out the travel arrangements.'

Monica smiled. Claire found this deeply annoying, she knew, but to her it seemed quite endearing. But she was well aware, from listening to her colleagues at the library moaning about their spouses, that what seemed endearing when you walked up the aisle could be the very thing that drove you wild after twenty years of marriage.

The meal was marvellous, as it always was. Zucchini flowers stuffed with ricotta followed by roast quail and a satisfyingly flinty dry white wine.

Martin, noting how small the birds were, elbowed Monica and pointed.

'I'm sure they're farmed, not shot while they migrate,' Monica reassured him.

'What are you two whispering about?' Angela asked crossly.

'Martin was telling me how many migrating songbirds they hunt in Italy. Seventeen million.'

'And did you know, they blind the canaries so they sing at night as well?' Martin added for good measure.

Angela put down her knife and fork. 'Can we not talk about this over dinner?'

Martin sipped his wine. 'So do you get fed like this every

night? Breakfast and lunch too? And given this great wine?' He looked at the label and got out his trusty guidebook. 'This one's about forty quid a bottle.'

An embarrassed silence descended on the table.

They all looked at each other.

'Stephen's a rich man,' Sylvie announced robustly. 'He seems to want to keep the place and let people come here as his guests.'

'Until now,' Claire reminded. 'Don't forget the offer he's had.'

'From Hugo,' reminded Monica.

Sylvie glanced at Angela, who seemed determinedly quiet.

'Why *wouldn't* he sell it?' Angela suddenly said irritably. 'According to the staff, he hardly ever comes here. His wife liked it but that was twenty-five years ago. Selling makes a lot of sense.'

Down-to-earth Monica was the first to fill the uneasy silence that followed.

'How much is beauty worth, and peace, and a kind of magic that's having an effect on all of us?'

They looked at her, startled. 'What do you mean?'

'I mean we're all changing, becoming different, something's happening to us.'

'What utter rubbish,' announced Angela. 'I'll see you all in the morning. I feel like an early night.'

They watched her depart.

'Come on, leave her alone,' Sylvie remarked. 'Did you see my flowers?'

They all trooped out to have a look. 'They're amazing,' Monica enthused. She loved flower arranging, but these were really special.

'I know,' Sylvie said.

'Does that smug smile mean that you're forgiving Tony?' Monica asked hopefully.

'It means I like the flowers,' Sylvie replied.

'And you're wearing his nail varnish,' persisted Monica.

'Monica,' Claire hissed, pulling her aside. 'Just leave it.'

'Those roses,' announced Martin, beginning to sneeze, 'are just like the ones in the garden.'

Behind them, Beatrice had suddenly appeared. '*Signori*,' she announced, shooing them towards the terrace. 'Coffee is on the *terrazza*. Immaculata has made special biscuits with amaretto.'

'Thanks for doing this,' Claire said quietly to Monica at breakfast on the terrace next morning.

'No problem. I wanted to go to Pompeii anyway.'

'At least Martin will sort out how you get there,' Claire added with an edge of bitterness.

Of course Claire was right. In fact, Martin was deeply irritated that a direct bus from Lerini to Pompeii had been axed and they had to go via Sorrento and then catch the Circumvesuviana train. Monica wondered if she should pass on the warning that this was the most pickpocketed train in Italy but, given that she'd been fine on the train and had lost her wallet on the ferry to an extremely handsome young man, there didn't seem much point.

At least the journey was along the lovely coast road. Monica smiled at all the tourists on the bus clinging on to the handrails, terrified of ending up in the crashing waves next to the road. Monica knew better.

At Pompeii they began with the grassy forum, its majestic columns proclaiming it to be the main piazza. 'I wonder if they had coffee shops here,' mused Monica. 'You know, early

Caffè Nero, where you could get a cappuccino and a muffin when you bought a slave.'

They wandered through the Temple of Apollo and on to the Temple of Jupiter. 'Not that their gods seem to have been much help when it counted,' muttered Martin. Next were the fish and meat markets. And then they found themselves at the small triangular building that formed Pompeii's famous brothel.

'I hear the frescoes are quite hot stuff,' Martin pointed to his guidebook. 'Too rude to feature in here. Designed to turn on the punters and show them what was on the menu. Are you up for it?'

'Why not?' Monica replied, thinking of past pleasures. 'I'm over twenty-one.'

And hot stuff they were. There was one lady with an enormous rear draping herself over the end of the bed so that she could offer free access to her ample amenities.

'Her bum's bigger than Kim Kardashian's,' pointed out Monica, proud of her up-to-date cultural references.

Another was being treated to fellatio by an enthusiastic toga-clad punter.

Martin was transfixed by a soldier with a two-foot penis while Monica's particular favourite was a lady about to pleasure herself with what looked like a ferret or some such furry creature. 'Ouch,' she commented to Martin, 'what sharp teeth you've got, Grandmother!'

Monica stared out into the heat haze already settling on the historic ruins.

Were love and sex over for her? Perhaps that was the reality for a woman in her position, but if so it was sad.

They decided to cool down in the shade and share the bottle of water they'd brought.

'Oh well,' Monica commented. 'Nothing changes, does it?'

'I think your experience must have been rather different to mine,' Martin commented a shade bleakly. 'Claire was always in a rush to put something in the oven. Sorry,' he apologized instantly, 'that was most inappropriate of me to make comments about my wife.'

They got up and headed for Pompeii's most famous landmark, The Garden of the Fugitives. Here were the world-famous plaster casts of thirteen men, women and children who had come for shelter from the burning lava and pumice stone raining down on Pompeii, only to find the lava too heavy for the roof, which fell in and suffocated them.

Monica stared at the grey figures silently. Their power lay in their utter immediacy and defencelessness. It was as if the deadly suffocating lava had killed them only moments before instead of in AD 79.

Some lay in the foetus position, hands over their heads, children on their backs as if they had died while they were sleeping, a man held one hand up as if he could prevent the imminent disaster. There was even a dog contorted in agony. Saddest of all was a family group, the father sitting up as if to try to protect the small child and woman lying next to him.

Monica noticed that Martin had turned away.

To her astonishment, she saw that he was silently crying. 'We all think we can protect ourselves from disaster,' he said in a low voice. 'And it's just as futile for us as it was for them.'

Monica found, without thinking, that she had put an arm round him to offer solace. Was this really the grumpy, selfish, unempathetic man Claire had described?

He smiled at her ruefully. 'I know Claire came here because she couldn't stand her life at home. I don't blame her. The thing is, it was only when she left that I realized how much she did for us all, and how little appreciation she got. Not from Evan, our son, he's a good lad, but from me and our daughter-in-law. That's why I came. But now I'm here, I get the feeling she wishes I hadn't.'

Monica desperately wished she could reassure him, but there was nothing she could say. It was up to Claire, not her, to break the news to him that things might be more serious than that.

'It may sound a bit crass,' she answered lightly, 'but after all this sex and death I think what we need is lunch.'

Martin stared at her and began to laugh. 'I couldn't put it better myself.'

For once everyone seemed to be busy and Angela, enjoying the peace by the pool, felt a stab of irritation at the sound of a car approaching up the drive. Beatrice could deal with it, she decided, and closed her eyes again.

The sudden shock of drips of cold water on her hot skin made her sit up with a start, to find Hugo laughing down at her. 'What's happened to the legendary workaholic Ms Williams?' he enquired.

'She seems to have stayed in London.'

'Excellent. That's what we'd offer the guests if the villa was a hotel. Only the most exclusive workaholics allowed.' He reached out a hand to help her up. 'Come and let me show you all my childhood haunts. I bet there are places in the grounds you didn't know existed.'

'I'd better put some clothes on.'

Hugo looked her up and down appreciatively. 'Must you?'

Ridiculously, Angela almost blushed. 'Two minutes.' She ran upstairs, quickly put on a shift and sandals and brushed out her hair. Unable to resist, she glanced down at Hugo.

He was standing looking at the nymph peeping into the half-hidden pool where Claire had been spotted in the nude by Giovanni.

He was still there when she went outside, taking a photograph of the statue on his phone. 'That's Claire's pool,' she told him smiling. 'She went skinny-dipping there when we all first arrived and got caught by the gardener.'

'He probably thought she was a mad old bird.'

'No, actually,' Angela insisted. 'It was all very romantic. He said there were two nymphs not one. And he didn't seem to think she was old at all.'

'I only meant because the Italians wouldn't dream of shedding a clout till June,' Hugo corrected himself swiftly. 'Pity it wasn't you.'

Angela bowed. Was she imagining it, or had the flirtation definitely gone up a notch?

They both stared into the clear pool, with its fronds of bright green weed and the wonderful statue, her marble skin glowing with light, as if she were a living, breathing woman. 'I expect my grandfather put it there for my grandmother.'

'To remind her of her previous career?'

'So, you two,' they heard Monica's voice shout from the terrace, and they wondered how long she'd been standing there. 'How about me taking one of both of you?' She skipped down the steps from the terrace. 'I saw you taking snaps of the nymph,' she told Hugo. 'She's wonderful, isn't she? Claire wondered if she was the work of a really good sculptor, she's so lifelike. There you go, nymph and satyr, smile!' Monica took a photograph of them both with the statue. 'Much better than selfies at our age. Too many pixels for comfort after fifty.'

'Come on,' Hugo gestured to Angela, 'I said we'd explore the gardens. Let's go!'

They walked off together towards the very top of the garden where there was a shaded colonnaded walkway.

*That man,* thought Monica, watching them with interest, *is making himself very much at home.*

Angela and Hugo passed a stand of yew trees, which always seemed so Italian to Angela, and round the corner, where there was a view of open headland.

'This place is so huge.' Angela looked around her, intrigued. 'I've never even been up here before.'

'Probably the biggest property on the whole coastline,' commented Hugo. And then, deliberately looking straight at her, 'and certainly the one with the best views.'

Angela laughed. He took her hand and led her into the hidden space under the colonnade. 'This was where we had our den when I was a little kid. We used to hide from everyone. We'd hear them calling us in to meals and stay put. The gardener knew we were here but pretended to be deaf.'

'You must—' she began, but didn't finish because he had pulled her into his arms and was kissing her.

Monica stood in her bedroom willing herself to open her wardrobe. Brian's ashes were in a wooden box with a cat carved on it. It was singularly inappropriate because Brian was a dog person, but it had been the only thing to hand the right size to pack.

She got the box out and put it on her dressing table. She'd been mulling over this idea for a while now, and as Martin had shown an interest too, the plan had crystallized in her mind. She would go to Mount Vesuvius, a place she and Brian had always planned to visit together, and scatter his ashes into the crater. She found herself smiling. What more perfect 'ashes to ashes' setting could there be than that?

She wanted to make the whole thing into a ritual that Brian would have appreciated. She wasn't sure how to do it yet, but there was a small local travel agency she'd noticed in Lerini. She would buy candles to bring as well. She had intended to do it alone but she had a feeling Martin wouldn't laugh at the idea, and that if she asked him not to, he wouldn't tell the others. It wasn't that she didn't trust them not to mock or laugh at her, she just wanted to keep the ceremony to herself.

She kissed the box and whispered. 'Still missing you. Not long now,' she promised, 'and you'll be blowing in the wind.'

This made her think of Martin and his desire so many years ago to be the new Bob Dylan. It seemed rather ludicrous, to look at him now. But time played tricks on all of us. And especially on our dreams.

Monica caught the bus into Lerini. The travel agency wasn't far from her friend the antiques dealer and she couldn't help glancing in the window. A musical instrument nestled among the stuffed birds, lacy shawls and statues of various Greek gods. Seeing her looking, the lady came out to say hello. '*Buongiorno*, Monica, are you thinking of learning the mandolin?' she asked in her breakneck Italian.

Monica laughed. 'Is that what it is? I was wondering.' She paused a moment. 'Though if you ever get a guitar, I might be interested.'

'Too modern for me. But my nephew or my second cousin might know of one. I will get them to ask around.'

Monica wandered on to the travel agency. When she announced what she wanted they studied her curiously. If she had been Italian, they would have shaken their heads and refused. But for the English it was different.

When she got back up to the villa, she found Claire and Martin locked in an intense discussion.

'But look, Claire,' Martin was arguing, 'I just want to see the place. You're spending all your time there and it sounds really interesting. I'd love to look around a lemon grove.'

'Garden,' Claire corrected automatically. 'They call them gardens, not groves.'

'Garden, then. I mean, you can't come here and not visit a lemon garden. Lerini lemons are famous all over the world.'

'I'll see if it's convenient. Of course there are other lemon tours you could take. Luca's isn't the only one.'

Monica had done all she could to help Claire out, but she was beginning to feel annoyed on Martin's behalf that no one was being fair to him.

'Ah, but that wouldn't be the same, would it?' she intervened. 'I mean, Luca's lemon gardens are obviously the best. And so conveniently near Lerini. I'm sure he would show Martin around the gardens and explain how it works. If you asked him very nicely.'

Claire shot her a furious look.

'Tell you what, I'll come with Martin, shall I? I mean, he and I seem to be doing an awful lot of sightseeing lately,' she added ironically. 'We could put this on our list.'

'Thank you, Monica. That'd be very kind.' Her tone was so acid that even Martin noticed and looked confused. Why should Claire mind so much if he visited her damn lemon grove?

Monica decided to make a quick exit and go for a swim. On the hall table, propped up against a Chinese jar, was a postcard of a small bird. Monica turned it over.

It was addressed to her and it was from Tony.

*Thanks for helping*, it read. *Sadly, no luck. I am going back to London. Love Tony. PS Ask Hugo Robertson why he was so diligently photographing* The Annunciation.

Monica put the card in her bag and stood thoughtfully in the hall for a moment. Hugo had been photographing the nymph too. And not just with Angela standing next to it.

# *Fourteen*

---

Luca was clearly feeling very guilty, because he went to some trouble for Martin's visit, sending a taxi to fetch them and standing outside the front gate of the gardens himself to greet them.

Surely Martin must suspect something, Monica thought, from Claire's uneasy manner and Luca's over-formal friendliness, but this was undercut by Luca's aged father, Bruno, who danced about like a sprightly leprechaun shaking anyone's hand and being so welcoming that everyone had to laugh at his antics.

Luca began with the family museum, which clearly held Martin spellbound. It was the era of history, just out of living memory, that most fascinated him, he insisted.

'I used to dream of setting up a bank of oral memories,' Martin explained, and asked yet another question about working practices in the nineteenth century.

'You still could,' Claire replied with more acid than was called for. 'You have plenty of time now you're retired.'

'Tell us more about what you do if the trees aren't producing,' chipped in Monica quickly.

Luca outlined in great detail how they grafted bitter orange onto the ailing lemon trees and still miraculously ended up with lemons, not oranges. 'Though people laugh very much,' he smiled round at them, 'when sometimes you get both lemon and orange on the same tree.'

He led them out onto the high, thin terraces of the lemon gardens, shady and cool and fragrant out of the hot sun. He plucked a lemon off a tree and bit straight into it. 'Lerini lemons are famous for being so sweet you can eat the whole fruit.'

'I thought the whole point of lemons was that they were sharp and acid,' whispered Martin.

Luca explained at great length, rather too great for Monica, how the branches of the lemon tree were fastened to the over-hanging pergolas that gave them shade and helped support the weight of the lemons with chestnut fastenings. But Martin was fascinated.

Strange, she thought, Martin and Luca weren't so different, after all, except that Luca had the sophistication and polish Martin lacked, though this wasn't a thought Claire would appreciate.

Claire, she could see, was visibly drooping, possibly with the underlying tension of the occasion, and when Martin and Luca disappeared up to the highest terraces, she suggested that Monica and she go back to the covered terrace for a coffee.

'When are you going to tell him?' Monica demanded as soon as they were alone. 'You'll have to tell him soon, you know. It really isn't fair just to string him along.'

'I know.' Claire looked suddenly vulnerable and guilt-ridden.

'And your son?'

'It'll be a shock but Evan's a grown man. Besides, I think he'll understand.'

'That's lucky.'

'Don't be mean, Monica,' Claire flashed. 'I'm not doing this to hurt anyone.'

'I'm sorry. It's just that Martin told me he knew you'd come here because you needed to get away from him and that he wanted you to be happy.'

'Martin told you that?' Claire asked incredulously.

'Perhaps he's more understanding than you think,' Monica said gently.

'Well, if he is, he could have shown it sooner.'

'Yes. I think he can see that himself.'

'You two seem to have done a lot of talking.' Was there a hint of jealousy in her voice?

'You can't read guidebooks all the time,' Monica pointed out.

'Thanks, Monica, for doing this.'

They could hear the two men coming back down the hillside, chatting away. Luca seemed to have forgotten the awkwardness of the situation in his desire to convey his love of growing lemons.

Claire began to lay out a cold lunch from the terrace fridge, letting herself imagine for a moment that this was her fantasy restaurant. Prosciutto, salami, cheese, olives and bread. They heard Bruno singing to himself as he approached with a bottle of the wine they made themselves and a fistful of glasses. He poured them each a glass as Luca and Martin arrived.

He raised his own, a gleeful expression lighting up his rheumy old eyes. '*A Chiara*,' he announced, '*la nuova fidanzata di Luca!*'

Martin nodded and sipped away. Thank God, Monica

thought gratefully, he doesn't speak a bloody word of Italian or he would have known he'd just toasted his own wife as Luca's new fiancée.

'Stupid old man!' The gathering was interrupted by a shrill and irritated female voice. 'You never know what nonsense he'll dream up next!'

'Graziella!' The word came out like an accusation. Luca stood staring at a heavily made-up woman with perfect Italian hair, in a well-cut linen suit and unsuitably high heels. 'What are you doing here?'

'I have come home, Luca. City living does not suit me. I have been yearning for the simple life. Who are these people?'

She looked around the group, clearly unimpressed with what she found.

Claire stood up, about to brazen it out, when Monica took her arm and gently pulled her down. 'We are on a lemon tour,' Monica announced diplomatically.

'You will not keep this place going on three visitors, with free lunch included,' Graziella commented acidly. 'Especially as your father will eat most of it.' She picked up her Prada bag and Max Mara trench coat. 'I am going to meet Bianca from school. My bags are at the house but I had to leave them in the garden as I had no key.' She held out her hand and Luca meekly gave her his.

As soon as she'd gone, Monica shepherded Martin and Claire out, leaving the shell-shocked Luca to work out what to do.

'You should have let me face her down, the horrible cow,' Claire whispered fiercely to Monica.

'I know the type. She'll only stay five minutes,' Monica insisted. 'Unless she thinks she's got a rival. Then you'll never get rid of her.'

Claire thought about this as they walked back to the piazza.

'What on earth was all that about?' Martin asked.

Claire looked at Monica helplessly.

'Italians,' Monica replied. 'Hopelessly emotional. I bet you don't get much of that in Twickenham.'

'No,' replied Martin, surprising them. 'I rather enjoyed it. Especially the old boy. Bruno, was it? Didn't seem like a stupid old man to me. Gave me some excellent advice on how to graft my roses.' He looked keenly at his wife. 'He seemed to think you'd got pretty friendly with his son Luca, as a matter of fact. I expect you'll get round to filling me in soon, but remember one thing: I'm not as daft as you say Bruno is.'

The journey back to the villa was spent in awkward silence. Even Monica couldn't think of anything appropriate to lighten the atmosphere.

As soon as they got back, Claire went straight up to their room and threw herself on the bed. Martin followed her.

'Are you all right, Claire?' he asked gently.

'I don't know, Martin.' She turned her head to the wall. 'I really don't know.'

'You didn't expect Luca's wife to come back,' he stated baldly. 'So when were you going to tell me about him and you?'

For an answer she just cried into the pillow.

'Look,' he answered, his voice hollow, as if he were fighting to keep from giving in to his emotions. 'I don't blame you for wanting to leave.' He sat down heavily on the bed. 'It took you coming here for me to see how your life with me must have been a prison. You're so lively and brave and I was behaving like Henny Penny as if the sky would fall in if I didn't plan every last thing. It must have been hell.'

Claire's amazement even penetrated her misery. 'You were pretty difficult.'

Martin laughed. 'Evan had a heart-to-heart with me. He said he thought you were pretty unhappy. But of course' – now it was his turn to look away – 'neither of us reckoned on a Luca.'

'Maybe there isn't going to be a Luca.'

'I'm afraid I'm not generous enough to say I'm sorry, but I do understand how horrible this must be for you.'

Claire smiled a small bitter smile. 'Maybe not as bad as having to choose.'

'Thank you for that at least.'

'And thank you for trying to understand, even if it isn't what you want.'

They sat in silence, neither knowing what to say next.

Claire sat up. 'I'd better get ready for dinner. I think trying to behave how I normally would is the way to go.'

Martin stood up. 'I'll leave you to it, then.' The habit of changing in front of each other and the everyday bathroom rituals seemed suddenly too intimate.

When Martin had gone, Claire began to cry in earnest. It all seemed so bloody unfair. Graziella with her expensive clothes and her city sophistication seemed almost like sacrilege in that simple setting where Luca was desperately trying to keep a traditional family business afloat after eight generations, and already finding it teetering close to bankruptcy without the addition of an expensive and disinterested wife to consider.

'Crisis on the Italian front,' Gwen Charlesworth told her son Stephen on FaceTime to alert him.

Stephen smiled back at her. He appeared to be on the top of a tower block. 'It's the twenty-fifth floor of the Shard, actually. We're announcing a new project up here. What's the problem?'

'It's bloody Mariella Mathieson. I bumped into her saintly husband Neville. She's planning a sudden visit to Italian gardens and has decided to surprise them at the villa en route. Neville thinks she just can't let Monica out of her sight this long.'

'Oh dear, poor Monica.'

'He's tried to dissuade her, but no dice. Neville's quite a good old sort. He's having to stay home with the drooling boxers. Actually, he looked quite relieved. Better than having to go with Mariella.'

'Come on, Ma, I think your duty's clear.'

'You're going to suggest I go with her, aren't you?'

'No one would be better than you at averting disaster.'

'Yes, but could I bear it?'

'You might enjoy seeing what they're up to. Beatrice left me a message that all is peace and harmony.'

'Not for long, it won't be.'

'I'll pay for you, Ma. Business class all the way.'

Gwen laughed. 'It'd almost be worth it to see Mariella's face. I bet she's travelling economy.'

Stephen smiled his twinkliest smile. 'You can take her to the VIP lounge. Really rub it in. Or maybe she'll be refused by one of those haughty hostesses.'

'I must admit,' Gwen replied with holy glee, 'you do paint a tempting picture.'

'Think of the good you'd be doing.'

'I don't see *you* offering.'

'Having me there would change everything. I'd be the host and they'd suddenly be guests. I like the idea they're feeling really at home.'

'You're a generous man, Stephen.'

'Thank you. I had a generous mother.'

'Go on, get back to ruining London's skyline.'

Stephen said goodbye to his mother then stood for a moment looking out at the dramatic London scene before him. The lights were just beginning to come on all over the city, giving it a magic of its own, different from Lanzarella's yet still powerfully alluring. He wondered how Angela was getting on and thought of calling Drew to find out. He thought again how he'd watched her progress, as well as her TV programmes, but had never had the nerve to approach her directly.

Come on, Stephen, admit it. It was because you felt guilty. He knew that, all those years ago, she must have felt abandoned by him while he enjoyed the heady thrills of being part of the smart set at university. He had become quite the party animal for a while.

What an irony, given that he now lived alone. Like Angela, without even a dog. Life had a way of turning out quite differently from the way you expected it to.

Monica drank her delicious Italian fizz and glanced across at Angela, sitting on the terrace looking out to sea, her face lit by the pink luminescence of the setting sun. But it was the inner radiance that was most obvious. Of all of them, Angela was the one on whom the siren call of this place had had the greatest impact. But it was the mythical sirens who had lured men to their deaths and she suspected it was Angela who was in the greatest danger, not of death but of heartbreak.

For the first time Monica faintly regretted coming to this glorious, beautiful, healing place. She, too, felt a different person but she was also the repository of too many secrets:

Claire's love for Luca and Tony's suspicions about Hugo, not to mention what Luigi and Giovanni and the others were up to.

Was there something strange and dangerous in this villa of the sirens? Would too many people she'd come to care for end up crashing on the rocks beneath?

She felt the need for Constantine, with his reassuring pragmatic cynicism, to get her feet back onto the ground and headed through the stand of holm oaks towards his house.

Despite the increasing heat, Constantine's clothes were unchanged. He still wore his trench coat and Russian hat but at least Spaghetti no longer peeped out of his pocket. Monica knew this because the little dog was snapping furiously at her legs.

'She's a fine little guard dog.' Constantine winked. 'I've taught her to go for journalists. Art critics especially; for those she gets a treat.' He led Monica through the studio, in which her own life-size nude portrait had pride of place.

'Oh, bloody hell!' She hid her eyes. 'Can't you put it somewhere a bit more discreet?'

He shook his head then rooted about for two bottles of, improbably, Fuller's London Pride.

'I import it specially. A true taste of London. Can't abide this bloody piss they call lager. Come on, try one.'

He looked the painting over. 'Anyway, I'm proud of it. As a matter of fact, I'm planning a little show.'

'Not with that in it, you're not.'

'My dear, don't be so prudish. Think of Picasso and Françoise Gilot, or Lizzie Siddal and the Pre-Raphaelites. What would Manet have done if Olympia had refused to let him show the painting that stunned the world just because she didn't have any clothes on?'

Monica tasted her beer and decided she didn't like it. 'Yes, but look at Sargent's *Madame X*. It ruined her life just because in the painting one of her straps had fallen down and everyone thought she was a whore.'

'No one is going to think you are a whore,' Constantine reassured her.

'I think I'm rather insulted by that,' Monica teased.

'And at least you don't look like a librarian.' He smiled wickedly.

'Touché.'

Now, we must go out on the terrace. It's time to feed my Venus flytrap.'

He led them out into the blinding sun of his amazing eyrie hanging right out over the sea. An unsettling green plant sat in the middle of a white table which opened its yawning red mouth and snapped shut its vicious-looking red spikes when Constantine fed it with flies.

'That is truly disgusting,' Monica complained.

'It's a metaphor for modern life. The Venus flytrap is the greedy capitalist and the flies are ordinary people like you and me. I am about to paint it for my next show.'

'Constantine, there is no one on the planet who would ever describe you as ordinary.'

'Thank you.' Constantine bowed with sudden dignity like an ambassador at the UN. 'Now to what pleasure do I owe this visit?'

'I wanted to ask what you make of something.'

'Fire away. Now we've fed my little carnivore Guido will bring us something to eat.'

As soon as they'd sat down, Guido appeared, smiling happily, and spread a feast of salt and pepper squid, tomato and olive oil bruschetta, a green salad and home-made bread in front of them.

311

'And a glass of local wine for the lady,' announced Guido gleefully. 'I cannot believe she wants to drink that nasty beer.'

Monica took it gratefully.

'You're becoming positively Italian, my dear.'

Like a dark cloud, the idea of home and the reality of no job and very little money swooped down on Monica. 'It's not surprising, considering the alternative.'

'Surely it can't be that grim in Great Missenden.'

'You haven't met my mother. Or her boxers.'

'But why do you have to live with your mother? You are far too old, if you don't mind me saying.'

'Something went wrong with our pensions. I'm not quite sure what, but it means I have what the state gives us and a tiny bit more, but I can't even claim it yet.' Monica went quiet. The idea was too depressing to contemplate.

'And you're thinking how can this one old man live in this house, which costs twenty million euros.'

'My God, does it?' She looked round reverently. 'I had no idea.'

'And think what your little property next door must be valued at.'

'Well, that's kind of what I came about. And, of course, for the delight of your company.'

'You don't have to waste your time on flattery. I've never cared what people think of me.'

'Even the ones who like you,' Monica dared.

'Well, maybe them a bit more. Now what's all this about?'

'I caught Hugo Robertson photographing *The Annunciation* and then one of the statues in the garden. Claire's always said she thought it had to be by an amazing sculptor.'

'We'll have to sneak up and have a look at nightfall. I had heard there were some important pieces up at the villa.'

'I do have some photographs on my phone, as a matter of fact.'

She produced the snap of Angela, Hugo and the nymph. 'It doesn't do her justice, of course. The workmanship is extraordinary. You could swear the statue's living and breathing.'

'My God!' Constantine's usual deadbeat style deserted him. 'That *is* something. I think it could be a Bernini! With his statues, you feel as if he's caught a fleeting moment. See how the statue is kneeling, staring into the depths of the pond as if she's just glimpsed something. Look at the intensity on her face! She knows in just a flash it will be gone.'

Monica caught his excitement. 'Do you think it could be quite valuable?'

'If it really is a Bernini, then yes, it could be worth a great deal. We need some expert advice.'

'But surely Stephen would know?'

'You'd think so, but Stephen Charlesworth is a curious owner. Guido tells me they picked up the statue in some little antiques place because his wife liked it. The gardener moans that it's difficult to keep clean.'

'And *The Annunciation*,' Monica persisted, 'I have this feeling that it's very special, not some run-of-the-mill fresco knocked up by some local artist.'

'All the more reason for Mr Robertson to want to get his hands on the villa.'

'The trouble is, Angela thinks it's her he wants to get his hands on.'

'That makes things tricky, I can see that, and if you open her eyes, she'll never forgive you. Well, we'd better watch him carefully, hadn't we?'

*

313

When she got back to the villa, Monica stopped for a moment to listen.

Someone was playing a guitar and singing 'Lay Lady Lay'. She stood entranced, all the years peeling back to when she was a lonely student of nineteen lying across her narrow college bed listening to the line about the man whose hands were dirty but his heart was clean and that she was the best thing that he'd ever seen, and yearning for someone to feel that way about her. When somebody did, he hadn't been at all a romantic figure; he'd been small, slightly plump, with glasses and a delightfully endearing smile, and a quite surprising talent in bed.

Of course, today's singer wasn't Brian but Martin, and as she approached she could see that the passion and delight he took in the music, and especially how well he played and sang, were both surprising and rather moving.

She didn't want to disturb him and make him suddenly self-conscious, so she went round the side of the house towards her room, hoping she'd be able to hear some more through her open window. In the hall Beatrice jumped on her, all smiles.

'The nephew of Signora Rosa in the shop in Lerini, he come with this guitar for you and Mr Martin, he borrow it.' Beatrice handed over a note from the antiques lady saying they were welcome to try it out and if they liked it, they could discuss a price later.

Claire, she noted, was reading in the salon, with the door to the terrace firmly closed. How very small-minded of her.

She jumped up when she saw Monica. 'Really, Monica, I think this is most peculiar and quite unnecessary of you to get Martin a guitar – at least, we assume it's for Martin since none of the rest of us play.'

'The lady in the antiques shop tracked it down through her nephew. I had no idea she'd be as efficient as this. And don't worry, it's only on approval.'

'Yes, but it's still rather weird of you, if you don't mind me saying so.'

But Monica found she did rather mind.

'Oh come on, Claire,' Sylvie had wafted in and was clearly as enchanted as Monica, 'anyone'd think you were jealous but for the fact that you've been so caught up with this Luca.'

'Oh shut up, the pair of you!' Claire closed her book and disappeared upstairs.

'We ought to be more sympathetic really,' the kind Monica was reasserting itself.

'Nonsense. You've been extremely generous looking after her husband for her when he was *de trop*, so she could go off playing Oranges and Lemons. Now it's all getting a bit sticky she'd be better off being nice to us instead of slamming off like a flouncy teenager.'

By supper time, Claire seemed to have worked this out for herself, and was being her old self again. 'Sorry for being a cow, everyone,' she murmured so Martin could hear.

That evening after dinner they all drifted onto the terrace, the sky above like dark blue velvet studded with flirtatiously twinkling stars, a kind of peace descending despite all the swirling tensions, and listened to Martin sitting in the shadows half hidden by a wall of fragrant wisteria.

'It's amazing how playing a guitar changes your image,' whispered Sylvie. 'Martin actually looks quite sexy.'

'Do you still want to come to Vesuvius?' Monica asked Martin as she helped herself to coffee and croissants next morning. 'I mean, now that Claire won't be disappearing off to Lerini all the time?'

'Hang around waiting to see if my wife starts to want me here, you mean?' he asked bitterly. Then laughed. 'And the answer is yes, I would very much like to come to Mount Vesuvius. It's firmly on my bucket list.'

'We won't need to leave till late afternoon, so I thought I'd have a swim.'

'Isn't it quite a big expedition? Why leave so late?'

'Hard though this is going to be for you, Martin, I am in charge today.'

'OK boss.' He grinned.

Angela had plans to go on a day trip to Ischia, so that left Claire and Sylvie.

'Why don't I come to Vesuvius as well?' Claire suggested.

There was an ominous pause. 'The thing is, Claire, it's a bit private.' Monica didn't want to tell them all she was going to scatter her husband's ashes yet she could see this must sound distinctly odd.

'But it's OK for Bob Dylan here to come along?'

'We made the arrangement when you were too busy to see me, you may recall,' Martin reminded Claire, which didn't seem to do a thing for her mood.

'So I have to kick my heels on my own all day?'

'Come for a swim this morning. And maybe later you could try out some more amazing lemon recipes with Immaculata,' Monica suggested.

'Are you trying to be funny, Monica?'

In the end, Sylvie dragged Claire off to look around the shops in Lerini.

Monica couldn't believe how nervous she felt. Everything needed to be done just right today. She'd even gone as far as ordering a taxi to take them there.

By the time it arrived at the back steps, Monica was feeling exceptionally anxious.

'A taxi all the way to Vesuvius?' Martin whistled. 'Isn't that ridiculously expensive?'

'Yes, but I thought the occasion deserved no less. Besides it's cheaper than hiring a car and bumping into an Italian on a motorbike.'

'So are most things,' Martin agreed.

'I still can't work out why we're going so late.' Martin, ever the organizer, could only see it as wasting half the day. 'What about lunch? Is there a cafe at Vesuvius?'

'Immaculata's made us a packed lunch.' Monica indicated the large carrier bag. 'I think she mistook us for a Roman legion. Ham, cheese, olives, pizza slices, caprese salad, a bottle of red wine and some water.'

'That should do us. Where do you want to eat it?'

'Hands off. Didn't I tell you I was in charge? I'll tell you when.'

'Forget librarian. You'd have made an excellent headmistress.'

'Thank you, Martin.'

The taxi caused great excitement in the kitchen as it was driven by Cesare, yet another second cousin of Beatrice's, so quite a large party assembled to wave them goodbye.

It took an hour to get to the lower slopes of Mount Vesuvius, still verdant even in the hot spring, with its bald crater on top like the tonsure on a green-haired monk.

Cesare dropped them in the car park nearest the crater.

'Crater very dangerous,' he informed them. 'Stay away from edge.' He agreed to return for them in three hours' time.

'What on earth are we going to do here for three hours?' Martin asked.

'You'll see. First, we're going to have a late lunch or an early supper.'

She led them away from all the other tourists, back down the slopes in the opposite direction from the crater.

'Monica,' Martin enquired. 'Aren't we going the wrong way?'

'Will you shut up and just follow me?'

'As long as you promise me this isn't going to involve me ending up in the crater as some pagan sacrifice?'

'Yes, Martin, I can promise you that.'

They walked down a surprisingly wooded trail following a narrow and quite muddy path, pushing brambles and over-hanging branches out of their way.

'Bad things happen in the dark forest,' Martin reminded her with a grin.

'Martin,' was Monica's brisk reply. 'Shut up and enjoy it.'

They kept up their ramble in silence until they came to an opening up ahead. Monica stood back to let Martin pass beneath the branches into the clearing.

'Sir, your table.' Monica indicated a grassy knoll.

They began to spread the food out on the cloth Beatrice had provided. As well as the rest of the food, there was crispy bread, and amazing ripe peaches.

They opened the wine and sat listening to the birdsong, savouring a moment of extraordinary peace.

'OK,' Martin said as they packed up, in a tone that in any-one else Monica would have taken as flirtatious, 'I'm in your hands. So, headmistress, what are we doing next?'

Monica laughed and, to Martin's amazement, led them, not back to the crater, but down another path. 'This is beginning to feel like a fairy tale. Will I find a princess who needs to be freed in the middle of the forest?'

'Not exactly a princess, more a prince,' Monica answered mysteriously.

They trudged on for another twenty minutes until they came out onto a plateau where, highly improbably, there was a row of what looked like wooden stables.

A man with longish hair, deeply tanned and wearing blue jeans and a faded waistcoat, walked towards them. 'Hi, I'm Nick. I gather you've booked a rather special ride today.'

'As far up as we can go,' Monica replied.

He nodded. 'You'll have to walk the last part, I'm afraid. It's only twenty minutes and you'll be grateful to know, there is a path.'

'Great,' Monica thanked him. 'Is that a Buckinghamshire accent?' she added.

He grinned. 'Born in Beaconsfield.'

'I live down the road. I worked at Buckingham University.' She waited for the laugh. There wasn't one.

'Well, this is strange.' He smiled at her warmly. 'Two folks from Bucks on the top of Mount Vesuvius.'

'There's only one problem.' Martin pointed out a shade testily. 'I can't ride.'

Nick shook his head. 'You really don't need to. Whole families do it with little kids. The horses are so used to the route they could do it blindfold. Plus, they couldn't be calmer.'

Martin only looked half convinced as they were led to the small ranch house. It was also entirely wooden, with a cosy wood-burning stove and colourful decorations, as if it would be happier in the Wild West than on Mount Vesuvius.

'The customers like it.'

'Do they stay here?'

'No, but we have dinners, Valentine parties, that sort of stuff. Are you just about ready to go? Let's go and saddle up.'

The ponies were black and white or brown with long fair fringes and they looked reassuringly gentle.

'No helmets?' asked Martin, shocked.

'They don't really go in for that sort of thing around here.'

'Come on, Martin,' Monica giggled, 'relax. It's an adventure!'

Martin smiled reluctantly. 'No wonder I didn't recognize it.'

'I'll take you along the trail to the crater path then let you get on with it. I gather you have something special to do.'

'Yes.' Monica didn't add any further explanation.

They headed out of the stables and up the overgrown path.

'You ride well,' Nick commented to Monica.

'I learned as a child. Pony club and all that but I didn't meet my mother's rigorous standards.' It was wonderful how she had finally managed to exorcise her mother while she'd been here and had started to become another person. The Lanzarella effect again.

For just an instant her pony stumbled in the mud then instantly regained its balance. She glanced round at Martin. He was hanging on for dear life. She couldn't help feeling disappointed. She'd seen a ride on Vesuvius at sunset as something wonderful rather than an endurance test, but, of course, she was a rider. Just as well the last bit was on foot.

After about twenty minutes, the dusk began to fall, pink and soft. Nick called the horses to a halt. 'Would you like me to wait here or can you find your way back?'

'We'll be fine, thanks, Nick.'

'I'll just tie them up to the post, then. See you a little later. Just remember, they close the path just before nightfall.'

'We won't be long.'

They headed up the trail, noticing that, rather strangely, they were the only walkers.

'All gone back to their hotels already,' said Monica.

Martin's silence implied that he wouldn't mind joining them.

Ten minutes later they were at the crater's edge, looking down into the lava pit that had caused so much death and devastation to Pompeii.

'You feel the power, don't you?' Monica shivered.

'I was just thinking it reminded me of the gravel pits outside Bognor where my brother and I used to play. I'm teasing. I'm teasing.'

Monica took the box out of her rucksack. 'I'm going to ask you something a bit weird, so promise you won't laugh.'

'OK.'

'Could you sing "Blowing in the Wind" for me?'

Martin started to laugh, then stopped. 'Of course. Though without a guitar I can't vouch for its tunefulness.'

He began to sing as Monica stood as close as she could to the edge and began to scatter Brian's ashes into the crater.

'Ashes to ashes,' Monica said softly. 'Dust to dust. Goodbye, my darling.'

And she found she was crying, a tiny bit of ash streaking her face.

'Would it be sacrilege to Brian if I just put my arm round you?' Martin asked. 'Thank you for letting me be here at this special moment.'

'Thank you for singing. He loved that song.'

'He had very good taste, then.'

'Time we got back,' she said, 'or I might accidentally push you into the crater in some weird pagan ceremony.'

They walked back to the horses in silence, taking in the beauty of the evening and the soft translucent mist that was quietly descending on the volcano. On the way back they came across a small portrait of the Virgin Mary holding Jesus, with the volcano in the background.

'I hope the horses have run away and we can walk,' Martin murmured.

But the horses were firmly tied up, nibbling quietly.

Martin climbed on and gave his pony what he took to be a gentle kick. The pony, delighted to be liberated at last, started to gallop back down the hillside to the stable with Martin terrified and clinging to its mane, convinced it would trip on a tangled root or lose its footing down a rabbit hole. About halfway down he willed himself to follow the animal's movement, to relax and lean forward. Miraculously, he began to actually enjoy himself.

Monica was just behind him. By the time they reached the stables Martin was laughing. 'Thank you, Monica,' he said softly as they both climbed down, 'for the adventure and for including me in such a personal moment.'

'Welcome back!' Nick was striding towards them through the gloom. 'How about a glass of something to commemorate the moment and I'll drive you back to the car park.'

'What a pity,' Martin laughed, 'I was hoping we could ride back in pitch-darkness.'

Inside the cosy warmth of the ranch house the stove blazed and there was a wooden table with an open bottle of wine and three glasses. Monica was grateful that no questions were asked about why she'd wanted to visit the crater at sunset.

'Tell me,' Monica sipped her wine, 'what is the painting of the Virgin Mary about?'

'It's a plea to the Mother of God to protect all those who live in the shadow of the volcano.'

Monica thought of her husband and how death had come to him without any warning. She raised her glass towards the fire. 'I suppose we all live in the shadow of the volcano one way or another.'

Nick offered to guide them back to the car park. 'You could lose your footing in the dark – though, to be honest, it's more likely to be a twisted ankle than falling into the crater.'

'Don't you find it a bit lonely on your own out here?' Monica asked.

'It's why I took the place. Besides, it's only for the season. Then it's back to Beaconsfield and a bit of supply teaching.'

'That sounds an interesting contrast, doesn't it, Martin?'

'Do you manage to make a living?' Martin asked, ever practical.

'Just about. I do some wildlife photography. That helps.'

'Now that *would* be interesting. What do you get around here?'

'Porcupine, marten, the occasional wildcat. And this year a pair of golden eagles.'

Monica listened, spellbound, thinking of the different ways people found to live. She was going to have to be more creative about finding work when she went home. She shuddered, suddenly feeling the chill, and decided she didn't want to think about that. Was it just because he was a man that Nick could carve out this seemingly romantic life? After all, he couldn't be much younger than she was. Monica glanced across at him. He had penetrating blue eyes and the self-contained air of someone used to his own company. And yet his occasional flashes of humour made her think that he might be a good teacher, guiding the pupils but knowing when to leave them alone.

Beatrice's cousin was waiting in the car park, with big news. 'Very worried about you at Le Sirenuse. Worried you are at bottom of crater. Talk of calling police but Beatrice say, no, Cesare will bring them home fine,' he added proudly.

'Damn!' Monica realized that the drawback of living in each other's pockets was that there was absolutely no privacy. She had seen tonight's ritual as concerning no one but herself. She was suddenly conscious of feeling hot and sweaty so she slipped into the car park toilets. Somewhat crazily, she'd brought her shift dress, thinking she might dress up for the scattering. She'd put it on now – might as well look her best to face a wave of disapproval.

When they got back to the villa, every light in the entire place seemed to be blazing, even though it was gone midnight. Beatrice hugged Monica as if she'd survived the Pompeiian earthquake rather than a few twilight hours on Vesuvius.

They walked into the salon to be leapt on by Claire and Sylvie. 'Are you *mad*, going up Vesuvius at this time of night? It's not as if you're irresponsible kids or anything. You could both be dead! What on earth possessed you?'

'As a matter of fact,' Monica summoned as much dignity as she could, 'I was scattering the ashes of my husband Brian into the crater. Ashes to ashes. And Martin very kindly sang me Brian's favourite song while I scattered.'

'Not "Blowin' in the Wind"?' murmured Claire.

'As a matter of fact, yes.' Monica refused to feel mocked.

'Cut it out, Claire,' Sylvie defended Monica. 'It's a touching gesture. Anyone would think you were a wee bit put out.'

Claire turned away in disgust. What an utterly bloody ridiculous suggestion.

'For goodness' sake, Monica,' interrupted a loud, imperious voice from the back of the room. 'What were you thinking, taking such risks? The crater of Vesuvius in the middle of the night! And how selfish to involve someone else's husband as well. Brian's been dead for over a year; couldn't you find somewhere more appropriate to scatter him?'

Monica swirled round to face her mother, Mariella, who she thought was safely in Great Missenden, hundreds of miles away.

# *Fifteen*

'Ma! What are you doing here?' Monica tried to keep the ludicrous disappointment from her voice. At the villa, amongst friends, she had felt a different person.

'What on earth are you wearing, Monica?' Mariella's gimlet gaze swept over the shift dress. 'Mutton dressed as lamb, if ever I saw it. You're over sixty, for God's sake.'

They all watched as Monica's new-found confidence seemed to deflate in front of them like a flat tyre.

'As a matter of fact,' Sylvie pounced to her defence, a lioness in orange and purple silk, 'I helped her choose that. We all think it looks wonderful.'

Mariella merely raised an eyebrow as her gaze swept over Sylvie's Bohemian outfit.

'As a matter of fact,' Mariella finally addressed Monica's question, 'I came with Gwen Charlesworth. Our plane was delayed. We were meant to be at a hotel down the road she particularly loved and now it's changed so much she can't bring herself to stay, so she decided to drop in on you.'

They all looked horrified, wondering how they'd fit everyone in.

'Don't worry, it's only for a few days,' she said cuttingly. 'I'm not sure we could stand it for longer. Is there any chance of something to eat?'

'I'll go and talk to Beatrice,' Sylvie conceded. 'How many is it for?'

'Just us two. I'm sure Monica will have eaten on her mountain.'

Monica nodded, still subdued. 'The stables owner gave us some food and wine. We're fine.'

'You mean you actually rode horses on the crater of Vesuvius,' Mariella persisted. 'Have you gone mad?'

'Martin couldn't, anyway. He loathes horses,' Claire commented scathingly.

'As a matter of fact, I did,' Martin challenged. 'I even had a gallop.'

Claire shook her head, stunned.

'You actually let a man who'd never ridden a horse gallop near a lethal crater?' Mariella made it sound as if it were one step away from first-degree murder.

'No helmet either,' Martin added provocatively. He'd taken an instant dislike to this overbearing old biddy.

Mariella's silence could have transformed the deserts of Arizona into an arctic waste.

'It wasn't like that,' Monica tried to protest. 'We were in absolutely no danger.'

They were distracted temporarily from the drama by the sound of a fast car racing up the driveway. Moments later a glowing Angela appeared in the salon.

'Everyone still up?' She sounded surprised.

'You look like you could dance all night, as the song goes.' Sylvie smiled.

Angela laughed. 'Something like that.'

They all turned as Gwen appeared from the kitchen, Beatrice and Immaculata clucking in her train carrying plates of cold meat and cheese.

'My dear,' Gwen shook her hand, 'are you Angela?'

Angela acknowledged that indeed she was.

'And you're Gwen. I've heard so much about you from Sylvie and Monica.'

'And no doubt you're bored already. But, my dear, what has your young man done to my lovely hotel?'

Angela stood, wondering angrily if the others had supplied this 'young man' business, while the torrent came inexorably in her direction.

'It used to be *such* a nice hotel; my favourite in the whole world. A genuine palazzo. A little run-down but only in the most charming way. It oozed character and friendliness. The owner would come and greet you and give you a glass of his own wine, grown on the terraces just below. The staff couldn't have been more helpful.' Angela attempted to stem the flow with a small defence of Hugo, but the flood continued unabated, picking up speed as it went. 'But they are all gone! And now it's like going into a hotel you could find anywhere from Singapore to Sydney instead of the most beautiful place on earth! My dear, it's a crime! A heinous crime! Excuse me for speaking frankly.'

Finally, the tide stopped. Obviously, Gwen wanted hotels to stay as they had been in the nineteenth century, Angela decided, with no bathrooms and a hot and cold British eccentric in every room.

'Hotels do have to move with the times.' Angela made the mistake of sounding ever-so-slightly patronizing. 'People want different things from them now.'

Gwen surveyed this tall, confident, slightly over-made-up

woman who clearly thought that since she'd been on TV she was a superior being, and conceived one of her rare dislikes.

'Is that the case? Obviously, we couldn't stay there, so my son insisted we come up here. I understand he left a message with Beatrice.'

Beatrice nodded enthusiastically.

'I'm afraid Beatrice got a little carried away and removed your things from the terrace room and installed me in it.'

Behind them, Sylvie and Claire exchanged a suppressed giggle.

Angela looked on, for once lost for words.

'And she's put Mariella in the second-best bedroom, laughingly called the Doom Room because of the painting.'

'Thank God for that,' muttered Martin. 'We can get away from that bloody awful painting.'

'But where are we going?' Angela asked, knowing she was playing this whole thing badly. She should have instantly agreed that Gwen have the best room.

'Stephen suggested you could have our rooms in the hotel. Or, otherwise, Beatrice tells me Sylvie has prepared two more guest rooms in the wing. I'm so sorry, my dear. I'm sure we can sort it out in the morning.'

'Come on, Ange,' Sylvie reminded her mischievously, 'you did offer to swap ages ago!'

'But there aren't any beds!'

'Beatrice's cousin has just arrived with camp beds in his pickup.'

'Right,' Claire announced. 'I'm off to find my new accommodation.'

'Me too,' Martin teased. 'As long as it isn't some TV makeover mock-up that falls apart when you touch it.'

'*Martin*,' Sylvie replied in wounded tones.

'I'm sure it'll be fine.' Angela made herself sound positive. This was Stephen's mother, for God's sake, the owner by proxy. 'This is virtually your house. What an awful guest I am after how incredibly kind your son's been.'

'Just as well,' Gwen twinkled, 'Beatrice has already hung up all your clothes in what I'm told is the Sylvie Sutton Seraglio!'

'Do I get a free eunuch to massage my temples?' Angela tried to redeem herself for her bad behaviour.

'I think eunuchs are extra.' Gwen softened. Maybe Angela wasn't *so* bad after all. 'I bet you could get them on room service at that smart hotel of yours.'

Monica, who'd been silent, suddenly thought of Tony and the accusation over the hen party. She was quite sure that with Hugo owning the hotel, you could order absolutely anything you wanted – probably things a lot more exotic than a eunuch.

She wondered how Tony was. Surely he hadn't given up on Sylvie completely?

Gwen slept extremely well, as she always did. The next morning, she sat out on the terrace with her iPad planning the day's activities before anyone else was even up, drinking her usual hot water and lemon. The sound of a splash made her look towards the pool. Whoever it was, they were an excellent swimmer, head in the water, perfect crawl for thirty lengths. Gwen enjoyed counting them. The swimmer then got out of the water, removed her cap and shook out her hair.

It was Monica. It struck her that it was a pity that they'd had to come here instead of the hotel, because Monica, without Mariella's baleful influence, seemed to be flowering just as bountifully as the lemon blossom that adorned the place.

Spring had come for Monica at last and she was damned if she'd let Mariella get out the bug spray to stop her turning into a butterfly.

She waved to Monica, who was walking along the path in a wine-red swimsuit which curved in all the right places. Who would have thought that? At home she always dressed in what looked like beige bin liners, but here her clothes had definitely taken a turn for the better.

'Monica, my dear, I must tell you I only came with your mother because I thought it might make things easier for you. You mustn't let her get to you. And, may I say, you look quite wonderful in that swimsuit?'

Monica felt a burden being lifted and hugged Gwen. She waved happily as she went up to change. Gwen was right. She mustn't let her mother undermine her. She wasn't Mousy Monica any more.

The next thing Gwen intended to do this morning was to go and see the old owners of her beloved Hotel Bellavista, now ridiculously named the Hotel of the Gods. What a pretentious name for a pretentious hotel.

At the breakfast table, Mariella took possession of the seat Angela had once sat in, causing just as much resentment.

If anyone should be sitting there, Sylvie thought crossly, it was Stephen's mother Gwen.

'I was just discussing the costs of running a place like this with Beatrice,' Mariella announced.

It was a question, they had to admit, which had fascinated them all.

'And what is an absolute scandal – and something Gwen is going to have to do something about – is that with all these vast gardens and two gardeners, they let their soft fruit go to waste.'

Monica glanced at her mother nervously and wondered how to head her off, but Mariella continued, 'Gwen may slag off expensive hotels but you do get a damn good fruit salad for breakfast. All they've given me is this measly peach.' She surveyed the peach that had come with their home-made croissants as if it were guilty as charged.

'But just look at it,' Monica enthused. 'And think of those "Ripen at Home" ones we get in England. I bet it's absolutely divine.'

'If I want your opinion, Monica, I'll give it to you.' She smiled a wintry smile at her own joke but since everyone round the table believed that was exactly what she did do, it didn't get much of a laugh.

After breakfast, Martin grabbed Monica's arm and pulled her onto the terrace. 'What's the matter with you, Monica? You're a wonderful woman. How can you let your mother treat you the way she does?'

Claire had glimpsed them slipping away and instantly followed.

'You should definitely believe your new admirer, Monica,' she said sharply. 'Martin's the Sigmund Freud of knowing how other people feel!'

Martin looked as if he was going to argue, but then he shook his head and disappeared into the gardens instead.

Monica faced Claire square on. 'Can't you see that you do to Martin just what my mother does to me? Put him down when he's trying to change? Or maybe you actually like things the way they are. It means you don't have to feel guilty about lovely Luca! It's all Martin's fault because he's the way he is, not yours. Martin isn't falling for me. It's just that I'm more sympathetic to him than you are. You should try it some time. And for what it's worth, I think he is trying to be different. Maybe you ought to notice now and then.'

Claire said nothing and went back into the house, leaving Monica on the terrace to ponder how true the observation was about her mother as well.

Her mother was being extra poisonous because her daughter was gaining independence.

In fact, Monica's words had had more impact on Claire than she thought. Martin did seem different here – less inflexible and kinder. The sensible side of Claire knew that she should try and piece her life back together with Martin. But was it too late?

Luca himself was behaving strangely and not replying to any of her texts or phone messages. She had even considered joining some other people on a tour of the lemon grove, if only to see how he was, but had rejected the scheme. What if his wife was there too?

She remembered that on one day of the week Luca picked up his daughter Bianca from school and they went for a cake and a hot chocolate, an old tradition from when Bianca was small that they both liked to keep up. What day did they do it?

She seemed to remember that it was today.

Making the excuse that she wanted to do some sandal shopping in the market, Claire caught the open-top bus down to the town. No matter how preoccupied you might be with other things, the beauty of the place always got to you. There were people on the beach today; no doubt they were foreigners.

Claire leaned back and let herself feel the warm rays on her skin as her hair tossed wildly about her face, and thought about the time they'd spent here. She had been on the brink of making this place her home. Had she been mad, deluded or dreaming? It had all seemed so very real: Luca, sharing his passion for lemon growing, being somewhere where she was needed and noticed. Given that she was only in her sixties, that meant she might have twenty years of work ahead. At home, that would have been mad, but it was different here. Look at Bruno. Look at all the old Italian ladies who still laboured in family businesses or did heavy-duty childcare so that the younger generations could work full-time.

*You're still young and fit,* Claire repeated to herself; *age is just an option now.*

She was still repeating it as she stepped off the bus and headed for the market.

The sandal stall was at the end of the row under a gaily striped umbrella. She did actually need some sandals, as a matter of fact. The pair she'd brought from home were last year's and the strap was about to fall off any minute. She stood for a moment looking around her, noticing a grand-mother who was managing a stall plus looking after three small grandchildren, the littlest of which she had attached by its baby reins to the leg of the table. In England it would have seemed cruel yet here it seemed just a sensible precaution. Two very old men played a game involving throwing dice on the ground. Back home they might just have gone to the bet-ting shop. A boy flirted with a young girl in an outrageously corny manner. And Claire loved it all. Was she just being a romantic sucker, a classic tourist who accepted Italy at face value, rather than looking at the real roots beneath?

She tried on several pairs of sandals. One, black leather straps, rather smart, but she didn't like the wide ankle strap;

the next, understated and sophisticated; and finally, a funky pair of high-heeled cork-wedges. She asked the price of all three then looked at them more closely. For all the much-praised Italian leather craftsmanship, two of the three weren't leather at all and came from China. So much for falling for all those Italian clichés. The third were indeed leather but almost triple the cost of the other two.

'I'd go for those,' a voice recommended. The voice's owner was in the deep shade of a next-door cafe and she couldn't see him properly. 'Class will always out.'

'Tony!' Claire gasped. 'I thought you'd gone home days ago. Sylvie thought so too.'

'I had a rethink. I decided I wasn't sure that I liked myself and I might have a short break from my ego. I do, on the other hand, like Lerini. Its unpretentious but lively nature appeals to me. I've rented a little room.'

'Does Sylvie know?'

'Nobody knows but you. Actually, I'd rather Sylvie didn't know. Till I'm ready.'

Claire thought about it. 'But wouldn't it be more intriguing – and annoying – for her to know that you're here but not know where?'

'If that was the game I was playing, yes.'

'Aren't you?'

He looked out at the horizon. 'I don't know. I don't know if it's a game at all. It might just be a brief break to recharge my batteries before I go and face the reality of separation.'

She studied him. He was thinner and browner. The slightly puffy look of a man who lives too well had left him. 'You look different,' was all she said. 'Better.'

'I've taken up running. How about that for a middle-aged cliché? But the mornings here are extraordinary. Before the dust lifts or the heat haze settles on the sea, you feel as if you can see tomorrow.'

'I'll keep your secret,' she promised, 'and I'll trust your taste as well.'

'Excellent. I'm very good on women's clothes.'

'I'm not sure that's something you should boast about in your new monkish state.'

A pretty girl passed and Tony's eye was instantly drawn. 'I don't know about the monkish.'

'Tony, I'm disappointed.'

He smiled at her engagingly. 'I'm as innocent as the day is long. Anyway, I couldn't sit here all day if I didn't appreciate the scenery. The Italians would think I was a weirdo. I'm actually a one-woman man. I just got temporarily confused over which woman.'

'Shall I give your love to anyone?'

'The time will come,' he remarked mysteriously. 'I've told the office I'm taking a break which suits them as they're not supposed to let me in. Maybe, if she thinks I've disappeared, she'll start missing me.'

'I'll ask her if she's had any news of you as soon as I get back.'

'Thanks.' He smiled again. 'And the shoes are great.'

As she walked down the street that led towards Bianca's school, Claire noticed a glamorous older woman eyeing Tony up with interest. He was going to have to try very hard to stay on the straight and narrow.

The school was in a wide street with wisteria hanging from every lamp post, filling the air with its heady sweetness. That was another problem with this damn place. Even the air tried to seduce you!

The little children came out first, running into the arms of mothers or nonnas, followed by the eleven- or twelve-year-olds, with the teenagers hanging back and dawdling as they did in every culture. There was no sign of Luca. Maybe they'd changed their arrangement. She'd give him five more minutes and then stop this unhealthy behaviour. She was about to turn away when she saw him walking towards her, talking into a mobile phone.

Suddenly she felt self-conscious. Hanging around his daughter's school! Only one step from bunny boiling!

But the sight of him stopped her in her tracks and again she was faced with that curious combination of sophistication and down-to-earthness which had so attracted her. It was even reflected in what he wore. Ordinary dark blue trousers with a sweater that was coming apart at the wrists. But what a sweater. It had to be Armani or one of those smart brands and yet he wore it as if it were something he'd picked up in the Italian version of Oxfam.

He saw her and without a second thought ran towards her, then checked himself and glanced around. Did he think Graziella was following him?

'Chiara! My God, I have missed you!' She felt he would have taken her in his arms were they not now surrounded by hundreds of interested schoolchildren. 'I have wanted to contact you so much but I could not.' He paused dramatically. 'Graziella made me go to confession.'

Of all the arguments she might have expected this was the least likely.

'Did you tell her about us, then?'

'No, no, but she knows there is something, not just from my father. She asked the pickers and the girl who showed you around. Everyone who works for me has been asked for an opinion! She did not want to force a confrontation so instead she sent me to confession. Very clever.'

'But surely you don't really believe . . . ?' Claire had almost blurted. But it was entirely obvious from his manner that he did.

For the first time Claire felt out of her depth. While she'd been musing on and on about the magic of Italy, there were cultural forces she hadn't even imagined working against her. How could she outdo God?

Bianca came out of the school gates and ran towards them. '*Chiara! Ciao!* Are you going to join us?'

Claire shook her head. Clearly, the one person who hadn't been given the third degree was Bianca.

After she'd said goodbye, she wandered back through the streets wondering if Tony was still there, but the cafe he'd been sitting in was empty. The doors to the big yellow cathedral were wide open, which was unusual, as they had been closed each time she'd passed before. Gingerly, as if she were about to encounter her rival in battle, she went up the steps and into the nave of the church. It was dark but surprisingly cool and fresh. There was the distant sound of an organist above her practising Bach, and the faint aroma of incense in the air. The child of enthusiastic atheist parents, Claire had only been to church for weddings and the occasional funeral.

Yet there was something in the atmosphere, some lingering sense of all the hope and suffering of hundreds of years of believers who, feeling they could trust nothing else in their uncertain world, chose to put their faith in God. It even got to down-to-earth Claire.

She sat back thinking about her own horrible situation. She'd believed she was beginning to feel for Luca what she had never felt for Martin. And yet what did that mean? Was love something irresistible that happened to you, a giant wave that swirled you around and might drown you or throw you back to the surface to go on living in a totally changed life?

She remembered how, when she was a small child in Cornwall, she had been grabbed by such a wave, felt the powerlessness of being tumbled and tumbled, trying to hold her breath, telling herself in a moment everything would be all right. And it had.

Or was she ignoring the fact that she had a choice? She had come to Italy to get away from Martin, from her life of too much responsibility. Was Luca just what one of her friends had rudely dubbed a 'last-gasp romance'?

For almost the first time she thought about Martin, and what Monica had said, that she didn't want her husband to change, because that would take away her justification for the way she was treating him.

Sylvie had even accused her of being jealous of Monica for uncovering the buried rebel in her conventional husband. The image of Martin playing the guitar that Monica had found for him came back to her. It was true, she'd resented Monica for being the one who'd noticed.

*Oh God,* she found herself suddenly on her knees, *if there is a God, which I very much doubt, can you help me see a way through all this mess and pain?*

She stood up, laughing at herself. How ridiculous of her. God had already been successfully signed up by Graziella to put the strong arm of Catholic guilt onto Luca.

Claire got back to find the house in a state of high alert.

'What's going on?' she asked Monica.

'My mother has demanded a tour of the house and gardens and is finding a great deal to criticize.'

'Can't you stop her? I mean, it isn't her house. Where's Gwen?'

'Off to do some detective work of her own. Fortunately, Immaculata can't speak a word of English and Beatrice, who can, has diplomatically disappeared.'

Mariella, it transpired, was explaining to the bewildered Immaculata a better way to run the kitchen, sort out the linen cupboards and organize the garden staff. Immaculata simply smiled and nodded without the slightest idea of what she was being told.

'Can't you take her off somewhere?' Claire suggested.

'I have offered Amalfi, I have offered Positano and even a day trip to Capri, but she is far happier here interfering.'

'I think we should Send in Sylvie!' Claire made this solution sound akin to deploying the Desert Rats.

'Claire, that is a brilliant solution,' Monica congratulated. 'Or at least it would be, if she weren't in hiding in case anyone suggested it.'

'Come on' Claire couldn't help laughing, 'let's go and smoke her out.'

Sylvie was not to be found in her usual haunt, painting old wooden furniture she'd found in the market to resemble something from the court of Louis XIV. Nor was she lying on a sofa in the salon with her laptop.

Finally, they found her staring miserably into space on a sunlounger by the pool.

'Sylvie!' Monica couldn't have sounded more shocked if Sylvie had announced she was pregnant via IVF, 'you're not wearing any make-up!' And if further evidence of crisis were required: 'And your nail varnish is chipped!'

'Oh, what's the point.' Sylvie turned her head away. 'I miss Tony. He may be a son of a bitch, but at least he's my son of a bitch.' She sniffed. 'At least I thought he was. The office rang to say he says he's going to be away for a while.' She paused tragically, then spat out, 'I bet he's back with *her*!'

Claire longed to tell her that Tony was a) alone and b) only three miles away but couldn't because of her promise to him.

'I'm sure he's not. He left her to drown in the pool, remember.'

'Some women like rough treatment.' Sylvie sighed as if she wouldn't mind some herself. Claire and Monica exchanged glances. Sylvie probably thought political correctness was something practised by dominatrixes in Westminster.

'Tony wouldn't like it if you let yourself go like this,' attempted Claire, avoiding Monica's reaction to this blatantly unfeminist line of argument.

'You're absolutely right, Claire.' Sylvie sat up and climbed off the lounger with renewed energy. 'I'll go upstairs and wash my hair.'

When she had gone Claire became thoughtful. 'Look, Monica,' she said finally, 'I owe you an apology. You helped me out by looking after Martin and I thanked you with my distrust. I apologize. And thanks for making me see what an effort he's making.'

'Don't mention it. I like him. I mean, I can see he lacks Luca's polish . . .'

'. . . or his complexity.'

'How is Luca being complex exactly?'

Claire paused, deciding whether to trust Monica. She was hardly the ideal candidate, given the tension between them, but Claire felt the need to share her emotions. 'I saw him today. He said he wanted to contact me but Graziella made him go to confession.'

'So now, if he phones you, he's betraying not just her but God too.'

Claire nodded.

'Does that bother him? Quite a lot of Italians seem to manage God *and* adultery.'

Claire flinched at the word adultery as if she'd been slapped.

'We haven't been to bed together. Only kissed.'

'God, Claire, you're risking an awful lot for a couple of kisses. Has he been unfaithful before?'

'How should I know?' Claire snapped back, beginning to wish she hadn't started this.

'In one way it's great if he hasn't, obviously; it means he's a good guy. But it also means falling for you may be harder to reconcile with his conscience – God – which isn't so good. Can I ask you a question?'

Claire nodded, dreading it all the same.

'I can see things would be easier for you, and for God, if Graziella just disappeared. But how long are you going to wait – and keep Martin waiting – to find out if she will?'

Claire's answer was to burst into tears and run from the swimming pool up to her room.

OK, Monica said to herself, you've been upfront with Claire about Martin. How about taking on your mother next?

The question was, how best to do it so that her mother realized once and for all that something had happened to her daughter – she had finally found self-confidence and couldn't be bossed around any more.

She decided to go and see how Immaculata was surviving her mother's onslaught and found Gwen, smiling and gracious as the Queen, attempting to counteract any serious damage that might have been done.

'My dear,' Gwen explained, 'Immaculata seems to have conceived the idea that your mother thinks her cooking is a little bit provincial. I can't *imagine* how she could have got that impression.' She winked at Monica. 'I have said I am sure it's all an accident of translation. Perhaps you could pour some more oil on troubled waters. Especially as I very much need Immaculata's help for a little luncheon party I am planning for tomorrow.'

Monica followed the unmistakable sound of her mother's voice into the kitchen where she found the tiny Immaculata positively quailing under Mariella's verbal assault.

'*Buongiorno*, Immaculata.' Monica then reeled off a lengthy greeting in her perfect Italian. Immaculata was suddenly all smiles.

Mariella listened suspiciously, unable to understand a single word. 'Tell me exactly what you've said to the woman, Monica,' she commanded.

Monica turned to her mother. 'I thanked her for hearing you out and informed her that you can't cook at all yourself and that's why you can't resist criticizing anyone who can and that she must pay absolutely no attention to anything you say.'

Mariella stood looking at her daughter, for once entirely lost for words.

'Excellent!' Gwen jumped straight in. 'I'm glad we've got that sorted out. Right, Immaculata, we'll keep things simple: asparagus with shaved parmesan; your wonderful pumpkin ravioli; saltimbocca and French beans; for dessert orange polenta cake. Perfect!' She turned to Monica. 'Could you speak to Beatrice about drinks and table settings. Inside, I think. White linen and fresh flowers. Let's not show Stephen up. If everyone can come we should be ten. Would that be all right?'

'Well done, my dear girl,' she whispered to Monica as they all trooped out of the room. 'I rather think your mother had that coming.'

The mystery guests turned out to be an elderly couple called Castellini, and they were by far the most popular they'd ever had at the villa. Everyone seemed to be waiting for them and came in to pay their respects, from Immaculata to Luigi and Giovanni. After the seemingly endless enquiries about their health, their new home and their daughter, Beatrice finally came round with a bottle and poured them a glass of wine.

They were, Monica guessed, in their mid-sixties. Both were grey-haired and not particularly smart or well-dressed yet they exuded welcoming charm and seemed far more interested in Sylvie, Angela, Claire and Monica than in talking about themselves. They were fascinated by the different careers they'd followed and sounded equally impressed by all of them. Monica found herself instantly warming to them when they congratulated her on her wonderful choice of being a university librarian, as if no other career option could have been quite as compelling and useful. Sylvie's interior design company sounded amazingly creative, Claire's cooking little short of perfection and as for Angela's fashion label! To build it up from nothing and sell it was staggeringly amazing! She must be like Miuccia Prada!

It was fascinating to watch how the others unbent in the sunshine of such attention. Sylvie told hilarious and very naughty stories Monica had never heard about her Russian clients and how one wanted special hand-holds so that they could have sex in the shower! Claire entertained them with tales of her most trying clients and Angela recounted the story of the tiny Hong Kong tailor who had introduced her to the soft material on which she based Fabric and insisted on stroking it – with Angela inside.

They had all but finished lunch when Angela asked the Castellinis what profession they'd been in.

There was an instant's silence and they both glanced at Gwen.

'Signor and Signora Castellini used to own my favourite hotel in Lanzarella, the Bellavista. You, of course, all know it as the Hotel of the Gods.'

A sudden silence filled the room as they all took in the significance of this information.

'My dear Angela.' Gwen had become acutely aware of how embarrassing their answer might be to her. 'Perhaps you and the Castellinis might continue in private?'

'There's no need for that.' Angela looked at her steadily. 'Sylvie, Claire and Monica are my friends.' Angela turned to them in her usual straightforward way. 'You might like to tell us how you came to sell the hotel.'

'We never intended to sell it,' blurted out Signora Castellini. 'We loved the Bellavista. We lived there for forty years, since our marriage, and ran it together. It was our daughter Caterina's idea. Caterina was not an easy child. She never liked any man who liked her. So she got to forty-five and was still single. Everyone else was married, they have children. And then she fell in love. And this man, a little older, his family was in the hotel business.' They all tried not to look at each other as they began to see where the story was heading. 'So she told us, Mama, Papa, it is a marriage made in heaven! Like us they can run the hotel together. We were getting older. We hoped for grandchildren. So we sold the hotel to this man's family.'

Signora Castellini stopped and sighed as if she couldn't go on with the story.

Her husband took it up. 'But once his family had the hotel they wanted to make so many changes; they wanted it to be grand international hotel. He and Caterina, they started to quarrel, and the fighting got so bad that one day she came to us and said she was leaving, she couldn't run the hotel with him, she was going to Rome. But they were not married yet, so she had no rights, and now we have no hotel.' He patted his wife. 'Maybe it is the way of modern life. Maybe our hotel was too old-fashioned.'

They all listened silently, not sure what to say.

'And what about the price you were paid?' Angela asked tonelessly.

'We have found since that it was much too little.' Signor Castellini shrugged, with a remarkable lack of bitterness. 'They said they must spend a great deal to make it a luxury hotel and could not afford more. We thought our daughter would benefit. It is not about the money. We are sad for Caterina. Now that she is in Rome we hardly see her. I think she is humiliated. She says people in Lanzarella think she was tricked. That this man did not want Caterina, he wanted the hotel, and now she will not come here.'

Angela got up from the table.

She nodded to Gwen. 'I think you've made your point. I'm going to my room. As a matter of fact, I'm probably going back to London. I've been here much too long already.'

The atmosphere in the room was distinctly strange, as if the barometric pressure had instantly dropped.

Mr and Mrs Castellini got to their feet, looking anxious, and announced they must go, that they hoped they hadn't created trouble.

Gwen thanked them and went with them to their car at the back of the house.

Claire, Monica and Sylvie looked on, shell-shocked.

'I think we're all being unfair to Angela,' Claire insisted eventually, thinking of Luca. 'There might be more to their relationship than Hugo wanting her to influence Stephen to sell.'

'Like wanting to get his hands on the art?' Monica couldn't help being truthful. 'Sorry, but I just don't trust him.'

'I was thinking of love, genuine liking,' Claire replied.

They glanced at Martin, obliviously studying the different cheeses with a view to making a selection.

'What do you know about art anyway?' Mariella reminded them of her presence with a dig at Monica.

'Not a lot,' conceded Monica, to Sylvie's annoyance. 'But, fortunately, I have a friend who does.'

'Come on, girls,' Claire suddenly announced. 'This calls for a wander in the garden. We'll leave Mariella and Martin to explain to Gwen. I think she'll understand.'

'Well, I think it's very rude,' announced Mariella.

'I know, Martin,' Claire smiled at him unexpectedly, 'tell Mariella about your movie poster collection.'

He looked at her sharply but she seemed to be entirely genuine. Forgoing the delights of the cheeses he launched into a chronological analysis of his collection while the three women disappeared onto the terrace.

'Oh God,' Monica whispered, 'how awful for Angela. And somehow the fact that it was Stephen's mother who invited them, it seemed more pointed somehow.'

'And Angela's so proud,' Sylvie pointed out.

'And actually a little bit lonely,' Claire said softly.

'Do you really think so?' Sylvie tended to take people at face value. 'She seems so confident and organized.'

'I think that's a bit of a cover.'

'Oh God, so Hugo really was a bit special.'

'She's a rich woman. If Hugo turned the villa into a hotel, maybe she would have run it with him, even put some money into it. It would have given her a whole new life,' Claire said. 'We've got to stop her going,' she announced, suddenly passionate. 'I can't bear both of us being unhappy. And besides,' she voiced a thought hanging unspoken in the air, 'if Angela went, then we'd have to ask ourselves what any of us are still doing here.'

# *Sixteen*

They sat on the bench under the pergola and looked around at the place that in a short time had become so real to them, that seemed almost more vivid than home. Could a place really possess a kind of magic? Through its light, its beauty, its remoteness, had Lanzarella woven a kind of spell? The villa was, in its way, a fairy-tale castle.

Yet, Sylvie thought wryly, there did seem to be a little problem with princes. Hers, the erring one, had gone missing. Luca belonged to someone else. Hugo was a false prince, it seemed, who might only want the keys to the castle rather than to win the princess.

Yet, Sylvie knew, she didn't want to go home yet, to face an empty flat and force herself to take up the reins of her business. Somehow demanding Russian clients seemed as weird a species as three-backed toads when you were somewhere as lovely as this.

Monica felt she'd come alive here, changed, been valued. 'I've stopped being passive,' she realized, 'I haven't been mousy Monica, dressing to be invisible. I even stood up to Ma!'

Claire knew that in leaving she would be renouncing her passion for Italy and all that she'd found here.

'I really don't want Angela to go,' Sylvie announced with sudden vehemence.

'Neither do I,' seconded Claire. 'I'm really fond of her. You don't get many chances at our age to make proper new friends, and coming here, that's what we've done.'

'And we're all so different!' added Monica.

'Yes, but isn't that great?' Sylvie grinned.

'And as Claire says, isn't it partly that if Angela goes, we have to ask ourselves why we're still here?' Monica, the realist, had to agree.

'Yes,' Sylvie conceded, 'but it's not just that. When she came she was a controlling cow and now she's . . .'

'One of us,' offered Claire.

'But how on earth are we going to stop her?' Sylvie asked. 'I mean, she's a pretty determined person.'

'Actually,' Monica stunned them, 'I do have an idea, but I just have to give a little more thought as to how it might work.'

'You'd better hurry up.' Claire shrugged. 'I bet you she's booking her flight right now.'

But actually, Claire was wrong.

On the floor above them Angela sat on a flat roof, hidden from the ground, but with an amazing view of the sea. From her secret eyrie Angela realized they were talking about her. Bitching, no doubt, remembering her need to organize everyone around her, relieved that she was leaving, feeling sorry for her, maybe even laughing at her.

Her mobile was in her hand ready to reserve a flight when, by straining her ears, she came to the amazing conclusion that far from wanting her to go, they were trying to think of ways of persuading her to stay!

She leaned forward, behind a chimney stack, and had to brush away a tear. She'd actually told them she didn't do women friends and by some miracle it seemed she'd acquired three of them.

And Monica had even dreamed up some scheme to get her to stay. She smiled at that, wondering what it could be.

In the distance, she could see someone walking towards the villa along the narrow path through the holm oak copse and she watched as Constantine burst dramatically through, still wearing his Russian fur hat.

'Ladies,' he announced, 'I come bearing an invitation. I am having a show.'

He placed a small painting on the stone table in front of them with the details scrawled on the back.

'But this is an original!' Sylvie insisted. 'It's probably worth a lot of money.'

'Quicker for me to knock them off, darling, than go down into Lerini and order a load of invitations.'

'Haven't you heard of email, Constantine?'

'I don't hold with that sort of thing. Anyway, what's more likely to get them flocking here? A free picture or an email?'

'I have to say,' Sylvie conceded, as Monica led him inside to meet Gwen, 'that man's a natural at self-promotion.'

'I think he's lovely.' Claire grinned. 'Except he does smell a bit.'

'It's probably the hat. Do you think he wears it in bed?'

Gwen seemed to rise above the smell and also his sartorial shortcomings. She and Constantine instantly bonded and dug up numerous mutual acquaintances, most of whom neither could stand. Monica saw a happy friendship and healthy respect emerging built upon the despised corpses of most of their acquaintanceship.

\*

The deal was sealed when Constantine carried Gwen off to his eyrie for afternoon drinks and to meet Guido and Spaghetti. The invitation was not extended, Monica noted, to the infuriated Mariella.

'Who's that frightful old scarecrow Gwen's gone off with?' her mother demanded.

'Constantine O'Flaherty, or more commonly known as Constantine O,' Monica replied. 'As a matter of fact, he's one of the most celebrated painters in the world.'

'A painter, oh well,' dismissed Mariella as if that settled the matter.

'And he's very kindly invited us all to his show. His house is absolutely amazing.'

'I'm not sure about that. Standing around talking about art isn't exactly my idea of a pleasant experience.'

'I think you'd really kick yourself if you didn't come to this.' Monica tried to suppress the laughter that threatened to overtake her. Her mother was in for a surprise. 'We could always find a seat, if it was too much for you.'

'I may be ninety but I have the energy of a woman half my age, thank you very much! Probably more than you, lying around doing nothing. Anyway,' Mariella didn't like Monica's tone, 'what *have* you been doing lying around here all this time? It cost us five hundred pounds to have the dogs looked after. It's high time you were thinking about coming home and making yourself useful.'

Monica saw Martin gesticulating at her from the other side of the salon and slipped across to see what the matter was.

'I can't bear listening to her any longer,' he almost spat. 'You're an amazing woman. You should be giving as good as you're getting from that old cow.'

'Don't worry about me,' Monica whispered, touched. 'I've

got a little plan to show my mother I'm not just a biddable daughter.'

She turned to her mother, guessing that without Gwen to distract her she would soon be up to some mischief. 'I'm just going down to Lerini on the bus, Ma. Do you want to come and look at the famous cathedral?'

'I don't like foreign cathedrals. So dark and smelling of incense.'

'There are some nice shops,' she lied.

The home-made crafts and created-on-the-premises jewellery she'd seen in Lerini wouldn't be at all to her mother's exacting tastes. On the other hand, she'd probably have a great time comparing them unfavourably with the products from Debenhams in Amersham.

Monica was pleased when the first bus to arrive was the open-topped one because it would give her mother a much better view of the landscape on the way down to Lerini.

How short-sighted of her. Instead, it gave Mariella the chance to brand the countryside as 'savage', the Americans three rows in front as 'coarse', and Monica herself as deeply selfish for not having considered her mother's hair, which would be ruined by the buffetings of the foreign wind.

By the time they got to Lerini, Monica was exhausted and suggested that maybe they should have a cup of coffee in the piazza.

Monica had just placed the order and waited while her mother went off in search of the Ladies' (probably another bad idea) when someone grabbed her arm.

'Tony! What on earth are you doing here?'

'Didn't Claire tell you I was still here? I suppose I did ask her not to.'

'That would explain it. Where are you staying? Not still at the degli Dei?'

'God, no. I'm renting a flat via Airbnb.' He wrote down the address.

'But why? Sylvie thinks you've gone off somewhere. As a matter of fact, I think she's missing you.'

'She won't for much longer.'

Monica noted Tony's wild-eyed look for the first time. 'What on earth's the matter?'

'It's Kimberley. She's threatening to sue for sexual harassment.'

Monica had been about to commiserate, but thought about it for a moment. 'Tony, that's terrific.'

Tony looked ashen. 'Did you hear what I said? I may be dragged through the courts and labelled a dirty old man.'

'Yes, but it's just the thing that will get Sylvie into your corner. She knows you didn't use your position of power to take advantage of Kimberley.'

Tony laughed hollowly. 'As a matter of fact, Kimberley rather took advantage of *me*, though that's hardly anything to boast about. I would never have dared suggest having sex on Sylvie's Russian's sheets. At home I'm not even allowed to make love on *our* clean sheets!'

'Hmmm . . . I need to think about this. Write your mobile down on that napkin. Oh my God, here comes my mother. Don't breathe a word of this to her.'

Tony took a look at the imposing matron dressed in top-to-toe caramel and decided to make a dash for it. 'Call me when you've decided!'

'Monica,' Mariella demanded, 'who was that weird man you were talking to?'

'Oh, just a friend, you don't know him.'

'Of course I don't know him. I must admit, I think you've made some very peculiar connections here. High time you came back to Great Missenden and faced reality. You're not getting any younger. If you leave it any longer, you'll never find a job.'

'I thought you wanted me to be on permanent standby to look after the dogs?' Monica asked, straight-faced. 'I could hardly do that if I had a full-time job, could I?'

Mariella looked at her daughter intently. What was the matter with her? For a moment Mariella had almost suspected sarcasm.

Monica sat in her new room, one of the Sylvie specials, and contemplated. Not long ago Sylvie, on hearing this news about Kimberley, would have announced that it was no more than Tony deserved. But that was before Tony had abandoned Kimberley and her exercise bike in the swimming pool. And also, this development could involve the reputation of Sylvie's business as well as her husband's.

If Monica knew Sylvie at all, she reckoned she was going to react to this like a lioness protecting her cubs – or, in this case, her mate. Did lionesses protect their mates? It would be even better if Tony actually seemed to *need* her protection. Monica was going to have to give that one more thought.

Martin and Claire knew by some long-married instinct when the other would want the shower or loo or basin to clean their teeth. It was a well-drilled ballet. But ever since Martin had arrived here and the Luca revelations had hit with full force, their ballet had turned into an awkward pantomime.

Tonight, when Martin collided with Claire for the third time, he sat down on the bed. Finally, he could take no more.

Martin grabbed his wife's wrist and pulled her down next to him.

'Claire, look at me. I know you weren't expecting me to come here and maybe I shouldn't have. I've got a simple question for you to answer. Do you want me to go home?'

Claire couldn't bring herself to return his look. She knew he had tried to change, to be more attuned to her feelings, and actually she had felt quite jealous of the closeness he had developed with Monica.

'Look, Claire, I'm no Luca. I've never had a high-powered job to give up. But if you ask me, giving up his lawyer's life-style, without even consulting his wife and family, which is what seems to have happened, is quite selfish. And you have to give his wife credit for trying to make it work again. I don't imagine it's easy for this Graziella. People like you and Luca, with all your belief in living a passionate life close to the soil or the lemons or whatever, you don't think about the people around you. Look at me, Claire!'

She turned at that, surprised at his vehemence. 'I love you, Claire. I think I was a selfish shit back home. I let you do everything. Maybe I felt a bit of a failure. But since coming here I feel different.'

'Maybe it's Monica's good influence.'

'Stop it, Claire!' And to her enormous surprise, her husband kissed her.

Angela dressed slowly; dinner wasn't for another hour and anyway she wasn't sure she could face them all.

The other, and far more serious, question was what she was going to do about Hugo. So far she hadn't replied to any of his texts or messages since the Castellinis' lunch. But if she stayed on here that could hardly last.

She sat at her amazing Sylvie-created dressing table which was sprayed with so much distressed gold it looked as if it were on loan from Versailles. Did she accept that the Castellinis' story applied equally to her? Caterina was their daughter, while Angela had no direct influence over Stephen other than that he had asked her to see if the villa would make a hotel. And even then she'd suspected it had partly been a gesture of protectiveness towards her. But why would Stephen Charlesworth still feel protective after all these years? Perhaps he was an exceptionally generous man. Drew seemed to think so, at all events.

There was also the question of her own money. It wouldn't be difficult in these days of Google for Hugo to know what she was worth down to the last fiver.

The funny thing was, Angela had never felt rich. She had built up her business out of an almost evangelical desire to bring that feeling of being cosseted by your clothes to other women. And while her business had been her passion, it had also protected her, if that was the right word, from ordinary women's concerns. Where they had husbands, she had the business. And the same with families. She had boasted to Drew that her business had given her everything she'd needed. But with Hugo she'd begun to see another future.

For the first time since the Castellinis' revelation she let herself face the truth. She'd thought she was in love with Hugo and had even – and she hadn't even admitted this to herself – imagined that if he bought the villa they might run it together.

She went over to the bed, lay down on it and wept.

A few moments later there was a soft knock on her door. She wondered whether to ignore it and pretend she was out, but the knock persisted.

Beatrice stood on the landing with a small tray on which stood a glass of champagne and a small bowl of rose petals.

'The other ladies say you must have bath before dinner with these flowers in it and drink your champagne as you bathe.' She carried the tray through to the bathroom, placed the glass next to it and began to run a bath, pouring in some bath oil for good measure. 'Is this a custom you have in *Inghilterra?*' Beatrice asked as she sprinkled the petals onto the scented surface.

'Absolutely,' Angela found she was smiling, 'we do it every day just before we have afternoon tea and scones.'

Beatrice went off to tell Immaculata what a curious country England must be, full of people having rose-strewn baths and eating scones.

'So what are you going to wear to The Big Event?'

'What big event is that?' Claire asked.

'Claire! Constantine's show, of course! The top date in Lanzarella's social calendar,' Monica tutted.

'Is it such a big deal?'

'Constantine is world-famous. There'll be art critics from all around the world – the beautiful people will be out in force.'

'For some silly exhibition of pictures?' protested Mariella. 'We only get twenty or so in the gallery in Great Missenden. And that's for The Samaritans.'

'You should put Constantine on to that, Monica,' Sylvie pointed out. 'I think he's missing a trick.'

'Well, I've only got shorts or my safari suit,' Martin protested. 'I wasn't exactly expecting the red carpet.'

'I'm definitely going to get something new,' Monica announced. 'And maybe not even from the market!'

'Then I hope it's more age-appropriate than the rest of the

stuff you've been buying here,' Mariella sniffed. 'Talk about laced mutton.'

'Do you know, Mrs Mathieson,' Martin exploded, 'I think we should be talking more old cows than laced mutton.'

They all stared at Martin in amazement.

Mariella chose to deliberately misunderstand.

There was a sudden screech from Sylvie who had gone to sit on the terrace with her laptop. 'The bitch! The calculating little bitch!'

'Oh God,' Angela murmured, 'she's on Stalkbook again!'

They all jumped up to see what had caused the latest upset on the Kimberley front.

'Sylvie, you should know by now that she only accepted you as her Facebook friend so that she could upset you!' Angela had long advised Sylvie that following Kimberley online was like biting into her own arm.

'Look at this! No make-up and a baby-doll dress – she looks like she's auditioning for the Brownies!' They all studied the deliberately innocent pose Kimberley had adopted. 'Little Miss Lolita from Basildon, saying she's lodging a sexual harassment claim against Tony! She taught him half he knew about sex! Oh my God. My poor Tony! Maybe she's only bluffing? I mean, would you go around telling everyone if you were bringing an action against someone? I'm going to have to go back to London at once and help him!' Sylvie insisted.

'But I thought you said he wasn't in London?' Monica asked.

She sat back down again. 'No, he's not. Maybe he's running away from this. I've got to find him and tell him that together we can fight this.'

'As a matter of fact,' Monica tried not to smile at how right she'd been over Sylvie's reaction, 'he's in Italy.'

'Where?' demanded Sylvie, looking for her handbag to go instantly and retrieve him.

'In Lerini, actually.'

'*Lerini?* Our Lerini?'

'I think there is only one.'

'But what the hell is he doing there?'

Monica felt herself getting out of her depth. 'I think you'd better ask him yourself.'

Sylvie's astonishment was so intense that even an emergency drive by Giovanni with Monica in the Mini Moke made no impression on her. They parked near the piazza and she trudged the last few yards on foot.

Tony, pre-warned by Monica, stood outside his apartment. She had even told him to lay on the rejected lover look and he had done so in spades. In fact, in Monica's opinion, he had rather overdone it and veered rather too much towards a scary Bela Lugosi than the stoical heroism of Humphrey Bogart in *Casablanca*.

But to Sylvie his appearance was perfection.

'Tony!' she screeched, flinging her large frame into his arms as if she were no more than a thistledown on the spring wind. 'You look terrible! What has that woman done to you!'

This did not appear to require any answer other than clutching Sylvie to his manly chest and patting her soothingly from time to time.

'But what I really don't understand is why you're still here?' Sylvie demanded when finally she let go of him.

'I wanted to be near you,' Tony stated simply. 'I've been so stupid. All men say that, I know. The cliché of all time. But I happen to mean it.'

If anything further had been needed for total forgiveness, it was this. 'It's all been a stupid mistake.' Sylvie beamed. 'Now let's get your things together and take you up to the villa. Giovanni's waiting in the piazza for us. I'll help you pack.'

An hour later, Tony, plus his suitcase, was being led up the back stairs of the Villa Le Sirenuse.

'It just struck me,' Sylvie joked, happy she had her Tony back, despite the less than desirable circumstances, 'Villa of the Sirens. *She*'s the siren, bloody Kimberley, luring you on. Do you think your lawyer, when we get you one, would appreciate the comparison?'

'I do hope not.' Tony grinned. 'And much as I would like to accept your scenario, my darling, as myself as helpless putty in her hands, I don't think it's entirely realistic. As you pointed out at the time, I had no business behaving like that with an intern.'

Witnessing this marital interchange, Monica couldn't help wondering at the complexity of adult relationships. Here was Tony doing his best to be honest, and Sylvie would have preferred his previous charming amorality.

No wonder so few marriages lasted.

Despite the awkward circumstances, Tony managed to inject a festive note into the gathering at the villa. In fact, the evening went so well that they all moved off after dinner onto the terrace to look at the almost-full moon.

'Why doesn't your son come here more often?' Tony asked Gwen when they were all in an especially cordial mood thanks to the wine and the moonlight.

'Sad memories, I suppose. Plus it's awfully big for one person.'

'Couldn't he bring friends?'

'Exactly what I tell him, but Stephen always seems to be

working. To be honest, I love him to bits, and you couldn't have a better son, but I wish he had more of a life outside of work.'

Angela sipped her wine thoughtfully as she glanced up at the moon. Gwen could almost be describing her instead of Stephen.

Stephen sat eating breakfast and watching the people hurrying along the riverbank to their various jobs. The post had just arrived, unusually early. He worked his way through the bills and reminders – his business mail went to his office address – and came across a letter from his old college at Oxford. A reunion was being organized of their year in the autumn term.

Of course it was probably about the dreaded 'd' word – development, i.e. getting money out of you for some new building or other.

Instantly he thought of Angela and whether she might like to go too. Or would she think he was one of those sad people who saw their time at university as the highlight of their whole life? He knew people like that.

How was his mother getting on out in Lanzarella with the awful Mariella? he wondered. Maybe he'd Skype her. It was about time for their weekly chat.

What he hadn't expected was to be greeted by gales of giggles. His mother was clearly having the time of her life with Sylvie, Claire, Monica and Angela.

'Hello, Ma, it sounds fun out there!'

'Yes, darling, great fun!' Gwen's face smiled back at him. 'Though the whole village is intrigued that there are now six ladies staying here! We're off to your neighbour's art exhibition tomorrow. It's quite the starry event of the year.'

'I'm glad you're enjoying it. Mariella not being too ghastly?'

'Sssh!' Gwen replied, stifling another giggle. 'But there is one thing. We're all trying to persuade Angela not to go home.'

Stephen sat up. 'Why does she want to? She doesn't feel that I mind how long you all stay, I hope.'

'Too complicated to explain on the phone,' was Gwen's mysterious reply.

'I was hoping to invite her to the reunion of our year in Oxford.'

'What a nice idea. I'm afraid she's not with us at the moment. Oh look, here comes Beatrice with coffee and croissants. I'd better go, darling. Say goodbye to Stephen, everyone!'

'Suddenly the screen filled with laughing faces and waving hands shouting, 'Thank you, Stephen. We're all having a lovely time!'

As he switched off his laptop, Stephen felt suddenly flat and rather alone.

Maybe he ought to get a dog after all. His mother was always telling him so.

On her visit to Lerini with her mother, Monica had glimpsed a simple black dress in one of the shops in the catacombs, not far from the hairdresser's. After breakfast she took advantage of the relative quiet at the villa to slip off to the bus stop. Outside the vegetable shop behind the piazza, the lady who ran it was dancing with one of her customers, both their heads thrown back in delighted laughter at their own antics. The sheer joy of their spontaneity enchanted Monica.

The dress shop didn't open till ten so she slipped into the hairdresser's to make an appointment for tomorrow.

A major discussion was taking place about Lerini's impending Wedding of the Year. This couple were from two of the biggest local families and the hairdresser's granddaughter was to be one of the bridesmaids.

The event was to be, of course, at the Grand Hotel degli Dei.

There was just one problem. The bride-to-be was unhappy.

'The management has allowed another wedding later in the day and Daniela, the bride, thinks this will spoil everything. She will have strangers in her wedding photos.'

The hairdresser turned to Monica to explain. 'In Italy it is all about *le foto di nozze*, the wedding photos.'

'It's the same with us. The photos are more important than the wedding.'

'They have paid a big deposit, or she would find some-where else.' She looked meaningfully at Monica. 'The villa is not available, is such a pity.' She shrugged and searched through her appointments book. 'You go to the big art show?' Monica was amazed that everyone in Lerini seemed to know about Constantine's party. 'We are very proud of our famous artist, even if he does look more like a *vagabondo*, how do you say – tramp?'

She wrote Monica's name in her book for the next day. 'But you are four ladies at the villa?'

'Six! My mother and the mother of the owner.'

'But I will make you big reduction! Would you like me to come up and do many hairs? Is big important party! There will be photographer from Rome!'

Monica felt slightly sick. She'd had no idea the show would be on this scale. Was Constantine still going to include her portrait? What had seemed rather a lark was now taking on threatening proportions. She would have to try and talk him out of it. But knowing Constantine's desire to stir things up, this might not be so easy.

'I will ask if any other ladies would like their hair done,' Monica reassured her.

By now the dress shop was open. The black dress was perfect. Ankle-length black silk, gloriously plain, with just a simple ruffle from one shoulder to the waist. It was a little longer than she'd hoped and twice as expensive, but what the hell. She was going to need all the confidence-boosting she could summon.

'Yes, let's go for it!' Angela laughed. 'I love the idea of a communal hair session!'

'Me too,' said Claire. 'My hair always looks quite different when I have it done.'

Sylvie shook her head. 'I just wash mine and let it dry in the air.' She demonstrated with a Carmen-like toss of the head.

'I'd love it,' Gwen agreed happily, 'though I've no idea what I'm going to wear.'

'Complete waste of money!' Mariella dismissed. 'I've no idea why you're all making such a song and dance about a few pictures being shown.'

'I wonder what the story is with Hugo,' Claire whispered to Monica. 'Angela hasn't even mentioned him since the fateful lunch.'

'I wish we could *do* something.'

'You know Angela, *not* doing anything is probably what she'd most appreciate.'

'I suppose.'

After they'd made the booking for the four of them, Monica slipped off through the gardens and down the path towards Constantine's hidden eyrie.

She was barely out of the bushes when Spaghetti bowled

towards her with bared teeth, then at the last minute jumped straight into her arms.

Monica hardly recognized the house Constantine had chosen for its extreme privacy. There were people everywhere. Publicists, photographers, journalists and caterers all laying the ground for tomorrow's big event.

She spotted Guido half hidden behind a life-size cardboard cut-out of Constantine.

'He *is* coming?' demanded one of the irritated journalists. 'I mean, it'd be just like him to have us all bust our arses getting to this ridiculous house and then find that thing,' he pointed to the cut-out, 'was hosting the evening instead.'

'No, no,' replied the harassed PR, 'he will definitely be here in person.'

'Is that true?' Monica whispered to Guido.

'Yes, yes.' Guido nodded. 'Cardboard figure is just big joke.'

'Can I see him now?' She handed the little dog to Guido.

'I go and ask.'

Five minutes later, Guido was back. He led Monica up staircases and down paths until they came to a small sun-room where Constantine lay under a blanket in the stifling heat, still wearing his hat.

'Monica, me darling, isn't it a grand day, to be sure. What can I be doing for you?'

'Apart from dropping that cod Irish accent, assure me you aren't displaying that painting you did of me.'

'I never decide till the morning of the show what I'm going to include.'

'But that's ridiculous. They have to be hung.'

'Now, Monica, what's happened to your art history? Tomorrow is the Vernissage, the day great artists like meself varnished their masterpieces to show them to the select few before the real opening.'

'Except that you've varnished yours already, and as for the "select few", I hear every room in Lanzarella has been booked.'

'I have an unorthodox hanging system. Wait and see.'

'Please, Constantine . . .'

'Now, Monica, courage.'

'I thought you were my friend.'

'I am your friend. More than you think. Now let's have a Pimm's, for God's sake. Guido!' But Guido knew his employer's tastes so well that he was already there with a jug. 'What happened to the Aperol?'

'A man can only take so much orange liquid.'

'I thought you came to Lanzarella to get away from this sort of circus.'

'I did. But the occasional circus keeps the old euros rolling in. I like to play the part of the colourful artist. I'm very dull in myself, as you know.'

This assertion was so funny that Monica got the giggles until the Pimm's started to fizzle out through her nose.

'Very sophisticated, I must say. Now off you go and bring all your lady friends with you tomorrow.'

'It's not my lady friends I'm worried about, it's my mother.'

'Wisht, now. Mothers are always proud of their children. It's in the DNA.'

'Not in my mother's it isn't.'

'To hell with her, then, and get Guido to bring me the dog. I don't want it trampled under the feet of all those hangers-on.'

Monica was about to leave when she screwed up her courage. 'Constantine . . .'

'Yes?'

'I think you should get Guido to wash your hat.'

*

The atmosphere in the villa next day was positively party-like. Luigi put extra flowers on the breakfast table, Immaculata baked her special sfogliatella buns and they could even hear Giovanni singing Neapolitan songs from the depths of the garden.

'It almost feels like the morning of a wedding,' laughed Claire.

Monica, spoon of yogurt halfway to her mouth, was struck by a sudden thought.

'For heaven's sake, Monica, don't sit there like a halfwit with your spoon in your hand,' Mariella commented acidly.

For once Monica didn't hear her.

Sylvie had just arrived with Tony, both of them looking fulfilled and rosy for reasons all the others could guess. 'Tell me, Mariella,' Sylvie asked pointedly, 'how long were you planning to stay?'

Fortunately, Beatrice arrived with the news that the hairdresser had arrived and Monica jumped up to meet her.

Claire felt a tap on her shoulder. It was her husband Martin. 'Would you like me to entertain the old bag while you're all having your hair done?' he asked.

Claire smiled at him gratefully.

'I'll try my best not to murder her. I'll take her to the Monastery Gardens, then we'll have lunch in the square. That should give you a few clear hours.'

The whole atmosphere changed without Mariella's forbidding presence, especially when Immaculata produced a bottle of the famous fizz with their lunch.

By five o'clock, they were mostly ready and Mariella and Martin still weren't back.

'Maybe they've eloped,' suggested Sylvie.

They finally re-emerged looking tired but pleased.

'We were just coming home when Mariella spotted a cardinal giving out blessings on the cathedral steps.'

'How very medieval.' Tony grinned. 'He wasn't selling indulgences as well?'

'The funny thing was, Mariella went off to buy one of those throw-away cameras.'

'I didn't know they even made those any more,' Angela commented.

'And when we got back to the cathedral, he'd gone.'

'Probably taken up to heaven on a cloud,' Tony decided.

'There was just a priest standing there shouting, "Who is responsible for this disgraceful charade?"'

'I bet it was Constantine,' whispered Monica. 'It's exactly the kind of thing he'd do just before his show. He really is very naughty.'

The show was due to start at six and by five forty-five they were all assembled on the terrace, except Martin and Mariella, who were still changing.

Sylvie took a long look at her three friends. 'I don't think we look too bad for a bunch of old broads!'

'I know,' Tony suggested. 'Photo opportunity. I'll do the honours. Sylvie, where's your phone? Come on, girls, say Lanzarella!'

The four women smiled for the camera and then passed over their own phones so that Tony could use theirs as well.

Gwen arrived looking elegant and just as they were about to leave, Martin slipped in among them.

Claire suddenly noticed what he was wearing. It was a brand-new extremely smart suit. Claire had to do a double-take; he looked so different from the usual Martin. 'That's a bit of a change from your safari suit. Where on earth did you get it?'

'There's a row of shops hidden away right round the back of the cathedral. I nipped in, tried it on and bought it. Ten minutes. Best shopping experience of my life!'

'You look really good in it.'

Martin raised an eyebrow. 'You've never said that to me before and don't say I've never looked good.'

'Oh dear, am I that much of a cow?'

'If you're a cow,' he said, looking at Claire in the pale-blue Fabric dress Angela had lent her, 'then you're the most beautiful cow I've ever seen.'

It wasn't exactly Casanova, but it was a start.

Of all the people going to Constantine's party, they were the lucky ones, because it took them five minutes to walk there through the stand of holm oaks. The house was so utterly inaccessible that even the richest, who normally didn't even walk to the pavement from their Rollers or Bentleys, had to clamber up the narrow, steep path from the back of Lanzarella.

The guests, a curious combination of young and beautiful or old and louche, looked to Monica as if they'd been cast by Federico Fellini.

'My God,' pronounced Sylvie, 'Rome and Positano must be graveyards tonight.'

Monica could see what Constantine had meant by his unusual hanging technique. It was actually no hanging technique at all. Instead, the giant canvases were propped up at interesting angles all round the large central atrium and the various galleried staircases. For some reason the water in the swimming pool had been dyed orange.

There was also an ugly murmur sweeping through the

massed ranks as the waiters circulated with glasses of bright red liquid.

'It's grenadine!' pronounced an infuriated guest with waist-length blonde hair and a latex dress that made Jessica Rabbit look positively nun-like.

No alcohol. Another Constantine joke but one the guests definitely didn't seem to be appreciating.

'Claire!' Angela leaned down. 'Call Luca. Get him to bring the Cellono and lots of glasses! This is the perfect audience for it! They're all desperate for a drink!'

Claire replied with a thumbs-up and instantly called Luca.

'Won't Constantine think it's rude?' asked Sylvie.

'He won't care. In fact, it'll amuse him. Let's hope Luca can get here before there's a palace revolution and everyone leaves!'

'Guido!' Monica saw him passing. 'Are you really not serving any booze?'

'Constantine has decided as a culture we are too dependent on alcohol.'

'Well, he certainly is!' commented a passer-by.

'Where is he anyway?' Monica asked Guido, nonplussed.

'He likes to create a little drama.'

'Well, he's certainly doing that, if not an outright revolt.'

It was another half an hour before the front doorbell sounded and Luca, backed up by Graziella, Bianca and even Grandfather Bruno, appeared with trays of the pale lemon liquid, which they topped up with Prosecco and soda water.

It was greeted like manna to the starving Israelites.

'Hey, what is this? It's great!'

'Wow, I've never had this before. What's it called?'

'Cellono,' announced Luca with a flourish. 'It is a brand-new aperitif.'

371

Luca winked at Claire gratefully and even Graziella smiled.

'Take a photograph and make sure it gets on social media,' Angela counselled. '"The night a new aperitif conquered the art world", or some such. I'm sure Bianca could do it. Look, there's the Fiat heir. Get him drinking it.'

Claire looked through the noisy throng, which had settled down at last. If this was the only drink available, they seemed more than happy to drink it. What a brilliant idea of Angela's.

She saw that Hugo had just arrived and was standing talking to Angela near the swimming pool. Claire edged closer in case she needed moral support.

'Why haven't you been returning any of my calls or texts?' Hugo was asking, visibly annoyed.

'Stephen's mother had a little lunch party. Very cosy. All of us and some people called Castellini. The story they had to tell us about you acquiring the hotel was quite eye-opening, I must say.'

'And you chose to believe those old dodderers rather than me? I suppose they brought out the story of their daughter and how I led her astray? They didn't tell you what a deeply neurotic woman she is? How hard I tried to make it work?'

Angela looked at him levelly. 'In the end I judge people by instinct.'

'And your famous instinct condemned me?'

There was a sudden commotion as Constantine, still dressed as a cardinal, appeared to loud Cellono-fuelled applause. He progressed towards them, arms extended, as if bestowing a universal blessing. As he passed Angela and Hugo, his foot seemed unaccountably to slip and he saved himself by leaning on Hugo, who fell in a spectacular arc into the pool.

This gave rise to a loud round of applause from the guests, who thought this was another of Constantine's con tricks.

Guido rushed up with a towel and helped Hugo, minus his dignity, out of the water. 'As if I care what you and your friends think of me,' he exploded. 'A bunch of boring post-menopausal harpies!'

Sylvie and Monica had arrived just in time to hear this and Sylvie burst into helpless laughter.

'And what's the matter with you?' demanded a dripping Hugo.

'It's just that, Hugo, you're so . . . orange!'

Hugo strode off through the sniggering crowds, leaving a trail of orange dye in his wake.

'I don't think we'll be seeing him again in a hurry,' murmured Constantine.

'You pushed him in deliberately!' accused Sylvie, delighted.

Constantine took up a pious pose. 'The ways of the Lord are many and various.'

He clapped his hands to get his audience's full attention. 'And now, the highlight of the evening: a new painting of which I am inordinately proud. He stepped back, revealing a large canvas on the wall above him, hidden by a curtain.

'Oh my God,' whispered Monica to him, in panic, 'I hope to God that's not what I think it is!'

# *Seventeen*

'Come on, Monica dear,' Constantine whispered encouragingly. 'This is just what you need. No more hiding behind Mrs Librarian from Great Wotsit.'

He signalled to Guido, who pulled a cord revealing the six-foot canvas of an entirely naked Monica.

Even the battle-scarred art groupies, when they saw that the painting was of the woman standing next to him, looked on impressed.

Monica tried to hide her face in her hands but was prevented by Angela, who forced her to stand up straight. 'Come on, it's safe to look. You're amazing!'

And then, from the back of the group, Mariella caught sight of the painting and gasped. 'Monica!' her voice rang out. 'How could you do it? A woman of almost sixty-five years old! Have you no sense of dignity?'

Monica looked up at the painting and saw what her mother saw – flesh that was no longer young or beautiful, if it ever had been. An embarrassment. And felt that everyone in the room must be laughing at her. A hand crept into hers. It was Angela's. 'You're part of the Lanzarella Women's Cooperative, remember?' she whispered. 'Proud post-menopausal harpies every one. Don't let us down!'

Monica turned her back on her mother and stepped forward.

'Thank you, Constantine. I am delighted to join the honourable tradition of *The Nude Maya*, *Benefits Supervisor Sleeping* and Stanley Spencer's *Second Wife*. Actually, I think I look bloody amazing!'

She took a bow to tumultuous applause. One thing the art world liked was a bit of modest irony.

But Constantine hadn't finished.

'Just one moment, ladies and gentlemen. I'm sorry that my experiment to lead you away from the demon drink has been such a failure, rescued only by the arrival of this mysterious new potion.' He grabbed a glass from Luca, who was standing by with a tray. 'Mmm, not bad. Monica here has been my muse and my friend, and I would like to present her with this painting as a token of my thanks and admiration. Monica, this truly is your painting!'

This time the gasp was genuine. Everyone in the room knew – if not the value of a genuine Constantine O, especially one as large and with such immaculate provenance – then at least that it would be a very large sum indeed.

'I recommend you talk to my dealer over there and put it on the market as soon as possible,' Constantine advised. 'You know my technique,' he added, sotto voce. 'I can always bang you out another one to hang above your fireplace. And you can tell that mother of yours to get stuffed; from now on, you'll be a lady of independent means.'

The others crowded round her. 'And do you know what, Mon,' Sylvie whispered so loudly that everyone in the room could hear. 'You really do look quite good. It must be all that swimming in your lunch hour. I knew I was going wrong somewhere.'

The next to congratulate Monica was Gwen. 'I'm so happy for you, dear. And don't worry about Mariella. I think it's time we moved on. There are some wonderful gardens in Sicily I'd like her to see.'

Monica smiled gratefully.

Last of all to approach her was Mariella. 'You do realize you've made an exhibition of yourself. I don't know what your father would say.'

'I think he'd be very proud. Just like all the people who love me. And if I've made an exhibition of myself, I'm delighted. That's what art is about. And the person people are feeling sorry for tonight isn't me, it's you,' Monica replied.

She turned back to Angela, who was waiting for her with a glass of Cellono.

'Well done. Actually, this stuff isn't too bad. If they market it right – and stress the secret ingredient so that everyone else in Italy can't copy them – they might even have a bit of a hit.'

They watched as on the other side of the room Luca and Graziella approached Claire, who was standing with the newly suited Martin. 'We'd like to thank you for giving us this opportunity tonight.' It was Graziella who spoke first. 'It might be the breakthrough we need.'

Claire could hear the enthusiasm in her voice and saw that Graziella had committed herself to Luca and his lemons.

'I wish you good luck.' Claire struggled to keep the emotion out of her voice. 'How do you say that in Italian?'

'You can say *Buona fortuna*,' Graziella replied, 'but what Italians would say is *In bocca al lupo!* Into the mouth of the wolf!'

'Into the mouth of the wolf, then!'

'Thank you.' Graziella held her gaze for just a moment longer than necessary.

Claire avoided Luca's eyes altogether.

After they'd gone, Martin slipped his arm around her. 'Are you OK?'

Claire nodded. 'I think so. She seemed nicer.'

'Maybe she's seeing the advantages of life in the slow lane.'

Claire sighed. 'Maybe she is.'

'Come on, let's go and find the others. You need cheering up.'

Monica was to be found chatting to Constantine's dealer. She wasn't going to ask him about the painting's value, that would be too crass, but, as it happened, he brought the subject up himself. 'Well, this is all a bit novel, isn't it? Who would have thought Constantine would develop a heart of gold? I was just thinking, if we introduced you to a few of his collectors, it might create a lot of interest. They all love something new.'

'As long as I don't have to take my clothes off.'

'Congratulations!' She turned to find Nick from the riding stable behind her. 'No more Great Missenden for you. You'll even be able to boycott Beaconsfield.'

Monica laughed. 'I didn't know you were a friend of Constantine's.'

'No one like our Con to hoover up all the interesting waifs and strays.'

She looked him over. 'You're wearing a suit.'

'Is that an accusation?' He grinned. 'I am British, you know, despite my occasional attempts to emulate the Wild Bunch.'

'Sorry, that sounded rude.'

'Not at all. Believe me, after fourteen years of wearing grey flannel of one sort or another at school, I hate suits as much as the next man. Probably more. But with Constantine you never know. He may be dressed as a tramp – or a cardinal. A suit seemed a safe option.'

'You went to private school, then?'

'Madam, I stand accused. My deepest secret is out.' He noticed Sylvie and Tony waving to her. 'I think your friends are trying to attract your attention.'

'Oh yes,' she was conscious of a moment's disappointment, 'time to go. Great to see you again.'

'And you.'

On the other side of the room, she saw Constantine twinkling at them and wondered what he was up to now.

Gwen was as good as her word. She announced the next morning that a taxi would be arriving later to take them to Naples, where they would catch the overnight ferry to Sicily.

'It has been such fun, girls! And Stephen would be touched, I know, at how seriously you have all been acting in his interests.'

'Come on now, Gwen,' Angela teased, 'it was you who opened our eyes to what Hugo would do with the villa. But surely it's Stephen you need to convince?'

'Stephen will listen to your advice, I'm sure.' Gwen helped herself to another croissant. 'I don't think the next part of our journey will be nearly as eventful, but a bit of calm can't do any harm at our age. What's happened to your mother, Monica? Perhaps you could go and see if everything's all right? She's usually down before me.'

Monica knocked on the door of the Doom Room. When she received no answer, she gently pushed open the door.

Her mother was sitting on the bed, still in her nightdress, with her iPad on her knee. 'Your father's seen your picture.

Somebody saw it on Twitter and sent it to him.' She looked up at Monica. 'You're right. He's very proud.'

Monica sat down next to her on the bed. Her mother looked older and sadder without her make-up and neatly coiffed hair, defenceless somehow.

'He thinks your painting is worth a lot of money. He asked his broker, who advises people about investing in art. You can get a place of your own. Have something proper to live off.'

'I think that was what Constantine had in mind.'

'But I don't understand why he wanted to paint *you*.' Her mother sounded genuinely puzzled.

'He said he saw something unusual in me.' Monica smiled at the memory. It seemed so long ago and yet it was hardly any time at all. 'Apparently, I have an elusive quality.'

Mariella studied her. 'I suppose you do. I could never understand why you said you didn't want to be noticed. And then you do something like this.' She shook her head in bewilderment. 'I suppose he felt sorry for you.'

Monica almost gave up. It was pointless to try and make her mother see her as anything but a failure, an object of pity. But Constantine didn't see her that way and neither did the Lanzarella Women's Cooperative.

She was damned if she was going to let her mother spoil things. 'I like Constantine. I suppose I knew he had my best interests at heart. He said I had to be more confident, dare to do things. So I did.'

'You seem very confident to me. I have watched you here. You are somehow the centre of things.'

'What?' Monica demanded, stunned. Surely colourful Sylvie or efficient Angela were far more the centre of things than she was? What on earth was her mother implying?

'I've tried to be the centre of things and people don't like me for it,' Mariella looked away, 'but you're at the centre and everyone likes you.' She took her daughter's hand. 'You've changed, Monica. I'm sorry about the art show. I should have been proud too. And not just last night.'

Monica found that tears were blurring her vision and she had to turn away. Her mother never apologized.

'I hope it's not too late,' Mariella added in a voice almost too faint to hear.

'You'd better come down' – Monica put her arms around her mother for the briefest of moments – 'before Gwen polishes off all the croissants.'

Angela looked at the message from Drew to call him as soon as possible.

It had to be something important. He'd handled everything in London up till now without any input from her.

She called Fabric's offices in St Christopher's Place.

Drew picked up the phone. She could hear incredibly loud music in the background and realized it was The Temptations singing 'Get Ready', one of her favourite songs.

'Hello, Drew, it's Angela. Are you piping Tamla Motown through the offices to keep up morale?'

Drew laughed. 'Actually, it's from the burger bar over the street. We have the windows open, shock, horror. Spring has come even to London.'

Angela imagined sunshine in St Christopher's Place, the pavement cafes filling up, tourists photographing the giant coloured elephant outside Jigsaw, and felt a pang of homesickness. 'So what's the big news?'

'They're ready for the signing. I assumed you'd want to come and do it in person.'

'Can't you Fedex the stuff to me and I'll sign it in front of witnesses here?' Despite the momentary lapse, she felt a curious reluctance to return to London.

'Wow, you've changed. What happened to obsessive Angela? I suppose I ought to be happy for you. You've found something that matters as much as Fabric.'

Angela smiled to herself. Friendship mattered as much as Fabric. And then the truth hit her – how much longer could they honestly spend here if the villa wasn't to be a hotel? Was she putting off reality, and with it loneliness?

It was as if he were reading her mind. 'Any thoughts of when you might come home? A nightingale may be singing in Berkeley Square by now.'

'I'll give it some thought.'

'Along with what you might do next with all that lovely money. I don't see you as the early retirement in Monte Carlo type.'

Angela shuddered. She'd visited the place once. It was full of sun-bleached old prunes of tax avoiders. It was the kind of town where you could buy gold necklaces but couldn't find a loaf of bread. But still, she'd have to think of something before too long.

'I'll keep you informed. But for now I'll email the exact address for Fedex.'

'Fine. You sound good, Angie. Relaxed. Happy.'

Angela laughed. 'You must be mistaking me for someone else.'

When Angela got back downstairs, everyone was gathered to wave off Gwen and Mariella in their taxi.

'Goodbye, dear. I'm sorry about Hugo,' Gwen said gently.

'I'm not, just grateful I found out sooner rather than later.'

It was a lie and they both knew it, but it offered a fig leaf for her pride.

Gwen squeezed her hand. 'Stay as long as you like. You're all doing a wonderful job here.'

'Have fun in Sicily!' they all chorused.

'Goodbye, Monica.' Mariella was still a shadow of her bossy self. Maybe the new humility was going to last. Although, from past experience, Monica doubted it. By Taormina she'd probably be the old Mariella. Thank heavens Gwen was well able to cope with it.

Somehow the departure of Gwen cast a small cloud over the villa, which Martin noticed at once.

'Why don't we declare tonight a party night and we can all get dressed up for dinner?' Martin suggested.

'Good idea,' seconded Tony.

'What, you mean a kind of fancy dress?' asked Angela, shuddering.

'No, no, just an evening of quiet sophistication,' Martin reassured her with a grin.

They all burst out laughing. 'Or we could go out somewhere.'

But nobody seemed to want to do that.

'How about sunset drinks by the pool?'

'Wouldn't that make dinner too late for Immaculata?' queried Monica.

'We could give the staff the night off and cook for ourselves,' offered Claire.

'What a good idea!'

So that was how they ended up having the villa to themselves for the first time since their arrival. Before they left, Beatrice came shyly up to Claire. 'I have to tell you, Chiara, how well this Cellono is doing. Luca and Graziella are so grateful to you.'

Claire tried to smile, then willed herself to get on with the cooking. A starter of asparagus from their own bed, with melted butter and home-made bread, followed by veal Parmigiana from the supplies of veal in the freezer, finishing up with her famous lemon tart.

They had dinner on the terrace while Tony, who was good at these things, sent the staff off in a taxi to his favourite restaurant insisting he would pick up the bill.

They had just started eating when Sylvie pointed up into the sky. 'Look! The sun's going down and the moon's coming up at the same time!'

They looked up at the magical sight above their heads.

'Is this the most beautiful spot on earth?' murmured Claire.

They all fell silent, contemplating the wonder of the villa and its amazing location.

And then, almost reluctantly, as if it were half dragged out of her, Claire asked softly, 'We're going to have to stop beating about the bush. How much longer is everyone staying?'

A hush fell as if someone had committed a sacrilege.

Finally, it was Angela who spoke. 'I don't know how much use we've really been to Stephen. I mean, sure, we may have stopped him selling to Hugo Robertson, but what about the other question he asked – should he open a hotel here himself?'

'I can't help feeling it'd be a pity,' Sylvie sighed. 'Even though I might get the contract to do it up.'

'Does he have to do anything with the place?' asked Martin. 'He seems to be extremely rich.'

'I think he's getting a bit of a conscience about keeping somewhere so lovely all to himself.'

'He could rent it out as a villa, I suppose.'

'Yes, but who could afford it? Only revoltingly rich types.' Claire made a face.

Monica screwed up her courage. Her mother had said she was at the centre of things. Time to be brave.

'There is one other alternative, something maybe we could do.'

They all looked at her, riveted.

'Fire away, then,' Angela smiled encouragingly.

'Before we came, the villa used to be rented out for weddings.' She got out the blurry leaflet showing a wedding taking place under the wisteria-covered pergola. 'The deal seemed to be that it was amazing value but it carried a risk: if Stephen turned up, it was off.'

'But did anyone agree to that?' Claire asked doubtfully.

'Yes, because it's so beautiful and such good value it was worth hoping you had it here but having a plan B.'

'Bloody hell!' Sylvie shook her head. 'And this involved little old ladies like Beatrice and Immaculata?'

'Remember what Constantine discovered. They always put half back for the upkeep of the villa. And remember, this *is* Italy,' said Claire.

Monica nodded. 'In fact, there's a wedding coming up. The hairdresser in Lerini told me all about it. It was supposed to be at Hugo's hotel, but the management is allowing another wedding later. The bride's so furious they're prepared to sacrifice a whacking deposit if they could have it here.'

'But how could they,' Sylvie asked, 'with us here?'

'I've thought of a way that Stephen could hang on to his wonderful villa and the lovely staff and salve his conscience at the same time. We make the place a wedding venue for local people. Not some ritzy destination full of hen parties from Texas but as a kind of community resource.'

'Like a posh village hall?' Claire asked.

'Exactly. In the long run Stephen would have to give his permission, and then he could feel he was contributing to Lanzarella, not just being an absentee landlord. We could start with this wedding coming up. Both the families are local people.'

'But none of us have ever planned a wedding before,' Angela objected.

'Not so far,' Sylvie conceded, 'but I'd love to have a crack.'

'I think we'd be brilliant at it, if we really worked together.' Monica started to get really enthusiastic. 'Angela in overall charge with her business brain, Sylvie doing the décor, Claire the food and I'd handle the flowers.'

They all sat in silence.

Finally, Claire said, 'I must admit, I rather like the idea.'

'But when is this wedding exactly?' Sylvie enquired.

'In two weeks from next Saturday.'

They all gasped.

'Well, if you want a male view, which I don't expect you do, I think you women could do anything you put your minds to,' threw in Martin.

'Hear, hear,' seconded Tony. 'Martin and I could be your barmen.'

'Don't be ridiculous, all of you!' Angela was as ever the realist. 'I think we've all had too much to drink or the moonlight's gone to our heads! Let's clear up now.'

'Maybe Angela's right,' Claire conceded as they put away the dirty dishes. 'Goodnight, everyone.'

Monica stayed up to watch the moon for a little while after the others had gone up to bed. Soon she was going to have to make a decision about what to do next. The only thing she was really sure of was how much she would miss this special place and these even more special people if they didn't follow her wedding suggestion.

The next morning, it was a very brisk Angela with a distinctly Boadicea-like air who joined them all at breakfast. She was holding an envelope with a sheaf of papers inside.

'Right,' she announced, 'I've been having a rethink. I've just received a very large bill from Hugo's hotel. It's for when Gwen and Mariella were supposed to be staying and it's of quite astronomical proportions. Normally, you would pay one night's cancellation but apparently they booked a three-day package. That, and the fact that Hugo's sent it to me, means one thing. War! We're going to have to make doubly sure that Stephen isn't suddenly intending to visit and, if he's not, then it's yes to this girl Daniela. We'll have to work hard as a team and start straight away – but hey, we're not a co-operative for nothing. So, Monica, go and see this hairdresser of yours and find out if the bride is serious. If she is, then *Andiamo*, everybody! We're going to organize a wedding!'

# *Eighteen*

---

'She asked you *what?*'

This time it was the unshockable Sylvie who was shocked.

'The bride would be absolutely thrilled to have her wedding at the villa,' Monica explained. 'Her entire family will also be thrilled. And her bridegroom and no doubt her second cousin. She also seemed especially keen to know if Giovanni would be around. Our Giovanni, it seems, is a bit of a local legend.'

'Oh my God!' Angela couldn't help biting her lip and giggling. 'That's not very bridal!'

'Right. Forget Giovanni and his magic wand. Down to business.' If Angela had had a gavel she would have banged it. 'Some of you have children. Haven't any of you helped organize their weddings at least?'

Sylvie sighed. 'My daughter just did it all herself, incredibly low key, register office followed by lunch in a pub. I just had to turn up. They didn't even want our money, which actually was rather hurtful.' The truth was, her daughter disapproved of Sylvie's old hippie style and had been terrified of joss sticks and a soundtrack of *Tubular Bells.* 'Please don't come in a kaftan,' had been her only communication. They had also firmly turned down Sylvie's offer of doing up their home for them. Sylvie had felt wounded and also a failure, but had allowed Tony to comfort her with the assurance that that was what they all did nowadays. They planned their own weddings and even cashed in their wedding-list money at John Lewis so that they could buy a single piece by some designer in Shoreditch.

Claire felt a stab of guilt about Belinda, her son Evan's wife. Maybe, if she could have liked Belinda more, they would have had a proper wedding and might even have wanted Claire's help with the catering.

Angela, spotting that she had opened a can of emotional worms, swiftly changed the subject.

'The first thing we'd better do is have them over and find out what kind of wedding *they* want.'

'With just a teeny bit of persuasion on our part,' added Sylvie, unable to resist. 'I imagine weddings in Italy are rather formal. None of that wilting wildflowers stuff that's all the rage at home. Twenty-five bridesmaids with bunches of cow parsley. This house would be perfect for something baroque and amazing, a real Medici-type wedding.'

'Didn't the Medicis go in for poisoning all their guests?' enquired Claire.

'I think that was the Borgias,' giggled Monica.

So it was agreed that the bride-to-be and her mother would be invited to view the villa and decide – with a little nudging from Sylvie – what kind of wedding they actually wanted.

'And strictly no mention of Giovanni!' insisted Angela. 'But first, we need to have a conversation with all the staff and make it clear what we're planning.'

\*

It was the oddest staff meeting Claire had ever been to. They sat on the terrace, amid the scent of jasmine, wallflowers and wild sage, with bees buzzing all around them and the odd butterfly landing on Angela's laptop.

Beatrice and Immaculata, Luigi and Giovanni all looked as though they'd been summoned to a firing squad. The two women and Luigi sat, heads bowed, as if they'd been waiting forever for this moment, while Giovanni was doing his Greek god number, head proudly erect, perfect profile much in evidence, buttons undone, showing the physique that seemed to be even more desirable than they'd hitherto suspected.

Angela sat at the head, with Monica at her right hand to translate anything tricky. This was one occasion when absolutely nobody minded Angela, with her habit of authority, being in control.

'I just wanted to start by saying what a marvellous, memorable time we've all been having and how grateful we are for your amazing care of us.'

Immaculata attempted a smile but the air of the condemned cell persisted.

'I'm sure you must have discussed many times what we are all doing here between yourselves, and what it is Stephen has in mind. The answer is, I suspect, that Stephen isn't sure himself. He loves this place, but feels guilty about keeping it to himself. Also, I'm sure you know by now about the offer from the hotel chain who own the degli Dei.'

Immaculata and Beatrice exchanged anguished looks.

'We feel, for what our advice is worth, that this place is far too precious and unique, and that a hotel chain would only ruin it.'

A loud round of applause drowned out her words.

'You do realize, of course, that Stephen doesn't have to

listen to us. We're not professionals, just friends and well-wishers who've fallen in love with Le Sirenuse. But we do have a plan. We believe that Stephen really cares about the villa and would like to keep it on, but it worries him that he uses it so little. But what if the villa were of use sometimes to the community? For example for weddings for local people? With Stephen's permission' – she looked beadily at each staff member to make sure they understood the subtext, no personal gain even if they gave half back – 'we propose to hold a wedding and see if we can make the idea a success, and if it is, we'll try and sell him the idea that he keeps on doing it. So in two weeks' time, with all your help – and, of course, we realize you have done this before' – the staff all looked nervously at each other at such a direct reference to their previous activities – 'the wedding of Daniela di Agosti and Marco Moretti will be taking place here. Daniela and her family would also like to stay the night here.' A slow, sexy smile appeared on Giovanni's handsome face. Angela looked straight at him. 'And she will be treated with the utmost respect appropriate to a bride-to-be. Is that clear?'

Giovanni glanced around innocently as if any alternative would be entirely alien to him.

'So, good luck to everyone. It will be very hard work.'

'*In bocca al lupo*,' added Monica, realizing that it wasn't long since they'd wished the same to Luca.

They laughed for the first time. '*In bocca al lupo!*'

'And you're going to need plenty of good luck,' Tony suggested, when they recounted the meeting to him afterwards. 'Two questions: how long are you planning to stay here to get this off the ground? And what are you going to do if Stephen suddenly decides to come and stay?'

'Pass and pass!' Angela collapsed with laughter. 'I have

absolutely no bloody idea. For the first time in my adult life I'm actually being spontaneous and it's absolutely terrifying. But I'll tell you one thing – I'm getting broadband installed tomorrow whether Stephen likes it or not!'

It was Monica's hairdresser who organized the meeting with Daniela and her mother the next day at eleven.

'I think Sylvie should be in charge, since you'll be doing most of the organizing,' Angela suggested.

Sylvie nodded. 'Last night I was so nervous . . .'

'The celebrated Sylvie Sutton *nervous?*' interrupted Claire, amazed.

'I do get nervous, as a matter of fact. Anyway, now I've looked at about a million YouTube videos on How to Organize Your Daughter's Destination Wedding, I feel a lot more confident.'

There was a palpable feeling of excitement among the staff as the pair arrived. Daniela, the belle of Lanzarella, was marrying the boss of a local factory and the fact that she was having the wedding at the villa instead of Lanzarella's premier hotel was seen as a Major Coup.

'I'd love to see Hugo's reaction when he hears what's happening,' confessed Angela with satisfaction. 'In fact, this wedding had better be absolutely bloody perfect!'

'Thanks for that reassuring encouragement,' Sylvie said as she passed her to go and greet the bride-to-be.

'*Ciao, Daniela.*' Sylvie held out a welcoming hand, as she stood on the back steps.

'*Buongiorno, signora,*' she greeted Daniela's mother, 'let me take you through to the salon.'

Daniela was one of those generously built Italian girls with soft, large bosoms and masses of glossy brown hair, wearing a slightly too-tight burnt-orange shift dress. She looked around critically, obviously comparing the unassuming villa entrance to the grand portico of the Grand Hotel degli Dei.

'For the wedding, we will put up an awning and lay down a red carpet,' Sylvie quickly reassured her, reading her mind. 'The delights of the villa are like a woman who reveals her beauty gradually.'

'Bloody hell,' Angela whispered to Monica. 'She's beginning to sound like Giovanni!'

'May we introduce ourselves?' Monica steered the subject away from the villa's slowly revealed beauty. 'This is the celebrated designer, Sylvie Sutton, who is very well known in London; Angela Williams, who is a famous businesswoman, will manage the costings; Claire Lambert, who will do the catering. My name is Monica Mathieson and I am here to help with any translation you might like and also to take care of the flowers. I have done a few arrangements from the garden so you can see some different styles.' She indicated various arrangements from the formal to the cottage-garden style she'd arranged earlier that morning.

'We are all friends of the villa's owner and we would like to welcome you to the wonderful Villa Le Sirenuse. Let us take you through to the salon and dining room. By the way, this is our proudest possession.' She pointed to the fresco of *The Annunciation*. Daniela only glanced at it; she had clearly seen enough religious art to last a lifetime.

Beatrice had laid out tiny coffee cups and a plate of equally tiny biscuits in the salon. They all sat down. Sylvie began proceedings. 'The major question, Daniela, is would you like to be married in Lanzarella Church, or would you prefer to have the ceremony here at the villa?'

Daniela was evidently a young lady who knew her own

mind. Which was just as well as her mother was a colourless woman who seemed permanently amazed that she could have produced such a feminine yet feisty daughter who was definitely marrying up.

'At the villa, of course,' she stated, as if any other idea were slightly mad. 'On the terrace next to the statues, with the sea behind me. That is the view that everyone will know at once. They will say, "Oh, Daniela is being married at the famous Villa Le Sirenuse!"'

'Have you thought about the look of the wedding at all?' asked Sylvie, knowing that every bride from Eve onwards spent all their waking hours thinking about nothing else. 'As the house has such amazing art and history, I wondered about a medieval-themed wedding? I have done a few sketches to give you a possible idea.'

She handed over a watercolour of a beautiful young woman in an embroidered dress looking like a Renaissance Madonna.

'*Assolutamente no!*' Daniela exclaimed, horrified. She turned a gaze on Monica that was starry-eyed and steelily determined in equal measure. 'With you four ladies to help me, what I want is an *English* wedding!'

She reached down into her voluminous handbag and produced a glossy magazine and an enormous folder of coloured photocopies.

'Oh my good Lord,' murmured Claire, trying not to catch Sylvie's eye, 'she's only brought the exact blueprint for Kate Moss's wedding!'

Claire could almost feel Sylvie's heart thud to the floor as Daniela handed over the reams of interviews with John Galliano about Kate's *Great Gatsby*-inspired wedding dress created by hand out of gossamer-like silk, chiffon and tulle and thousands of sequins.

She turned to Monica. 'You are the lady doing the flowers?' Monica nodded.

'I want only apricot and lilac roses in my bouquet. And for the tiara only ivy and flowers from the garden.' She turned to Claire. 'And you are the cooking lady? Then here is the menu. I have been on the Internet and found exactly what Kate had!' she announced proudly. 'Toro tartare with caviar . . .'

'What is Toro tartare?' whispered Angela. 'Is it something to do with a bull?'

'Some kind of sushi, I think,' Claire whispered back.

'Longhorn veal with grilled peaches, strawberry granita dusted with gold leaf, wine from Sesti and champagne. Oh, and a cake where every layer is a different flavour!' she added, and sat back smiling contentedly.

'*That* is a young lady who knows her own mind!' Angela announced, impressed, when Sylvie had led them off on a tour of the house and garden.

'There'll be a lot more on her list, you wait; Diptyque candles at seventy quid a pop,' Monica smiled, 'love birds in cages, white butterflies—'

'Not unless Kate had them,' Angela giggled. 'But doesn't she realize Kate's wedding wasn't exactly happy-ever-after?'

'Daniela's the determined type who doesn't give a hoot,' Monica shrugged. 'She just wants the fairy-tale dress and all the trappings. And good luck to her, I say.'

Sylvie joined them after Daniela and her mother had left. She looked exhausted.

'That young lady should be running a multinational company! What an eye for detail. I suppose it's just as well, given how little time we've got. One thing, though. I am definitely trying to talk her out of Kate Moss's wedding dress. It was made for a waif and Daniela is built like a sofa.'

'Talk *that* young lady out of her dream dress?' The others laughed till tears ran down their faces. 'Even John Galliano himself couldn't manage that.'

'But she'd look so much better in something that flatters her size!' Sylvie wailed. 'It could take a stone off her at least. If she copies Kate Moss, she'll look like a fat auntie borrowing her little niece's clothes!'

'Then I'll just have to make a bouquet – out of apricot and lilac roses – so big it hides most of the damage!' Monica suggested. 'Besides, I like her. I just wonder if the bridegroom knows quite what he's in for!'

'Let's hope he doesn't find out before the big day, then.'

'Well, my job's easy – all I have to do is source toro, whatever that is, longhorn veal and gold leaf! To think I was hoping for asparagus, rare beef and strawberries!' Claire picked up one of the photographs Daniela had left. 'Look at the veil, though. That could hide a few curves. See how clever it is. It has a short part that goes over the face like a mantilla for the ceremony that gets tied back by those little rose clips after the kiss, but the long part is about nine feet! Enough to cover three Danielas!'

Just in case life might have got dull, Monica spotted Constantine and Spaghetti, the former thankfully no longer dressed as a cardinal, appearing out of the bushes.

'Causing trouble again, ladies?'

'Constantine,' protested Angela, 'can you not call us ladies? It makes us sound like the committee of a golf club in Guildford.'

'Girls, then?'

'Better.'

'Golden girls?'

'*Definitely not!*'

'Anyway, in what way are we causing trouble?'

'Your bride has been tweeting away. Guido brought it to show me. She has been showing off about the new venue for her English country wedding. The degli Dei were rude and old fashioned as well as outrageously expensive, she says. Your friend Hugo isn't going to be happy about that. Weddings are his number-one earner. In fact, if rumours are true, about his only earner.'

'Well, that's hardly our problem,' Angela pointed out. She didn't want to think about Hugo. It was still too raw.

'But why – if his hotel isn't doing that well – would he have been making an offer for this place?' Monica asked, puzzled.

'That's the way capitalism works.' Constantine shrugged. 'If your business is doing badly, you buy another and hope that it will rescue it. Usually with other people's money. I expect Hugo Robertson can be extremely persuasive.'

Angela got up quickly. 'I'm going for a swim.'

'Angela . . .' Sylvie began, 'what if Stephen sees it?'

'I think that's pretty unlikely. And Gwen said we should do what we want, that he would appreciate any efforts we made.'

'Right. Good.' Sylvie got up, suddenly all decision. 'Well, I'd better go and think about how to turn an eleven-stone bride-to-be into a Pre-Raphaelite wood-sprite. Easy peasy.'

Angela dived into the green depths of the villa's pool and tried to think only about the feel of the enveloping water and the beauty of the sunlight splintering the surface above. When she was a child, she used to spend hours at the local pool, amazing her father with her determination to swim faster and faster. While other children splashed about, Angela competed with herself.

She knew it was a dangerous emotion; despite her efforts,

she was feeling sorry for Hugo. She knew he didn't really care about *her*, probably never had done, but he had penetrated her defences and for the first time in years, she had imagined a proper life together in this beautiful place. But maybe her dreams had been no more solid than Claire's when she had fantasized about leaving Martin for Luca and his lemon groves.

She had got to like Martin. He seemed different from the man Claire had described. Were they all mad, thinking they could still make crazy choices at their age? It was something their parents' generation would never have considered. Throwing everything up and starting again at over sixty; instead of being happy with retreating to the man-shed and bowling club, they still thought they could start whole new lives.

How wrong she'd been. Pathetic even. Duped.

She pulled herself out of the pool and shook the wetness from her. Drying herself briskly she made herself think of practical things. They needed a budget and Daniela and her mother were going to have to sign it.

A happy bustle took over the kitchen at the Villa Le Sirenuse the next day as Claire, with Immaculata and Beatrice to help her, surveyed the tableware, glasses, serving platters and candelabra. Daniela had invited a hundred and forty guests and they would have to order a lot of stuff in. Nevertheless, the villa possessed some very fine artefacts which would make perfect showpieces.

Immaculata, Claire noticed, was quietly weeping as she polished a silver rose bowl which would look lovely with a centrepiece of the bride's apricot and lilac roses.

'Immaculata, what's the matter?' Claire enquired gently. She'd become very fond of both of them over their stay here.

'The last time we use this bowl is for the wedding breakfast of Stephen and Carla.'

'Oh dear, that's sad.' Claire sat her down and produced a glass of water. 'You're very fond of Stephen, aren't you?'

Immaculata nodded. 'He is very good man. He say to us we can always work here. You do not think Stephen would sell his house to be a hotel?'

Claire realized what a terrible shock it must have been to someone who had worked here most of her life.

'We hope not, no. Let's make a big success of this wedding and show him he should hang on to it!'

'I think the sooner the wedding happen the better with that one.' Immaculata nodded ominously towards Daniela and her mother, who were sitting in the salon.

Trying not to think what this pronouncement might mean, Claire started to draw up some costings. 'Toro' or 'O toro', she discovered rather to her dismay, is the fatty part of the Bluefin tuna – naturally the most prized and expensive bit. And then there was the caviar, all of which would have to be sourced at the fish market in Naples. She thought longingly of all that free asparagus in the gardens and wondered whether to have another go at persuasion. The veal, she suspected, would be a lot easier as Daniela probably didn't know what Longhorn Veal was. She'd only got this information from the Internet. It probably wasn't what Kate Moss had anyway. Claire would do her best and Daniela would have to lump it.

Strawberry granita she could manage, but where the hell did you get real gold leaf? A browse around the cook's friend YouTube told her a list of suppliers and, amazingly enough, it wasn't that expensive. Maybe it could help fund the tuna.

The wedding cake she could also manage. The biggest challenge would be dreaming up seven different flavours and finding enough lilies of the valley to decorate it like Kate's in the time they had to do it.

While Immaculata and Beatrice sang and polished, it struck Claire again how sad it had been that Evan and Belinda hadn't asked for her help with their wedding. Evan would have, she knew, but had Belinda sensed Claire's hostility and thought screw you? Here was a wedding she was helping to organize for a complete stranger and already she felt that it was going to be enjoyable because it was a shared venture. Maybe if she had been nicer to Belinda, Belinda would have wanted to ask for her help.

Claire sighed. Too late now. Much too late. But when she went home she would make a deliberate effort. And she must stop right now thinking of Belinda as her 'difficult daughter-in-law'. She started to hum without realizing it was 'Blowing in the Wind'.

'You sound happy,' Martin commented. She'd joined him out on the terrace in the sun where he was doing the crossword.

'You know me, I like to be doing.'

He put down the paper. 'Well, I think you're all amazing. To even think of doing this in the time you've got. But then, you're a pretty impressive bunch.'

Claire wished she felt herself as confident in their abilities as Martin seemed to. She started to make a list out loud of things to do. 'Trestle tables, whatever they are in Italian. Monica would know. I need twelve of them, and a hundred and thirty chairs. In fact, it would be amazing if you and she could go to Lerini and consult her antiques lady and see if we can get mismatched ones. That would be very boho. Though Monica's doing the flowers as well, so I don't want to take up too much of her time. Martin . . .'

'Yes?'

'I've decided I'm going to be much nicer to Belinda when I get home.'

Martin took her hand and held it surprisingly tightly. 'You *are* coming home, then?'

'Of course I'm coming home,' Claire replied, taken aback.

'Don't mess with me, Claire,' Martin's sudden anger startled her. 'There's no "of course" about it. If Graziella hadn't come back, you might have stayed here.' He pulled her to him, squashing her notebook. 'For whatever reason, I'm very glad.' She thought he was going to kiss her again but this time he didn't. Maybe he didn't want to be taken for granted.

Sylvie studied the celebrated vintage-style wedding dress Kate Moss had worn. The fabric was beautiful, with its panels of silver- and sequin-embossed lace. There was no way she could find anything similar except in Milan, Italy's fashion capital, yet the thought of braving the frenetic urban atmosphere was too much after the peace and remote magic of Lanzarella. It wasn't her bloody wedding after all.

That made her think about her daughter again. Salome seemed to have defined herself in opposition to Sylvie's personality by being ultra-conservative, calling herself Sal and dressing entirely in Boden. Perhaps Sylvie should never have called her Salome in the first place. It must have been an awful lot to live up to. When she'd got married, she'd turned not to Sylvie, who would have enjoyed nothing more than creating an original colourful wedding for her daughter, but to *his* mother, who'd more or less bought one off the peg in Harrods, it was so dull and conventional.

Sylvie suspected Sal was simply embarrassed about her flamboyant mother. Of course, stupid gestures like sending incriminating pictures of Tony with a girl younger than Sal herself couldn't have helped. Her daughter seemed to spend more and more of her time these days with her parents-in-law in deepest Surrey. And since she'd had children of her own, Tony and Sylvie hardly saw them at all.

Sylvie had tried to convince herself she didn't mind. After all, being a grandmother was so ageing. But the truth was, she did. Very much indeed. Sylvie sighed. Sending out that email of their father would hardly have helped. When she returned home, she was going to try much harder to be what Sal wanted her to be.

She willed herself to go back to the dress. She stared at it, trying to see how it was made, and how she could produce a convincing copy.

A sudden thought struck her that slip dresses, which she would need to go underneath the transparent lace, had been all the rage in last year's collections. A version had been produced by all the big-name designers from Dior to Marc Jacobs. It was just possible that she might find something suitable in Capri.

The island of Capri, less than an hour away by sea, was a wonderful mix of yachties and Eurotrash, all prepared to blow a few thousand euros in the smart boutiques – Dolce & Gabbana, Vuitton, Prada – that graced the island's capital.

'Anyone fancy a day in Capri?' she asked the others. 'I'm going to scour the shops there for anything that could be converted into a boho wedding dress.'

Angela, who, with her usual efficiency, had already drawn up a budget and whisked it over to Daniela and her mother to sign, decided that this sounded a lot of fun, so they set off together to catch the next hydrofoil.

Angela, despite running Fabric, had never witnessed the

art of serious shopping before and was about to be humbled in admiration before one of its foremost proponents. Sylvie could enter a shop, take in an entire rail at a glance, demand to see anything that was being stored in the back, occasionally actually go into the stock room herself to make sure that nothing had been missed, and be out again in under fifteen minutes.

With Daniela's ample measurements stored in her phone she sampled every boutique in Capri Town. There was a promising moment when an Alexander Wang dress was discovered in a cupboard but it was a size 10, and a raised heartbeat when the name Calvin Klein was mentioned, only to find that the dress was short and champagne-coloured.

Angela could take no more and went to have a coffee. She was joined by an exhausted Sylvie an hour later. 'Nothing. The only thing that was Daniela-sized was a cheesecloth monstrosity that reminded me of those covers for spare loo rolls.'

'Well, as it happens,' Angela, cool as usual in a linen dress and silver sandals, sipped her Bellini, 'how about this?' She got her iPad out of her bag and opened a website. A pretty natural-looking model appeared in a floor-length waft of satin with spaghetti straps and a small self-train. 'It looks just like that Alexander Wang, only longer. It's a hundred per cent silk, fully-lined.'

'Don't show me,' Sylvie half covered her eyes. 'They'll never have her size!'

'As a matter of fact, they do. Of course, you'll have to add all that lace and beading and make it look vintage, but I'm sure that isn't beyond your talent.'

'How much is it?' The other dress had been two thousand euros.

'You're not going to believe this. Two hundred and fifty-seven pounds, plus twenty-four-hour delivery costs!'

'I think I'm going to faint.'

'Well, have a Bellini first. They're delicious.'

To Sylvie's utter amazement, the dress arrived the next day, as promised, and she began to add all the antiquey bits she'd found in Lerini, old lace, faded silk and beading, which she stole from an evening bag the wonderful antiques-shop lady had produced for her. 'It belonged to my mother,' the lady had explained, 'but my daughter remembered it and thought you would find it useful for Daniela's dress.'

Sylvie loved the way the whole community was getting involved in Daniela's wedding. Chairs of all different styles and sizes kept mysteriously arriving at the house via pickup, Fiat 500 and even a scooter. The word was out that Claire wanted chairs and chairs she would have!

'God knows what we'll do with them afterwards,' Claire shook her head, 'since I've absolutely no idea where they've come from.'

Martin came good with the trestle tables too. The truth was, he mentioned it to Luigi and Luigi went off on a mission to Lanzarella, where the cafe owners put their heads together and remembered that someone had some stored in a barn. They were used once a year when there was a Christmas fair in an area famous for specializing in Nativity crib scenes.

Feeling pleased with himself, Martin stood gazing out at the wide blue horizon, viewed through the purple framing of the wisteria-covered pergola. 'She's got good taste, this girl. I can't imagine anywhere more romantic than this to get married in, can you?'

'You're turning into an old softie,' Claire teased. 'It's certainly one up on Twickenham Town Hall where we did the deed.'

'Still, it's not the location so much as who it is you marry.' Martin looked at her penetratingly.

But before she could answer, Angela put her head out of the salon. 'Before you get too sentimental, there's something of a surprise waiting for you round the back.'

Claire shot a look at Angela. If it was Luca, she wouldn't have this rather curious teasing tone, surely?

They both followed Angela through the dark, cool interior, past *The Annunciation* and out to the back steps. There were two people standing in the shade of a holm oak tree leaning on what looked like a hire car.

'Oh my God,' Claire rushed forward with her hands out, 'it's Evan and Belinda!'

With all her newly polished good intentions, Claire made sure she gave her daughter-in-law a big hug. Belinda looked surprised, but smiled back.

'Hey, Mum!' Evan put his arms round her and then turned to Martin. 'Hello, Dad. We thought as we'd been abandoned by the pair of you we might come and see what the attraction of this Shangri-La-sur-mer is. I must admit, I can see it beats good old Twickers!'

Claire's mind was whirring about where they could put her son and daughter-in-law with all these mad wedding preparations going on.

Evan, always closest to her, read her mind. 'Don't worry, we're not expecting to stay here. We've got an Airbnb in Lanzarella, just round the other side of the town.'

'I'm sure we could have sorted something.'

'We want our independence too, you know!' His eyes twinkled. 'We've been quite enjoying having the place to ourselves, as a matter of fact.' He caught his mother's eye. 'And don't worry, we've been keeping it tidy; haven't we, Bel?'

'Even the liquidizer!' Belinda grinned. 'And the Kitchenaid.'

'Oh dear, am I that much of a domestic tyrant?'

'Yes!' they chorused.

'On the other hand,' Belinda conceded, 'they are the tools of your trade, so it's fair enough.' She glanced round. 'I'd love to see inside the villa. It looks absolutely amazing.'

'We wondered what had kept Dad here so long.' Evan grinned at his father. 'We thought the sirens had got him.'

'Maybe they have.' Martin flashed a look at Claire which made his son raise an intrigued eyebrow.

'Right, let's have the tour,' Evan said eagerly.

Claire and Martin took them around the house first, up the stairs past *The Annunciation*, which made a big impression on Belinda. She grabbed Evan's hand and stared at the Madonna. 'She actually looks happy about being pregnant in a quiet Madonna-kind of way. Do you know, I've never seen that before? They usually look like someone's slipped them the short straw.'

Evan squeezed her hand. 'Instead of seeing it as the beginning of a big adventure, as Lou Reed put it.'

'Well, Mary was going to be an unmarried mother; I don't suppose that was such hot news two thousand years ago in Galilee.'

The doom painting just made them fall about with laughter. Evan stared at the demon who was poking the naked women with a red-hot pitchfork. 'I'm not sure it would work as an effective contraceptive, but I suppose it might make you stop and think, "Is this really going to be worth it?"'

'Women have wondered that ever since the dawn of time,' Belinda teased him.

Sylvie's mad bordello rooms enchanted them. 'Definitely got some design ideas from those.' Evan grinned.

'Well, that would make a change from magnolia,' his wife pointed out.

'How is the flat-hunting?' Claire instantly wished she hadn't asked that. Did it sound as if she were trying to get rid of them?

'Good. We've found somewhere at last,' Evan announced. 'Your spare room may very soon be liberated.'

They went back down to the salon and out onto the terrace.

Belinda stopped, rooted to the spot, staring at all the trees with their froth of blossoms against the perfect blue sky, with the misty heat-haze of the sea beyond. 'My God, this is one of the most beautiful places I've ever seen!'

'I think that's what we're all feeling,' Claire conceded. 'Even Martin.'

Behind them the ever-smiling Beatrice appeared with a tray and an inevitable bottle plus some little nibbly things. 'For your guests.'

'More than just guests.' Claire put an arm round each of them. 'My son and lovely daughter-in-law, Belinda.'

They sat down under the wisteria-clad pergola as Beatrice poured the wine.

'Are you having some, love?' Evan asked Belinda tenderly.

'Oh, I think so.' She smiled at him. 'Go on, spill the beans.'

Claire watched them, unable to stop smiling herself.

'OK, Mum and Dad, we've got something to tell you . . .'

# Nineteen

'We're going to have a baby,' Evan announced, beaming with fatherly pride.

Claire was instantly out of her seat. 'Oh, Evan, Belinda, that's wonderful!' She had never really thought much about being a grandmother, she realized, but suddenly the prospect seemed entirely delightful.

'Well done, son!' Martin was hugging him.

'Quite clever of Belinda too,' Claire teased.

'Absolutely! Congratulations, absolutely bloody brilliant!'

'And when's the EDD?' Claire found the jargon – the all-important Estimated Delivery Date – came flowing back.

'The beginning of October.'

'Gosh, and you've had a scan?'

Evan reached for his wallet and removed a blurry grey-and-white scan photograph. 'Look,' his enthusiasm bubbled over, 'there's the head, and there's the back.'

He handed it to Claire who found her eyes were misting over.

'Grandmother alert!' Evan teased affectionately. 'Mum's tearing up!'

'You'd better give it to me, then!' Martin gently removed it then reached out a hand to hold Claire's. 'It is amazing, isn't it?' he asked, awed. 'A whole new life.'

'This is a great reaction.' Evan grinned at Belinda. 'I think we can book up the babysitting now.'

All Claire's hopes suddenly flooded into her mind, her feelings for Luca, her desire to make a life here – and all without the slightest suspicion that anything like this was waiting to ambush her. She turned away for a moment, to find Martin watching her, obviously guessing what she was thinking, and she felt at a loss, as if by even thinking such things she were betraying Evan and Belinda's trust, and somehow tramping on their happiness.

'Any idea if it's a boy or girl?' she managed finally.

'Evan would quite like a boy to fill his head full of football, and I'd quite like a girl to come shopping with me.' Belinda smiled at Evan tenderly, relishing her own joke. She was not one of life's shoppers. 'But actually we'd both be happy with either.'

'And you say you've found a flat?' Martin asked.

'Yes, we've actually paid the deposit, amazingly. We couldn't afford Twickenham, obviously, but the flat's not that far away.'

'I hope you didn't think we wanted you to move!' Claire blurted suddenly.

They all looked at her and Claire realized she must have sounded oddly vehement.

'Don't worry,' Evan teased, 'I'm sure you'll see plenty of us once we've got the baby.' He smiled at Belinda. 'We'd better head off. We've got a busy schedule while we're here. Belinda wants to see Pompeii and Vesuvius.'

'But you'll come to dinner?'

'Tomorrow would be good. We're here till Friday. Your housekeeper said you were planning a wedding. Not yours, I assume. I mean, you only got married in a register office so you're due a party.'

'Not ours, no.' Claire avoided Martin's sceptical gaze. 'It's for an Italian girl. Quite a big do. We're all pitching in.'

'Let's hope there's no bloodbath. *The Godfather* and all that.'

With perfect timing, Beatrice arrived to announce that Marco, the bridegroom-to-be, and his family would like to come tomorrow and have a look at the villa.

'What's his surname,' Evan quipped, 'not Corleone, I trust?'

Beatrice, on whom this literary reference was entirely lost, smiled helpfully. 'I think is Moretti.'

'Oh well, at least he makes a good beer.'

'No, no, is making parts for washing machine.'

'Evan,' his father chided, 'stop it.'

After they'd gone off down the hill in their little car, he turned to Claire. 'Well, they seem happy.'

'They do, don't they?'

'And you did very well in your be-nice-to-Belinda campaign.'

'She did offer an olive branch about cleaning the Kitchenaid.'

'So it's peace and happiness all round, then . . .'

What most surprised them all about Marco Moretti, when he arrived for an inspection tour with what seemed like a full delegation, was how much older he was than Daniela.

'I'd say forty-five,' said Martin.

'Surely more like forty,' argued Tony.

'Fifty,' chorused the women.

'Funny how you men all see him as younger than we do.'

'Too old for her, anyway,' suggested Claire. 'She can't be more than twenty-five.'

'What's wrong with that?' began Tony.

'Careful, mate.' Martin elbowed him. 'Shaky ground. Ladies of a certain vintage always distrust the younger model, and in your case . . .'

'Point taken.' Tony nodded humbly, but with a residue of twinkle. 'He is far, far too old for her.'

At that point the delegation rounded the corner and the portly bridegroom strode towards them. 'Whatever Daniela has told you,' he greeted them, 'we must be married in the church first, for the sake of my family. All my family have been married in Lanzarella Cathedral. I will fix this personally with the parish priest. He can read out – what do you call them? – the banns this week and get a special dispensation to marry the week after. He did the same for my cousin.'

'Mr Moretti, this is for you and your bride to decide,' Angela replied diplomatically. 'We will do whatever you wish. We just wish you to have a peaceful happy wedding.' And good luck to you persuading your fiancée, she almost added.

Marco nodded his thanks and re-joined his family just as an agitated Beatrice rounded the corner, attempting to prevent a very angry Hugo from bursting in on their conversation.

Seeing Marco Moretti in no way calmed him.

'This is all *your* doing, of course,' he accused Angela. 'You had some pathetic design on me and then when it wasn't going to happen, you steal my business from under my nose.' He really didn't look at all attractive when he was angry, Angela noticed. His charm was obviously just a cover for a domineering nature. 'I wonder what your precious Stephen thinks of the way you've all been behaving up here, eating his food, drinking his wine. How much of his money have you all blown on your five-star lifestyle?'

The Moretti party were witnessing this interchange from a distance, looking shocked that civilized people could behave so badly.

Angela maintained her calm with great difficulty. 'I don't think Stephen measures friendship in the same way you seem to.'

'Clearly not. But then perhaps he doesn't know the extent of your indulgence. Wine before dinner, wine with dinner, and, no doubt, wine after dinner. A nice little number for a group of—' he paused, looking for the appropriate insult.

'I think post-menopausal harpies was the delightful expression you used before.'

'Quite.' Finally, he noticed the Moretti party approaching.

'Mr Moretti,' Hugo turned on the charm like a tap, 'I hope you appreciate that you have placed the most important day of your life in the hands of rank amateurs.' He turned to Angela. 'How many weddings have you, or indeed any of you, organized before, Ms Williams?'

Angela looked at him coolly. 'That is hardly the point.'

Claire decided it was time to speak up. 'As a matter of fact, Mr Robertson, I have organized dozens of weddings, and funerals, and anniversary parties over a thirty-year period. Is that enough experience for you?'

Hugo looked her up and down. 'For some tin-pot catering company with absolutely no style or elegance. Rather like yourself.'

Which was when Martin hit him.

'Oh my God,' Sylvie, the one member of the quartet who hadn't been present, asked after they had all calmed down and

Hugo had been requested to leave, 'what did this Moretti man do? He's not going to cancel the wedding, is he?'

'I have absolutely no idea.' Angela was still feeling rather shocked herself. She'd seen unpleasant behaviour in business, but never seen anyone lose it like Hugo.

'Is Hugo OK?'

'I think his dignity was wounded more than his face, but he'll need a raw steak tonight. Maybe he can get one from his empty restaurant.'

'What do you think we should do?'

'I think we wait till tomorrow and then go and see Mr Moretti, all calm and professional, and reassure him it'll all be fine. Meanwhile, we have to hope he's persuaded Daniela and the priest that the ceremony ought to be in church.'

'Hey,' Sylvie brightened, looking up from the *Vogue* photograph she was using as a pattern for the dress. 'Didn't our Kate get married in church too?'

'Sylvie, you're a genius,' Angela congratulated her. 'Of course she did. This is going to be easier than we thought. Though if I remember Lanzarella Cathedral, we're going to need an awful lot of apricot and lilac roses.'

'Just tell her it's not in the budget,' Monica insisted. 'We'll do the whole thing from the garden. An English country Italian cathedral. No problem. No problem at all.'

By the time Evan and Belinda came to supper the next night, things had calmed down. Daniela had gone for the Cotswold cathedral number, her bridegroom had been assured Hugo only behaved like that because his business was going down the tubes, and the parish priest was delighted to welcome his strayed sheep in the form of Daniela, a rather over-endowed strayed sheep, it had to be said, back into the fold. Luckily for them the cathedral was free and the priest prepared to take a curiously Italian view of the canon law.

Monica was thrilled to relate tales from Pompeii and Vesuvius with the parents-to-be and they were genuinely impressed to hear from Martin of Monica's private scattering of her husband's ashes in the crater.

'How amazing to see Vesuvius on horseback,' enthused Belinda. 'Do you think we could do that, love?'

'Do you think that's a good idea?' replied the cautious Evan.

'In my condition, you mean? How do you think ladies got around before the motor car?'

'Maybe they stayed at home lying on their chaises longues being fed grapes by their husbands?' suggested Evan.

'I promise only to walk, not even trot, how about that?'

Monica gave them the details of Nick's riding stables and they booked themselves in for the day after tomorrow.

Stephen Charlesworth looked out of his latest high-rise, glass-fronted development on the River Thames and could feel spring in the air, even in this ever-growing, global city.

He loved London and though some people were convinced he and developers like him were trying to destroy the vistas that Canaletto had captured in the eighteenth century, he cared very deeply about the London skyline. It was just that he also believed in growth and change. He had laughed and listened when the actor Damian Lewis had asserted that London was becoming Dubai on the Thames, but also maintained that London had always evolved from Christopher Wren's time onwards. But this year spring came to him with an unusual sense of restlessness, something he could not remember ever feeling before.

This sense, he had to admit, had been exacerbated by the

curious letter he was holding in his hand. It had arrived yesterday. It was unsigned and written in a strange kind of stilted style as if trying to sound deliberately translated from another language.

*Dear friend,* it read (who was this curious anonymous friend anyway?), *you are being cheated by people you trust and your good name is at stake. It is time you visited the Villa Le Sirenuse immediately to put stop to corrupt and abusive actions.*

Stephen's first response had been to laugh, and then to imagine that it was some kind of practical joke.

Instead he rang his mother.

Gwen, sitting on the terrace of the Grand Ticino Hotel in Taormina, had no idea who this strange missive might be from or what it referred to.

'Sounds like a crackpot to me. Or someone who's been reading too much Conan Doyle.' Gwen thought about the situation for a moment. Who would be making trouble for the villa's residents?

A thought struck her, not for the first time, that it wouldn't do Stephen any harm to get over this strange relationship he had with the villa, rarely going there yet not being able to let go of it. How could he have even considered selling it to become an anonymous chain hotel? It was time Stephen experienced the Lanzarella magic again for himself. Who knew where it would lead?

'Go,' she counselled her son. 'I think you should go. Beatrice and Immaculata would love to see you.'

'But what about the others?' Stephen sounded suddenly hesitant. 'Wouldn't I be intruding on their peace?'

'It's spring in Lanzarella, sunshine and lemon blossom, remember? It would be good for your soul.'

Stephen came to a decision. 'Do you know, I think I will?'

'Excellent.' An even better idea occurred to Gwen.

Angela.

Gwen hadn't liked her at first. But Angela had definitely grown on her. Friendship had mellowed her and stopped her needing to be in charge. The only trouble was, after the Hugo situation, Angela had been making noises about going home.

Stephen hadn't told her a lot about their relationship in Oxford all those years ago, but she suspected it had been Stephen who had ended it. Angela was the proud type.

The position with Hugo had been humiliating enough, but if she knew Stephen was coming as well, someone who had also rejected her, even if it had been a very long time ago, she would probably jump on the first plane back to London. She was too proud to want to be pitied by Stephen.

Gwen thought that would be rather a waste. Stephen had been on his own for far too long.

'Tell you what, darling,' she advised her son, 'don't warn them you're coming or they'll pull out all the stops and make a huge fuss to say thank you.'

'I'd hate that.'

'Exactly. So I'd just turn up, if I were you. Tell them you're passing through. Give them all a nice surprise.'

'Do you think it would *be* a nice surprise?'

'Darling, of course it would!'

Stephen found his mood had changed. The restlessness had evaporated like mist in spring sunshine.

He would just tie up the ends of the deal he was working on here then he would go to Lanzarella. He'd book a flight for next Saturday morning.

Stephen found he was quietly whistling as he reached for his laptop. Which was quite surprising, as he'd never been able to whistle before.

*

415

Now that the church ceremony had been resolved, things were going along swimmingly with the wedding preparations. Marco felt he had successfully put his foot down and that this boded well for his marriage to the feisty Daniela, plus it was keeping his relatives happy. He was also relieved that the festivities were not happening in a hotel that was on the slide, managed by a man given to erratic behaviour.

Daniela adored the idea of her dress, and felt there was absolutely no problem with a size 16 damsel wearing a dress designed for someone literally half her bulk. Her mother thought the back scandalously low, but as Daniela argued, that would be covered up by the nine-foot veil.

The toro, the veal and the gold leaf had all been sourced and ordered, as had the outrageously expensive apricot and lilac roses. The bridesmaids, all twelve of them, would just carry flowers from the garden so that would save on the budget. And Sylvie, now hooked on the Internet, had managed to find bridesmaid's dresses for a fraction of the cost of shop-bought versions, which she could cleverly customize to complement the bride's.

What could go wrong?

Evan and Belinda only had two more days and there was still so much they wanted to do. Evan wanted to spend a day in Sorrento and Belinda wanted to go to the famous museum of Neapolitan Nativity scenes. They compromised by going on the horseback ride on Vesuvius. They were amazed to find what looked like Wild West stables on the slopes of a volcano in Italy. And to Evan's relief, the ponies looked both small and friendly. In fact, he reckoned, his long legs would almost touch the ground.

'You must be Monica's friends,' Nick, the owner of the stables, greeted them.

'Yes, she told us all about scattering her husband's ashes here,' Belinda replied. 'We thought it was so amazing. And I'd love to see Vesuvius from horseback. As long as you can promise there won't be an eruption.'

'I think I can pretty well guarantee that.' Nick grinned. 'There are well-known warning signs from the scientists. Unfortunately, they didn't have them in AD 79, or history might have been a bit different.'

He helped them saddle up.

'Can you make sure Bel gets the docile one?' Evan couldn't stop himself adding, 'Only she's four months pregnant.'

'Right. Maybe I'd better come with you, then, if you don't mind. I won't intrude.'

'We'd love our own private guide, wouldn't we, Ev?'

They set out on their black-and-white ponies, a bottle of water strapped across Nick's saddle in case it got hot later, following the path of the lava, through trees, passing small vineyards and curious rock shapes, all in the shadow of one of the world's most famous slumbering volcanoes.

Halfway up, they stopped to admire the amazing view of the Bay of Naples.

Belinda twisted round to get her camera from her backpack. The sudden movement spooked her pony and it started forward. Belinda, holding her camera rather than the reins, found herself slipping from the saddle, twisting her ankle as she fell, hitting the ground with a yelp of pain.

Nick instantly jumped off his horse and took her foot out of the stirrup so that there was no chance of her being dragged, but she was worryingly pale. 'Right,' he announced instantly. 'You just lie here on my coat and I'll go back and get the four-wheel drive. I won't be more than ten minutes. Here, have a drink of water.'

Evan had climbed down too and was kneeling next to her. 'My God, darling, are you OK?'

Belinda, with a shade of Claire's own sharpness, snapped back at him. 'I don't know, do I? My ankle hurts like hell but I think that's all.'

The ten minutes seemed to go on forever until finally they heard the sound of a car. Belinda was still pale and looked sweaty.

Nick had had the foresight to bring a hand from the stables who could lead all three ponies back. 'I'm taking you straight to the hospital in Naples,' he announced. 'They'll kill me at the villa if I don't! I'm sure it's only a precaution but I think it would set all our minds at rest.'

Belinda and Evan climbed into the back of the car, grateful that someone else was making the decisions. Evan insisted she lie down as flat as she could while he did his best to support her.

'I promise I won't drive like an Italian,' Nick joked, trying to keep the atmosphere as light as possible. 'Evan, I think maybe you should ring the villa once we get a signal. Your mum and dad will want to know what's happening.'

They stopped briefly at the ranch to pick up a blanket which Nick insisted Belinda have over her.

They were lucky that the traffic on the motorway was quite light. It would only take them half an hour to get to central Naples.

Evan wanted to ask if Belinda was having any cramps but realized it would only make things worse. She'd soon tell him if she was.

*

418

As soon as they got the news, Monica blamed herself. 'I should never have mentioned the riding stables to them in the first place,' she insisted.

'According to Evan she's only twisted her ankle. It may be absolutely nothing,' Claire tried to reassure her. 'Martin's going to the hospital now. They didn't want both of us because they've no idea if they'll even be seen for hours.' She paused, not wanting to even consider it. 'Unless it becomes an emergency.' She tried not to think of the blurry scan and their delighted happiness.

The truth was she'd been a little hurt that they'd wanted Martin rather than her, though it was true Martin was calmer. She knew she had a tendency to overreact, like pouring that coffee into the horrible banker's lap. And too many people hanging around might make the situation more tense.

Martin's taxi arrived and she made him promise to call her the instant there was any news. At least she had a million things to be getting on with here that would thankfully take her mind off the situation.

He had only been gone ten minutes and Claire was beginning to sort out her ingredients for the bottom layer of the wedding cake, when Luca arrived. He had the good judgement to ask for her to come out rather than come into the house, but, of course, everyone would still know.

'Chiara,' he looked rather wild, the restrained elegance that had characterized him nowhere in evidence, 'it is Graziella. She has gone and says this time it is forever.' He grabbed one of Claire's hands. 'Everything has been going so well. The business is turning round. The Cellono, thanks to you, is beginning to really sell. It was all over the Internet after your friend's party. A magazine wishes to write about it as the new Italian aperitif and yesterday a big distributor asked to come and see me! But Graziella says she knows that you are the one I love! *Chiara mia*, will you come with me and share my life here in Lerini?'

Claire listened to him, but it was as if he were talking about someone else. His words, the words she had longed to hear such a short time ago, seemed hollow and unreal.

Reality now was Belinda lying in a hospital in Naples. Reality was her son Evan trying not to mention the chance of a miscarriage. Of them both waiting desperately for the doctor to examine her and say that everything would be all right.

'Luca, I'm sorry,' her eyes searched his, trying to make him understand, 'I will be going home to England soon. With my husband. Once I have gone, I am sure Graziella will come back and you will save the business together. Your way of life is right for you, you are part of a family, a tradition, but my family and tradition are in England.' She reached out a hand to him. 'Goodbye, Luca. And good luck. I'm sure before long I will be reading about your big success with Cellono and I will feel glad that I had a small part in it, that all of us here did. And, most of all, that you can keep the tradition alive of Lerini lemons.'

She turned and walked back into the house.

As she got to the top of the steps, her mobile started to ring. It was Martin.

'It's all right, Clairey.' He used the pet name she hadn't heard in thirty years. 'Belinda's going to be fine. She'll be hobbling about for a week or two but the baby's in absolutely no danger.'

Claire was so relieved that she didn't even see Luca walk away and get into his car. 'Oh, Martin. Thank God. We can all breathe again. Monica will be so relieved too. She's been blaming herself for ever mentioning her ride on Vesuvius.'

'You can tell her that that friend of hers, Nick, was brilliant. He drove them straight to hospital himself. He's here still, as a matter of fact. He's going to give us all a lift back. Belinda says there's one good thing: she can get wheelchair assistance on the plane tomorrow and not have to walk miles from some ridiculously remote gate at Heathrow!'

When she went back into the house, she passed *The Annunciation* and stopped for a moment. Of course, the medieval Madonna had had absolutely nothing to do with Belinda being fine, but Claire found herself thanking the glowing depiction of the pregnant Virgin anyway.

Beatrice and Immaculata were busy in the kitchen but when Immaculata left to get a serving platter, Beatrice took Claire's hand. Claire had almost forgotten that Luca was her nephew. 'Is a good thing you do,' she said softly. *Grazie.*' They both knew what she was referring to.

Beatrice went back to the task of making sure the hired plates were clean, as if she had never spoken.

'Any news from the hospital?' Monica was almost as anxious as Claire had been.

'All fine, she's just twisted her ankle. That's all.'

Monica launched herself into Claire's arms. 'Oh, thank God! I have been *so* worried.'

'I know you have. One good thing. Your friend Nick was brilliant, apparently. He's dropping them all back.'

'I must really thank him.'

'I expect he'd enjoy that,' Claire added mischievously. 'How are all the flowers going?'

The flowers had been the last thing on Monica's mind. 'I'm storing them in the potting shed round the side of the house. It's cool and dark in there, perfect for blooms. One drawback of this wonderful wildflower look is that we can't pick them till the actual day of the wedding or they'll look like they've got brewer's droop, so it'll be up early for me and Luigi and Giovanni. In fact, a delivery has just arrived. I'd better take them round there now.'

Monica picked up two huge boxes that had been delivered from the flower market.

The fragrance of the flowers hit her the moment she opened the door of the shed. At one end there was a wall of terracotta pots and behind it a narrow space where the wheelbarrows probably once lived. Now there were simply some old blankets and yards and yards of cobwebby fabric which Luigi must use as protection for the plants if they ever got a severe frost which, given the climate here, must be almost never.

Monica had bought a dozen brushed-steel florists' buckets from the market and row upon row of roses waited to be made into bouquets and table centrepieces, each tied with ribbon for the big day. Timing was everything with flowers, Monica had learned. The wildflowers would be a headache, but, on the other hand, there was such a plethora of wildflowers from pale-washed anemones and wild irises, to white cyclamens and tiny blue hyacinths in the gardens and nearby wood. They would have plenty to choose from. Weaving those into headdresses with ivy should be straightforward and very striking. For the pew ends she planned narcissus, creamy camellias and orange blossom.

For the big showy displays, white peonies, lilac, and her favourite white hydrangea, Madame Emile Mouillère, all bought in the market. She'd toyed with pinks and lavenders to look like an impressionist painting but had decided an English country wedding should be white, white and white.

*

Gwen sat outside, sunning herself on the balcony of her room adjoining Mariella's. She felt like an old lizard lying silently, watching out for flies. It was a very good feeling.

The time she was spending with Mariella was drawing to a close and she was thrilled. Rarely had she felt more grateful. Mariella's selfishness was of epic proportions. She seemed, through her long life, to have acquired no self-knowledge at all. Gwen imagined that her husband Neville must be grateful to be deaf so that he could ignore all her demands.

'Gwen!' Mariella called out from inside the next-door room in a faint self-pitying tone. 'I really don't feel at all well. I've been up half the night in the lavatory. In fact, I'm suffering from both ends. It must be that restaurant you took me to last night. I thought there was a strange smell in the place. I bet it's their hygiene standards. Can you come in?'

Gwen knocked on the door and a shuffling Mariella came to let her in. As far as Gwen remembered, she'd eaten a very hearty meal last night – in fact, hearty enough for a con-demned man. She'd probably just overdone things.

'I don't think I'll be well enough to fly tomorrow,' Mariella protested. 'You'll have to get Monica over here. She can wait a day or two till I'm better and fly back with me. She's spent quite long enough in the villa with all those women. I don't think too many women together is a good thing. It starts to affect their hormones.'

'What, like nuns all having their periods at the same time?'

Mariella sniffed. She didn't like personal references. The less said about hormones or sex the better, in her view.

'Anyway, it isn't all female. Tony and Martin are there.'

'It's still high time she came home.'

'No,' stated Gwen simply.

'What do you mean, no?'

'Just no. As in No, Mariella, I will not try and get Monica out here to stay with you. There is absolutely no need. Monica has her own life to lead. We've had our turn, now it's theirs. Besides, you'll probably be fine by tomorrow.'

'But it's the responsibility of the young to look after the old.'

'It's a responsibility that has to be earned. What have you ever done for Monica?'

Mariella was looking at her incredulously. 'I have been giving her a roof over her head. It's time she did something in return.'

'Yes, but she won't need a roof from you any more, thanks to her friend Constantine. If you need someone to look after you, we will find you a nice carer like everyone else has.'

'A stranger in my home?'

'As you've often told me, your home is very large. You could fit in a stranger and only see them when you chose to. You'd enjoy it. Someone new to boss about. Now, are you going to be well enough to come down to dinner? If you recall, it's the manager's cocktail party tonight.'

The news of this gruesome event had the immediate effect of cheering Mariella up.

'I suppose I might make it down with a lot of help.'

'Excellent news. I will call the concierge and get them to send somebody. Personally, it's an occasion I prefer to avoid, full of social climbers, so I will read my book on the terrace and watch the sun going down before we return home tomorrow.'

Gwen got up and bustled to the door before the astonished Mariella could stop her.

Once in her room she sent a message to Monica.

'Your mother fine. Ignore all calls for assistance. We are returning home tomorrow. Enjoy the rest of your stay. Gwen.'

Gwen smiled as she helped herself to a Prosecco from the minibar.

Any day now Stephen would be arriving in Lanzarella.

Martin and Claire decided to go and see their son and daughter-in-law off at the airport in their hire car and get a taxi back. It was a big extravagance as the wedding with all its last-minute preparations was so soon but seeing them off seemed a lot more important than some stranger's wedding anyway.

Claire sat in the back with Belinda while Evan drove and Martin chatted to him. Despite Belinda's bandaged foot there was a festive air in the car. No doubt it was down to extreme relief.

'Monica's been nearly as worried about you as me,' Claire told her. 'Seeing as it was she who gave you the details of the stables.'

'You may have noticed,' Belinda replied teasingly, 'that when I decide to do a thing, I do it, irrespective of what anyone else advises. I'd better watch out for that. What seems like engaging feistiness in someone young could easily turn into shameless bullying!'

Claire thought of Mariella and how true that was.

To her surprise, Belinda took her hand. 'You seem so much more relaxed here, which is odd, seeing as people are usually most relaxed in their own homes. Maybe it was not having your home to yourselves that made you so spiky.'

'Was I spiky?'

'*Claire!*' Belinda teased, 'Yes, you were spiky. But then I was selfish.'

Claire squeezed her hand. 'I'm so glad about the baby.'

Belinda patted her tummy. 'Yes. He/she seems to be pretty determined too.'

'Anyway,' Belinda dropped her voice so that her father-in-law, happily chatting in the front, wouldn't hear, 'you may be more relaxed but what about Martin? He's a new man!'

'Maybe we all need to get away from ourselves sometimes.' She leaned towards Belinda and whispered, 'He actually hit someone the other day!'

'No! Defending your honour?'

'It was an unpleasant man who insulted my friend Angela and then turned on me. It was too much for Martin.'

'He seems ten years younger. Everyone talks about this Lanzarella magic. Pity you can't bottle it, I'd like to take some home! When are you coming back, by the way?'

Hearing this perfectly innocent question gave Claire a shock like an electric current running through her. Once they'd proved that the villa could be a successful wedding venue there was nothing more to keep her there. And now that she'd made her decision about Luca she ought to go home and make some changes so that she never again felt the kind of dissatisfaction that had made her come here in the first place.

She had chosen Martin and her family over Luca. Now they had an obligation to make their life together worth the sacrifice.

Without any sign that he'd heard a word she'd said, Martin reached back, took her hand and squeezed it, still looking forwards and talking to Evan.

Belinda raised an eyebrow and grinned. 'You seem pretty well tuned in anyway.'

Their flight was on time and the wheelchair was duly waiting to whisk Belinda off.

'I think I'll pull this stunt every time,' she laughed, eyeing the long queue at the check-in.

'Bye, darling!' Claire called to Evan.

'Bye, Mum, Dad. Have fun.'

Claire got her iPad out on the journey home to go through the last-minute preparations.

'Everything under control?' Martin asked.

'I hope so,' Claire snapped the cover shut. 'The trouble with spontaneous Bohemian weddings is that they're far more fuss than the formal kind. You have to do everything at the last bloody minute!'

Claire had taken the decision to turn down Beatrice's offer of roping in every second cousin and niece three times removed to do the waitressing in favour of using professionals. This had caused disappointment among the local maidens but great relief to Claire. She needed people who knew what they were doing. Waitressing at weddings was an art. She had seen occasions where some people had finished their meal before others were even served, and where one lot of guests had had so much wine they were drunk while others had empty glasses. All this had to be managed with experience and delicacy. Especially with the explosive Italian temperament. She had no desire to start a blood-feud that would last generations because the bride's family thought the bridegroom's was getting priority service.

When they got back, they found Sylvie, Monica and Angela all gathered in the garden.

'Claire, the weirdest thing,' Monica explained, 'your nymph's disappeared.' They were standing staring into the palm-fronded pool cut into the rock where Claire had had her dip on the first morning in Lanzarella.

'It can't have!' Claire peered into the watery depths, half

expecting to see the nymph staring back up at her like the victim in a Swedish noir thriller, but the pool was empty.

'She must weigh a ton! She's life size and pure marble! What do Luigi and Giovanni have to say?'

'Just as flummoxed as we are. She hasn't been removed for cleaning or anything. She's just straightforwardly disappeared.'

Staring at the empty space where the nymph had been, Claire found she wanted to cry. Without being aware of it, the statue had taken on a significance for her, an emblem, somehow, of how short a time she had been here, and what changes had happened to her since she had.

'I hope it doesn't end up in some garden centre or Italian scrapyard, I couldn't bear to think of it. She always struck me as a genuine work of art, not some British aristo's mad folly.'

'Luckily, I took some photographs of her on my phone,' Monica put an arm round Claire, seeing how upset she was. 'I'll see if Constantine can help.'

'OK, but that can wait. Let's get this wedding sorted. I think we should have a meeting later this afternoon: everyone should come and we can draw up a timetable. Rule one of successful entertaining – always have a timetable.' Monica looked at her, impressed. 'Yes,' Claire grinned, 'I'm channelling my inner Angela. Four p.m. here. I'll make sure the staff are all assembled, plus our head waitress. Can you organize Sylvie and Angela? Luigi and Giovanni will be here in a minute anyway to put out the trestle tables and chairs. If you want me, I'll be in the kitchen.' She grinned at Monica. 'For about the next thirty-six hours!'

The next thing Claire did was to check the weather forecast. She was never happier to see a perfect yellow sun smile back at her from her phone. Tomorrow was going to be beautiful.

# *Twenty*

'Quiet, everybody.' Trying to shut up a room full of excited Italians was a fresh challenge to Claire but she found a new and effective technique. Pointing her wooden spoon accusingly at anyone who didn't toe the line.

The trestle tables were all assembled on the terrace under the awning together with the wondrous assortment of borrowed chairs which were covered in every fabric from imperial purple velvet to a garish copy of Royal Stuart tartan. Claire just hoped Marco's family understood the concept of laid-back boho. Otherwise, they'd just think the villa had been sold a job lot in a junk shop.

'I think they look terrific,' Angela congratulated. 'Very Kate Moss. Especially with the white tablecloths and the silverware.'

Claire had to admit that she agreed. They had gone with the shabby chic idea and sourced non-matching plates and brightly coloured napkins. The whole look seen against a bright blue sky had the festive air of a country fete which she hoped the families would appreciate. It was certainly different from the stuffy formality she had seen in the photographs she'd studied of Italian weddings.

'How are the flowers coming along, Monica?' Angela enquired.

'Excuse *me*,' Monica teased her, 'but I think Claire's running this meeting!'

Angela smiled and sat back down, not in the slightest bit offended.

'As a matter of fact, they're gorgeous, especially the bouquets. Luigi, Giovanni and myself are getting up tomorrow at six a.m. to pick the wildflowers.'

There was a snigger from Giovanni which made Monica think of naughty prep-school boys telling each other dirty jokes.

She looked at him quellingly. Really, if he undid another button of his shirt it would fall off.

'I hope you're at your best in the early morning, Giovanni. I don't want to spend hours trying to wake you up.'

'*Chiara mia*, I am always at my best.' Giovanni slouched sexily forward, looking so much like the local bounder that he was that Claire wanted to laugh out loud.

'Excellent. Luigi, can you make sure the church will be open so that we can decorate it? Make extra sure we have their permission. Mr Moretti will help out if there are any problems. He seems to be an old friend of the parish priest.' Claire produced a timetable and seating plans, agreed by the bride and groom.

'Here is the list of what needs to happen when. I will put one outside as well. There are very few places for cars to stop, so we have organized valet parking round the back of the villa. 'Sylvie, what is happening with Daniela and the bridesmaid's dresses?'

'I have created a Bride's Room in the wing. Daniela and the bridesmaids can get changed there. They will then be driven to the church for the wedding. But, coming back, Monica has booked a little Italian band to accompany them as they walk back with all their guests. A touch of the medieval.'

'They always used to do it before weddings got so formal,' Monica explained. 'Then all the village can come out and cheer them on their way.'

'What a lovely idea,' congratulated Claire. 'Now. Daniela says she has a special surprise for her husband.'

'She is full of surprises, that one,' Giovanni murmured.

'After they cut the cake, she is going to release a dozen white doves to celebrate the purity of their love for each other.'

Behind her Claire heard Giovanni distinctly snigger.

'Well, I think it's a very sweet gesture,' Sylvie looked at him darkly, 'but where are these birds going to be kept?'

'They come with their own handlers, thank God. They'll stay round the side of the house until they're needed, but we need someone to make sure they aren't seen. Can you do that, Giovanni, or are you going to stand there behaving like a lounge lizard?'

'What is lounge lizard?' smouldered Giovanni.

'Oh forget it. Martin, could you take on the doves of purity?'

Martin nodded, grinning.

'What *is* the matter with Giovanni?' Claire hissed at the others. 'I mean, he's not exactly the subtle type, but he's ten times worse than usual. The cat that got the cream is the image that's springing to my mind.'

'Maybe weddings excite him,' suggested Sylvie. 'The thought of all those marital high-jinx probably sets off his testosterone.'

'Giovanni's testosterone levels are already a health hazard. I think someone should keep an eye on him.' Claire looked at Giovanni suspiciously.

'Well, he's hardly going to run off with the bride. Not at this late stage. Anyway, he's nowhere near rich enough. Daniela's far too mercenary.'

'I certainly hope so.'

Soon, however, they had other more pressing problems to worry about. They were all sitting on the terrace, exhausted but satisfied, feeling that they had done all they could achieve for today.

'I don't like the look of those,' Angela suddenly commented, leaning out on the balustrade. Over on the horizon were unfamiliar thick grey clouds that, to English eyes, looked ominously like rain.

'I'm sure they'll blow over,' Claire said hopefully.

But half an hour later the clouds had arrived in Lanzarella. They weren't, in fact, rain but a thick pea-souper of a fog.

'Oh my God.' Claire's optimism was finally evaporating. 'It's like London in the forties.'

'Apparently, it's quite common at this time of year.' Angela had been doing some investigating. 'It's a well-known local weather phenomenon. Last year they were shooting a big Hollywood movie here and they had to stop for a day.'

'Why do I not find that comforting?' Claire demanded.

'The locals in the piazza say it'll be fine for the wedding. They're all booking their places in the queue to watch.'

Claire dropped her head into her hands. 'Here am I trying to achieve *The Darling Buds of May* and we'll end up with a *Hammer House of Horror*.'

Angela hugged her. 'Time to go inside, pull the curtains and open a nice bottle of something.'

'But what happens when we open the curtains tomorrow and it's still like this?'

432

'It won't be. You just wait and see. You'll wake up and it'll be a beautiful morning.'

Stephen felt ridiculous. All this time he had visited the Villa Le Sirenuse only for brief moments, and with mixed feelings. Now that, finally, he had decided to go, and was feeling a childish excitement, what happened? His flight got diverted to Bari because of localized fog.

Of course, the sensible thing to do would be to get a hotel room in Bari then hire a car tomorrow and drive to Lanzarella. But if Stephen Charlesworth was known for one thing, it was his determination and his occasional wild decisions that had a habit of paying off.

So he didn't do that. Instead, he got in a taxi and asked it to drive him the three hours or so to Lanzarella. Then he went to sleep.

When they reached the villa, it was pitch-dark. The picturesque arches of the old convent and the square tower which housed the main rooms were shrouded in an eerie mist. There was utter silence apart from the call of an owl to its mate in the holm oak trees.

Stephen thanked and tipped the driver and got out his key to the large back doors. The silence inside matched the total quiet outside. In the kitchen, he realized how starving he was and helped himself to ham and cheese from the fridge plus a glass of white wine from an open bottle.

He took his meal through to the salon where an amazing sight waited him on the terrace. It was like the stage set of a country party. Thomas Hardy meets Glastonbury festival. Even Stephen, who didn't aspire to be fashionable, recognized the trendy vintage vibe.

Some people, coming back to their house and finding a

large party about to happen, might have felt aggrieved. But Stephen was an exceptionally generous man. He was delighted they all felt at home enough to throw a party. He had told them to make themselves relaxed here, and clearly they had. Besides, Stephen liked parties, especially if he didn't have to organize them. Finding him here would give them all a bit of a shock but it looked like they could find a space to fit him in.

He sat down on the sofa, hoping the fog would lift for them. He noticed his own wedding photograph in its silver frame. Someone had put a single red rose in a bud vase next to it, probably Beatrice.

He picked it up. 'Time I started to love this place again, Carla,' he confided to the photograph. Then he kissed it lightly. 'I wish we could have had children, you and I. Though we were so crazily young they would have been middle-aged by now.' The thought made him laugh. 'Fancy having forty-year-old children!'

Extreme exhaustion suddenly came over him. He washed up his plate – years of living alone had made him well house-trained – and picked up his carry-on bag. He always slept in the front room when he was here, the one his mother had slept in, she told him, when she'd stayed here. There were plenty of rooms to choose from now, Gwen had said, since Sylvie had done three up in her inimitable decorating style. He couldn't wait to see them.

The curtains were partly open in the room, lending that strange other-worldly sense, exacerbated by the owl. Why did owls always sound so mournful when it was just their normal cry?

He threw his clothes off and climbed into bed.

To his horror, he encountered a warm, sleeping body.

The body sat up and took a swing at him.

'If that's you, Giovanni, you can bloody well fuck off!'

Stephen ducked, just avoiding a black eye.

'Actually,' he explained apologetically, 'it isn't Giovanni. It's Stephen Charlesworth.'

'*Stephen!*' Angela almost passed out as she snapped on the light. 'What are you doing here?'

Stephen, naked apart from the sheet, seemed to think the whole thing was extremely funny. He surveyed Angela admiringly. 'God, Angela, you hardly look any different! And who's Giovanni?'

'Giovanni is your under-gardener. And the local stud. He's been behaving very oddly and we all thought he might be up to something. Sorry I nearly hit you.'

'Perfectly understandable when caught in a lady's bed. We do have a slight problem. Neither of us seems to be wearing anything.'

'I'll put the light out, 'Angela volunteered, 'and then go and get my wrap.'

'You always were delightfully practical,' he recalled. 'I'll get my T-shirt and boxers. Maybe we could count to twenty before we put it back on.'

In the disguising darkness Angela began to giggle. 'This really is the most preposterous situation!'

'All my fault, or rather my mother's. She suggested I come and surprise you all.'

'Well, you certainly did that. You can go back to bed. I'll go and sleep in the Bride's Room.'

'The Bride's Room?' Stephen asked, stunned. 'Is one of you getting married? Not Monica, surely?' He paused a moment. 'Or you?'

'It's a girl called Daniela. Lanzarella's wedding of the year, if only the bloody fog lifts. It's a long story but basically we wanted to show you how the villa could be useful to the village – by holding a local wedding.'

'I look forward to being convinced.'

'Goodnight, Stephen. I'll try not to wake you when I come and get some clothes, only as you can probably imagine, we're going to be pretty busy.'

'Any way I can help, I'd be delighted. I'm just pleased the house seems happy again.'

'It's a wonderful place. I think we've all fallen in love with it.'

'Fingers crossed for sunshine.'

Angela had to move the wedding dress off the chaise longue where Sylvie had draped it so that Daniela could change into it tomorrow.

She looked at it as she did so. It was a real work of art. Weddings were ridiculous events, really. The expense, the mad planning, all for one day that had little relationship to the life that would follow. All the same, there was a part of her that felt sad she would never be a bride herself. There were rites of passage she had denied herself. As Drew had pointed out, even owning a dog. 'But I'm not some frosty old maid,' she reminded herself. 'I have friends!'

As she tucked herself uncomfortably underneath a bolt of unwrapped fabric, all that she could find that was remotely like a bedcover, she smiled. Stephen was here and instead of being livid he seemed to think the whole thing was funny. The last image she had before she closed her eyes was Stephen, his long frame covered in only a sheet, grey eyes twinkling with humour at finding himself in bed with her again after all these years.

*

The next thing she knew it was morning. 'Angela, what on earth are you doing here? Where's the dress?'

'On the back of the door. Sylvie, the weirdest thing, Stephen arrived in the middle of the night. He actually got into my bed.'

'Oh my God!' Sylvie panicked. 'He's not going to call off the wedding?'

'Actually, he seemed to think it was quite a good idea.'

'Why did he get into bed with you?'

'He didn't think I was in it, obviously. In fact, I socked him one. I thought he might be Giovanni. You know how weirdly he was behaving yesterday.'

'Forget about Giovanni, we have a bigger problem on our hands.'

'Not the fog still?'

Sylvie threw open the curtains and brilliant sunshine streamed in.

'We've lost the bride.'

'What do you mean, we've lost the bride?'

'Her mother's downstairs having hysterics. She went out with her girlfriends last night and hasn't been seen since.'

'Oh my God,' Angela leapt up, 'you're not imagining anything sinister?'

'I very much doubt it. She messaged one of the brides-maids at eight a.m. this morning not to forget her gold stilettos.'

'Well, then, she has to be somewhere. You don't think she's had second thoughts?'

'I'd be extremely surprised. Now if *he*'d had second thoughts, it'd be much more credible.'

'We'd better start playing Hunt the Bride, then.'

'Angela . . .'

'Sylvie . . .'

They both had the identical idea at the same moment. 'Giovanni!'

'Oh my God, surely he wouldn't be that stupid?'

'Do you know what, that's exactly the kind of thing he'd do. Where the hell is he? He's supposed to be up with the lark picking wildflowers with Monica.'

'Maybe Daniela's gone with them,' Sylvie suggested hopefully.

Downstairs in the kitchen, a major war seemed to have broken out. Daniela's father was screaming at his wife that Daniela was a *puttana*, a whore, and it was all her fault. Claire, ignoring them, was up to her elbows in dough; Beatrice was weeping quietly in the corner.

'Luigi,' Monica tried to introduce some calm, 'please start picking in the upper garden. Anemones, wild irises, and ivy. Where is Giovanni?'

Luigi shook his head. 'He arrive with me to pick flowers then he disappear.'

She slipped into the shed where she was keeping all the precious roses, and picked up the large baskets to fill with wildflowers for the headdresses and bridesmaids' bouquets. She was about to leave when she heard a sound coming from behind the stacks of pots.

'Daniela,' Monica said coldly, 'your mother is hysterical and your father says you are a *puttana*. I imagine by now word will have got back to your bridegroom that you are missing. You had better think very fast of a convincing excuse or all our hard work will be very much in vain.'

'*Che cazzo!*' Daniela pushed Giovanni off her with impressive speed. 'Fucking hell!'

An Italian Holiday

Giovanni, who, like many promiscuous men, was shocked at women using bad language, looked away primly.

'I can handle Marco,' she announced with more confidence, in Monica's view, than the situation warranted.

When they arrived in the kitchen, Marco, his mother, and the best man had all arrived and were all standing round Claire yelling at each other and at Daniela's parents. Marco was insisting that the wedding was off.

'Marco,' Daniela adopted an impressively queenly manner, 'have you lost your mind? I went out to the shed simply to choose the loveliest roses for my headdress.' She looked modestly down at the flowers she had had the presence of mind to pick up.

Monica had to admit she was good.

'And that prick helped you, I suppose?' Marco glared at Giovanni who, for once in his life, had the sense to look innocent.

Into this melee strode Tony. He quietly announced that his wife would like some coffee on the terrace, then carried Marco away from the maelstrom of family accusations.

'Look, Marco, give her the benefit of the doubt. Giovanni tries to pretend that every woman in the world is after him. Daniela wouldn't fall for that cheap routine of his; she's much too classy, especially when she's marrying a proper man like you. I mean, let's face it, Giovanni is the gardener and you own a factory. And Daniela loves you. Look how she gave up her dream of getting married here and agreed to having the ceremony in church to please you.'

The logic of this seemed to be making an impression on Marco, who valued himself quite highly.

'È vero, this is true,' he conceded.

Marco, Tony quickly decided, *wanted* to be convinced.

Marco suddenly looked at Tony suspiciously. 'You believed her story about the flowers?'

'Absolutely,' lied Tony.

'Perhaps you are right. She did go and look for flowers.'

If he believed that, he'd believe anything, but that was love for you. Tony himself had believed Kimberley thought he was wonderful.

'I will go and talk to her.'

In the kitchen, Tony went straight up to Daniela. 'Go upstairs to the bride's room. Put on your beautiful dress. I'll send Marco up in ten minutes. The rest's up to you.'

'But if the bridegroom sees the dress on the day of their wedding, it will bring bad luck,' pouted Daniela.

'If the bridegroom catches his bride with the under-gardener on the day of the wedding, it is much worse luck, I can tell you!' Tony replied unsympathetically.

Tony was as good as his word. He dispatched the bride's and bridegroom's parents off back to their hotels for coffee and sent Marco upstairs.

There was absolute silence. They all waited for war to be declared and objects thrown.

But the sounds that emerged five minutes later were re-assuringly conciliatory. As well as extremely noisy.

'Oh my God, her dress!' wailed Sylvie. 'When I think how long it took me to alter it!'

'You can mend the odd rip for the sake of marital harmony.' Tony slipped a reassuring arm around his wife. 'I hope that stupid girl *has* learned her lesson. I rather like Marco.'

'Whether it works or not, thank you for trying.' Sylvie kissed him gratefully. 'You've probably saved the day.'

'And sentenced a nice man to life with a trollop. Oh well, that's marriage for you.'

'I hope you're not drawing parallels with me,' Sylvie teased.

'More with myself actually.'

'You know, I think I'm going to rather enjoy today. Wedding or not.'

Angela could see that Sylvie and Tony's reunion was looking like more and more of a success. 'Oh my God, that reminds me,' she suddenly remembered. 'I'd better go and wake Stephen.'

'What are you talking about?' Claire demanded.

'Today, of all days,' Angela announced, 'our mysterious host has decided to join us!'

'Why?' demanded Claire anxiously. 'And we hadn't even told him about the wedding! What on earth will he think of us?'

'The funny thing is, he seems quite happy.'

'It must be really weird for him, coming back into all this.' She gestured at the festive tables, flowers and candles. 'I mean, the last wedding here he went to might have been his own.'

They were all quiet for a moment, thinking about Stephen's young bride and all the hopes and dreams she must have had in this house.

In the silence they noticed that the noisy reconciliation between bride- and bridegroom-to-be had also gone silent.

'I hope she hasn't completely wrecked her dress. The hours I spent on it . . .' Sylvie protested.

'Ripped lace could be the latest look for the boho bride,' laughed Angela. 'Very Kate Moss. Just tumbled out of bed in my wedding dress could definitely catch on. Where's Monica, by the way?'

'Out picking wildflowers.'

441

The kitchen doors opened and Monica came in followed by Luigi and his little grandson, carrying baskets of ivy, pale-coloured anemones, irises and wild clematis. 'OK, who's up for making the headdresses? The bridesmaids will be here in half an hour. Thank God we did the pew-ends and the big church arrangements last night. By the way, I sent Giovanni home. He's caused enough trouble already today. God knows what would happen if he met the bridesmaids, even if they are only ten.'

They were all busy twining ivy with the wildflowers when Stephen arrived in the kitchen. Monica, who hadn't been warned, almost fainted. Beatrice and Immaculata both screeched like mating owls and threw themselves at him.

'Stefano, *santa madre di Dio*! You did not warn us you were coming!' Immaculata couldn't decide whether to weep or cover him in kisses.

'But your room!' Beatrice was beginning to realize the full horror of Stephen's unexpected arrival. 'Signorina Angela sleeping in your room.'

'Yes,' Stephen smiled, 'it was quite a shock when I tried to get into my bed.'

'And not just for you, I can tell you!' Angela agreed.

Sylvie, Monica and Claire looked at each other and then back at Angela.

'Shut up, you lot!' Angela commanded.

'Did we speak?' asked Sylvie. 'Did we make the slightest implication?'

'You didn't need to. I understand the post-menopausal harpy brain.'

Stephen listened to them, amazed. 'Women are wonderful,' he marvelled. 'If men talked to each other like that someone would get hurt.'

'We've spent quite a lot of time together, thanks to you. Besides, it's a reference to something the delightful Hugo Robertson said.'

'He sounds charming, I must say.'

'So charming that we'd go to any lengths to stop you selling him the villa. Including holding a wedding to show you why you shouldn't.'

'Right,' Sylvie announced. 'I'm going upstairs to repair the bride.'

For some reason all the others fell about.

Tony held out his hand to shake Stephen's. 'Time we left them to it. I'm Tony, by the way, Sylvie's husband.'

'Right.' Stephen tried not to stare at him since the last time he'd seen him it had been in the infamous email attachment.

'I know,' Tony smiled ruefully, 'I'm famous. Thank you for letting us stay in your beautiful house. It's been quite an adventure one way or another.'

'So it seems. I'm beginning to wish I'd been here too.'

There was a sudden eruption of small girls as the gaggle of bridesmaids made their appearance.

'*Andiamo!*' Monica adopted her librarian persona. 'Upstairs! Everyone pick up one of these headdresses on the way.'

There were whoops of delight as each little girl grabbed a flowery crown and dashed after Monica.

'Right,' Claire insisted, 'less of the mini-Glastonbury. I need a clear kitchen! Thank God we'll have an hour for all the last-minute stuff while they're tying the knot. I love that man Marco for insisting on a church service.'

Once Sylvie had appeared upstairs the bridegroom took himself off as fast as possible, much to general relief, since the bride's parents had reappeared.

'This is going to be a classic wedding,' murmured Sylvie, 'everyone hates each other already.'

But when Daniela descended from the Bride's Room with her little bridesmaids in tow, wearing the ingeniously repaired dress and a headdress of ivy and wildflowers, all they could do was watch in admiration. She even managed to convey, with the help of her nine-foot veil and the strategically placed lace inserts, which played down her ample chest, a surprising air of maidenly modesty.

'And given what she's been up to this morning that's quite an achievement,' Sylvie whispered.

The cars were waiting outside to transport the bridal party to the cathedral.

As soon as they had gone, Claire consulted her timetable. The waiting staff, in black skirts or trousers and white tops, were ready to dive into action; someone was dispatched to brush down the red carpet that had been quickly laid on the back steps where the reception line would be; glasses were polished and champagne checked. Claire had decided that the wonderful Sesti wine from Montalcino came in such beautiful bottles that it ought not to be decanted. The water and white wine would be put out just before the guests arrived. The canapés were arranged on serving platters for the waiting staff to hand out with the champagne. The caviar and toro could only be plated at the last moment, but the garnish was already assembled, and the veal roasting in the hired catering ovens. So far, so familiar.

'Is Martin ready with Daniela's little surprise?' Claire asked Monica.

'I would have thought we'd had enough surprises from Daniela,' Tony commented.

'She's going to release a flock of white doves as a symbol of the purity of their love for each other.' Claire tried not to giggle.

'I do hope she's not going to say that or she'll bring the house down,' Tony pointed out. 'I imagine this morning's escapade is all over Lanzarella by now. Giovanni's probably in the bar in the piazza embroidering the story as we speak.'

'Men are so pathetic,' commented Angela waspishly while Stephen and Tony looked apologetic. 'Now, Claire, what can we do or would you rather we were out from under your feet?'

'To be honest, I'd love a little space,' Claire agreed. 'But stay somewhere we can find you. Judging by this morning, anything could happen.'

'I'll just finish the table arrangements and make sure the seating plan's where it should be,' offered Monica.

'I think I'll hang on upstairs in the Bride's Room just in case the dress does need adjusting,' Sylvie announced.

'And I'll make sure Martin's OK with the doves,' said Tony.

'Just you and me, then, Stephen,' Angela teased. 'It may be your home, but we need to make ourselves scarce for a bit. You know that little pagoda thing right at the top of the garden? Why don't we steal a bottle of wine and hide ourselves up there? I don't think any of the guests will penetrate that far but Claire can yell if she needs us.'

'That'd be perfect,' Claire thanked her. 'Stephen, I'm so sorry at shooing you out of your own house.'

'If the wine Angela's talking about is that delicious Sesti, you can shoo me out anytime.'

Angela led the way to the pagoda. It was a perfect hideaway since they were within earshot of the wedding yet hidden from sight themselves.

Angela sat down and left Stephen to open the wine.

'My mother had such a good time with all of you.' Stephen handed her a glass. 'She loved being one of the girls. And thank you for rescuing her from the degli Dei. She was so disappointed at how much the place had changed.'

'That was why we couldn't let you sell the villa to Hugo Robertson and see him turn it into a posh mausoleum.'

He smiled. Despite all the time that had passed since their Oxford days he still had the same smile. Boyish and enthusiastic. It would probably be the same at eighty. 'I'm glad you and my mother sorted him out. I gather he turned out to be rather a shit.'

'She told you about that? I don't seem to be very lucky in my relationships.' As soon as she'd said it she regretted it. It was too personal. And it sounded as if she was trying to make him feel guilty for something that had happened when they were in their twenties.

'I don't think I behaved very well . . .'

'Stephen,' she interrupted, 'we were very young. We had no idea even what kind of people we were. That was what university was for. To find out.'

Stephen held her gaze intently. 'I've thought about you a lot over the years, Angela. Even watched your TV shows,' he confessed, looking suddenly sheepish. 'I actually saw you at a couple of events. I almost came over. But I thought I'd look like I was impressed by your fame.'

'I wish you had.'

A moment's silence fell between them.

'But you've been so successful yourself.' She felt suddenly shy. 'I followed your career too.'

'Yes, it's gone well but, lately, I've been bored by it. That's why I came. Hoping for the Lanzarella effect. Maybe it's age. I

446

keep thinking I'd like to do something different. God knows what.'

'I was so sorry to hear about your wife. Everyone here seems to have loved her very much.'

Stephen smiled. 'Even though she was Sicilian. That was quite a feat.'

'Was it losing Carla that made you so ambivalent about the villa?' She somehow knew he wouldn't resent such a personal question.

'Yes. But I couldn't let the place go. Of course, it cost so little when we bought it.'

'And it must be worth so much now.'

'That wasn't why I considered selling it. It was that I couldn't work out my feelings for the place.' He looked around him. 'I'd come here and realize how special it was, how extraordinary. But it always made me feel more alone. I tried bringing friends, girlfriends even, but it always seemed to be Carla's place.' He glanced down towards the garden. 'You know the statue by the hidden pool, the Venus bathing . . .'

'We thought it was just a nymph.' Angela jumped guiltily. Oh God, they would have to tell him it had gone.

'Carla bought it. It always reminded me of her. She was such a happy person yet she could get this sudden wistful look of sadness, as if she were seeing something no one else could see, almost as if she could tell what would happen. Just like the marble statue. Stupid, really.'

'Stephen, something awful's happened. Someone's stolen it. The statue.'

Stephen looked stricken. 'But why?'

'It just went the other day. Monica has asked your neighbour Constantine if he can find out anything. He knows everyone, apparently. Now we know the value it has to you, we must look properly, get the police in.'

Behind them they could hear the happy cheering and clapping from the bridal party as they took their places for the celebration.

'Signora Gwilliams . . .' Beatrice ran up through the garden looking anxious, 'there is someone to see you.'

'Can't they wait until after the wedding?'

It was Hugo Robertson, with Tony pursuing him, and behind them two large types, who looked like doormen from the hotel, carrying something very large wrapped in a white sheet.

They put it down and Hugo removed the sheet. 'Your missing statue.'

'Oh, thank God, it's your Venus, Stephen. But where the hell has it been?'

'I saw it in Lerini market this morning,' Hugo replied silkily, 'and lucky for you I recognized it and assumed you might want it back.'

He glanced back at the wedding that was in full swing, the trestle tables and non-matching chairs with the deliberately planned air of a relaxed country wedding.

'I can't believe she'd actually prefer all this tat to the kind of elegant wedding we'd have given her, but then from what I've heard, she's pretty damaged goods herself.'

For the second time in quick succession Hugo Robertson found himself at the other end of a commanding punch.

This time it was Angela who delivered it.

Stephen was watching her, deeply impressed. 'You really do have a powerful left hook.' He smiled at her teasingly.

'I've been wanting to do that for some time,' Angela announced to Hugo with satisfaction. 'As a matter of fact, we were wondering if you had anything to do with its disappearance.'

Hugo laughed, nursing his rapidly swelling chin. 'Then why the hell would I bring it back?'

'No doubt to get back into Angela's good graces,' Tony commented nastily. 'For some reason of your own.'

'This is entirely bloody ridiculous.'

Behind them, the moment had arrived to release the doves of purity. Martin and the handler had assembled their cages so that when one opened the others would follow. To thunderous applause, Daniela opened the first cage and a flock of terrified doves took wing in the direction of the pagoda.

With impressive precision, the lead dove shat over Hugo's head and shoulders, staining his Armani suit with a fetching green which, as Angela was tempted to point out, went well with his eyes.

'What the fuck . . .' he shouted.

'Probably a female,' Angela murmured. 'Possibly damaged goods.'

'Actually,' Stephen pointed out, 'a bird shitting on your head is supposed to be good luck. Something to do with the odds against it happening being a million to one.'

Behind them, a figure in a trench coat and Russian hat, with a small dog tucked inside yapping furiously, shambled towards them. 'Where's Monica?' he demanded, almost bursting with excitement.

'Down amongst the wedding guests.'

'Only she showed me this photograph of the missing nymph—' He stopped, noticing the wandering statue. 'Oh, she's back. My friend thinks she may indeed be by Bernini, but much more important is this!'

He got out his phone with the photograph of *The*

*Annunciation* which Monica had taken. 'He's pretty sure it's a real Filippo Lippi and if so, it'll be absolutely priceless!'

'Constantine, this is Stephen, the owner of the villa.'

'So you're the eccentric gentleman who owns a slice of paradise and never shows up? Well, if this *is* a Lippi, you're an exceptionally rich eccentric.'

'Actually,' Angela was finding things too funny to contain herself, 'he's pretty rich anyway.'

'I'm getting out of this mad house.' Hugo tried to achieve a little dignity and failed. Being covered in green bird poo didn't help.

'Good idea,' Tony congratulated him, hugely enjoying the situation. 'Before we call the police to look into what really happened to this statue.' He considered Hugo's red and rapidly swelling jaw. 'Of course, you may want to explain your own generous part in its rescue and why you got hit by a woman.'

'Or press for assault,' Hugo said nastily.

'From what I hear of how the statue made its way from here to the market, I very much doubt that,' Constantine challenged. He turned towards the sounds from the wedding party which was getting decidedly riotous. 'Seems like people are having a good time. He addressed Hugo again. 'You know, you really ought not to be such a sore loser, as our friends the Americans put it.'

'Losing a slag of a bride and her pathetic husband? I prefer clients with a bit of class.'

'Perhaps you soon won't have any clients at all,' Constantine purred as Hugo started forward.

'Time you left.' Stephen introduced his long body between Constantine and Hugo. 'In fact, I don't recall inviting you here in the first place.'

'You're just a rich idiot who inherited his money and

doesn't even know the value of his own property,' Hugo accused.

'As a matter of fact,' Stephen was beginning to enjoy himself, 'I didn't inherit any money at all and I got rich by knowing exactly the value of property. I just don't happen to value this one in monetary terms.' He handed Hugo a handkerchief. 'You may want this. It's easier to insult people when you aren't covered in green slime. Now please leave before I ask someone to throw you out.'

They all had the satisfaction of watching Hugo walk towards the wedding party, then think better of it and ignominiously dodge round the side and into the trees to avoid Marco, in case he had somehow heard his comments about the bride.

'What a delightful character.' Stephen grinned. 'No wonder my mother didn't want to stay in his hotel.'

Across the lawns they saw a swaying Daniela walking towards them, smiling blissfully.

'It is a wonderful wedding,' she enfolded Angela in an enthusiastic embrace, 'but where are your friends? I want to thank them also.'

'I'll go and find them.'

Moments later, Angela was back, one arm linked into Claire's, the other into Monica's. Tony had fetched Sylvie from the midst of the happy throng and Martin, freed of dove duty, came along behind.

'Thank you all,' Daniela announced, her ample chest heaving. 'It is just what I dreamed of. It is the best day of my life.'

'She sounds as if she actually means it,' Angela whispered, as the bride stumbled back to find her bridegroom.

'For today anyway.' Monica shrugged.

'Monica, you've got so cynical!'

'You heard what she got up to in the potting shed!'

'Come on, Claire quite fancied Giovanni herself once.'

'Correction,' Sylvie pointed out, looking slyly at Martin, 'it was the other way round. Giovanni fancied Claire. Don't you remember, he called her his nymph?'

'Well, he can't have her.' Martin put his arm round his wife. 'Because she's my nymph.'

Stephen, sensing this might be a moment to leave the friends together, suggested the men all help him move the marble Venus back to her natural resting place.

'So,' Monica asked the question they were all asking themselves, 'now that Stephen's arrived, what are we all going to do next?'

# Twenty-One

'We've booked our flights.' Sylvie threw in the bombshell and stood back to see the reaction. 'For tomorrow.'

They all knew it was inevitable, and yet it was a decision none of them had dared to make. Until now.

'Time I got back to my business. I've stayed away far too long.' Sylvie stood up and shook out her brightly coloured skirts. 'There're only so many excuses my staff can make to clients about why I'm not there.' She glanced across at the three men who were trying to decide if Venus was back in the right position. 'There's one thing I've been thinking about: I want to build bridges with my daughter. Persuade her I'm not *always* an embarrassment. Get to know my grandchildren better. And I'm planning to include Tony more in the business instead of treating him as a slightly annoying encumbrance. After all, he does have useful skills.'

'Charm,' agreed Monica.

'Negotiating skills,' Angela agreed. 'It was he who persuaded Marco to go ahead with the wedding.'

'Humility,' Claire pointed out. 'He's ready to admit when he thinks he's wrong.'

'Another thing I've learned,' Sylvie smiled happily, 'is that I'd never make a wedding planner. I'd rather face a roomful of rich Russians than plan another marriage. It's too damn stressful. Unless,' she glanced meaningfully at Angela and Monica, 'it was one of your weddings.'

They both laughed uproariously. 'Well, that isn't going to happen!'

Claire and Sylvie exchanged a meaningful glance. 'Of course it isn't,' Sylvie agreed. 'Absolutely no way. How about you, Claire? Back to catering anniversaries and funerals?'

'As a matter of fact,' Claire announced, 'I rather thought I might open a cafe. Just lunchtimes, you know, and ask Martin to help me. I do think Martin's mellowed.'

As if in confirmation, they could hear Tony and Stephen laughing at some joke Martin had made.

'It's the old Lanzarella magic again,' Monica agreed.

'I suppose the big test will be whether he comes over all grouchy when we get home. But I sort of think he won't.'

'And you're absolutely sure about Luca and the lemons?' Angela asked gently.

Claire nodded. 'I realized it when Evan and Belinda came, and then when she might have lost the baby. It isn't that I'm gagging to be a granny but it reminded me of reality. We're all told change is good, even at our age, but the change has to be rooted in something more than a fantasy. So, for me, change will be opening a cafe.'

'You do realize,' Sylvie pointed out, 'that opening a cafe is the most popular fantasy in the UK and even more stressful than being a wedding planner? How about you, Angela?'

Angela sighed. 'The funny thing is, I really don't know. I thought I would want to start another business, but coming here has changed that.'

'That old Lanzarella magic . . .'

'I feel a bit adrift, which is not like me at all. I might do some travelling – after all, there's nothing to make me go home. No commitments apart from my mother. I felt quite sad about that and then I remembered – I've got you lot!'

'Yes!' seconded Monica. 'The Lanzarella Women's Cooperative will still be together! Maybe we could even take on some tasks. Thank God I've got the painting Constantine gave me. It means I can stop worrying about money all the time and have some choices – like not living with my mother!'

'Will you go back to Great Missenden? What about the big city? We're quite near, me in Chelsea, Angela in Marylebone, apart from Claire, who insists on living in Twickenham for reasons best known to her.'

'It's very nice in Twickenham!' protested Claire.

'I'm not really the big city type. I like the wide open spaces and fresh air.'

They saw that the men were heading back towards them.

'Shall we all go out to dinner tonight? Our last night together in Lanzarella?' Sylvie suggested. It hardly seemed possible that they had got so used to having each other around. 'And then tomorrow Tony and I will head back to reality and the Riskovs. You do know, husband dear, that Mr Riskov offered to bump you off for cheating on me?'

Tony looked seriously shaken.

'Naturally I turned him down,' Sylvie said with a twinkle. 'This time.'

'Could I have a word, Angela?' Stephen asked.

'Come on, you lot, time to pack,' Sylvie chivvied, looking knowingly at Claire and Monica as she did so.

'I just wondered if you were planning to stay on?' Stephen

asked as soon as they found themselves alone. 'Or will it be too strange without the others?'

'To be honest, I've no idea what I'm going to do,' Angela admitted truthfully.

'I'd like to spend some time together catching up,' Stephen smiled shyly, 'it's been such a long time.'

'I'd enjoy that too.' In a blinding flash she realized how much she'd wanted him to say that.

'I've even hired a sports car so we can see the scenery properly.'

'Just like the old days, do you remember your old Austin Healey?'

He laughed. 'Do you know, I'd forgotten that car?'

'But you loved it so much.'

'I hope this one will be a bit more reliable. I'd really like to go to Caserta, to see the English Garden. Carla used to love the place.'

Angela hesitated, hurt. Was this going to be a trip to keep alive his love for his wife?

Stephen instantly understood. 'I was happy with Carla and will always love her, but it was a very long time ago, and I've been quite lonely, as a matter of fact.' He took her hand. 'I think maybe you have too, though you'd die rather than admit it.'

'Now what would make you think that?'

'Updates from Drew. He's a very good friend of mine, and before you protest, there was nothing creepy about it. I only asked him now and then. So are we on for the road trip? After Caserta, we can go wherever you like.'

'Naples!' Angela replied instantly. 'I want to feel the buzz of a city. Eat pizza in the street. Watch kids playing football. See the nonnas hanging up the washing between the buildings. Get my pocket picked.'

'That doesn't sound like Angela Williams, scary business-woman.'

'Maybe I'm a bit bored with being a scary businesswoman.'

'Next question, a big one, this,' he looked at her searchingly, 'one room or two?'

Angela smiled and took a step towards him. 'Oh, two, I think, don't you? I wouldn't like to have to administer another punch, though I must admit we did make a promising start on the bed-sharing. At least you've had the good manners to ask me first.'

'But, Miss Williams, it is my house.'

'And outrageously wasteful you've been in making use of it.'

'Perhaps,' she was a tall woman who liked to wear high heels, so finding his lips level with hers was a rare pleasure, 'we could put that right,' he offered generously.

'We could hold the annual convention of the Lanzarella Women's Cooperative here for a start.'

'At the very least. Perhaps we might even consider turning it into a hotel after all.' Angela looked shocked. 'Run by you and me as the best boutique hotel in the Med. Sylvie could decorate and my mother could advise on old-fashioned charm.'

He pulled her firmly into his arms.

No ghosts from the past came between them, only the promise of happiness in the future.

She raised her head for a moment. 'Another question. Did you suggest to Drew I come here because you felt sorry for me?'

'Absolutely. I always feel sorry for terrifying blondes who sell their companies for a big profit. It's a definite weakness of mine.'

*

Monica, taking a quick peek out of her window at Stephen and Angela in the pagoda, smiled. She liked Stephen and thought there was a good chance he and Angela could be happy. Especially now the cooperative had taught her not to be so bossy.

What would she go back to herself? Thanks to Constantine's generosity, she would no longer have the depressing life she'd had before she came, living with her parents as if she were still a teenager, scraping together the money for even the smallest treats. Coming here had been by far the greatest extravagance of her life and without Gwen to make her, she probably would have turned the offer down. Now she would have choices. She could buy new clothes, maybe even ones that would get her noticed, have a garden, go to classical concerts. She would be leaving Brian here, but at least he was in a fitting resting place.

There was a knock on the door and Tony put his head round.

'Sorry to disturb your packing, Monica, only the staff are still busy with the last of the guests. There's a man downstairs with a rather curious message. He says to tell you his name's Nick and is there any chance you might like to meet up back in Beaconsfield?'

Monica laughed. She wasn't sure if she wanted another man in her life. The idea of independence, paid for by Constantine's painting, was too tempting. But then, you never knew. Monica smiled to herself.

Leaving Lanzarella wouldn't be so difficult after all.